This is a work of fiction. The characters, incidents, and dialogues are products of the author's imagination and are not to be construed as real. Any resemblance to actual events or persons, living or dead, is entirely coincidental.

Cover design 2024 by Alice G. Bjornstedt.

Cover image courtesy of iStock, contributed by breakermaximus.

Image ID: 484296164

Ship Diagram 2023 by Alice G. Bjornstedt

Map: "Southern Coast of Daffodalion" 2023 by Alice G. Bjornstedt

Section of "Break, Break, Break" by Alfred Lord Tennyson, published 1842. Public domain.

ISBN: 978-1-7375262-9-2

Also in the Orlell Chronicles

Book 1 - Guardians of Gayrile

Book 2 - The Jewel of Power

Book 3 - The Quest for Drisilas

Book 4 - The Shard and the Shadow

Book 5 - The Curse of the Compass

Book 6 - *coming soon!*

THE ORLELL CHRONICLES

Book 5

The Curse of the Compass

Alice G. Bjornstedt

THE BURMAN MARIE

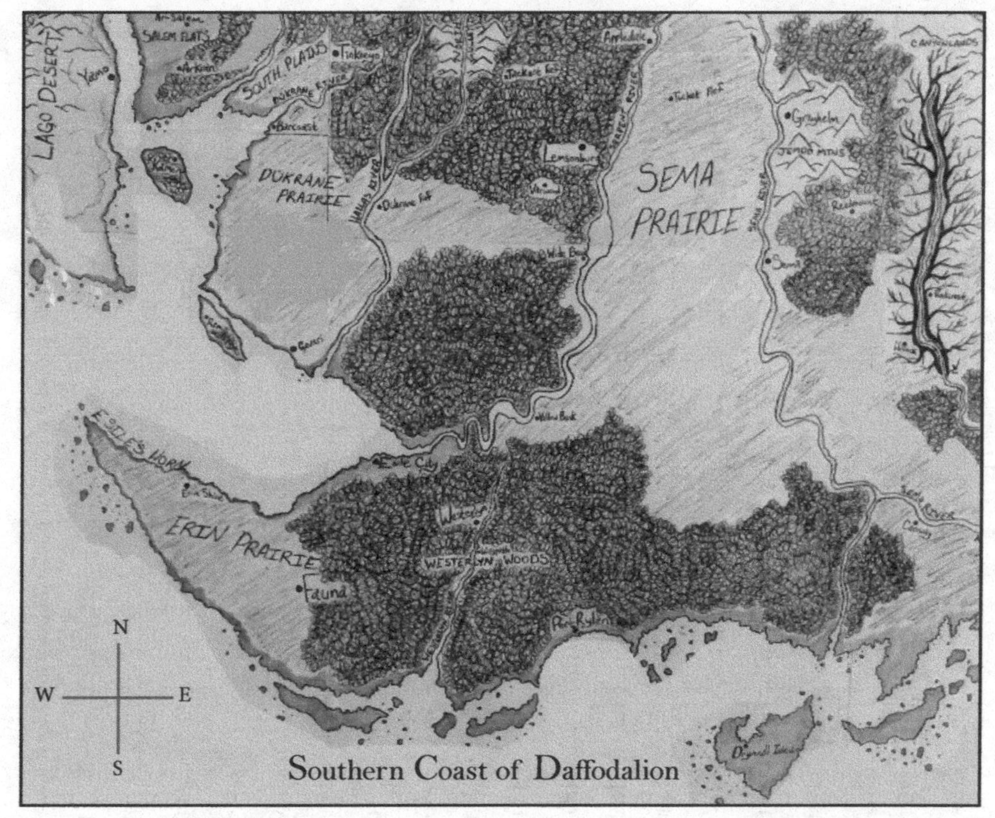

Southern Coast of Daffodalion

Table of Contents

Break, break, break,
On thy cold gray stones, O Sea!
And I would that my tongue could utter
The thoughts that arise in me.

And the stately ships go on,
To their haven under the hill;
But O for the touch of a vanished hand,
And the sound of a voice that is still.

Break, break, break,
At the foot of thy crags, O Sea!
But the tender grace of a day that is dead
Will never come back to me.

—Alfred Lord Tennyson, abridged

PART 1

The Rylander Spy

Prologue

The port of Esile City, on the eve of the New Year...

The clock read five minutes to midnight, and thus three people were marked for death.

Snow spotted the dark wood of the ships in the harbor. A winter gale caught the canvas sails of an approaching ship, sending them billowing. Inland, the starry sky outlined the tall buildings of Esile City. Cheery yellow light filled the interiors of the buildings, occupied by boisterous crowds celebrating the coming of the new year. On the streets below, a few beggars huddled beneath the awnings of the large structures, drawing their ragged garments closer about them as the first flakes fell.

A midnight snow on a midwinter's night, lovely and deadly at once, stealing the warmth and breath of the beggars as they drifted in and out of dreams.

The beggars were the only ones who might have seen Bryn Valetown moving from rooftop to rooftop, agile as a cat.

The winter wind caught her black cloak, sent it billowing behind her, but never enough to reveal her face beneath her hood. The darkness concealed her features well enough, but one could never be too careful. The lantern light from the streets below glinted off the small red pin in the lining of her jacket, the mark of a Dricaster Ringmember.

From her vantage point, the sprawling mass of Esile City appeared as nothing more than a trail of snow-speckled shingles and chimneys belching gray smoke. Aside from the faint conversations within a few inns, all was calm. By day, the city bustled and thundered with traffic and activity, common in a principal Daffonic port.

By night, it was another thing entirely. By night, the Dricaster Crime Ring ruled all.

Bryn slipped into the shadow of a chimney, next to the upstairs window. Through the curtains, the sleeping inhabitants were barely visible, apparently not much interested in the New Year's celebrations. Ignorant, fat, happy homeowners fast asleep in their towering mansion. Their home, like others nearby, was right next to the oil factories and sweat shops, where the poor lived and worked and died in the rancid smoke.

Three minutes to midnight.

She sprang to the next rooftop, gathered her balance, and kept moving, silent as the falling snow. Snow was dangerous. It made the tiled roof slippery under her boots, threatened to send her sliding to the road below. That would mean certain death, of course, whether or not she survived the fall. The town guard might be preoccupied with holiday festivities, but they would seize the opportunity to catch an assassin in the act.

She leapt to another rooftop and crouched in the shadows. The filthy, grease-streaked window at her left elbow caught her reflection in the pale light, her dark eyes shadowed beneath the hood covering her black hair. She heard soldiers patrolling the block behind her and thought briefly how much they'd pay to see her face, to include it on the wanted posters and increase the chance of her arrest.

Bryn turned her gaze from the dirty window and looked across the street. The clock tower loomed before her. A triumph of technology and the pride of Esile City, it overlooked the rest of the township. No matter where one stood in the city, its chimes were audible.

Next to the clock stood Merrit's Front, a three-story, first-class inn sought after by every visiting well-to-do. She was level with the inn's top story windows. Bright light filled the room nearest to her, and she could hear the loud excited voices of men inside.

They spoke the Gevarian tongue, which confirmed what she had assumed by now. Crime lords. Gevari Fief had been built on mining, but the highest form of wealth came from the empire that was the greenstalk trade. The illegal drug brought in high profits for crime lords. They had gathered tonight to celebrate another good year of business. At this hour, their enjoyment was at its peak, heightened by food and drink and other, stronger substances.

A man reeled against the open window sill as she sat watching. His face was flushed with mirth in the lantern light as he inhaled the night air. It was the same face carefully drawn on the scroll she had taken upon accepting the job. She smiled slightly to herself as she recognized him. There was the target, unsuspecting of the danger.

It would be a straight, clean shot if she took it now, but there were other factors she must consider. Two guards stood on either side of the balcony of the clock tower next to the inn. Both had crossbows. In the dim light, she doubted they would see her, but it was not a risk she was willing to take.

She nocked a black-feathered arrow to her string, drew back, sighted, let out a breath. Released. The arrow spanned the twenty-yard distance and passed through the neck of the guard on the right; his knees buckled and he fell against the tower railing with a faint rattle.

One minute to midnight.

She noticed with irritation that the target had gone back inside the inn. She would deal with him later. The second guard had glanced around uneasily as he heard his companion fall, raising his crossbow slightly. Her second arrow felled him before he could see his fallen comrade or sound the alarm. He slumped forward against the railing. Unluckily, his crossbow slipped through the gaps in the rail and fell, clattering loudly on the road below.

Two guards dead. A sudden thought seemed to barge into her mind, surging from a distant corner of her conscience that usually remained silent on missions like tonight. They hadn't been a threat. They hadn't even seen her, crouched where she was on the opposite roof.

No. She shook herself slightly, as though to clear the thoughts from her mind. Where had those doubts come from? The guards were a security threat, she reminded herself. They interfered with her ability to successfully execute the crime lord and, thus, complete the job she'd been hired to do.

The target had returned to the window, having heard the clatter of the crossbow falling. He stood there, looking dazedly at the clock tower, his inebriated mind trying to make sense of what he had heard.

She raised her bow a third time and let the shot fly with a dull thrum.

The crime lord jerked back under the impact; already dead, he reeled forward and toppled through the open window.

The chimes of the clock striking the first hour of the new year concealed the sound of his body hitting the ground. Lilting notes rang through the snowy air. Cheers rose from within Merrit's Front, joining the joyful voices that rose over the city.

Bryn leaned back against the roof, unsure where that moment of weakness had come from. Years of service to the Dricaster Crime Ring should have snuffed out any such concerns. She could not feel regret for what had been done, not after all this time.

All the same, that moment of uncertainty and doubt had stifled the victory she usually felt after completing a mission.

She listened for a few moments until she was certain her presence was unnoticed. Then she turned and headed back the way she had come, slipping through the shadows toward the harbor.

No one seemed to notice the sudden disappearance of the crime lord inside the inn. Nor, she assumed, would they notice for a good while. Not until the excitement of their celebrations had died down, or someone tripped over the body on the street. Then they would call for the town guard, examine the black-feathered arrow, remove the body. Perhaps they would seek for signs of the suspect on the surrounding roads and roofs, signs that would be covered in minutes by snow.

By then, he would be yesterday's bounty. She'd be long gone.

1

Opportunity

The wind had changed. Now it blew northward, away from the restless sea as though fleeing from the coming storm. Bryn heard the sailors in the square speaking in muttered tones. "Bad luck, that is," one of them commented, shaking his head.

His companions agreed. "Aye. Bad luck to have a north wind this early in season."

"The way to Mata City will be nigh impassible—you'd hardly get up the Strait in a gale like this," another sailor commented grimly.

Bryn shifted her position on the snow-dusted bench on the edge of the square. The wind was no more gusty than last night, but it was an old Esilian superstition—starting the new year on a northerly breeze was bad luck.

Bundled forms brushed shoulder to shoulder, hurrying through the haze of damp to different stores and vendors that made up the city square. To the left, the main road of Esile dipped downward toward the harbor. The sea stretched on in an endless carpet of gray water, the horizon muddling with the gray of the sky.

Bryn watched the sailors disappear into the crowds. A breath of cold air chilled her neck, and she drew her cloak closer, both guarding against the chilly breeze and to hide the bow and quiver at her side. The wind brought the strong salty scent of the sea, accompanied by the lingering smoke from the busy factories. The bustling city was far different from the small forest town of her childhood.

She allowed herself a wry smile. First her hesitation during the mission last night, and now these reminiscent thoughts. She attributed it to the long night. At least the late mission had kept the dream away; that recurring dream made it impossible to feel rested. A dream without a palpable start or ending, where she found herself in the middle before realizing it had begun.

She closed her eyes for a moment, and images swam through her mind. A house burning around her. A figure speaking to her, scolding, the words muted. Her hand closed around someone else's, gripped in an unspoken promise.

I'm not going to leave you.

Yet before the dream ended, she felt the hand leave her own, and she stood alone in the burning room until waking, thankfully, ended the vision.

"Got the stuff, Valetown." Mads' drawling tone made her sit up. The Dwarve shuffled forward, hunched under the weight of two sacks of flour. His left leg was permanently twisted from an old injury, the toe trailing uselessly in the snow behind him. The injury, Bryn thought, had made him even more bad-tempered, though she couldn't imagine him ever having an agreeable mood.

"What're you doing, napping?" he asked dryly, setting the flour sacks on the bench and stretching. "Give me a hand here, and let's get out of this wind."

Bryn stood. "I was keeping watch. Not a bad thing to do now that it's daylight, you know."

"Eh, the Dricasters own the town either way," Mads said absently, straightening his woolen cap.

"Maybe. But the town guard patrol for the Capital nonetheless." Bryn adjusted her cloak so that it still covered her bow and quiver, then picked up one of the flour sacks. "Besides, our names are still on the post, so it pays to keep an eye out."

She nodded at the post, which stood in the center of the square. Numerous sheets of paper had been tacked to it by the town guard. Esile City, as a principle port of the west, carried information from all parts of the world: who was king and where, new rules and regulations at the start of the new year, ships or items available for sale. And, as ever, posters displaying criminals and outlaws, wanted for a variety of crimes.

Mads stole a worried glance at the wanted posters. But he recovered quickly. "Naw, they won't have my name. I haven't been out in the field for years, you know that. Not since that Light-blasted cart accident." He spat on the ground angrily, as if the very mention of the injury was a foul taste, then glanced up at Bryn. "Still, makes sense you're careful. You took out that Gevarian Mudger last night, didn't ya?"

"Keep your voice down. The town guard might be incompetent, but they aren't deaf."

"And they wouldn't be inclined to like you, neither. Heard you got two guards along with the Mudger." Mads raised his eyebrows, his weathered face holding a light of interest. "How much was the bounty on him, anyhow? Three hundred? Four?"

"Not enough to keep me from killing you, if you don't shut it." Bryn strode ahead of him, shifting the flour sack to her other shoulder. The older man shuffled after her, cursing under his breath as his bad foot dragged in the snow.

By daylight, no one would know they were Ringmembers. Civilians moved past them without a second glance—an irritable, shabbily dressed cripple, and a dark-haired woman whose worn cloak concealed her weapons.

The three bodies had been removed from the scene, but Bryn felt a twinge of uneasiness as she and Mads passed Merrit's Front. Five town guardsmen stood at attention by the door while their captain spoke with the inn keeper.

Reason reasserted itself in her mind before the unease spiraled to anxiety. The town guard were nothing to worry about. The target had been a wanted criminal himself. The death of a wealthy Mudger—the common term for a greenstalk dealer—might raise the interest of the Esile Council, but they would pay little attention to the event besides that. Mudgers killed each other all the time. Waging invisible wars with their competitors, they placed high bounties on the heads of their rivals. The bounty she'd killed last night must have had powerful enemies, enemies wealthy enough to enlist the help of the Dricaster Brethren.

More posters peppered the wall next to the inn. Bryn's eyes landed on one—a familiar sight by now. The poster was written in Erinian runes, which she was still learning, but she knew it read the following:

WANTED

DEAD or ALIVE

A miss BRYN VALETOWN

On accounts of SMUGGLING and MURDER

REWARD of 500 lupin

"You've gone up in price, Valetown," Mads muttered from behind. "Last one said only two hundred lupin, weren't it?"

"It doesn't matter," Bryn said. The Esile Council had her name by now; a past employer must have let it slip. Her reputation as an archer, and the illegal oversized broadheads she used, would connect her to the crime. But the Council did not know her face. No town guardsman could identify her unless they saw her in action, and no bounty hunter would come after her without a face to seek.

The latter thought was an unnecessary fear. Working for the Dricasters meant that she was protected from other bounty hunters along most of the southwestern coast. The Dricaster Brethren were a powerful Crime Ring, able to protect their own, as long as their own remained loyal.

Bryn turned onto Third Street and stopped in front of the hat shop so Mads could catch up. The building was a little shorter than the rest of the shops, two stories tall, and so old that the roof bowed downward from the weight of the snow. Its front windows were streaked with grime, the sign within barely legible: *Closed for Repairs.*

"We've had that sign up for years," Bryn commented. "You'd think people would expect to see construction."

"Take it up with Dakrind, then," Mads said, unconcerned. "Maybe he'll put up a new sign."

Bryn followed him inside. The sign was only there for effect, of course. As far as she knew, no one ever paid much interest to the hat shop in the first place. Placed just off the main thoroughfare, it hunched in the shadows. Hidden in plain sight. Much like the group that inhabited it.

The bell above the door gave a dismal ting as she and Mads entered. Large crates covered in dust filled the front room. Mostly empty bookshelves occupied the space behind the counter. A few shelves held hats, the style of which were so outdated that Bryn guessed they had been here back when the shop had been in business. But that would have been decades ago.

A fat man sat behind the counter and looked up dully as they entered. "Name?" he grunted.

"Mads and Valetown, reporting back," Mads said.

"Mads who?" the fat man asked.

"Me," the Dwarve snapped. "Now get on with it, Noll, so we can warm up. It's cold as caskets out there."

Noll shrugged. "Sorry about that. Chief wants extra security now. On account of them Rylanders, ye know."

He pulled a hidden lever under the table top. The second bookshelf down the row behind him clicked and swung forward.

"Rylanders?" Mads repeated, looking at Noll with a frown. "What do you mean?"

The fat man shrugged again. "Eh, maybe talk to Chief about that. Don't know much. Just know that there's extra security now."

Bryn held the door open with the toe of her boot, only mildly interested in the news. The Rylanders—a rival Crime Ring to the south—frequently caused trouble for the Dricaster Brethren. But they rarely came as far west as Esile City.

Thoughts of Rylanders were driven away as they descended into the brightness and activity below. A short flight of stairs led from the hidden door above into a wide room. The basement of the hat shop was much larger than the shop itself. Doors led away from the central meeting hall to separate rooms. Rows of tables and benches lined the walls. A scattered crowd of Ringmembers milled around the room, some eating, others talking in lowered tones.

The pantry was directly to the left, and they deposited the flour sacks inside. Mads stretched his back painfully. "I'm off for a drink now. What've you got left?"

"My day's nearly done," Bryn told him. "I just have to check in with Dakrind."

"Not bad," Mads snorted enviously. "The night shift agreeing with you, then?"

"Well enough," Bryn replied curtly. She turned and swept through the meeting hall. The far wall held a solid wooden door leading to the office of their supervisor. *Supervisor*, her mind echoed. That was far too tame a word for this type of work.

She squared her shoulders and knocked briskly on the door in the same way she had for the last fourteen years.

"Come in, Valetown." Dakrind's low drawl reached her ears, and she obeyed. His uncanny accuracy to predict whoever was at his door was normal to her now. Some of the younger recruits called it magic, and said he could see the future. Bryn highly doubted that—but then again, she had never believed in such things anyway.

Hawk Dakrind, the leader of the Dricaster Crime Ring, sat in a wide-backed armchair sharpening his curved sword. He was clean-shaven, his long black hair twisted into a mane of braids with golden beads that clinked slightly. His skin was deep brown, and his amber eyes echoed a desert-dweller's heritage. While his height and muscular build made him intimidating by outward appearances, the only part of him that truly chilled Bryn were those eyes. Not for what they held, but for what they lacked—not a trace of regard for life or pity for others. His was a bloodthirsty, cunning nature, and it showed in his eyes.

"Ah, Valetown," he said, setting his sword and whetstone aside. "I assume your task has been completed?"

Bryn nodded. "Task completed around midnight last night. No

witnesses. Two additional hostiles taken down in the act."

"Two hostiles?" Dakrind repeated, arching an eyebrow.

"Yes, sir. Two guards on the clock tower. They were a potential security risk and interfered with the shot." Bryn fidgeted with the small red pin within her coat, the badge of a Dricaster. The words felt stiff and formal. It was a polite way of saying *"I had to kill them so they didn't sound the alarm."*

"Well, then," Dakrind said, leaning back in his chair. "That was well done. I shall contact the employer about your reward. It was quite a bounty."

"Yes, sir," Bryn replied. The statement helped her forget about the lingering regret over killing the guards last night. It was unpleasant. But it had been necessary so that her task would be successful. It was a truth that had been drilled into her in the last fourteen years—nearly fifteen years, she thought absently—as a bounty hunter.

Dakrind stood and turned up the oil lamp, allowing yellow light to fill the room. "Have you any news you wish to share?"

Bryn thought for a moment. "The wind's changed—a north gale. You know the superstition, I assume."

Hawk Dakrind was a pirate captain himself. As such, he paid far more attention to the wind's patterns than Bryn did. But he looked unconcerned as she mentioned it. "Indeed. But I have never trusted luck to the whims of the wind. I believe our luck is quite good, as times would have it."

"Even with the border patrol tightening again?" Bryn asked.

Dakrind glanced at her. "The news has come this way at last, then?"

"Mads mentioned it on our way to the market. Something about jobs being harder, now that Caer Sia is back on its feet." Bryn studied him carefully, trying to read his expression. There was no reaction. Dakrind only nodded.

"That is to be expected," he said. "What have you heard thus far about the situation in Caer Sia, Valetown?"

Bryn pushed a loose strand of dark hair away from her face as she thought. Different news about the Coonsian capital had circulated for months, each report more far-fetched than the next. "No one knows for sure what happened. All we know is that the city was out of action for a month or so." She adjusted her quiver strap. "There's been all sorts of guesses, as I'm sure you've heard. Some people blame the Jenna, some people said it was a warlord. And, of course, there are all sorts of theories that it was something… otherworldly."

"There are indeed," Dakrind said with a chuckle. "Well, whatever it was, it's no matter to us. What matters is the fact that during that month, the Rings were able to do business freely across the border, within Coonsia. Now that the Liznees have regained control, they have tightened security again, and that means fewer jobs for the Rings."

Bryn nodded. During that one-month period, activity over the Coonsian border had become easier between Crime Rings. Now that things were getting back to normal, most business within Coonsia had ceased. But the Dricasters were powerful enough in this part of Daffodalion to stay in business. She guessed this was what Dakrind was getting at. "Are there any missions available now?" she asked.

"Only a few, and I doubt anything worth your while," Dakrind said, sinking back into his chair, causing the many gold beads in his hair to clink. "But I have a proposition for you. One of our Ringmembers has recently accepted a rather… unusual task. He's gathering a team, and he needs one more member."

Bryn frowned slightly. "I don't work in teams."

"I know you don't," Dakrind drawled. "But you might want to consider it, at the very least. The Ringmember is providing the ship. It's protection he needs for the venture, and I think you'd be up for the job." He smiled. "He'll be here come evening to talk it all through. Pass it by or accept, but I can assure you, it might be some time before you get another assignment that pays this highly." He paused, clearly waiting for her to ask the question.

Bryn hesitated until her curiosity got the better of her. "How much?"

"Six hundred lupin," Dakrind said, drawing the words out slowly to add emphasis.

Bryn raised her eyebrows. "Per Ringmember?"

"Per Ringmember," Dakrind confirmed, smiling again. "I can't tell you much more, naturally—Ringmember security and all that. But think about it."

Bryn nodded slowly. His mention of security reminded her of the guard's words earlier, and she turned back to him. "There was one other thing, sir. Noll mentioned extra security because of Rylanders?"

Dakrind's face darkened, as it always did at mention of the rival Crime Ring. "There are spies among us, Valetown," he said shortly. "As ever, you are to report any suspicious activity to me. For the good of the Brethren."

"The good of the Brethren," Bryn echoed in agreement, then added, "Are the Rylanders so bold that they come this far west? Esile City is miles from their territory."

Dakrind scooped up a stack of papers on his desk and sifted through them. "I'm not entirely certain what the Rylanders are planning. As I hear it, the Rylanders are interested in a bounty—the very same bounty I ask you to consider." He smiled coldly. "Perhaps you should consider it further."

Bryn's interest was piqued, but she tried not to show it, only nodded to Dakrind and left the room. She had never collaborated with any other Ringmembers. Except for Mads, but that was just to escort him through town because he was too afraid he'd be arrested otherwise. These tasks, these jobs… they were too dangerous for more than one person. Dangerous for both herself and her potential partner.

But this job must be something different, she mused as she entered the snow-flecked streets again. Something that needed multiple able-bodied Ringmembers to successfully complete it. Something that needed a ship and a crew. Something that the Rylander Brethren was interested in, too.

Something important enough that the employer would pay anyone who completed it six hundred lupin.

That fact nagged in her brain as she thought. It was too much. No
one paid that much for bounties—not even the Esile Council, who
dabbled in Ring activity every now and then. Perhaps the entire job
was a scam, and the employer planned to run before paying up. That
happened occasionally, which provided frequent jobs for a bounty
hunter like herself. Maybe the employer didn't plan to pay them at
all.

Or maybe he was counting on another factor all together. Multiple Ringmembers working on the same job never ended well, no
matter if they were all paid equally.

Bryn remembered a situation in the past. A crime lord had placed
a large reward on the job. Thanks to the temptation, multiple Ringmembers had accepted the task. But, as was to be expected, the hunters
eventually turned on each other, each eager to complete the bounty for
his own reputation and gain. In the end, the crime lord had only one
man to pay—the hunter who had killed all his other companions.

The fact that rival hunters were after the bounty made Bryn almost certain in her guess. Likely, the nature of this job ensured that
only one Ringmember would return alive.

2

Ringmember Trelawney

By evening, Bryn had returned to Dakrind's office.

She had spent the afternoon alone, as usual. She'd left the Dricaster Headquarters and headed to her quiet little apartment downhill from the hat shop. She had boarded up the cracks in the windows to keep some of the damp out, but a bitter chill filled the flat. After she lit the fire, she managed a few hours of rest in the smoke-filled room.

The dream came in brief fragments. The little cold hand gripped in her own, the flames at the end, and the brisk scolding voice. The voice had seemed louder this time, familiar, reminiscent of another, long ago.

"Fear is weakness. Hide it away or you offer your opponent a valuable advantage."

Her voice had trembled, her eyes wide, filled with the nervous curiosity of her six-year-old self. "I'm ready, Papa."

"Not you, Brynlee. Not now." His heavy hand rested on her tousled hair, brushed her aside. The hand she held vanished as her companion was pulled away by their father. Her father's attention was not for her. It never had been.

Fear is weakness, her father's voice echoed in her brain as she entered the hat shop. How true that had become over the last few years of working for the Dricaster Brethren.

The fat guard, Noll, sat in his usual place. He seemed more on edge than normal. "Name?" he asked briskly as Bryn entered.

"Bryn Valetown, come to meet with Dakrind," Bryn said with an impatient sigh. "Honestly. You saw me this morning."

"Can't be too careful," Noll muttered, pulling the lever. "You should hear what's going on down there…"

Bryn frowned in thought as she descended into the hidden lair of the Dricasters. The room was noisier now, filled with people. With the coming night, Ringmembers operated freely, anticipating the hours of darkness that cloaked their sinister actions. By night, the Dricasters ruled Esile City.

There was an audible difference in the atmosphere of the room tonight, though. The conversations were hushed and hurried, urgent and irritated. She caught snatches of words as she walked.

"There'll be Rylanders here by morning, I warrant, coming after Chief."

"It's not a man they're here for." That was Mads.

"No, they don't want Chief," someone agreed. "They're looking for something, same as the crew of the *Marie*."

"The Rylanders haven't come this far west in decades. What's got 'em brave enough to do it now, I wonder?"

"Something important…"

The conversation faded as Hawk Dakrind walked through the

room, his black cloak sweeping around his tall frame. He threw a withering glance at the whispering Ringmembers, nodded curtly to Bryn, and walked into his office. Bryn followed, confused but growing more interested. "Sir…"

"Sit, Valetown," Dakrind ordered shortly, and left the room again.

Bryn remained standing but didn't ask any more. Dakrind's desk was messier than usual; she glanced at the upside-down pages and could make out a few words. One word appeared multiple times—what was it? *Wavers.*

She frowned. Mads had mentioned the Wavers once, but she didn't know much about them. They appeared often in pirate legends; legends that she tended to ignore. Why was Dakrind interested in such stories, especially when there were more important things to deal with? If a rival Crime Ring—the Rylanders—were on the move…

The thought remained unfinished as the door opened and a man she had never seen before peeked inside. "Where's Hawk? It's nearly six." His voice was quick, with a Northerner's accent that might have been called elegant if his tone were not so breathless and hurried.

"He'll… be back soon," Bryn said briefly, rattled by both the sudden appearance and his casual reference to the Ringleader.

"Well, obviously. This is his office." He sauntered inside and leaned against the desk. "Who're you?"

"Ringmember," Bryn said shortly, studying him. He stood an inch or two taller than she did but looked about the same age. His eyes were blue, bright and sharp as they took in the room. His unkempt hair was caramel-blond, tied back by a brightly colored cloth. He had a small beard and mustache, a slightly darker shade than his hair. The facial hair was uneven on the right side, adding a slight quirk to his mouth like a permanent smirk.

"Good to meet you, Ringmember," he continued without missing a beat. "You're number five in our party, I assume?"

"Don't. Assume, I mean, because I haven't taken the job yet," Bryn informed him.

The man grinned, then looked down at Hawk's desk, reading the pages there without much interest. His clothes were simple and lightweight—a long-sleeve shirt under a thigh-length water resistant coat and weathered boots. He wore a curved sword, similar in make to Dakrind's, on his right leg. Left handed. Judging by his quick, agile movements, she guessed he knew how to fight, too. Along with the sword was a leather holster, half-hidden by his coat. That was interesting. Firearms were hard to get in Daffodalion under regular circumstances, much less a pistol. She wondered where and how he'd gotten it.

"Bounty hunter, aren't you?" he said suddenly, looking at her again. "Got a name, or just Ringmember?"

Bryn raised an eyebrow. She'd made it quite clear she had no interest in a conversation… and he kept *talking*. He was unbelievable, she thought. "Valetown. And you?"

"Trelawney. Robin Trelawney," the man replied smoothly. "And you are a bounty hunter, aren't you?"

"At the moment, yes." Bryn eyed him carefully. "And you're a smuggler?"

"Privateer, Miss Valetown, an honest sea-farer."

Bryn smiled wryly. "There are no honest Dricasters, Mr. Trelawney."

"Captain, please."

"Ah, so you're a pirate."

"You flatter me," Captain Trelawney said with a wink.

Hawk Dakrind entered and closed the door behind him. "I see you've already met. Saves the time of pleasantries, then. There are more important things to discuss."

"How much have you told her?" Trelawney asked.

"Only enough to interest her." Dakrind turned to Bryn, his amber eyes meeting her dark ones. "I'm glad to see you took my advice. Thank you for coming."

Bryn squared her shoulders, careful to keep her expression neutral. Curious or no, she promised herself that she would neither accept nor decline anything until some of her questions were answered. "I admit you've intrigued me, sir. What exactly is the job?"

Dakrind sat down. "Do you remember our business with the Rylander Brethren?"

Bryn let out a breath. A month or so before, she had accompanied Hawk Dakrind to Drynrall Island, passing through Rylander territory to get there. The rival Crime Ring had been none too pleased to let them pass, and they had been forced to fight their way out. "I remember," she said aloud. "I take it they've grown bolder in the last few weeks."

"Indeed," Dakrind said darkly. "As I mentioned earlier today, we have received word that Rylander spies have infiltrated Esile City. They want to know Dricaster secrets and steal our bounties before we can take them." He paused. "This particular job has piqued their interest as well as ours."

"Ah," Bryn said, nodding slowly. Then, as Dakrind paused, she asked, "Why?"

Dakrind jerked his head towards Robin. "Captain Trelawney has recently accepted a job—the employer of which happens to have a rather large bounty on his own head."

"Then why not turn him in for the reward?" Bryn asked.

"Because the job itself pays four times higher than the employer's bounty," Robin Trelawney replied. "My guess is someone's trying to pay off their own debt."

Bryn nodded thoughtfully. This happened frequently enough. "Who placed the bounty on the employer's head in the first place?" she asked.

"Caer Sia itself," Dakrind replied. Bryn stared at him, startled. "This is why the job has resurfaced," the Ringleader continued. "I assume the employer was free to escape whatever fate the Coonsian Capital had planned for him, while Caer Sia was under siege. Now that the Liznees have control again, he needs to move."

"So we're smuggling someone?" Bryn guessed.

"Not quite," Robin said. "The employer doesn't seem to want to run and hide. He's looking for something—some sort of weapon he can use against his pursuers."

"A weapon against the Liznees?" Bryn said, confused.

"So it seems," Robin said.

Bryn frowned. This job was beginning to sound more and more unusual. An outlaw on the run, looking for something that would protect him from the Liznees. Paying anyone who returned alive six hundred lupin. With that amount, she could practically retire. Buy a ship. Get out of Esile City. All the same…

"Why do you need me?" she asked bluntly, looking Captain Trelawney in the eye. "I imagine you and your men can handle this easily."

"Which we probably can," Robin said, smiling again. "But if we're playing hide-and-seek with Rylanders the whole trip—and probably Capital soldiers, too—I'd like a decent archer at my back."

"Captain Trelawney's ship is unknown by the Capital fleet," Dakrind said. "But he believes the Rylanders will recognize it and pursue him. Our sources indicate that the Rylanders are determined to get the bounty too."

"So you want me to protect you," Bryn said slowly, allowing her meaning to sink in. "You want… a bounty hunter… to protect you."

For the first time, the smirk faded. "You're thinking you could kill me, and take the bounty for yourself?" Robin crossed his arms over his chest. "Ever been on a ship in a hurricane, Miss Valetown? Do you know the difference between a Nøkken's song and a Siren's? Do you know the route to and from Port Rylan without being pinned down by Rylanders? Because *I* do," he stated, as Bryn said nothing. "And I promise you, it'll be a heck of a lot harder to survive the southern coast on your own. So, if you keep those oversized arrows turned *toward* the Rylanders, and not my neck, I'll ensure you return safe and sound to Esile, and we'll *both* get paid."

Bryn took a deep breath. She had wanted to see how Trelawney would respond to her subtle challenge, and she was satisfied by his reply. He was not daunted. He genuinely wanted her help. They had mutual need, which made her feel more secure than anything else. And if protecting him throughout this mission got her the reward, then she would do what she could. "Fair enough," she told him, then looked at Dakrind. "You mentioned the Rylanders are after the bounty too. Do we know who's hired them?"

"I'm afraid I don't know much," Dakrind said. "The Rylanders are as wary of spies as I am. What our men have managed to gather is that someone else wants this weapon too. A second employer has hired a Rylander Ringmember to complete this bounty—looking for the same thing you are. Who this second employer could be, and why they want this object, your guess is as good as mine."

Bryn nodded slowly. It made sense. All the Crime Rings kept their secrets close. The fact that a Dricaster spy had gathered even that much information was impressive. Perhaps they'd find out more about the second employer on the mission. Whatever they were looking for must be important—important to two different employers.

She realized one vital question had been left unanswered. "So, what exactly are we looking for?"

Dakrind was silent; a dark look flickered briefly across his face. It was gone just as fast, leaving Bryn wondering if she'd imagined it. But Robin Trelawney met her gaze, a slightly manic gleam in his blue eyes.

"A compass, Miss Valetown. We're looking for a compass."

3

The Informant

The same evening in Lemsonburg…

"Get on with it, will ya?" The prisoner's voice echoed in the small interrogation room, leaving a cloud before his lips. The silent stone of Lemsonburg's prison muted his angry words, but his face showed confusion and frustration at being summoned.

The warden watched through the thin pane of reflective glass that divided the interrogation room from the watchers. It was bitterly cold in the stone room. He stuffed his hands into the pockets of his thick fur coat and threw a glance at the two cloaked figures standing beside him.

Two rangers.

The warden knew about rangers, of course. Stationed in different towns and cities all across the Mainland, they protected civilians and maintained order. There was the ranger stationed in Lemsonburg who reported to the Daffonic king. The warden knew him quite well.

He'd never seen these two rangers before, though. They had arrived yesterday, requesting to interrogate this prisoner. Why, the warden had no idea at all. He had assumed at first that they had come from the Capital in Fauna, which made little sense. The Daffonic Crown couldn't care less about prisoners. Definitely not enough to want to question them. It only added to the strangeness of the visit.

But these two were not from the Capital, he realized. The Liznee crest, embroidered in silver on the breasts of their jerkins, told him they were from the neighboring country of Coonsia. They had come from Caer Sia.

The two rangers stood patiently, cloaked and hooded. The warden studied them for a moment, then looked to the older, who was clearly in charge. "Right, well, you're free to start, ranger," he said, nodding toward the door to the interrogation room. "Go easy on him," he added.

The tall man nodded, but did not move forward. Instead, the shorter hooded figure stepped toward the door. The warden felt another surge of confusion. So the tall, dark ranger had not come to do the questioning; he would send that fresh-faced youth instead. This day was getting stranger and stranger.

"Good luck, lad," the warden said awkwardly. The boy turned and grinned his thanks. Light above, he couldn't be much older than eleven or twelve. Tawny red hair, a shock of freckles across his honest face. It was not the face of an interrogator.

The warden turned his attention back to the window and watched as the boy entered the cell.

The prisoner looked up as the door opened. Confusion, then

disdain, crossed his face. "If you've come to bring me a drink, I want something hot. Be quick about it, it's taken you long enough."

"Sorry, I'm not the serving boy," the young ranger replied, looking around with interest before sitting. The prisoner watched him. There was something vaguely familiar about the lad, but he couldn't place it.

"What're you here for then, boy?" he snapped, his impatience turning to irritation.

"To talk. Just to talk." The boy spread a leather folder on the table between them and studied a page. "You're Curtis Bregg, from Tackert Fief?"

"If that's what your papers say," the prisoner grunted, scratching a patch of stubble on his square jaw.

"And you were previously employed as a butcher, right?"

"A while back."

"Your charges—disturbing the peace, manslaughter, resisting arrest, treason to Caer Sia, treason to the Daffonic Crown." The boy raised his eyebrows. "Sentenced to life in prison on the twenty-second of the twelfth month, year 1128. Been here for about twelve months now. Is that correct?"

"Has it really been a year already? Time flies in here," Bregg said sarcastically. "Now hurry up and say what you want to, boy, so I can go warm up."

The young ranger looked at his papers again. A slight flush had colored his face, but it was hard to tell whether it was from the cold or from the taunts. The warden looked at the other ranger next to him, but he couldn't read any expression in the shadowed face.

"He's doing pretty well so far," he offered. The tall man nodded but said nothing, keeping his eyes on the room beyond.

Bregg bumped his chair against the table. "Get on with it, I said," he snapped. "I've got things to do."

"You have plenty of time with a life sentence," the boy said mildly, and looked up at him. "Now, your crimes. You didn't commit them on your own. You were hired by an Elven prince, right?"

For the first time, a flicker of uncertainty crossed Bregg's face. "Don't remember. It's been a while."

"Let me remind you, then. You were hired by Terrax of Elvengate. You led a battalion of his followers. You went with him to steal the sword Drisilas from Caer Sia. You helped him place the sword in Appledale's market and went west again. But after that, you traveled to the area around the North Gully caves, a few miles south of Elimar, because you'd decided to help him get the sword back."

The lad stated each sentence without even a glance at the papers before him, his eyes penetrating the disdain in Bregg's gaze. Bregg stared at the youth as recognition dawned. The tawny hair, the inno-cent face… but that was impossible. "I don't… recall that we…"

"You helped him face off with the group led by Dandio Ki in the North Gully. Your men and the Black Dwarves fought them. You drove them into the caves. Do you know what happened then?"

"They… got away," Bregg muttered. "Took the sword and got away."

"We did," the boy said, placing both hands on the table and leaning forward so his face was inches from the prisoner's. "But not all of us."

Bregg looked at him as familiarity dawned. His shock came not from the realization, but from seeing the change. The lack of fear. The fire in the lad's eyes. The stone in his gaze. What a year of living hell could do to a child.

"Focus."

Bregg jumped at the low voice. A tall ranger stood in the doorway, a few paces behind the boy. The warden stood behind him, watching with intense interest. Bregg hadn't seen them enter. He felt a flash of satisfaction. Clearly, the other ranger was worried for this boy's safety. He'd come just in case he needed to interfere if Bregg tried anything.

At the other man's voice, the young ranger took a ragged breath and leaned away again. The emotion was locked away just as fast. Bregg realized suddenly that his assumption was wrong. The older ranger wasn't here to protect the child. The ranger was there to protect *Bregg* from the boy.

That thought unsettled him more than anything else. "You got more questions for me?" he grunted.

The young ranger closed the leather file. "Terrax led you north then. Your men were ordered to lie in wait in the wilderness outside of Caer Sia."

As he spoke, the warden, watching at the other ranger's side, saw a new look enter Bregg's eyes. Not anger, nor confusion, nor surprise by the boy's fire. Fear. A raw, primal fear borne of something seen that could neither be explained nor forgotten.

"Tell me what happened then, Mr. Bregg."

Bregg looked up at the young ranger and shook his head slowly. "You wouldn't believe me if I told you."

The boy met his eyes. In the silence that passed between them, Bregg relived the memories. Saw them reflected in the stony face of this—child—dragged into a struggle that had not been his to fight. But fought it he had. Bregg sensed images in the boy's eyes that he remembered too. Darkness in the woods. Black fog. Soldiers screaming and writhing in the haze. Empty eyes. Charred skeletons. Essence rotted, withered from within.

"Believe me," the young ranger said, "I've seen worse."

From the look in his eyes, Bregg didn't doubt that. He leaned back, covering his fear with anger. "Is there a point to all this, boy?"

"Your employer, Terrax. You escaped with him—I watched him and the rest of his followers disappear into the forest. Where did you go then?"

"East," Bregg grunted, fidgeting with the sleeve of his filthy coat. "We went east. Terrax had heard of a weapon that could help us. But the town guard caught us south of Carna, brought us here." He gestured vaguely around him.

"But they didn't catch all of you? Terrax isn't here, at least."

Bregg snorted. "No, he got away with a few of his guys. Trust me, if you find out where he went, I'd like to know too. Thank him for the mess he got me into."

"So you don't know where he's gone?"

"As if I would, boy," Bregg said dismissively. "I was just a soldier in his group. Even if I'd been higher ranked, I wouldn't have been told. Terrax was paranoid about traitors then and he's probably more paranoid now."

"And the other men with him? How many soldiers would you guess he still has?"

"Dunno. He probably got away with, oh, I'd say ten or twelve men. But he has more followers, supporters, in other places. I bet he has close to thirty men with him by now," Bregg said.

"I assume he didn't go northwest again," the young ranger said, half to himself. "Maybe he kept going east."

"Your guess is as good as mine," Bregg said, fidgeting with his sleeve again. He smirked. "Ironic, isn't that. You going after him now. A year later and the roles have reversed."

"A lot can change in a year," the boy said simply. He picked up the folder.

Bregg watched him stand, the smirk lingering on his face. At least he would get some benefit out of today's interview. "So, how much do I get off my sentence? For cooperating so well?"

The young ranger glanced at him. "That's for the Capital to decide. Cooperation now doesn't change what you did then, not in my mind."

Bregg's face darkened in anger. "Is that all?" he spat. "You have your blasted information and I get—nothing?"

"You have a life sentence. That's better than a hanging, which I'd say you deserve."

Bregg stared at him, speechless with anger for a moment. Then, in a burst of fury, he slammed the table forward, knocking the other chair to the ground and making the boy step back. "This is about that bloody business in the Gully, yeah?" he snarled. "All about that stupid Elf what got himself killed?"

He started forward, ignoring the chains that bound him to the chair, towering over the young ranger. Something changed in the boy's face, and he held his ground. One hand slipped into his pocket, the other pointed at Bregg as he moved. There was a brilliant flash of blue that seemed to radiate from the boy's fingers, hitting Bregg like an invisible wall. He faltered, stunned for an instant. "What on—"

The young ranger straightened and lowered his hand, his expression hard as flint, his eyes blazing. "His name was Llyrion."

"Mel."

The hooded ranger by the door crossed to the boy, taking his shoulder firmly. The boy moved back, his hand still inside his pocket, hatred on his face. Something small and blue glowed through the fabric.

Bregg stared at the rangers wide-eyed. The strange stories he'd heard about the happenings in Caer Sia over the last few months filled his mind. Slowly, he pieced together who they were.

The warden cleared his throat, not quite sure what he had just witnessed, but no longer doubting the young ranger's skill in the slightest. He nodded to the guards, who forced Bregg back into his chair, then looked at the tall ranger. "Will, ah, will that be all, Master Hummingbird?"

"One more thing." The tall ranger placed his hands on the arms of Bregg's chair and looked him in the eye. His face was far different from the boy's. Not a shred of doubt or hesitance. "Where would Terrax have gone?"

"Your boy already asked that," Bregg muttered, adverting his gaze from the dark eyes.

"So he did. And you didn't answer him. But you will answer me."

"If I get a decade or two off the sentence, maybe," Bregg snorted.

"I could end your entire sentence and kill you now, if you like," the tall ranger said calmly, one hand resting on his sword hilt.

"Fine," Bregg blustered. "Terrax talked about going south. He talked about finding a weapon. He mentioned the Crime Rings. I don't know anything more than that."

"Thank you," the ranger said. He turned and nodded to the warden, then swept out of the room. The boy trailed behind him, one hand still in his pocket, closed over the small orb of blue light.

. . . . . .

"Anger is a greater weakness than fear," Aryion stated when they were back at the inn.

Mel sat across from him on his bed, holding the Stone. Its glow had faded slightly, but Aryion could still see the fire in its core.

A strange choice to have Mel guard it, but Aryion chalked it up to yet another of Iriam's unexplainable decisions. It had been months ago, and he still wondered about it.

Mel didn't meet his eyes. "It worked," he mumbled.

Aryion raised his eyebrows. "Worked, in what way? Oh yes, you stopped a chained criminal from taunting you. You also revealed one of the most valuable assets we have, which made for some interesting questions from the warden when we left, and wrongly showed the Blue Stone's power to half a dozen watching guards— who will *also* have tales to spread now."

His apprentice seemed to wither under the criticism. Aryion regretted his blunt tone. He took a breath, softening his voice. "Were you afraid?"

"No. Not really. I knew he was chained. He just… he wouldn't take me seriously," Mel said, looking up at his mentor in frustration. "Kept calling me *'boy.'*" He mimicked Bregg's voice with irritation.

"So you felt as though you needed to prove yourself," Aryion guessed. Mel nodded. His face was still flushed with anger, but there was another look in his eyes, one that Aryion recognized. A grief and helplessness, feelings weary of being pushed away, threatening to rise to the surface.

"He brought up the Elf," Aryion ventured after a pause. "Your friend from the quest to find the sword?"

"Llyrion," Mel said dully.

Aryion sat on the bed across from Mel's, silent for a moment. "Did Bregg kill him?"

"No. No… I barely remember Bregg being there that day at all. Just Terrax and the Black Dwarves, and then… and then the Darkness came later."

"So you have nothing to prove to Bregg. No vengeance to pursue."

"I guess not," Mel admitted. "I just… wanted him to know… what happened." He seemed to push the emotion away, taking a shaky breath. "What do we do now?"

There was more behind his words, Aryion could tell. He could guess most of it. Of course Mel wanted Bregg to know what he had caused. He wanted him to know the same pain he had gone through. To see what it had done to him. To suffer the way he had.

How well Aryion understood that feeling.

"For now, get some sleep," he said, standing. "We're going south tomorrow."

"We are?" Mel asked, surprised. "Where?"

Aryion paused, thinking. "If Bregg told the truth, Terrax went to enlist the help of one of the Crime Rings southwest of here. There are several Crime Rings, but the direction he indicated narrows it down. I'd assume Terrax went to Esile City. Our next move will be to take a boat down river."

"All right. Aryion?" Mel called as the ranger started for the door to the lavatory. "How did you know he was lying to me about where Terrax went?"

"He didn't meet your eyes, and he was smirking while he said it. Sure giveaways that he was lying."

"I didn't notice that."

"You'll learn," Aryion said. "Good night, Mel."

Mel started to lie down, then sat up again. "Aryion?"

"Yes?" Aryion asked patiently.

"Maybe you should have done the interrogation today."

A slight smile crossed Aryion's face. "Maybe. But I must say, it *was* entertaining to watch." With that, he left the room.

4

The Burman Marie

The following morning dawned wet and cold over Esile City. The temperature had risen just enough to turn the falling snow to rain, but that only made everything muddier.

The single window in Bryn's flat allowed a dim view of the harbor. The glass was mostly obscured by grease and soot thanks to the factories nearby, but she could just make out the ships docked at the piers. Hawk Dakrind's tall, hulking warship, the *Black Raven*, was nearest to the harbor mouth, her sides painted black so that she appeared as a shadow through the rain.

But they weren't taking Dakrind's ship. Bryn, and the other three Ringmembers assigned to the mission, were to meet Captain Trelawney in a half hour to board his ship.

"Fastest ship south of Caer Sia," Robin had said last night. "Not as big as the *Raven*, maybe, but the *Burman Marie* will get the job done, I can promise you."

That's what all captains say, Bryn had thought, but she hadn't said it out loud. She guessed that Trelawney, though a little overconfident, was probably right. The *Black Raven* would be easily recognized thanks to her size and color. If they were traveling into enemy territory, they

50

would need to blend in. No matter how fast the *Burman Marie* was, they couldn't afford a fight with the Rylander Brethren. Not when their mission was a simple retrieval—find the compass, and get out.

A compass, she thought incredulously.

That was the object this secret employer needed so desperately. Why, Bryn had absolutely no clue. Still, a job was a job. It might be unusual, but it would hopefully be easier than the other missions she usually completed. If they avoided the Rylanders, it would be over soon, and they'd all walk away alive and rich.

She shouldered her pack, which contained her few belongings, and slipped her quiver over her other shoulder. Then she took her bow in her free hand and locked the door behind her. This flat had been offered to her after the Dricasters had evicted the previous occupant from the premises. These apartments were too close for comfort to the Dricaster base. Nearly everyone that lived here nowadays were Ringmembers.

She slipped the key in her pocket and started down the muddy road toward the harbor.

"So, you're the fifth one they wanted, are ya?"

Mads sat on the curb across the street, smoking his pipe and looking mildly interested.

"Why are you here?" Bryn asked without stopping.

"Need ya to get me past the guards on our way to the harbor. Don't trust 'em. They've put up new posters—these ones got color on 'em." The Dwarve stood stiffly and shuffled after her.

Bryn glanced at the post as they moved through the square. Sure enough, the guards had put up new posters. She noticed there were more with her name than there had been yesterday. The assassination of the Mudger two nights ago must have been traced back to her. She could remain a faceless criminal, thanks to working with employers through Dakrind only. But her reputation and name would have been known by the employer. He must have let something slip to the wrong people.

Just to be safe, she adjusted her cloak to hide her quiver. The longbow would be inconspicuous enough. Unstrung, it looked like a warped staff.

"Give the town guard credit for their artistic ability," Mads muttered, glaring at the posters.

Bryn waited until they had left the square behind to throw him a look. "You're coming on the trip too? I thought you hated working in the field."

"M'dear, six hundred lupin is enough to persuade anybody to come out of retirement," Mads informed her. "Besides, don't have much better to be doing, do I? Get the groceries, run the errands, get the lunch orders."

At least that's safe, Bryn thought. But Mads was already on edge about the new wanted posters without her mentioning the danger of this mission. He was clearly willing to risk that danger for the re-ward. Or maybe he just wanted to escape Esile City and the monotony of life here for a little while.

They left the smoky haze behind as they reached the harbor, and Bryn filled her lungs with the brisk sea air. Two parallel piers jutted out into the water, ships moored on either side. The harbor was packed full this time of year. Now that the winter holidays were over, people would travel back to their homes, or go north to the warm tropics.

"You know where we're meeting?" Mads asked as they walked down the pier on the left.

"Number eleven," Bryn replied. Captain Trelawney had talked through most of the details last night with Hawk Dakrind. Each mooring spot was marked by a number—eleven was at the very end, on the right.

The ship waited in place. A three-mast frigate made of deep brown wood, her clean gray sails bustled up on the masts. People moved around, loading supplies and preparing the ship for the journey, as busy as an anthill.

"Not a bad looking boat," Mads commented, hands on his hips. "But she looks tipsy. Do you think she'll capsize?"

"Not the *Marie*," came Robin's voice. The pirate captain strode down the pier behind them, carrying a large roll of parchment. "She's slimmer than your average warship, sure. But she's fifteen guns to a side and she'll fly fast once she's got the wind behind her."

"Eh. So ya say," Mads grunted, but Bryn could tell he was impressed as he walked up the gangplank.

"How many are we waiting for?" Bryn asked Robin.

"Two more. Out of the Brethren, five agreed to the venture. Me, you, the Dwarve, and two of Hawk's brain-dead stooges. But they're providing the muscle and that's good enough for me." Robin strode on deck and called a few orders to the crew.

Bryn followed, not quite sure where to go or what to do. The activity and noise around her dizzied her for a moment. Mads was talking to a tall, burly fellow with bushy sideburns. Sailors moved rapidly over the ship, brushing past Bryn to tie down lines and move barrels of supplies below.

Bryn caught up to Robin, who had stepped to the port side. "Captain, where should I…"

"Oh yes, your lodging—first come, first serve, might want to claim a hammock below deck while you can," Robin said. "The boys get noisy down there sometimes, so maybe grab one on the edge."

"Where…" Bryn began.

"I'm joking, Miss Valetown, we had a nice little place set up for you once we knew you'd be on board. Nice and private."

Bryn flushed angrily. "Captain Trelawney, that's not at all necessary."

"Miss Valetown, it wasn't any trouble. Where's John? John!" Robin bellowed up at a man in the crow's nest secured to the central mast. At Robin's call, the man climbed down and came smartly to attention before his captain.

"Yes, sir."

"There you are," Robin said, pushing the roll of parchment into his arms. "Take that down to my office, and get the crew ready for departure."

"Naturally, Captain. They're quite prepared," the other man reported with a slight nod. He was a little shorter than Robin but seemed a few years older, though maybe that was just his mature manner. He had a well-trimmed mustache and wore a cable knit sweater, the same canvas breeches as the other sailors, and a simple wool cap. Everything about him seemed put together and painstakingly clean—he would have looked more at home onboard a Capital yacht, not a pirate frigate.

"Busy morning. You got the guns oiled down last night, I hope," Robin said.

"I assume that is a rhetorical question, Captain."

"Once again, very on top of it, John," Robin said, pleased. "Give me a moment and I'll find something else for you to do that's probably already been done."

John's attention turned to Bryn for the first time, and he smiled and tipped his hat. "Welcome aboard the *Burman Marie*, madam. John Tailor, First Mate."

"Thank you."

"Proper enough to be a court lady, isn't he," Robin said. "Don't worry, he's got the same vocabulary as any sailor, just better grammar."

"I'll take the charts below," John said, ignoring Robin's comment.

Robin stepped up to the tiller and turned back to face Bryn, who had just drawn breath for her question. "Oh, right, your cabin.

Take it or leave it, but don't complain about Richard's snores if you choose the latter. Oliver!" he called to a boy passing by.

The lad could hardly be older than eleven, with deep brown skin and wide eyes. "Aye, Cap'n?" he asked.

"Show Miss Valetown to her cabin, will you. If she doesn't want it have her call dibs on a hammock quick—the best spots'll be gone fast."

Oliver looked up at Bryn, a little confused. "The cabin will be fine," Bryn told him, deciding to abandon the argument.

He nodded, and his eyes lit up as he saw her longbow. "Where'd you get a bow like that?" he asked eagerly.

"Elimar," Bryn replied shortly.

"Oh. I hear the Elves in Elimar make the best bows. Did you get it from one of them? But you're not an Elf." The cabin boy scrutinized her carefully. "Don't have them pointy ears."

"It'll be three lashes for dawdling, Oliver," Robin said without a hint of malice—Oliver grinned and led Bryn below decks.

Bryn followed, hiding a smile. "I'm not an Elf. I grew up near Elimar, though—that's where I got the bow."

"Wow," Oliver breathed, as if it were the most interesting thing he'd ever heard. "I've never been to Elimar. It's kinda close to Caer Sia, right? Didja know that Richard—he's the bosun—he said that Caer Sia got attacked by… Aces." The boy shivered at the word.

"Yes, I've heard that too," Bryn said noncommittally.

"I don't know if it's true though," Oliver said, his brow furrowed slightly. "Ya know, no one can really say what happened. Them Coonsians keep their secrets close. No offense," he added, looking at her.

"None taken. It's been a long time since I considered myself Coonsian," Bryn said.

"Oh. Well, you don't sound like one. No accent—at least, not like Cap'n's."

Bryn raised an eyebrow. "Where's the Captain from, then?" she asked. Robin's accent was somewhere in between the elegant Caer Sian dialect and the quickened syllables of the coastal fiefs to the north, though she couldn't decide where he was from.

"North," Oliver said with a shrug. "One of the coastal towns, I think? I don't know. You don't talk like them." He paused, perplexed. "But you don't really sound Esilian either."

"I suppose not," Bryn said, not quite sure how to respond to the observation. "So… what do you do on the ship?"

"Cabin boy, though I'm fixin' to be mate one day," Oliver informed her proudly. "Cap'n says I will be, once I'm older, anyway. Till then I get to sleep on the big bearskin rug in Cap'n's cabin."

"Sounds nice," Bryn commented. "Where does the rest of the crew sleep?"

"In the hammocks below starboard and port," Oliver said. "There's a spare storage room down here that we set up yesterday after Cap'n said a lady was joining us."

He led her to the spare cabin. It was mostly empty except for a few barrels of water and some sacks of corn meal and potatoes. A hammock had already been slung in the opposite corner, with a blanket inside.

"You'll want that blanket," Oliver told her. "It gets cold down here at nights."

"Thank you," Bryn said, setting her pack down. The cabin boy grinned and jogged back up the steps.

The room was snug but tidy. An unlit lamp was set on one of the crates, and Bryn checked the oil. Plenty of fuel. That was a relief. The light would help ease her fear of confined spaces.

The ship began to move, rocking in the gentle waves of the harbor. She heard Robin giving orders on deck as they drifted out to sea. The venture had begun.

Bryn left the room and started up the steps. A furry gray shape headed downstairs tangled with her legs, and she nearly fell. The animal let out a meow of protest.

"I see you've met Whiskers," Robin said, catching her hand before she fell forward. Bryn pulled away, detangling herself from the gray tabby cat that now rubbed contentedly against her legs. "Not much cunning for a cat," Robin commented. "She tends to sleep on the stairs, so watch your step. We keep her on board to keep the rats down."

Whiskers retreated downstairs, and Bryn looked out over the deck. The gangplank and anchor had been lifted, the mooring lines hauled in, and the *Burman Marie* pulled away from the pier. Esile's Horn, a large rocky peninsula, carved through the sea to the left.

Bryn glanced behind them—Esile City sat in the crook of the bay, a cloud of gray smoke hovering over it. The wind picked up, catching the sails, and she drew her cloak closer around her.

"Even colder out here," Mads grumbled. He stood by the port rail, looking out over the water. "Days of sailing ahead in the wet and wind."

"It'll be less wet in the south, at least," Robin told him. "Now, if you two don't mind coming below decks to my office, it's time to discuss our plan."

5

ട ട ട ട ട ട ട ട

A Course Southeast

Robin Trelawney led Bryn and Mads below deck. Once out of the biting wind, Bryn warmed up almost immediately. At the base of the steps, instead of turning left toward Bryn's cabin, they went back and into another small room.

A large round window in the back of the room looked out over the water, splattered by the frigid rain. Lanterns lit the room, casting yellow beams on the roll of parchment spread upon the small table.

John Tailor stood inside with two other sailors. Two Ringmembers Bryn recognized but didn't know by name waited silently. They stood apart in distinct groups—sailors and Ringmembers. Bryn studied the faces of the two Ringmembers, seeing the tension in their stance. The total loyalty to the Dricaster Brethren and the fear and distrust of outsiders were ingrained in every fiber of their being. Trelawney might be a member of the Brethren, but his crew weren't. Bryn doubted any camaraderie would ever come about.

Then she thought about the crew, who had been civil so far. John Tailor had been welcoming. Oliver had been friendly. No, she may not trust them, but she could at least accept them as allies for now.

She stood slightly behind Robin's shoulder and looked around.

The nearest Ringmember to them looked to be in his mid-sixties. He was tall and burly, with a square face and bushy beard. He wore utilitarian armor made of steel and leather. His eyes were dark and set close, darting around the room. The blade of the sword at his belt was nearly the width of Bryn's arm.

The other Ringmember was a Hymian. Easily identified by his pale blue skin and rust-red hair, he stood silent and observant, a little taller than Robin. His armor was Hymian by make, too, finely cut and crafted steel as light as scales. This warrior was vaguely familiar, and she remembered that he had joined with the Dricasters a few years ago.

Once everyone was gathered and the door closed, Robin spoke. "Well, then. Let's get introductions over. As you know, I'm Robin Trelawney, captain of the *Burman Marie*." He gestured around the interior slightly, as though to reiterate that the ship was very much his own. Bryn rolled her eyes.

"These men," Robin turned to the three sailors, "are my principle officers on board the *Marie*. John Tailor, first mate. Richard Darvi, bosun. Matthew McCreery, second mate."

The three men nodded as they were introduced. Richard was the oldest: muscular, bearded, and built like a bull. Matthew was shorter and stockier, with straw-colored hair and a glass eye where his left one had once been. John's tidy appearance and slim build stood out from the other two.

"These four," Robin said, turning to the Ringmembers behind

him, "are our hired help for this venture. Harven Drike of Sikhazi." The sword wielding giant nodded slightly. "Roragan Cliadell of Kilee." The Hymian did not react at all to his name, only stared unblinking at Robin.

"Mads Moda, and Bryn Valetown," Robin finished. "You don't have to like each other, but try your best to get along. There's reward enough for all of us."

Is there? Bryn wondered inwardly. She was still confident in her earlier theory—about their employer expecting them to kill each other off so he only had to pay one person.

"What specifically is required of us for said reward, Cap'n?" Richard Darvi asked. His low voice held the faint burr of a Southerner's accent.

Robin reached into the breast pocket of his coat and pulled out a faded piece of paper. "We're going to find this," he said, and slapped it on the table. Bryn peered around his shoulder to see a slightly smudged drawing bearing a decent rendering of the compass. Black and shiny, with a strange star-like emblem etched under the arrow hand.

Bryn noticed the three sailors exchanged excited yet worried glances. They seemed to recognize the object. "A compass, Cap'n?" Matthew McCreery asked slowly.

"A compass," Robin confirmed with a nod. "And if you ask me why, I'll tell you honestly—I don't know. I have some guesses, sure, but that's not important. What's important is that our elusive employer has promised to pay us each six hundred lupin if we can deliver it."

"Are we assured of that?" Mads asked. They all looked at him. Bryn realized this question hadn't been answered yet. Usually, when someone hired a Ringmember, they offered some form of insurance—a physical promise that the job would be paid. Half-pay up front. Valuable information. Something.

"I don't know," Robin admitted. "The employer did the deal with Dakrind. Dakrind's assured us that we'll be paid."

That was hardly reassuring, but Bryn knew they couldn't do much about it.

"Do we have a heading?" John asked.

Robin put the drawing back inside his pocket and bent over the map. "According to our sources, the Rylander Crime Ring is determined to get the compass too. Unfortunately for them, the Dricasters' spies picked up news on their movements. The compass was intercepted by a Dricaster Ringmember a few weeks ago, hidden somewhere along the coast near Port Rylan."

Bryn eyed the map uncertainly. A dot marked Port Rylan, about halfway down the coastline. That only narrowed down the search a little, though. "Where?" she asked.

Robin unfolded a smaller piece of paper. "This is a map of the port and surrounding area. According to this, the man hid the compass in an apple orchard, about five miles within the city limits."

Bryn bit her lip. That meant they would have to pass through the city gates and walk the bustling streets of the Rylander port town before gaining the compass. More importantly, it meant they would have to leave the same way.

"That doesn't help us much," Mads muttered, evidently thinking the same as Bryn. "He couldn't have gotten the compass any closer to the city edge?"

"Maybe," Robin said mildly, "but considering he was killed in the act of getting this map to us, we'll never know."

An uncomfortable silence followed this statement.

"Well, then," Mads said briskly. "How long before we reach Port Rylan?"

Robin traced the jagged coastline of southern Daffodalion. "Once we round the Horn, we'll have a decent stretch of water before we enter Rylander territory. At that point, the going will be especially tedious."

"You think the Rylanders will recognize the ship, Cap'n?" Richard Darvi asked uneasily.

"Hopefully not," Robin said, "but they will have checkpoints or scouts that will patrol the southern waters. They tend to move those checkpoints periodically." He scanned the map, then looked up. "Who's gone south most recently?"

No one spoke, so Bryn cleared her throat. Everyone looked at her, as though remembering she was there. "I went that way last month, with Dakrind. We stopped just west of Port Rylan, and we went through two check points... here," she tapped a small cluster of rock islands, "and here." She indicated a distinctive outcrop of rock that jutted off the coast.

"Those may be problematic, Captain," John said warily. "The Rylanders will insist on inspecting the cargo, and they will likely recognize them." He nodded at Bryn and the other three Ring-members. All five Dricaster Ringmembers were wanted criminals, and their bounties would be higher if they were caught in Rylander territory.

Bryn noticed the nervousness in the eyes of the other three. Likely, none of them had ever gone that far into enemy territory. She felt critical of their fear until she remembered her own fright during the mission with Dakrind last month. Her pride faded. The trip had been harrowing. Aside from being an enemy city, Port Rylan was crawling with Capital soldiers, ordered to arrest any known criminal on the spot.

Dakrind had managed to avoid any Capital notice by steering clear of Port Rylan, but they'd had to fight a Rylander frigate on the way out. Since the *Black Raven* was equipped with cannons, they had won the fight, but it had been a frantic race to escape the Rylanders' territory.

"We'll probably get in fine," Robin said after a moment. "Getting out may be harder, especially if we have the compass with us." He exchanged a glance with Mads. Bryn frowned, wondering what he was implying.

The Hymian, Cliadell, spoke for the first time, his voice cold and dry. "You believe those tales, Trelawney?"

"Maybe," Robin said simply. "It's something to be aware of. Unlike you, I *have* been in Port Rylan before, and I've seen them myself."

"You've seen who?" Bryn asked, feeling a little left out.

Robin faltered. "I'll... tell you later," he said vaguely. He turned back to the map. "This strategy will keep the *Marie* well clear of Port Rylan. We'll anchor a mile or so off shore, row in, and walk the rest of the way into town." He indicated the route on the map. "Hopefully, we'll retrieve the compass fast and rendezvous with the ship and crew on the other side of the port—here."

Cliadell raised an eyebrow. "You intend to leave us stranded on your paltry ship while you claim the bounty for yourself, Trelawney?"

Robin smiled. The expression never reached his eyes. "Nope. We five," he nodded to the Ringmembers, "will go onshore ourselves and get the bounty all together."

"And most likely, get killed by Rylanders all together," Drike grumbled.

"Naw, they won't kill you," Mads said casually. "Rylanders are too broke to afford killing prisoners. They'll probably sell ya to the Jenna, more like."

That was not reassuring, but it shut the other two up.

"After we leave Port Rylan, we'll meet Hawk Dakrind on Drynrall Island," Robin continued, indicating a large island on the map. "We'll pass on the bounty and receive our pay."

Bryn frowned. "Wait—we're giving Dakrind the compass? Not the employer?" That was unusual. As the Ringleader, Dakrind often organized payment, but he never handled the bounty itself.

Robin shrugged. "Dakrind's the only one the employer even

agreed to work with. Whether he's paranoid or antisocial I can't tell."

Despite his casual words, Bryn found she could read his tone. *I don't like it either,* his voice said. *But don't bring it up here.* The prickle of unease she'd felt before had grown into a ripple of worry running through her veins. There was some other layer to this, something else they had yet to learn about this mission.

"We'll get to Port Rylan in four days, maybe three," Robin said. "In that time, keep ready. We know the Rylanders are onto us, and there's a good chance they'll try to intercept us before we get to the compass."

They cleared out of the room. Bryn fell behind Robin as they left and moved close enough to whisper under her breath. "Dakrind didn't say anything about meeting us in Drynrall."

"Really? I thought he might have told you. He told Mads and I," Robin replied quietly, sounding mildly interested. "I wonder why he didn't tell you."

"Dakrind probably had a reason," Bryn said shortly. It wasn't unusual for the Ringleader to withhold information from certain people. But as hard as she tried to ignore it, she found the thought troubling. "Why is he the one taking the compass at all?" she asked instead, pausing on the steps. "Why is he the only one to work with the employer?"

"Maybe," Robin said in a low tone, "he wants the compass for himself, and plans to take it before the employer gets it."

That idea pulled Bryn up short. She hadn't considered this possibility—not in the slightest. Dakrind had his own compass. He probably had several compasses—he was a pirate captain, after all. Why would he double cross the employer to gain this compass in particular?

Unless this compass wasn't just a compass, of course. Dakrind had talked about it almost reverently. Like it was a relic. Like it had… special powers.

This thought was laughable. Impossible. Dakrind was firmly grounded in fact—he wouldn't stake so much on a legend. More importantly, he was bound by the rules of the Brethren. He'd never turn on an employer, no matter the bounty.

Unless…

She shook the thought out of her head. She should know better than to question Dakrind, to question the Dricasters. No, knowing the Ringleader, he wanted to impress their secret employer by being the one to hand the compass over himself.

"Storm to starboard!" Richard's shout drew her attention back to the present. They were heading into a roiling wall of gray clouds. The water had grown restless, rocking the *Burman Marie* side to side and clawing at her hull as they neared the tip of the Horn.

Bryn moved up the steps on deck and caught up to Robin, who looked unworried. "Is that a hurricane?" she asked.

Robin glanced at the ominous clouds. "That? Oh, that's nothing. It's not hurricane season yet, you know—it's still too cold."

Bryn stared at him incredulously. Robin noticed her shocked expression and shrugged slightly. "It'll be a little rough for a while, so you might want to go below. But the *Marie's* gone through worse waters before. She'll make it through a little ripple like that without a problem."

With that, he gripped the wheel and steered the ship into open ocean.

6

∽ ∽ ∽ ∽ ∽ ∽ ∽ ∽ ∽ ∽

A Whisper of Wavers

As Captain Trelawney had predicted, the ominous black clouds caused no damage to the ship, but Bryn could hardly call it a "little ripple." As they left the shelter of Esile Bay and rounded the Horn, the warm Kamo Sea in the north clashed with the chilly waters of the south, creating a thundering tempest. Towering waves rolled the ship from side to side for hours as rain poured down in sheets and lightning raked the sky.

Bryn sheltered in her cabin for the first few minutes, but the pitching and tossing turned her stomach in a way that her voyage on the *Black Raven* never had. She was soon back on deck, dreadfully sea sick.

At least she wasn't alone. The other Ringmembers were no better off than she was, and clung to the port rail soaked to the bone. Mads adjusted to the tossing and rolling fairly quickly. "You'll get yer sea legs soon," he grunted to the others. "Keep an eye on the horizon, it'll help yer mind ground." This might have helped, but the horizon was impossible to glimpse clearly between the gray sea and gray clouds.

The crew worked tirelessly and calmly enough, which eased Bryn's initial nervousness. If the worse storms congregated at the Horn, the crew must be used to this. For the most part, the sailors sympathetically ignored the discomfort of the other four. Oliver offered them some water; they thanked him but declined. It was too shaky to drink anything, and they were all so wet from rain and seawater that no one felt thirsty.

Robin, on the other hand, found the entire scene amusing. When they finally broke clear of the storm several hours later, he threw the queasy group a smirk and commented, "There, that wasn't so bad, was it? I mean, aside from you four hurling your insides into the sea at every bump, it was just fine."

Bryn glared at him, but her uneasy stomach kept her from coming up with a scathing reply.

Once the sea had settled, Oliver brought them water and biscuits. Bryn didn't feel particularly hungry, but the food and drink helped.

"That's probably the baddest it'll get," Oliver informed them cheerfully as they ate. "Now we've come round the Horn of Esile. It's normally not too bad in the Southern Seas."

"How long have you had this kid with you?" Mads asked Robin.

"A few years. Keep him around to do the washing," Robin said absently. Oliver grinned at him.

Bryn was sopping wet and the wind set her shivering, but her stomach was still settling and she didn't want to retreat to the stuffy quarters below. Instead, she sat on the deck with her back against the gunwale, catching her breath.

The low voice of the Hymian, Cliadell, drew her attention. He was speaking with Drike. "This mission reeks of treachery. We are to trust the word of a roaming pirate, the captain of a crew who are not of the Brethren. Have you noted this?"

"You think they're a threat?" Drike grunted.

"Perhaps under certain circumstances. They believe the legend of the compass. Their fear may lead to foolish decisions."

"You think they would take the compass for themselves?" Drike asked, his tone dark. "Do you think they'd turn on the Brethren?"

"I cannot say. I do not trust Trelawney." Cliadell noticed Bryn watching him, and his eyes narrowed. "Is there a problem, Vale-town?"

"That's what I wondered," Bryn said steadily. "Dakrind trusts them."

"Dakrind trusts no one," Robin said. "That's probably why he's still alive." They turned sharply, realizing he had been listening. The pirate captain studied Cliadell carefully. "What are you implying I'd do with the compass?"

The Hymian looked at him for a long moment, a gleam of distrust in his eyes. "You say you have been to Port Rylan," he said finally. "You claim the Wavers indeed exist."

Bryn frowned at the term, but both Drike and Mads reacted, looking at Robin with a fear and wariness that surprised her. She didn't know Drike well, but she knew he had been a Ringmember for a while, and had likely seen plenty of frightening things. As for Mads, she'd never seen him react like this. He was nervous around the soldiers, sure, but the look in his eyes was a different, deeper fear.

Robin folded his arms over his chest. "I've been to Port Rylan," he said casually. "I don't claim anything about the Wavers at all. I do think the compass does things to people, but that's just my opinion."

Cliadell eyed him and shook his head slowly. "Say what you will, captain. There is something strange about this mission, and I intend to find out what."

"Only thing strange is what you're imagining," Mads said, his fear disguised again.

Harry, the cook, had prepared a savory stew. Bald and beardless, he remained below decks, cutting up meat and occasionally tossing a scrap to the cat. The crew headed below for a quick meal as night fell. Bryn and the other Ringmembers joined them.

Bryn sat in the corner of the room, eating and observing. The soothing broth helped dispel the last traces of nausea and warmed her up.

She kept a careful eye on both Robin, who was sitting at a table near her, and Cliadell who sat on the opposite side of the eating room. She doubted the Hymian would act on his suspicions and turn on Robin. Whether or not they trusted one another, they were both Ringmembers, working for the same purpose.

But what about Robin? Was he actually after the compass for his own gain, as Cliadell had implied? Would he really betray them?

Cliadell and Drike clearly sensed something was amiss—not just in the unusual nature of the mission. No, they seemed to believe that the entire crew of the *Marie* would turn on them for the compass.

Robin noticed her scrutinizing gaze and threw her a slight smile. "Something on your mind, Miss Valetown?"

"What are Wavers?" Bryn asked quietly.

Robin hesitated. Mads, who sat across from him, looked at Bryn intently. "Figured you would have run into them when you went south with Dakrind last month," the Dwarve mused.

"We kept to the sea. We never went inside Port Rylan. From what you've implied, these Wavers are only in the city," Bryn said, keeping her eyes on Robin. "What are they?"

Robin took a slow drink of ale. "Depends what you believe," he said vaguely. "What do you believe about the compass?"

Bryn shrugged. "Nothing more than what's been told. Our employer seems to be willing to pay a lot for a simple compass, if you ask me."

Robin leaned back. "In that case, the Wavers are a population of madmen. Nothing more than that. Ask the Capital, they'll say greenstalk is to blame."

Bryn frowned doubtfully. From what she had heard, Port Rylan was a relatively safe city compared to Esile. It was much more law-abiding, with far less corruption than the Esile Council. She found it very unlikely that a population of drug-driven madmen lived there.

"Greenstalk don't do that to people, and you know that, Trelawney," Mads said shortly.

"What are the Wavers like?" Bryn asked.

Robin thought for a moment. "Like a shell. Most of their conscious thought has rotted away. Most of them starve to death simply because they forget to eat, if they live that long. Before that, they lose any sensation of pain, any memories. They're driven by one purpose."

"To get more greenstalk?" Bryn guessed.

"We wish," Mads snorted.

"I just told you what the Capital would call the Wavers," Robin said after a pause. "What others think would be different."

"I don't care what the others think," Bryn said flatly. "I want to know the truth."

"Then we agree on that," Robin said. He said nothing further, only studied Bryn carefully. Bryn had the odd sensation that she was missing something, but she couldn't think what it could be.

She studied the table top, trying to figure out what Robin meant. She had never heard of Wavers before yesterday. If there was supposedly a large population of madmen living in Port Rylan, she would have heard of them before, wouldn't she? Then again, maybe not. The compass was important, but she'd never heard of it before now either.

The compass. Thinking of it reminded her of Robin's words earlier today. He'd said that he believed the compass did things to people.

What kind of things? Drike and Mads' fearful reaction implied that it wasn't good. If it was indeed some kind of weapon, that explained why the employer would pay so much for it. He could then use it to fight his enemies. Yet Bryn couldn't see how a compass could do anything besides its intended purpose.

For another matter, why did the Rylander employer—whoever they were—want the compass? She thought through a few possibilities. Perhaps the Rylanders had been hired by the king of Caer Sia. That would explain why they were trying to stop the Dricasters from getting the compass. But that didn't make much sense either. If Caer Sia wanted to stop the Dricaster employer, they'd send their own soldiers to do it, not hire out a rival Crime Ring.

Whatever the truth of it, Bryn could assume the Rylanders would fight to get the compass. Someone had hired them to find it, and they certainly wouldn't let it go easily.

7

The Blood Swan

Bryn lay awake, thinking long into the night. So many questions had been roused in such a short period of time. The strange interest everyone seemed to have in the compass. The fear in the sailors' eyes upon hearing of it. Mads' genuine concern upon the mention of the Wavers. Robin's vague answers. The fact that they were to give the compass to Dakrind, not directly to the employer.

Maybe Robin's theory was right, and Dakrind wanted the compass for himself…

None of it connected. Bryn spent the night deep in thought, wracking her brain to come up with an answer. *Never find satisfaction in the unknown. There's a logical explanation for everything.* That was something her father used to say. Cold-voiced, stone-willed, unimpressed, uninterested. He had always been the same, her father. Right up until the moment he'd been killed.

Fire in the house, voices in her mind, a little hand gripped in hers, torn away…

Bryn sat up stiffly, realizing she must have drifted off sometime in the night. The slow rocking of her hammock and the rolling of the ship had lulled her to sleep. Dawn light streamed through the small round window of the cabin. She pulled on her coat and boots and went up on deck.

The *Marie* moved at a brisk pace, her sails filled by the northern breeze. Robin stood at the helm, squinting against the rising sun.

"Have we passed any checkpoints yet?" Bryn asked him.

He shook his head. "None so far. We're close to the first checkpoint you indicated on the map."

"Unless the checkpoints have moved since then," Bryn pointed out. It had been at least a month since she had last sailed this way. There was a chance the Rylanders had relocated the checkpoints.

"True. Never know how much has changed in the time since you were last here." Robin glanced at her. "Speaking of which, what brought you south last time?"

Bryn shrugged slightly. "Dakrind had a deal with an informant, and he needed protection to get through the Rylander territory."

Robin nodded, processing. "Where?"

"Drynrall Island."

"I wonder what brought Dakrind to Drynrall Island," Robin mused. His tone implied a question. Bryn realized, to her chagrin, that she had forgotten the details of that mission—if she had ever been told them. The latter was more likely, she decided. Dakrind rarely told her anything. But that thought was traitorous to the Brethren, and she couldn't admit such a thing to Robin.

She avoided answering the question. "Dakrind was meeting with someone. I don't know anything more," she replied irritably.

"And yet you agreed to take the job."

"I agreed at the request of the Ringleader," Bryn informed him. "The same reason I agreed to take this job. Why do you ask?" she added suspiciously.

Robin only shrugged again. "Only thinking. Hawk tends to leave out important information. I like to know what information and why. Helps me connect the dots about him, and about you."

Bryn stared at him, not sure if he was joking or not. He seemed serious, which confused her. She had never heard anyone talk so casually about the Ringleader. Though she'd never trusted Dakrind herself, she certainly never mentioned that to her fellow Ringmembers. Such thoughts harmonized with the doubt she infrequently felt during her missions, the same uncertainty she'd felt after killing the two guards a few nights ago. That doubt was joined with the more dangerous ideas of leaving the Ring altogether, of unclasping the Dricaster pin and walking away from it all.

"What dots do you connect about me, then?" she asked instead, turning her attention to the buttons of her coat. It helped hide the notes of both unease and interest in her voice.

"Nothing much more than what you've told me," Robin said. "You're a straightforward person. Skeptical too. You see things as they are. That's good. But it confuses me about this."

Bryn frowned. "About what?"

Robin gestured at their surroundings. "You being a Ringmember at all. You don't question what you're doing, or what you're being ordered to do. It doesn't seem to line up with that part of your character."

His statement was almost exactly what she had first asked herself when she had joined the Dricasters. She had long grown used to shoving those doubts aside, but hearing them aloud now made them real to her, forced her to face them. *What are you doing here, Brynlee?* her inner voice wondered.

Bryn felt her face warm. "I'm here because I choose to be," she said, half to convince herself. "And you should be careful voicing those ideas, Captain Trelawney. That sort of talk could get you expelled from the Brethren."

"I'm allowed to talk," Robin said coolly.

The voice of Matthew McCreery interrupted the conversation. The second mate crouched in the crow's nest, peering out to sea. "Ship to bow, Cap'n!"

Robin looked up sharply. Bryn peered out over the waters ahead. Silhouetted against the sunrise was the distinctive shape of a sail. From this distance, it was difficult to tell if the ship flew the colors of a Crime Ring, but Bryn had no doubts that it was a Rylander scout.

From Robin's expression, he had the same thought. "Now why would they send a scout to meet us?" he muttered, confused.

"That's a Rylander ship?" Bryn asked for confirmation.

"It'd be safe to assume," Robin said. His joking manner was gone now, his face serious. "We can't avoid them. They will only give chase."

John Tailor had emerged from below decks the instant he had

heard Matthew's warning, and turned to Robin. "Shall we run up the cannons, Captain?"

"Ready the guns," Robin confirmed.

Bryn looked at him uncertainly. "Captain Trelawney, that isn't a good plan. If we engage in battle, the Rylanders will know who we are. Even if we escape them now, they'll be ready to catch us the instant we reach Port Rylan."

Robin drew breath to argue, stopped, and thought for a moment. "That's true, but what else would you have us do? We are, five of us at least, wanted Ringmembers in enemy territory."

Bryn glanced back at the oncoming vessel, hesitating for a moment. Robin was right. If they didn't prepare to fight, the Rylander ship would subdue them in an instant. Then the Ringmembers would be captured, and either be turned in to the Daffonic Capital of Fauna, or sold to the Jenna.

But if they fought, all elements of stealth would be lost. If they weren't simply killed here, the Rylanders would kill them as soon as they made berth in Port Rylan.

Neither were appealing options, and neither brought them any closer to gaining the compass.

The rest of the crew were up and active by now. The wind drove them on, as though urging them to confront the Rylanders. John Tailor jogged to the prow, shouting orders to the crew on his way there. The other three Ringmembers had come above, watching the other ship warily.

Slowly yet surely, the ships drew nearer together. Bryn could see details now. The ship was larger and leaner than the *Marie*, made of pale silver wood that gave her a ghostly quality. The Rylander's violet and silver flag fluttered from her central mast.

"We do not need to fight them, Trelawney," Cliadell said. "If your ship is half as fast as you described, we can flee and avoid the confrontation all together."

"And run where?" Mads asked dryly. "This is their territory." He looked at Robin. "All the same, if you're planning to fight them, it'll make our entrance into Port Rylan that much trickier."

"We don't have an option," Robin said. "If they catch us, there's no getting into Port Rylan at all. Get below, you three. I'll handle the confrontation, and Miss Valetown will watch my back."

"Your face is known just as much as theirs," Bryn pointed out.

John returned to the tiller, his face drawn. "Captain, that is not a frigate. That's the *Blood Swan*."

"What?" Robin demanded, real fear showing on his face. He snatched the spy glass from John and peered through it for a moment. "Curse it all, you're right. What's she doing out here?"

"What's the *Blood Swan*?" Drike asked.

"The Rylanders' flagship," Mads said grimly. "Their Ringleader will likely be on board too."

Bryn looked at the ship. The Rylanders were closer now, nearly within arrow shot. The *Blood Swan* glided toward them with a chilling grace. The water drew back before her prow, exposing a gleaming ram attached to her hull. Judging by the ship's swift, agile movements, once in range, she could ram the *Marie* before they had time to fire a single round.

"Get below," Robin ordered again, regaining control of his thoughts. "Wait there until we're clear."

"You know they will want to inspect the ship," John said doubtfully.

"Can they do that?" Bryn asked, wondering if there was some sort of loophole to avoid a full inspection.

"The Rylanders are allowed to stop any ship that comes through their waters for inspection, with the exception of Capital vessels," Robin said, irritated. "It's their territory, after all."

"The Rylanders frequently deal with the Jenna," John pointed out wearily. "They may not recognize the *Marie*, but they will want to inspect the cargo and see if there is anything they can buy or trade."

"Either way, the Rylanders will recognize you," Bryn said. An idea came to her as she spoke. "I don't think they'll recognize the *Marie*. Mr. Tailor—can you bring me four sets of chains?"

John threw a confused glance at Robin, who shrugged. "Can't hurt to try. I think I can guess what she's getting at."

"They're coming up," Mads warned. "You better act quick, Valetown, before they take us as prisoners after inspecting the cargo."

"Not if you're the cargo," Bryn said urgently. John reappeared with four pairs of handcuffs. The others finally realized what she was implying, and drew back warily. "This is the best way we'll get through," Bryn insisted. "There's any number of slavers that come this way normally. Presenting you as prisoners will be easier than explaining why you're here, and I'm the only one whose face they don't know."

"So we act as your captives?" Cliadell said slowly.

"That's right. Now hurry, before you get captured for real," Bryn urged them, stepping forward with the chains. No one moved. Cliadell and Drike looked openly distrustful.

Robin finally stepped forward with a sigh. "Hang it all, you're right." He offered his wrists, and Bryn set to work chaining him. At his example, the others did the same.

"This is a terrible plan," Cliadell growled.

"This is a great plan," Mads said with a short chuckle. "They don't know Valetown's face. If she's a half decent actress, she'll act the part of a slaver, and the Rylanders will believe her." He scowled. "Which unfortunately means we have to play the part of beaten Dricasters."

"Well, play that part well," Bryn said. "This whole mission depends on it."

They headed below decks as the ship drew nearer. The berth decks were lit only by three lanterns, aside from the faint daylight leaking through the gun ports. Robin and the other three men knelt to the left of the stairwell. Bryn stood slightly in front of them, listening tensely.

"Did they inspect the *Black Raven* the last time you came this way?" Robin asked in a lowered voice.

"No," Bryn whispered back, trying not to show her uncertainty and fear.

"It'll be quick," Robin told her quietly. "Keep your head down and do what they say. They'll want to inspect the whole ship. Don't stop them. Any resistance or argument will be suspicious."

"All right," Bryn said, reassured slightly by his words.

"Here they come," John murmured down the stairs to them.

There was a distant rush of water and creaking of timbers as the *Blood Swan* drew level with the *Marie*. A voice called across the water, echoing downstairs. "Halt! These waters are the domain of the Rylander Brethren. Your ship must be cleared before you proceed."

"You may board," came John's returning call.

Bryn heard the slap of the mooring lines as the sailors secured the *Marie*, locking her in place beside the *Swan*. Then came the clatter of boots as the pirates swung easily to the opposite deck.

John's polite voice came to Bryn's ears again. "Madam Ida. Welcome aboard."

A woman replied crisply. "You are captain of this vessel, I assume?"

Robin inhaled sharply. Bryn glanced a question at him, and he whispered, "The Ringleader herself. Be careful, Bryn. She's dangerous, even for a—"

"Shh!" Mads hissed.

"Correct, my lady," John answered, his voice drifting down the stairs.

"Then I assume Captain Trelawney finally received his due," the woman answered, sounding slightly amused. "Let us go below."

Footsteps paced the length of the deck to the stairs. Bryn glanced at her companions, who knelt on the floor, their shadowed faces not quite hiding their uneasiness.

John appeared down the steps, his pale face the only indication of how nervous he was. Three Rylanders Bryn recognized from other wanted posters came downstairs, their leader wearing a blue coat.

A tall, wiry woman entered last. She wore a long coat, but the rest of her body was covered in dense fur speckled gray and white, the color of ash. One flashing green eye surveyed the ship, the left one was covered by a patch that did not conceal the scars on that side of her face. Her hair was cropped short, and her catlike ears and the slight upturn of her face affirmed Bryn's guess. The Rylander leader was a Wildkid.

John nodded at the Ringmembers, chained in a line by the starboard rail. "Our cargo is grains and drink. You are welcome to purchase any if you so choose."

"Indeed," Madam Ida answered shortly. "Search the ship," she ordered the other Rylanders. The pirates crossed to the cargo hold, bumping past Oliver, who was walking the opposite direction. One of the Rylanders shoved the cabin boy out of the way with a curse. Oliver glared at them, but Richard gripped his shoulder.

"What is your destination?" Madam Ida asked, ignoring the interaction behind her.

"Drynrall Island, madam."

"Very well," Madam Ida said, seeming satisfied. "No firearms among the cargo?"

John hesitated for a split second. "No."

Bryn noticed Robin and John exchanged a quick, nervous look. She had never stopped to take stock of the cargo the *Burman Marie* was carrying, but she guessed they were indeed smuggling firearms. Such cargo would be of great interest to the Rylanders—they'd probably insist on taking it.

"You neglected to include the slaves, Captain," she said quickly, drawing Madam Ida's attention away from John. The Rylander Ringleader studied her for a moment, and Bryn tried not to react. Her gaze held the same lack of empathy as Dakrind's, but there was a wildness blazing there that chilled Bryn.

"These are your bounties, I assume?" Madam Ida asked.

Bryn nodded. The Wildkid studied her thoughtfully. "Your face is familiar, but I do not think we have met."

Cold fear clutched Bryn's stomach for an instant. Could the Rylanders know her? Had they somehow connected her face to the reputation of the feared bounty hunter? No, no, that was impossible. She gave a slight shrug and what she hoped was a casual smile. "I just have one of those faces, ma'am."

Madam Ida nodded shortly and studied the chained Dricasters. "Quite a catch," she commented. "They will fetch high prices from the Capital, as I am sure you know."

"The Jenna know their bounties," Bryn said slowly. "They'll match the price, and if they don't, I'll take these four to Fauna."

"Wise choice," Madam Ida murmured. She studied the prisoners with mild interest. "Mads Moda, it has been a while since we saw you in our waters. Was your retirement so short?"

Mads glared at her. "Not long enough, Ida. I hear your people have been busy. Dealing with Jenna, chasing Dricaster bounties—you must be swamped."

Disdain crossed Madam Ida's face. "The Jenna will have little use for this one, slaver," she informed Bryn.

"They could have him for a jester," Bryn said. "I hear Jenna have notoriously bad senses of humor."

Madam Ida moved down the line to Robin. "Well, well, Trelawney. I believe the Viriki have senses of humor." She smiled coldly. "How much is your bounty?"

Robin returned an easy smile. "Oh, probably not as high as yours. It's delightful to see you, Madam Ida. Your company is such an improvement from Hawk Dakrind's. I might turn Rylander just to work for you."

His smooth compliment was so casual Bryn worried it would seem suspicious, but Madam Ida only laughed shortly. "It is far too late for such charms, Trelawney. Still, you might be useful." She turned to John. "How much will you have for him?"

John nodded to Bryn. "They are her bounties, madam. We are only ferrying the slaves east."

Bryn felt a stir of unease. She should have expected this. As a Dricaster captain, Robin would be a coveted prisoner among the Rylanders. "Two, three hundred, maybe," she answered with a slight shrug.

"I will give you one seventy for him, and save you his silver tongue the rest of your journey," Madam Ida offered.

"Can't do it," Bryn said, shaking her head. "Besides, I've already promised him to the Jenna."

"Did you?" Madam Ida said, irritated. "Two hundred, then."

Robin looked alarmed. Bryn pretended to think about it. "I'm hoping for two fifty from the Aikala Jenna tribe," she said after a pause. "If they don't want him, I'll bring him to you."

Madam Ida glanced between Bryn and Robin. "How did she catch you, Trelawney?" she asked abruptly.

The unexpected question caught Bryn off guard, and for an instant, she froze, unable to imagine what answer he could give.

Thankfully, Robin was quick. "It was embarrassing, really," he said. "I had no idea she was a bounty hunter. She met me in a tavern, had me buy her a few drinks, flirted and flattered me like I was the High King. All the charms and tricks. Quite a cunning little flirt, she is. You know how women are," he added to Mads, who looked like he was about to break a rib trying not to laugh.

This was so outrageous that Bryn almost started protesting, but she forced herself to go with the story. "You're easy to flatter, Trelawney," she told him. "Maybe pick your company better next time."

Madam Ida looked impressed. "Very well. You are free to pass, slaver."

The pirate in the blue coat strode up to the Ringleader. "Nothing to report, Captain. No weapons aside from those arming the ship, and none in the cargo hold.”

“Good,” Madam Ida said, and turned to John. “Sail on. I will order the second checkpoint to allow you through.”

“Thank you, my lady,” John said, tipping his hat again.

The Rylanders walked back up the stairs. Bryn waited until she heard the mooring lines hauled loose and the sound of the *Swan's* oars pushing away before she unchained the others. But she waited several more minutes, until John peeked down at them, a nervous smile on his face. “They have gone. You can come up.”

Bryn felt herself exhale, the tension fading as she walked back up into fresh air. The *Marie's* crew stood above, all with the same hesitant relief that they had escaped. The *Blood Swan* sailed west, and the *Marie* moved away in the opposite direction.

“By the Light, that was slick,” Richard said with a wide grin.

Bryn looked at Robin. “You think the second checkpoint will let us through?”

“They have no reason to stop us now,” Robin said with a shrug. “We’ll get to Port Rylan that much faster.”

“What about the Jenna?” Cliadell asked warily. “Do you believe the Rylanders will double check your story with them?”

“The Aikala Jenna hardly ever do business with the Mainland,” Bryn said. “Even if the Rylanders talk to one of the other tribes, I doubt the news would come up that quickly.”

“Smart,” Mads said.

"Humph," Cliadell snorted sullenly. He and Drike moved away. Bryn ignored them, too relieved they had escaped the Rylanders to really care about their irritation.

"They didn't notice the guns?" John asked Richard.

"They might have, but wouldn't have known it," Richard chuckled. "It was Oliver's idea."

"Whiskers was sleeping," Oliver broke in excitedly. "So I put her on the sack with the guns, and the Rylanders just thought it was her bed."

"Now that's slick," Mads said, throwing the boy a genuine smile.

"Not as slick as Miss Valetown," John said to Bryn. The other sailors echoed their compliments.

Bryn hid a smile, pleased by the successful plan and by the admiration in the eyes of the crew. "We should keep on the lookout all the same," she told the enthusiastic sailors. "I wouldn't trust a Rylander as far as I could throw one."

"Let's get moving," Robin said, moving to the tiller. "Hard to starboard. Send her east."

John repeated the orders to the crew, who leapt back into action. The *Burman Marie* turned slightly to the right, then began moving forward, the wind filling her sails again.

Robin watched the retreating *Blood Swan* and shook his head slowly. "Decent plan, Miss Valetown," he said to Bryn, the crooked grin returning to his face. "But to make one thing clear—I am worth more than three hundred lupin."

Bryn rolled her eyes. "To make another thing clear, I am *not* a flirt."

"Oh, you both tell good stories," Mads told them. "If you weren't constantly bickering, I'd say you make a decent team." He sighed and took a draw on his pipe. "Of course, what do I know."

8

Stone and Ship

The snow began again as Aryion and Mel headed south. In this part of Daffodalion, with the high road skirting the foothills of the Diamond Cap Mountains, winter came swiftly, swirling through and freezing the forest before moving north. The road was slick with ice and slush.

Aryion and Mel had left Lemsonburg the day before and traveled steadily toward the ferry station several miles southwest. They had spent the night cold but sheltered in a stable, and continued south at dawn. The slippery road made the going painfully slow.

"We should have borrowed horses," Mel said for the second time that morning.

Aryion drew his cloak tighter around his shoulders, shielding himself from the falling snow, and shook his head. "As I told you, the road would be too treacherous for them. Besides, where do you think we'd find horses to borrow?"

His apprentice thought for a moment, brow furrowed. "I don't know. A farm or something. I thought rangers could just… borrow horses."

"Well, you could, I suppose. But you would have to explain to an exceptionally angry farmer that you would bring them back, which, in these parts, is unlikely."

"We could pay him, couldn't we?"

"We?" Aryion repeated dryly. "Right now I need to pay for our boat ride south, and places to stay along the way. Unless you have some spare change, then no, I don't think we can pay for horses." He skidded slightly and ended up ankle deep in a large mud puddle. Cold water sloshed inside his boots, and he swore under his breath.

Mel nearly lost his footing on an icy patch and used the same word.

"Don't say that. Your mother will kill me," Aryion said.

"My mom's too happy that you offered to train me at all," Mel said, unworried. "I think she was afraid I'd go into some low-pay trade school otherwise."

"Rangering isn't exactly a high-end profession, you know."

"Yeah, but we get paid by Caer Sia for doing missions like this," Mel pointed out. "And it's better than a boring trade like… I don't know, banking or something."

"Which would probably be safer."

"Well, I don't want a different trade."

"I know," Aryion said with a smile.

Six months ago, Mel had officially chosen to train as a ranger. Though not a traditional trade school, it had satisfied both the expectations of Mel's parents and Mel's own desire for adventure. Aryion knew the boy would have been miserable doing anything that separated him from this strange world of adventure that had become his life ever since the incident with the Darkness.

Since then, of course, there was their latest quest, the one that had brought them together. This had changed their relationship from guard and charge to master and apprentice. And it had led them both to the face of death—quite literally.

"How's the Stone today?" Aryion asked.

Mel reached in his pocket and produced the Blue Stone. One of three Star-Stones—well, two, now that the Jewel of Power was destroyed—it drew its power from the Land Immortal. After joining the Shards into one, Mel had been appointed as the Keeper of the Stone. The Blue Stone was different than its sisters. In the hand of a worthy wielder, its power flowed through the person, allowing him to channel its pure magic through his body for defense and protection.

It was definitely not the sort of power you used against an over-bearing yet defenseless prisoner.

"You don't think the Aces will… come after us, since I used the Stone?" Mel asked nervously. "Rygal said that the Serventiri used to track the Jewel's magic. What if the Aces do that?"

"I doubt the Aces will come after it. They know you have it either way," Aryion said. "But don't use it to intimidate someone like that again. It just causes more problems."

Mel slipped the Stone back into his pocket, his shoulders slumped. Aryion felt a twinge of guilt over his blunt words. It was hard scolding Mel; he was usually harder on himself than Aryion ever was. Still, he would learn. He was only twelve, after all.

"The Stone will defend you if you ask it," Aryion told him, softening his tone. "And I hope you will use it in situations where you need to protect yourself or others. But you need to learn to use your own skills, too. You can't use the Stone for every issue that comes up."

"I know. I just—didn't want to look weak. In front of the warden, or the guards, or the prisoner," Mel admitted.

Of course you didn't, Aryion thought. For a boy who had faced off with wraiths and Aces, being taunted by a rude prisoner must be infuriating. "You are not weak," he said. "And Bregg knew it. You didn't rise to his challenge right away, and that made him angry, so he kept pushing you. You need to resist the urge to fight back. Don't let your sense of honor cause you to make poor decisions. Wise men are patient men."

Mel nodded slowly, digesting this. They walked in silence for a few minutes, occasionally skidding or sliding in the slush.

"Aryion?" Mel asked finally.

"Yes?"

"Why are we going to Esile City? I mean—couldn't we just search for Terrax' trail ourselves, instead of doing what Bregg said?"

"We could," Aryion said, "but it would probably take longer. No one's quite sure where Terrax is. He might have gone south, as Bregg said. Or he could be roaming the forests in the north. We could take a guess at where he could be, but it's easier to follow the trail he left—and for the time being, that leads us to Esile City."

"So we're going to search for the Crime Ring he went to?" Mel asked.

"No, not quite," Aryion said. "I'm hoping we can avoid a confrontation with the Crime Rings all together. We'll contact the authorities in Esile City and see if they have news regarding Terrax. If he went there after the battle with the Darkness, they might have information about where he is now."

There was a brief pause. Aryion could see Mel's brow furrowed slightly, a sure sign that he was coming up with more questions. Finally, Mel said, "I'm still not sure why we need to bring Terrax in at all."

Aryion nodded, pleased. He had been waiting for his apprentice to voice this question. Knowing their motives were an important part of any mission. "Aside from it being a request of the High King, you mean?"

"Well, yes. Why would Jan want us to find Terrax? We already beat him, right before we destroyed the Darkness. Why would arresting Terrax change anything?"

Aryion thought for a moment. "Terrax may have been defeated, but I doubt he has simply faded into the background. He wants Star-Stones, Mel—that was his mission before and it probably still is now."

"The Ace-Lord wants the Stones too, though."

"True." A brief pause. The name sobered them both. Aryion began again. "The Aces have been driven back for now. Whatever their next plan is, we have to take advantage of this time before the war begins again. Now is the ideal time to track Terrax down and stop him. He is a variable we can't afford in these times."

Mel frowned thoughtfully. "That's true. But wouldn't it be easier to just… track him down and kill him? It's not as if we need to question him."

It was a simple question, but Aryion felt a prickle of unease as Mel said it. He glanced at his apprentice. That gleam of pain and hatred he had noticed in Mel's eyes during his confrontation with Bregg was present, though subdued. Whatever Mel said, Aryion could read his apprentice's tone and expression. He could tell Mel wanted Terrax to pay for the pain he had caused. He wanted him dead.

"It's better practice to bring in prisoners alive, instead of killing them," he answered slowly. "We are law-abiding rangers, not bounty hunters."

"All right. I just thought it might be… easier." Mel shrugged. "Still, Terrax doesn't seem like our biggest problem. Shouldn't we be more worried about stopping the Aces instead?"

"Terrax is not the Ace-Lord," Aryion agreed. "But look at what he managed before, Mel. The uncertainty he caused within Caer Sia, working for Drona, sending a deadly force to attack the city—if that were to happen now, the Aces would capitalize on it. Our fight with the Aces has paused for now. Both sides will mobilize and prepare, and we must be ready."

Mel nodded slowly, though he still looked doubtful. "It feels weird. Like we're just waiting for the Aces to make the next move. You always say it's best to strike first in a war."

"Not this war," Aryion said. "Not when the Prophecy states otherwise."

Mel's expression grew thoughtful at the mention of the Prophecy of Three. Aryion knew little about the Prophecy, which had changed from a long-forgotten legend to a vital piece of both information and advice from the High Light. Despite this, few people had read the Prophecy at all. While Mel had had the option to read it after joining the Shards, he had chosen not to.

The Prophecy, from what they had been told, predicted three events or stages, with key figures within each. Mel's role in the Prophecy had been to join the Shards and to resist the Ace-Lord— which had happened, down to the last detail.

Aryion had doubted the Prophecy initially, but he figured he might as well start believing in it now. The dark side of the supernatural had made itself abundantly known in the last few months. They would need every bit of light.

"Sometimes I think I should have read the Prophecy when I had the chance," Mel admitted.

Since the second stage of the Prophecy was yet to take place, Mel had decided to wait before he read the whole thing. The uncertainty in the ancient words would only add unneeded worry to the boy's mind. According to Iriam, the leader of the quest for the Shards, several key events had to happen before the second part of the

Prophecy would begin. Mel could read the Prophecy once the time was right.

"It wouldn't change when the second stage begins," Aryion pointed out. "Still, it might have been helpful to know what we're waiting for."

"Iriam says there will be people from both sides—some from the Aces, some from our side—that have to enter the war," Mel said.

"Mm," Aryion murmured. Mel had discussed his conversation with Iriam many times since they had left Caer Sia. Aryion secretly agreed that Mel's decision not to read the Prophecy had been a good one. No one really knew what the ancient words entailed. Besides that, he felt it was better to focus on one task at a time. The next part of the Prophecy—and the war—would happen eventually, and when it did, they and their allies would be ready.

For now, they had to find Terrax.

The hours passed slowly as they continued their journey south. At last, around midday, they reached the town of Wide Bend. Here, the Serpent River curved between the foothills and the eastern prairies, creating a three mile long lake that gave the town its name. As one of the larger rivers of the Mainland, the Serpent River allowed ships and barges to travel to and from Esile City, supplying and trading with the smaller villages in the Lemsonburg area.

Wide Bend was quiet and restful this time of year, since the merchant season had ended. Snow dusted the tidy streets. A cluster of houses and shops were built next to the river's edge. The main road led directly to the harbor, where a few elegant sailboats waited.

Aryion scanned the village as they walked. The houses, though quaint, were well-made, adding to the clean, put-together appearance of the town. The simple yet artistic feel of Wide Bend told him that it was likely exclusive to the wealthy merchants and traders who made their homes here in the off-season.

He slipped a hand inside his pocket, fingering the coins as he and Mel reached the harbor. A man stood near one of the skiffs, and moved to meet them as they approached.

"Afternoon, rangers," he called, his accent a mixture between the lilting Gevarian and the broad, rural tones of the east. "Can I help you?"

"Good day," Aryion returned. "We're hoping to buy passage south to Esile City."

The captain frowned slightly and made a *tsk-tsk* sound between his teeth. "Ahh, can't take ya all the way to Esile. But I can getcha halfway, and drop ya off at Yellow Bank, if that'll do."

Aryion hesitated for a second, then realized that would be better than nothing. Yellow Bank was twenty miles south, another small riverside town. It would be a slight delay, but they could make up the time. "That will be perfect," he agreed. He handed the desired amount over to the captain, who nodded in satisfaction.

"We'll be off in a half hour or so. Got a few more passengers on their way. Might be faster if you'd help us prepare," he added as an afterthought.

"Of course," Aryion said, following him to the sailboat. Mel trailed behind them. The boat was small and simple, with a large square-shaped sail tied to the center mast and two triangle sails at either end. In addition to carrying passengers, the little sailboat was to ferry a cargo of grain south to the town of Yellow Bank. The two rangers dutifully helped the crew load the remaining barrels on board. By the time they had finished, the other passengers—two hulking men who looked like twins, and a family of Dwarves—had arrived.

There was no room for seating below with the grain loaded, so they sat on the benches at the back of the boat. The captain called orders to his small crew and the boat swung away, moving steadily down river.

Aryion wrapped his cloak tighter around him, scanning the terrain of trees and prairie. The day was cold but clear. The sun shone periodically through the thin shroud of clouds. To his left stretched the endless expanse of the prairies, empty land and yellow-green grass waving in the breeze. Occasionally, he could make out herds of cattle on the east bank scattered among villages. The wide, grassy terrain in this part of Daffodalion was ideal for cattle farming.

To his right was the dark green of the western forests. Further southwest, he knew, those woods joined with the Magno Forest of Coonsia. He and Mel had traveled that way only months ago. The monotonous green made it hard to pay attention, and the rocking of the boat had a lulling effect. It had been a long walk.

"Eyes up," Aryion murmured, nudging his apprentice lightly. Mel had begun to nod off—he shook himself awake and looked around.

"How far are we from Esile City?" he asked.

"A day's journey, maybe more," Aryion replied. They were making good time; the steady wind in the sail and the river's gentle current moved them south. "Tell me what you notice here," Aryion said after a pause.

This was a drill he incorporated occasionally on their journeys. Much of ranger training involved observing and analyzing the places and people around them. "There's no such thing as a small detail," Aryion had told Mel more than once. "Anything could be important. Make note of it."

Mel surveyed their surroundings for a moment. "There are some cows over there across the river," he said after a pause. "I think I see a farmer with them on a horse."

Aryion squinted across the river. From this distance, the cows looked like a cluster of rabbits. "I think you're right. Even if you didn't see a farmer, it would be smart to assume he was there. Cattle farmers usually stay close to the herd in this area."

"Because of predators?" Mel asked.

"Sometimes. Pirates will sail upriver too, and steal livestock."

"Wouldn't the cows just run away?"

"The cow wouldn't know it was being stolen," Aryion said patiently. "What else?"

Mel was silent for a moment. His next observation was closer. "Those two men are talking about a Crime Ring, I think."

Aryion nodded slightly, glad Mel had thought to keep his voice down. The conversation of the sailors around them and the sounds of the river made it hard to hear, but he could catch fragments of the conversation across from them. The two large brothers were speaking in lowered tones, but he overheard the occasional word: *Esile. Bounty. Pirate. Randuin.*

That last word was familiar to him. Mel looked at his mentor questioningly, and Aryion answered in just above a whisper. "The Randuin Order. They're an elite group of warriors in eastern Daffodalion. They even have a cavalry of dragons."

"Dragons?" Mel repeated, fascinated.

"Yes. The Randuins were the main reason that Daffodalion won the War of the Strait, and the Jenna didn't invade," Aryion said, smiling slightly at his apprentices' interest. "Nowadays, the Randuins operate from their base in Reedmount and monitor the Jenna movements."

Since the Jenna—a few tribes, at least—had joined with the Aces during the Kamon battle, Aryion guessed the Randuins had had their hands full. But after Caer Sia had been reclaimed, the Jenna had left the Ace-army and returned to the east.

He glanced at the two men, trying to follow the conversation. Perhaps the words he'd overheard weren't connected. But it was strange that news about the Randuins had circulated this far west if it wasn't Jenna-related.

He strained his ears, trying to pick up anything else of interest. The conversation seemed to have moved away from the Randuins.

But he did hear one more word of interest—*Dricaster*.

Mel didn't recognize this word. "What's Dricaster?" he asked quietly.

"One of the more prominent Crime Rings," Aryion replied in the same lowered tone. He kept his eyes on the deck, giving no indication of how hard he was listening to the conversation across from him. "They mostly operate within Esile City, and occasionally do business with the Gevarians in the north, too."

They sat in silence for a few minutes. The wind picked up, and any news of interest was lost in the breeze.

Aryion's thoughts returned to planning. Originally, when they had accepted the task at the request of Jan, he had assumed it would be a simple enough job. Track down Terrax, apprehend him, bring him in. Yet he had begun to realize it was more complicated than that. Bregg had mentioned that Terrax wanted to involve one of the Crime Rings in his plot. If Terrax succeeded, Aryion and Mel would have to somehow maneuver around the Crime Rings to capture him.

That could be difficult. The Dricasters practically controlled Esile City, and it would be nearly impossible to avoid their notice. He'd dealt with the Crime Rings before, in a time he did not like to remember. A time he could not yet bring himself to recount, not even to his apprentice.

"What's the plan when we get to Esile?" Mel asked after a long pause.

Aryion took a breath, dismissing the heavy thoughts for now. "We need information to continue our hunt for Terrax. But we must be very cautious who we talk to. You must do exactly as I say—is that clear?"

Mel nodded seriously. "Do you know who we'll talk to? Does Esile City have a baron or anything?"

Back in Lemsonburg, they had met with the baron before interrogating the prisoner. But Aryion shook his head. "No. Esile City operates under a Council of eleven men, similar to Elimar's. Unlike Elimar, though, the Daffonic king has less influence and interest in Esile City. The Council can run the town however it pleases, provided business is good."

There was another major difference between the Elimar and Esile Councils. Elimar's Councilors tended to be pompous, a little hesitant to engage in dangerous business, but they were still loyal to Caer Sia. From what he knew of Esile, however, the Council was loyal only to itself. With plenty of independence, it was rumored they dealt with the Dricaster Crime Ring for a profit. Such business was highly illegal, but no one had been able to prove it for decades, and so the Council got away with it.

Aryion guessed questioning the Esile Council would be useless. They wouldn't risk handing over secrets about their business partners. It would make finding information on Terrax that much harder. He leaned back against the bulwark, racking his mind for a strategy.

When they arrived at Yellow Bank a few hours later, he was no closer to a plan. The afternoon was growing old, and gray storm clouds hulked in the west.

The township of Yellow Bank was only a little larger than that of Wide Bend. The sailboat coasted in neatly beside the pier and the passengers disembarked. Wood smoke hung in the air, and a few lamps lit the dirt streets. Past the buildings, the rolling hills of the prairie stretched on to the east, as far as the eye could see.

"Now what?" Mel asked.

Aryion studied the small harbor. "Let's find our next ride, and then we'll decide what to do." He led the way to the ferry master's office. The next boat to Esile City left early in the morning. Aryion was loathe to delay that long, but there was nothing to be done about it.

Aside from a quick breakfast that morning, they had eaten little all day. Mel had been very patient not bringing it up so far, so they headed to a tavern for a meal.

The pleasant smell of roasting meat and baked bread greeted them as they opened the door. The tavern was small, hardly the size of the Smallbutton's home in Appledale. But it was cozy and welcoming after the long journey.

Mel practically inhaled his food. Aryion ate slower, keeping his eyes up. Welcoming village or not, Yellow Bank was still an unfamiliar town. The broken conversation he'd overheard on the passage here lingered in the back of his mind. Clearly he was missing information. Maybe he'd heard wrong. But still, there had to be something connecting the rumors. What did the Crime Rings of Esile City, Terrax, and the Randuin Order have in common to be in one conversation?

He glanced at Mel, who was peacefully munching bread. The cold air reddened his cheeks, accentuating the purple scar next to his nose that was still healing. Mel had received that injury from Irshkhan during the Kamon fight—the Jenna had kicked Mel in the face and knocked him unconscious. Thankfully Rygal had been there to save him from the maddened Jenna chieftain.

The Jenna.

Aryion paused mid-chew. He knew the Jenna no longer wanted to work for the Aces, but that didn't mean they were out of the area. Terrax needed hired muscle, and he needed enough of it to feel confident dealing with the Crime Rings.

What if…

What if Terrax was planning to hire Jenna warriors?

"Aryion," Mel whispered, his voice tight.

Aryion looked up, following his apprentice's line of sight. Three men were sitting at the table in the corner near them. They wore dark clothes and cloaks.

At first glance, Aryion thought his guess had come to life, and there were a trio of Jenna warriors sitting there. But then he realized he was wrong. The faces were different—not quite the wolf like shape of a Jenna's face, but not quite human either. Tilted up noses, catlike green eyes, pointed ears half hidden by their shaggy hair. They all had spears resting against their chairs.

Wildkid warriors.

Aryion studied them carefully until one—the leader, presumably—spoke in accented but clear Coonsian.

"You, child," he said in a soft rasp, his eyes going from Mel's face to the small lump of blue in his pocket, "you have something very valuable."

Mel put a hand on his pocket instantly. Aryion loosened his sword in the scabbard. "You know of the Stone?" he asked, trying to remain calm. His mind was reeling. What on Orlell were Wildkids doing this far west? How did they know about the Stone? Why were they here, of all places?

"We are aware," the Wildkid said levelly. He leaned closer to them, into the light. His hair was black, as was the thick fur that covered his body. He and his companions all seemed very young, but they carried themselves with visible confidence. They wore jackets and breeches, which disguised their fur somewhat. Of course. The Wildkid Clans had not been welcome on the Mainland for decades, out of the Capital's fear of them more than any wrongs between the two countries. If people knew Wildkid warriors were here—Aryion wasn't sure what would happen.

"Why are you here?" Aryion asked slowly. "Has your tribe allied with the Daffonic Crown?"

The three Wildkids snorted disdainfully. "We have no dealing with the human king. These lands were once ours," the leader said.

"We come and go as we please. We have traveled west more often in recent months, on account of strange rumors we are trying to make sense of."

"Have you?" Aryion said, not sure what to make of this information. He knew next to nothing about the Wildkid Clans. They kept to themselves in their own land. He guessed the rumors of the Aces had brought them west again. "What brings you here, then?"

"The child called Mel. The Stone he possesses," the Wildkid said, turning his vivid green eyes on Mel.

Aryion started at the words, prickles of unease running down his spine. He drew his sword halfway. Seeing his motion, the other two Wildkids straightened, reaching for their spears.

"Wait," Mel said before anyone moved further. He looked more surprised than fearful as he turned to the lead Wildkid again. "How do you know me?" he asked slowly, studying the strange faces before him.

The Wildkid warrior glanced at Aryion's sword disdainfully, then looked back at Mel. "Tell us, young Mel, do you know one called… Dusty of the N'Tell?"

9

≪ ≪ ≪ ≪ ≪ ≪ ≪ ≪ ≪

News From the Far East

Aryion slid his sword back into the scabbard, his mind echoing the name. Dusty of the N'Tell. It was vaguely familiar to him, but he didn't know where he had heard it before.

Then he remembered. The name belonged in the story of Rygal's first adventure in Coonsia, years before, during the rise of Kado. Rygal had told Aryion this story a few times—Dusty had traveled with Rygal, then returned to her home in Kasabren after the defeat of Kado.

But Dusty had been on the Mainland more recently since Kado. She'd joined the quest for Drisilas and traveled with Mel. She had been present during the Darkness' defeat. That had been the last time she had been heard of in the Mainland, Aryion was sure. But if that was true, then what were these Wildkid warriors doing here?

For his part, Mel looked stunned. "Dusty—yeah, I know Dusty. I met her almost a year ago, when we were trying to return Drisilas."

The Wildkid leader looked pleased. "She told us of you and your actions against the Darkness. That was quite a feat. You are now the one to guard the Stone?" he asked.

"I am," Mel said, still sounding surprised.

111

"Who are you?" Aryion asked, finally finding words. "What brings you this far west? You know the Capital does not trust you, and the Crime Rings will not hesitate to find quarrel with you. It's not safe."

The Wildkid smirked slightly. "We know the dangers. Our mission is important enough to risk it."

"Then why are you here?" Mel asked, echoing his mentor's question.

"Our sister's report of the Darkness' defeat was met with great interest among the Clans," one of the other Wildkids explained. His fur was a rusty red. "News of the Ace-Lord's return has sparked the urgency to act. There are many Clans now who are considering the renewal of the old alliances with the Mainland kingdoms in resistance of the Aces."

"Wait, wait," Mel broke in. "Sister? Dusty's your…"

The first Wildkid nodded. "I am Joesp. My brothers are Nellioh and Newuel. We are warriors of the Mara-N'Tell, and currently, our sister's espionage team to the prairie area of Daffodalion."

"Espionage?" Aryion repeated, his mind staggering under the information. Wildkids in Daffodalion, thoughts of alliance among the Clans—such things had not happened in decades.

Joesp nodded. "Many Clans are hesitant to enter this war. Our father is among them. He insists we need additional evidence that the Aces' reappearance is as much a danger to us as it is to the Liznees."

"Which it is," Mel said, frowning. "You have to know that."

"Indeed we do," Newuel said, shaking his head. Judging by his voice, he was the youngest of the group. His pale silver fur and curly dark hair gave him the appearance of a young wolf. "But without proof, no action will be taken. Dusty is determined to help the Coonsians, however, and so we have come to the Mainland to scout and observe."

"Dusty's here?" Mel asked hopefully.

"No, she is in the east, near Caroway fief," Nellioh said. "We have come to investigate the prairie areas before further action can be taken."

"We will not send warriors in blindly," Joesp said. "That is why we must find proof of the Aces to convince our father and the other Clans to act."

"If you need proof, you should go to Caer Sia," Mel said immediately. "That'll assure you that the Aces are real."

"Mel," Aryion said, quieting his apprentice. His thoughts were swirling in confusion at the unexpected appearance of the Wildkids. Their presence here, and their possible involvement in the war, was a variable in their mission he had never expected. "There will be answers in Caer Sia," he told them. "Mel is right. You will find little this far south."

"We have few allies that far north," Joesp admitted. "We are already risking much by being here."

"Then why come to Yellow Bank?" Aryion asked. "What's in the prairie lands that brings you here?"

The three Wildkids exchanged glances. "I assume you have heard of the actions of the Randuins, ranger?" Nellioh asked finally.

Aryion's heart skipped a beat. "We overheard a rumor on our way here, but not much besides that."

Joesp nodded slowly. "We have heard more. That the Jenna have crossed the Strait and entered Daffodalion, seeking to join with another."

"Terrax of Elvengate," Aryion guessed.

All three Wildkids scowled at the name. "Dusty told us of Terrax," Newuel said darkly. "We thought he was defeated."

"So did we," Mel muttered.

"We were sent to find him," Aryion said. "Our sources point us to Esile City."

"That is where the Randuins are said to be currently," Nellioh said. "So say our informants."

"Then the Jenna could be there too," Aryion murmured. The pieces were beginning to connect, aligning with his guess from earlier. Terrax needed more men to aid his cause—skilled soldiers to fill the ranks of his once numerous fighting force. Now that the Jenna mercenaries had cut ties with the Aces, they would be looking for a new employer. If the Jenna were an option, Aryion had no doubt that Terrax would hire them.

But the Wildkids were frowning. "That is where the details become muddled," Nellioh said. "A squad of Randuins rode to Esile City—we assumed to follow Jenna movements. But now we have received different news—that the Jenna are not in Esile City, but have settled near the southern coast."

Aryion frowned slightly. "Then why are the Randuins in Esile City?"

"We are uncertain. Either they are there for another reason, or…" Nellioh hesitated before finishing, "the Randuins have been led astray in going to Esile City."

Aryion leaned back in his chair, thinking. He doubted the Jenna could have so successfully evaded the Randuins. From what he knew of the Randuin Order, their informants were almost as good as the Red Dawn's. The Wildkids' news about Jenna in the south must be wrong.

And yet that thought didn't sit right with him either. The prickling unease in the pit of his stomach told him that there was another layer to this mission that they had yet to uncover.

"Either way, we can assume that Terrax does have Jenna warriors joined to his cause," he said aloud. "Your news seems to confirm that."

"I agree," Joesp said. "The question I would like to know is, how many warriors?"

Aryion took a slow drink while he thought. That was an important question. If Terrax had Jenna warriors, apprehending him would not be something he and Mel could do alone. Maybe if they had help—the Randuins in Esile City would be willing to aid them, he was sure.

If Terrax was in Esile City at all, a nagging question reminded him. But he pushed it away. That was not a doubt he could consider right now. For now, they would proceed to Esile City until the trail led them elsewhere.

"What do you plan to do now?" he asked Joesp.

The Wildkid warriors exchanged a glance. "We are to return to the Westerlyn Woods in two days' time," Newuel said. "Our sources state that there are Jenna in the south, and if the Randuins are unable to track them down, we must do so."

"We appreciate that," Aryion said.

"It's no favor for the Mainland kingdoms," Newuel told him flatly. "The Jenna have threatened Kasabren's waters for many moons. We are not about to accept an invasion now."

"Either way," Aryion stated gently, "we appreciate it."

"We will keep watch for any signs of Jenna on our way south," Nellioh said. "Do you truly believe they have come this far west?"

Aryion took a breath. "I'm not sure. It would depend on where Terrax is—and at present, no one knows his location. But the surest path leads us to Esile City at this point, and so to Esile we will go."

"I wonder," Joesp said quietly, "if the path seems sure for unpleasant reasons."

Mel looked at him. "You think it's a trap?"

"Perhaps. The Randuins seemed to fall for it rather quickly," Joesp said uneasily. "It seems rather convenient that all paths lead to Esile City."

Aryion felt Mel's eyes on him, sensed the question in the boy's gaze. Part of him wanted to agree with the Wildkids and head south to look for Terrax. Still, following the rumors of Jenna movements was not their mission. Their assignment had been to go to Esile City and find Terrax. Other questions would have to wait.

Mel looked at the Wildkids. "Where did you hear the news about the Jenna?"

"The Jenna slavers are active in the southern islands," Joesp said grimly. "They will sell captured warriors to the tribes, or to furriers."

Mel paled. "Furriers? You mean people…"

Aryion nodded. "The Daffonic King shut down the fur trade decades ago, but it's still common among the criminal underworld. Bounty hunters will seek Wildkid pelts and sell them for a high price."

"It is often a better fate than being a Jenna slave," Nellioh said. "At any rate, escaped slaves are our best source of news. Many reports of late have stated that there are Jenna camps on the outskirts of Port Rylan."

Port Rylan. Another town, another layer. "Are there Randuins in Port Rylan, then?"

"None that we have heard about," Newuel replied. "It is strange. The Randuins have gone to Esile City, and yet there don't seem to be any Jenna there at all. Nellioh is right—either the Randuins are there for a different reason, or they received inaccurate information that brought them there."

Aryion rubbed his brow tiredly. Maybe his theories were all wrong. Maybe Terrax and the Jenna were two separate incidents entirely. "Perhaps we'll find the answers in Esile City," he said.

Joesp studied him for a moment. "I do not know your orders, ranger, but if you have the choice, I would suggest not going to Esile. Come southeast with us and see what is happening in the Westerlyn Woods. If Jenna are there, Terrax may be too."

Aryion considered this idea for a moment. The Wildkids had a point. Any trail he and Mel found in Esile City would likely be several months old. And what if Terrax was indeed gathering Jenna warriors? If that was true, it was crucial that they find out as soon as possible.

All the same… their orders were to apprehend Terrax, not get involved in a Jenna infiltration. He and Mel weren't equipped for that. Besides, following a rumor was hardly worth traveling over a hundred miles in the wrong direction.

"Our orders are to find Terrax," he said slowly. "The Randuins can handle the Jenna. If there's trouble, we'll come east after we catch him."

Joesp nodded slowly, still looking doubtful. "Very well. We will wait for your report before we send any alert to Reedmount."

"Can we plan to meet you in Waypath?" Aryion asked. "It's a pirate town, but it's hard to find, so it should be safe enough for a Wildkid squadron."

"This Wildkid squadron can protect itself, ranger," Newuel said with a slight smile.

"That's not entirely what I meant," Aryion said wryly. "I trust you can keep yourselves safe. But be aware that most Mainlanders don't trust you."

"We are aware," Joesp said. He stood and paused, still looking uncertain. "We will plan to meet you in Waypath in five days' time. That will give you ample time to apprehend Terrax—if he is indeed in Esile City," he added with a meaningful glance.

"If he's not in Esile City, then I will owe you each a drink," Aryion said with a half-smile. "Travel carefully."

"You as well," the Wildkid replied. "Be aware what you carry. Be aware of who you protect." He glanced briefly at Mel, then drew his cloak around himself and followed his brothers out of the tavern.

The two rangers set up camp on the outskirts of town. It was dark by now, and frost coated the ground. Mel lit a fire while Aryion set up the tent. The tent would be cramped, but it would be significantly warmer than laying out in the open. Aryion could tell his apprentice was practically bursting with questions, but Mel focused on his task for now. This was good, because Aryion wasn't sure how he would answer Mel's questions. The day had taken a twist he had not expected.

He tried to organize all the information they had about the case so far. Terrax had gone south. Terrax was trying to contact the Crime Rings—from what Aryion assumed, Terrax would contact the Dricasters. There was a rumor about Randuins in Esile City. There was another rumor, this one about the Jenna in Port Rylan.

The stories didn't connect. Had the Randuins received incorrect information, as Joesp guessed? Aryion had doubted it at first, but now it seemed to be the most logical explanation.

Perhaps the Crime Rings were involved somehow. The Dricasters owned Esile City. In Port Rylan, a rival Ring, the Rylanders, ran business. Strange that the two cities mentioned in the rumors happened to be the lairs of two prominent Crime Rings. That couldn't be a coincidence. Maybe the Dricasters—or the Rylanders, whoever Terrax was actually working with—had sent the Randuins a false report that brought them to Esile City. But why would they want to do that?

Something connected it, Aryion knew. That connection might be Terrax, but he couldn't justify how or why. He hoped he and Mel could catch Terrax in Esile City. If they could interrogate the Elven outlaw, their questions might be answered.

If they could catch Terrax…

The doubt and growing worry nagged in his mind as he took first watch, crouching by the fire and watching the falling snow.

10

The Bosun's Tale

The *Burman Marie* saw no sign of the Rylanders the rest of the afternoon nor into the night. By the following morning, Bryn allowed herself a sigh of relief that her plan had worked. Despite her hope, one could never trust a Rylander, and she had lain awake late into the night fearing that the *Blood Swan* would be waiting just over the next wave. But they saw nothing, and the voyage to Port Rylan continued.

Bryn was startled to realize how much the dynamics onboard had changed in a day. The crew of the *Marie* seemed cheerful and friendly. They nodded to her when she passed them below decks, and called to her by name from their perches in the rigging. It seemed that the chilling confrontation with the *Blood Swan* had created a camaraderie that Bryn had never expected.

Cliadell and Drike were as sullen as ever, but Mads seemed to have picked up on the new alliance too. He chatted with the crewmates and seemed in as good a mood as Bryn had ever seen him.

The evening passed in jovial conversation and good-natured, off-key shanties from the sailors. Relief of escaping the *Blood Swan* was felt by everyone on board, Ringmember or no. As she sat at the table with Mads, John, and Robin, talking of simple, trivial things, Bryn was surprised to realize that she was enjoying herself.

That night, as she lay in her hammock, her distrust returned. She could have allies, sure, but making friends was dangerous in her line of work. People were unpredictable, and trust was inadvisable for a Ringmember. People would mistrust her, would lie to her, would betray her. People would leave.

People would die.

The dream came in its full horror that night, details she had not noticed before. The bodies on the floor of the burning house—small bodies, mercilessly cut down. An urgency as she pulled someone from the fire, a clenching in her chest as she cried out for help and coughed in the smoke. The hand she knew to be her companion's taking her shoulder, a young voice asking if she was all right.

Yet, as ever, her companion left her alone.

She slept very little. Morning came as a welcome relief. Bryn swung out of her hammock, dressed, and headed up on deck for another day at sea.

The heavy clouds of Esile City had been left behind, and the sun shone clear and bright as they continued the voyage east. The sailors went about their tasks until midday, when a steady breeze allowed for a break in the work. Bryn leaned against the port rail, watching the distant line of the Mainland pass by.

"Pretty, ain't it?" Richard commented. The bosun sat on a barrel, Whiskers dozing on his lap.

Bryn nodded. "How far are we from Port Rylan?"

"A ways off yet, but we're getting closer. I'd say we'll make it there by tomorrow morning," Richard said. There was a slight note of fear in his voice as he said it. The confrontation with the *Blood Swan* had ended well, but that had been lucky. It would be a miracle if they made it in and out of Port Rylan unscathed.

"I doubt it will take us long to recover the compass," Bryn said, trying to sound confident. "The Rylanders don't know we're coming, so it should be a simple enough task."

"Knock on wood," Mads grunted, sitting down beside Richard.

Richard managed a grin. "Well, I hope so, Miss Valetown." He sat up straighter and patted Whiskers, his confidence returned. "Now, if there's trouble, the Cap'n says we're to sail into the harbor and get you five out safe. The *Marie's* guns should discourage any Rylanders from following you."

"Where did you get the guns?" Bryn asked, interested. Firearms, once an experimental weapon, were becoming more widespread across the mainland. She knew the Red Dawn of Caer Sia were equipped with firearms, but they were the only army in Coonsia that had them. As for Daffodalion, only one or two armies were supplied with firearms. Not even the capital city of Fauna had such weapons; they were still too rare and expensive.

Among the Crime Rings, acquiring firearms illegally was possible, but uncommon. Dakrind was quite proud of the cannons aboard the *Black Raven*, which was one of the few ships that carried them. Bryn had noticed yesterday that the *Blood Swan* had no such weapons.

Richard winked. "Depends who you ask. The Cap'n maintains he bought them fair and square off a Liznee merchant."

"We're not idiots, Darvi, we know merchants don't sell cannons," Mads said, exasperated.

"From Caer Sia, then," Richard said, grinning wider. "Either way, we got 'em up north a few months ago."

"During the occupation of Sia?" Mads asked, surprised.

"Aye," Richard said with a nod. "There were orcs and Jenna that raided the city then, you know. They stole a bunch of weapons and tried to sail them back to their homelands. Most of the ships were intercepted by the Coonsian navy, though. Or by pirates." He nodded to the ship, better implying where they had come upon the cannons.

Bryn frowned slightly, interested by what he had said. "Orcs and Jenna in Caer Sia? Is that who actually did it? Took over, I mean." There were many circulating theories about what had happened in the Coonsian capital, but this was the first she had heard of the orcs being involved. She knew orc tribes traveled west, raiding Coonsian cities. But she doubted they could have defeated the Liznees, even if they'd had Jenna on their side.

Richard leaned forward conspiratorially. "Ask any Coonsian you like, they'll tell you the truth—orcs and Jenna were there all right. But they didn't lead the attack. I've got my own ideas—everyone does, since no one in the south knows what happened."

"Then what do you think?" Bryn asked.

"I believe the first reports of it. That it was something... other-worldly. Something supernatural. Something very dangerous, mark my words."

Bryn raised an eyebrow. "And what do you think it could be?"

Richard started to reply, stopped, and frowned. "Well... I don't rightly know for certain. But that's my opinion. Maybe someday we'll get the true story."

"True story to what now, Rich?" Robin asked from behind. He stood at the tiller and seemed to have overheard the last part of the conversation.

Richard turned. "Oh, we're talking about the Caer Sia incident, Cap'n. Sharing theories and the like."

"Ah," Robin said, glancing at Bryn. "What do you think happened? Are you with Richard, that it was some sort of otherworldly being?"

Bryn shrugged slightly. "No, I don't think so. There's no evidence of that. If anything, I think the Coonsians have a tendency to label any defeat a supernatural one, so they feel better about it."

Mads snickered, and Robin actually laughed—not mocking her, but genuinely amused by what she'd said. It surprised her and caused a slight smile to break through before she could hide it.

Richard looked at her curiously. "Are you that skeptical of your own countrymen?"

Bryn frowned, startled. "How did you know I was Coonsian?"

Oliver, who had been standing by Robin, looked down guiltily.

Bryn remembered mentioning that she had grown up near Elimar when the cabin boy had asked about her bow a few days ago.

Richard confirmed her guess. "Oh, Oliver mentioned something about it yesterday," he said. "I was just wondering."

Bryn threw a look at Oliver. That boy. Who knew what sort of tale he'd spread.

"I—sorry," Oliver said, ashamed. He looked so distraught that Bryn had to hide a smile. She shook her head, dismissing the matter. It wasn't as if her entire history had been exposed by that simple fact. Still, it felt odd to know that the sailors associated her with Coonsia now. Maybe they'd think she was some sort of Caer Sian outlaw.

"Better mind secrets, Oliver," Robin said. "Loose lips sink ships and all that. You might have been keel-hauled for that if we were a Capital vessel."

Oliver brightened. "But we're not a Capital vessel, are we?"

"No, which means I'll have to think of something creative. Better get back to work before I do."

Oliver fled downstairs, grinning impudently over his shoulder.

"I didn't know you were from Coonsia," Robin said to Bryn once Oliver disappeared.

"Well... I was," Bryn said, wishing for a change in conversation. "I grew up outside of Elimar, right near the border."

"Past tense 'was' Coonsian?" Mads noted with a chuckle. "What, you trade your heritage for a Crime Ring membership?"

"No—I mean—I guess I still am. I came south to Esile when I was sixteen." Bryn stopped herself. She was talking too much. She barely knew these men, and she trusted none of them. Nor had she ever talked this much about her past.

Thankfully Richard changed the subject. "So, you've got no belief in anything magical or anything of that sort, then?" He chuckled. "Should be an interesting voyage for you, then. Wait till you hear the compass' story."

"Oh, she won't believe a word of that, Rich. It's too far-fetched," Robin said. He was studying Bryn carefully. Bryn couldn't tell if he was joking or not, but her interest was piqued.

"What about the compass?" she asked.

Richard leaned back against the mast. "The compass we're looking for—it's a rather interesting piece of lore among us honest sea-farers, you see. Now, take what you will as truth, but here's what I know of the story."

He paused, enjoying the suspense. "Legend has it that there was a great sorcerer who, with his power, crafted a compass. This was no ordinary compass. The tales claim that this compass tells the future, warning the user of any potential threats. It points to your future enemies. Whether or not they *were* your enemies was never to be determined. Anyone who had the compass got pretty used to killing without question."

Richard smiled grimly. "The compass was soon sought after by every person in power throughout the southeastern seas. What no one knew, though, was that this compass came with a terrible price. A curse. Its owner assumes he possesses it, though in truth, it possesses him. The compass shows the owner's hidden enemies, one by one, whether they be friend or foe. But it takes something from him, too, something deep inside. Eventually, the compass becomes his master, the only reason for living, and its owner will do anything he can to keep it."

He finished. Bryn noticed that several other sailors had stopped to listen. "That's the legend?" she asked finally, for lack of a better question.

"Aye, that it is," Richard said, looking pleased with himself. "Trust what you will of it, Miss Valetown. But if it's in fact true, it explains why the two employers want it so badly."

"Does it?" Bryn said.

"Oh, come on, Valetown, think about it," Mads said. "A compass that points to all your threats? Threats to your empire, hidden spies, future usurpers? That's something a man in power would pay a pretty penny for, I can assure you."

Bryn thought for a few minutes. "How would a compass know those things?"

"Magic," Richard said simply.

"But even if that's true, magic always has its limits, doesn't it?" Bryn pressed. "How would it keep track of thousands—if not millions—of people at once, knowing where they are? How would it know every person's role in those places?"

Richard shrugged, nonplussed. "That's the mystery of it."

He genuinely believed it. Bryn shook her head slowly and looked at Robin. "What do you think, Captain? Do you believe it too?"

"Parts of it are a little far-fetched," Robin said. "Still, all legends have their roots in truth. It should also be said that this isn't an old legend. The compass itself only showed up around twenty years ago, and the stories came after."

Bryn frowned, surprised to hear this. She had always assumed that legends became less and less believable the longer they had been around. They aged like cheese—give it enough years, and they were riddled with holes. For this story to become so popular and so wide spread within such a short time was odd.

Somewhere in the back of her mind, she remembered their earlier conversation about the Wavers. They too seemed to have sprung from the pages of pirate mythology, just as the compass had. Maybe the two were connected somehow. Maybe the compass did indeed hold some sort of power.

John swung down from the crow's nest. "We are nearing the mouth of the Westerlyn, Captain. It may be a good place to anchor for the night."

"That it would," Robin agreed. "Hard to starboard. Bring us to the river mouth."

Richard stood and joined the rush of movement as the sailors carried out Robin's order. Bryn returned to her place by the rail and was startled as Robin moved to stand beside her.

"Elimar, you said you're from?" the captain asked quietly. "What part of Elimar?"

Bryn glanced at him. There was a slight frown on his face, a thought behind the question. "The outskirts of the city," she replied vaguely. "One of the little villages."

"Which town?" Robin asked, looking into her eyes.

Bryn hesitated for a moment, taken aback by this direct route of questioning. By the inquiring in his eyes. By the fact that, for the first time in years, it had happened. Her carefully crafted identity questioned.

"You came from Valetown, didn't you?" Robin said at last. "Nice little place. I visited it once, growing up. Had a few friends there."

"That's nice," Bryn murmured, wishing she could escape.

"It's a small village," Robin continued. "If you left it on bad terms, I couldn't care less. What I am interested to know is your real name."

Bryn looked at him briskly. "My name is Bryn of Valetown. Take out the 'of' or add it in. I don't prefer either one."

"But you prefer that to your surname, I assume," Robin said, frowning deeper. "Whatever your true surname is."

Bryn took a deep breath. "It doesn't matter anymore. I can promise you, at least, that the truth won't affect this mission."

Robin studied her a moment. "Truth always affects things," he said at last. "Whether we realize it or not, it's always important."

Bryn nodded shortly. Robin waited for a few moments, clearly hoping she would answer. Part of Bryn wanted to. To her own surprise, she found that she longed to trust him. To hand over the truth of who she was. To let the ruse fall away.

But the risk of that was too great.

The silence stretched between them before Robin returned to the tiller and the *Marie* swept toward shore.

11

∽ ∽ ∽ ∽ ∽ ∽ ∽ ∽ ∽

Esile City

Morning dawned cold and white. Snow fell softly upon the prairie. Aryion and Mel packed up camp and headed back to the harbor. They saw no sign of the three Wildkid warriors. Likely, they had moved on to the next river town, hoping to learn more information before they headed south again.

"Do you think the Wildkids will go to Caer Sia?" Mel asked as they waited by the harbor.

Aryion had not thought much about the Wildkids' potential involvement in the war against the Aces. With the Ace-Lord already amassing an army, the Liznees would need all the allies they could get. "I'm not sure," he admitted. "It is interesting that they are considering it. Do you suppose Dusty can convince them to help?"

Mel nodded rapidly. "Yep. I just hope she can do it soon. It'd be great to have the Wildkid Clans on our side."

"It would," Aryion agreed, staring out at the water. That alliance would be significant, yes. More importantly, though, he knew the Red Dawn army was drastically outnumbered by the Ace-Lord's forces. The more warriors that joined with the Liznees, the better.

"Dusty saw the Darkness attack," Mel said. "I bet Rygal filled her in

132

on everything that happened with the Aces. With that knowledge, the Wildkids will probably help." He leaned against the harbor master's shack and yawned. "You've never met Dusty. I think you'd like her."

Aryion nodded, only half listening. His thoughts had strayed back to their current task. A nagging voice in the back of his mind told him that they should take Joesp's advice and go east to Port Rylan, instead of Esile City. Otherwise, they could be following the same false trail that the Randuins had fallen for. Maybe Bregg was mistaken, and Terrax had actually gone to the Rylander Crime Ring for help. If that were true, he and Mel could meet with the Wildkids in Waypath and take down Terrax as a team.

But if he was wrong… if he was wrong, they would have traveled miles and miles in the wrong direction for nothing. No, the trail they followed led them to Esile City. Following new rumors and speculation might just slow them down, and they had orders from Caer Sia.

There was no way to be certain. He tried to tell himself it would be fine, and Esile City was the safer option. If there were indeed Jenna amassing near Port Rylan, he didn't want to bring Mel into that.

Their ride arrived a few moments later. The sailboat was a little larger than the one they'd taken yesterday, built to weather the rougher waters near the coast. The two rangers stepped on board.

The journey continued in silence. The forest fell away before more snow-dusted prairies on either side of the river. Aryion knew he needed to come up with a better action plan for Esile City, but his mind was distracted by other concerns. The possibility of a Jenna invasion near Port Rylan was one.

And then there was the fear that Esile City was primed to erupt into a war zone. He'd begun to worry about that after everything they'd learned about the Crime Rings. The Dricasters were planning something, and while their war would be a silent, invisible conflict, fought in the shadows, that made it no less deadly. Nor any less dangerous for he and Mel to traverse Esile City, Jenna or no.

Mel was evidentially thinking the same thing. He studied the distant skyline of buildings that marked Esile City, his jaw set in both determination and fear.

"Calm down," Aryion told him quietly. "Try to relax. It looks suspicious the way you're all wound up."

Mel let out a tense breath and relaxed his posture slightly. "What will we do when we get there?"

"Find answers," Aryion said simply, though he was still working on an exact strategy. "Try not to worry. Esile City has its fair share of interesting characters, but it is still a Daffonic port. People pass through it often, so it's used to newcomers."

He left out the fact that the Esile Council had total control of the town, and that they would probably pass anyone suspicious to the Crime Ring to handle. But he knew he didn't need to remind Mel of the danger, and he didn't like worrying his apprentice any more than was necessary.

A few hours later, the river widened and opened out onto the wide expanse of the Esile Bay. Aryion sat up stiffly, studying the city as they sailed into it. Gray brick buildings lined the roads and river mouth. Pungent black smoke filled the air, courtesy of the oil refineries and factories on the industrial side of town. Ships crowded the harbor mouth, and they passed two slow-moving barges loaded with goods on their way into the Bay.

The harbor itself was filled with ships of all sizes and purposes. Some flew the flags of the Capital army—warships, probably, stationed here for security. But several other ships flew a red banner with a golden bear, which Aryion recognized, with a prickle of foreboding, as the crest of the Dricaster Brethren.

"That's a lot of Dricaster ships," Mel murmured as they docked in the harbor.

Aryion nodded, leading the way down the pier. "I imagine their crews are in the city, waiting for new orders or having a rest." He knew, from a past experience he did not like to remember, that the Dricaster Ringmembers operated mostly at night. With this in mind, he and Mel could hopefully avoid the Crime Rings altogether. Then again, that might be hoping for too much.

"Wouldn't they worry about being arrested? I thought you said most of the Ringmembers are wanted criminals," Mel said.

"They are, but the town guard can do very little to stop them—they just don't have enough men," Aryion said. "And then there's the Esile Council. It's long been rumored that the Council works with the Dricaster Brethren, taking a percentage of the profit. The town guard must answer to the Council, and I doubt the Council would want the soldiers tracking down their business partners."

Mel frowned. "That seems wrong."

"It is wrong, but there's very little the Daffonic Crown can do about it. Not without proof," Aryion said. "As it is, well, the Council's dealings with the Dricasters are deemed wild theories."

He turned onto a quieter side road. Esile City was filled with people, bustling from shop to shop or hurrying to work. Merchants drove wagons laden with goods through the crowded streets. Soldiers patrolled the marketplace.

"Aryion?" Mel asked after a pause.

"Yes?"

"Are you sure we should meet with the Esile Council? If they're as corrupt as you say, won't they just lie to us or worse?"

Aryion let out a long breath. Mel had a good point. He doubted they would be able to speak with the Council at all, and even if they did, it seemed unlikely that the Council would give them accurate news. "I don't like it either," he said. "But it's either speak to the Council, or speak to the Dricasters. They are our two best options of news within Esile City. At least the Council is safer."

"And if they don't want to tell us anything?" Mel asked with a frown.

"We'll deal with that then," Aryion said. "Remember what I've told you?"

"Right. One thing at a time," Mel said with a sigh.

Aryion hid his smile. "We'll find Terrax, Mel," he said. "The Council won't affect that."

Mel said nothing. The set in his jaw and stony look in his eyes caused Aryion's slight smile to fade. This errand was a personal mission for Mel, he could tell. He wondered if it had been a wise choice to involve him in this. But then, Mel was an apprentice ranger now. It was pointless to shelter him. The world was a cruel and strange place, and it would grow harder and stranger the older Mel got.

They threaded their way through Esile City, passing through bustling roads and quieter side streets. Heavy smog hung in the air, mingling with the gray storm clouds. The babble of conversation was present everywhere they walked. Aryion followed the street signs that pointed to the Esile Council Hall. The low chimes of the clock tower striking the hour hailed them as they reached a large, two-story building made of red brick. A troop of guards stood posted outside the doors, stiffening as the rangers drew close.

"Good morning," Aryion said civilly. "We've come to speak to the Esile Council, or whoever represents them."

One of the soldiers, whose uniform bore the markings of a captain, shook his head. "Sorry, sir. The Council is occupied for the rest of the day. Perhaps you could try tomorrow."

"We don't have time…" Mel started.

Aryion quieted him with a look. "We will return tomorrow," he told the captain. "Perhaps you could answer some of our questions, though." He nodded toward the harbor. "What do you know of the Dricaster Crime Ring?"

The other soldiers looked at their leader worriedly. The captain glanced between Aryion and Mel as he studied them. "You're… rangers?" he guessed finally.

"We've been sent from Caer Sia," Mel said.

Now all the soldiers looked interested. "Caer Sia?" one of the other guards repeated. "We've been hearing strange stories about what's been happening up in Caer Sia. None of 'em make sense, though."

Aryion, who had been about to berate Mel for dropping this piece of news, decided to let it pass. Technically, there was no harm telling the guards where they were from, not after Aryion had asked about the Dricasters. That question was suspicious enough.

"We are only here to gather information," Aryion said. "We had hoped to speak with the Council about a Coonsian criminal we believe has come here. Maybe you know of him."

The captain nodded thoughtfully. "There are posters all throughout town. My men know the names of most of the prominent criminals and outlaws."

"Of course, there's not much we can do about the crime here," one of the other guards said bitterly.

"How so?" Aryion asked carefully.

The captain threw a worried glance at the guard who had spoken, but shook his head. "It's not exactly a secret. Unless we can catch the outlaws, we can do very little. The Council even controls which posters we are allowed to put up and where. Now, there may be something we don't know, but…"

"But?" Mel prompted, as the captain trailed off with an uneasy expression.

The captain looked at Aryion. "From our perspective, it looks like the Council has allies among the Dricasters—people they don't want to be arrested. People that pass on profits to them."

"You are not alone in that line of thought," Aryion said slowly. He hesitated, interested to learn more but not wanting to get these soldiers in trouble with their superiors. "There's a man we've been sent to track. Terrax of Elvengate."

The captain frowned and shook his head slightly. "That's a name I don't recognize. Any of you men?" he asked the guards behind him. The other soldiers shook their heads. "Sorry about that, ranger," the captain said.

"You've never seen him here?" Aryion asked. "A tall elf, dark hair, dark eyes—tends to wear silver armor, right, Mel?" he added to his apprentice. Mel had, of course, actually seen Terrax in person—Aryion was going off the sketch they had been given in Caer Sia.

Mel nodded, looking hopefully at the captain. The captain still looked uncertain. "I can't say I have. He's a person with a high bounty, I would assume?"

Aryion nodded. After escaping Caer Sia, the Liznees had placed a high reward for Terrax' arrest. With both Terrax' crimes and his wealth taken into account, he would fetch a high bounty now.

The captain frowned. "He might have been here, of course, but it's odd that we never heard of him or saw a poster for him. Especially if he had a large bounty on him."

"The Dricasters would know," one of the other guards said. "Maybe they went after him."

"Maybe," Aryion said, but he doubted this. Bounty or no, Terrax wouldn't have allowed himself to be easily captured by the Dricasters. He may have had some sort of plan to hire them.

"Well, I'd say you have two options," the captain said. "Your man Terrax was either never in Esile City, or he is protected by the Council."

Mel looked at Aryion sharply. Aryion said nothing, his mind working over those probabilities. Hopefully he was right, and Terrax was indeed in Esile City—but if that were true, it meant that the Esile Council was hiding him. Keeping his name off the streets as long as they received some profit from whatever Terrax was doing.

"How fares the town?" Aryion asked instead. "The Council seems busy, at least."

The captain gave a slight shrug. "Business seems usual, ranger. But a group of Randuins got here three days ago, requesting to meet with the Esile Council. It seems there were rumors of Jenna on the outskirts."

"Jenna this far west?" Aryion asked, feigning surprise. "That's strange."

"Well, don't count on it yet. It's been three days now, and no one's seen head or tail of any Jenna at all," the captain said wryly. "Typically, the Randuins would leave by now, but it seems they've started investigating another form of business." He nodded to the Council Hall behind him, implying the real reason for the Council's flooded schedule.

That's interesting, Aryion thought. The Randuins must have realized something was suspicious, and were now investigating the Council's dealings with the Dricasters. Perhaps the corruption would finally be exposed. It was a weak hope, but hope nonetheless.

"Thanks for the news," he said, extending a hand. "If you hear any news of Jenna or Terrax, send for the Hummingbird. Captain…?"

"Jackson, sir," the captain replied, shaking Aryion's hand. "And we'll do that. Good luck, rangers."

Aryion turned away, heading back down the road. Mel jogged to catch up, frowning. "This doesn't make any sense," he said finally. "I know Terrax might just be hiding, but someone would have seen him at some point."

"True," Aryion said, thinking.

"Besides," Mel continued, "didn't Caer Sia alert the Capital that Terrax came this way again? Why weren't the guards told to watch for him?"

Aryion moved to the side of the road to allow a wagon to pass and let out a breath. "As far as I know, yes, the High King sent a report to Fauna warning them about Terrax. I imagine most cities across Daffodalion are aware of Terrax, and would arrest him on the spot if they saw him."

"Then why—" Mel started.

Aryion raised a hand, gently interrupting his apprentice's flow of questions. "I said most cities, Mel. As I explained earlier, the influence and control of the Esile Council allows them to do whatever they want, as long as they avoid the Capital's notice. No one has been able to prove their corruption for certain."

"But they can control whose posters are up?" Mel said skeptically. "That seems pretty corrupt."

"It is," Aryion said. "But they could easily excuse it as a lack of information. Since no one can prove it, they can get away with it."

Mel leaned against the building, arms crossed, frowning deeply. "So… that means the town guard here can't do anything about Terrax, even if he is here."

Aryion glanced at him. Despite the short time he'd been with his apprentice, he could tell when Mel was thinking hard. "You think he is elsewhere?"

"I don't know," Mel said slowly. "Something about this whole trail of clues feels… off."

Aryion felt the same way. From the moment they had interrogated Bregg back in Lemsonburg, he had sensed that they were beginning to uncover something much bigger than they had expected. Rumors, inaccurate reports, the meddling of the Esile Council, the threat of a Jenna invasion… it was all connected, he was certain. Whatever connected it, he and Mel were in the middle of it, and there was no telling where it would lead them.

"I don't think Terrax is here," Mel said after a pause. "I feel like the guards would have at least heard of him."

"Unless the Council is covering up for him, of course," Aryion pointed out.

"Right. But… I don't know, that doesn't seem right either," Mel said, sounding frustrated. "I don't think Terrax would trust the Council at all."

"And yet he seems to trust the Dricasters," Aryion mused. "At least, if Bregg's report is accurate."

He wondered if the Dricasters had requested Terrax' presence be kept a secret, and that was why the Esile Council was covering it up. But from what he knew of the Crime Rings, they rarely protected outsiders. What would have motivated them to shelter Terrax? What was Terrax really after?

He rubbed his brow tiredly. All this information, but no solid answers. They seemed to come to a new dead end every day. "Let's go get something to eat," he said. "I'll think of a plan. For now, we had best prepare to speak with the Esile Council tomorrow morning."

Mel brightened at the mention of food and they turned another corner down a road lined with shops and inns. The dreary gray and smoke-filled skies added to the ominous feeling in Aryion's chest. He had reassured himself all day that the mission was safe, that there was nothing to worry about, that he and Mel would be fine. Now, he'd begun to fear that they were both in over their heads.

12

Port Rylan

"Port to prow, Captain!"

Bryn's eyes flew open at John Tailor's shout. The thunder of many feet moving above decks grew louder as the crew tried to glimpse their destination. Her hammock rocked gently to and fro as the ship gradually slowed. They had arrived.

Bryn had spent the remainder of the day before thinking over what Richard had told her about the compass. She had to admit that parts of the story made sense. If an artifact out of pirate legend had suddenly appeared, it was logical that many people would want it. No matter if the compass actually did what it was fabled to—it'd be a matter of bragging rights to own it. Perhaps they'd just been hired by an eccentric collector eager to claim the compass.

Yet something about that line of thinking didn't add up with the fact that people had *died* to get the compass. A Dricaster Ring-member, in fact, had risked everything to hide the compass in Port Rylan—and had lost his life in the process.

Ringmembers could be superstitious, yes. But they all had a solid sense of self-preservation. Bryn doubted that any of them would willingly die to gain a pirate artifact… unless said artifact really did have the powers it was said to.

She decided it didn't matter whether or not the story was true. Their employer would pay them for the compass, not for the powers it supposedly had.

But in that case, why risk life and limb on this venture at all? Why not just find a similar looking compass and turn it in? Dakrind had never objected to such strategies before. They had turned in faux jewelry and gold in the past.

Maybe Hawk Dakrind believed in the legend too. Maybe that was why he had been so secretive about this mission. Yet that didn't sound right to Bryn either. Dakrind was so logical, so grounded in reality. He was easily the least superstitious pirate she'd met among the other Ringmembers. It was unlikely he believed in the legend of the compass. Still…

Bryn had mulled it over most of the night and come to no satisfactory explanation. At least it kept her mind off her brief conversation with Robin. The look of curiosity and distrust in his eyes as he questioned her story and name lingered in her mind. People that used their hometown as a surname still had a family name, or at least the name of their father. Bryn had hidden both long ago. By the look on Robin's face, he probably thought she was a high-profile bounty, an escaping noble maybe, who was hiding behind a false identity.

The truth was less exciting. It was grim and dark and sad.

The truth would have to stay hidden for now.

Someone knocked on the door, and she swung out of her hammock. Whiskers, who had been asleep next to her, dropped to the floor. The cat looked up at her in annoyance, then promptly jumped back inside the hammock.

"Miss Valetown?" Oliver's hesitant voice came from outside.

"You can come in," Bryn called, scooping Whiskers out of the hammock before the cat could continue shedding on her blankets.

The cabin boy opened the door holding a bundle of clothes under one arm. "Sorry for blabbin' yesterday," he said sheepishly. "Didn't know you didn't want me to tell the boys about where you're from."

Bryn shook her head. "It's not a problem, Oliver. What's that?"

Oliver looked relieved and held out the bundle. "Cap'n says these are for you."

Bryn frowned slightly. "For me?"

"Guess so. He says your clothes won't blend in at Port Rylan." Oliver glanced back nervously—clearly, he was worried about their destination.

Bryn took the clothes from him without further objection, shooed Whiskers out of the cabin with her toe, and dressed promptly. She realized what Robin had meant as she saw the clothes. Her black woolen outfit from Esile City was too warm. It was also cleaner and better made. Her new trousers and shirt bore black stains from the ship's tar, weathered and worn. The simple leather vest smelled of tobacco. They were the clothes of a pirate, not a bounty hunter.

She drew her cloak around her shoulders, not willing to abandon the security it afforded her, then grabbed her bow and quiver and walked up on deck. The air outside was warmer than before, carrying a scent of pinewood and soil. They must be close to Port Rylan.

The crew were hard at work. A rowboat had been prepared for the five Ringmembers going ashore. The fear and nervousness of the sailors was almost a palpable thing. They were deep in enemy territory, near land and exposed to any watching eyes.

The coast stretched out a mile or so away. Dark trees reflected off the water, which was flecked in white where the waves lapped the rocks. There was no sign of civilization in sight, but Bryn knew the city was not far.

"Let's get going," Robin called, bringing Bryn's attention back. The captain appeared on deck with Mads. He seemed calm, but there was no sign of his usual swagger. This confirmed what Bryn had assumed—he was nervous, too.

"Not a single bloody thing," Mads said, shaking his head. "No sign of any scouts. You'd think the Rylanders would come to investigate, with us so close."

"Lazy Rylanders," Drike snorted.

"Rylanders are not lazy," Robin said levelly. "I assume our friend Madam Ida told the checkpoints to let us pass."

"She couldn't have got word to Port Rylan, though," Mads pointed out uneasily.

"They must know," Cliadell said darkly. "They would not allow us in so easily, if not to trap us."

"We're still a few miles from the city," Robin said. "The Rylanders might send scouts to inquire after the *Marie*, but we won't be here to see that."

He turned to John and Richard. "Fly the Daffonic flag only. Anchor off shore on the other side of the city and wait for us there. If we aren't there by nightfall, send a group ashore to investigate, but don't stick around and get arrested by Capital stooges."

"Aye, Cap'n," the two sailors grunted. They both looked worried.

The sailors lowered the boat to the water, and Bryn and her four companions climbed down into it. Drike began rowing toward shore, his powerful arms carrying them at a swift pace. Behind them, the *Burman Marie* turned slightly and continued her course east.

"What's our strategy?" Bryn asked after several minutes of tense silence.

Robin produced the map of the city and passed it to each of them in turn. "Here's Port Rylan. We'll enter by the coastal road, here. The compass is hidden near the coast midway through the city, in an apple orchard by the cliffs."

"Do the Rylanders know that?" Drike asked.

"If they do, they already have the compass, in which case our plan will need some adjustment," Robin said. "Our sources have stated they don't."

"What about the Wavers?" Cliadell asked in a low voice.

Robin let out a breath. "I assume wherever our informant hid the compass is out of the Wavers' reach. However, I think it's safe to assume that the Wavers will pursue us once we have the compass."

Bryn looked at Robin with a frown. This was the first she'd heard about the Wavers wanting the compass, though Robin had inferred it before. What did a population of madmen want with it?

Cliadell studied Robin carefully, a gleam of distrust in his eyes. He finally spoke, his voice still low. "This is a trap, I am certain of it. The Rylanders would not allow us so easily into their territory otherwise."

No one could prove him wrong, and the sense of unease grew. Bryn fingered her bowstring, her mouth suddenly dry. She had fifteen arrows. Enough shots to protect herself and Robin fairly well. What about the other three? They would be on their own against the Rylanders. This was why she hated working in teams, because inevitably, difficult choices had to be made of who to save and who would die.

She straightened and shook the thought away.

The boat coasted up to the rocky shoreline and they dragged it into the forest, concealing it in the underbrush. If the plan went awry, they had this as a backup escape route.

After hiding the boat, they found the road and began to walk east. Deep ruts furrowed the road, signs of frequent carriages. They passed a few groups of travelers on their way. While the population of Port Rylan was not particularly large, it was one of the only ports in this part of Daffodalion, allowing access to the eastern cities. That meant it would probably be crowded, which could make retrieving the compass even harder.

On the plus side, she reminded herself, it meant they could blend in with the other crowds of travelers.

"You've come this way before?" she asked Robin quietly.

"A few times," Robin said. "Not usually by road. There's a small bay on the other side of town that we usually anchor in."

"And the Rylanders let you?"

"They didn't find out we were Dricasters until recently," Robin said. "Before that, we were safe to enter."

Bryn frowned. "What were you doing in Port Rylan then?"

"Ringmember business," Robin said vaguely. "Nothing too interesting."

Something about this story made Bryn uneasy. The Dricasters avoided Port Rylan—any business to the east was done in Drynrall Island, which was neutral ground. What sort of business had brought Robin deep into enemy territory—multiple times?

"You're sure the Rylanders won't recognize the ship?" Bryn asked.

"They might, but if they see her sail past, they'll probably think we're just passing through. I doubt they'd spend time pursuing her."

Bryn thought for a moment. "Do you think they'll recognize you?"

Robin smiled faintly. "That, Miss Valetown, is why you're here."

Bryn nodded shortly. Whether or not Robin believed her story about her name, he still seemed to trust her enough to protect him from the rival Crime Ring. That was better than nothing.

In a few minutes, they reached the outskirts of Port Rylan.

The coast bowed inward in an elongated half-moon shape. The land sloped gently downward toward the water, as though trying to tip the clusters of buildings into the sea. The coast rose in a series of jagged cliffs by the water front, waves spraying white foam against the stone. The city was built up to the edge of the cliffs. The slant of the land allowed for a better view of the township—shingled roof-tops, winding roads, carriages and people making their way around.

From this view, it looked like a typical coastal town, Bryn thought. But then, so did Esile City. At a glance, no one would know that the city was ruled by a Crime Ring.

"There are guards at the entrance to the city," Drike warned from up ahead.

"We should break up the group," Mads said as they paused. "Not all five of us at once. You two let us go ahead."

"As you like," Robin said, then added casually, "Just remember, the *Marie* is your only ride out of here, so don't think of running with the compass."

Mads nodded shortly, but Bryn noticed the irritated look that crossed Cliadell and Drike's faces. She wondered if that had been their plan, if they wanted to flee with the bounty once they found it.

This compass. What was it doing to people? A few days ago she had been assured in this mission, strange though it was. Now she was questioning her fellow Ringmembers, questioning Hawk Da-krind, questioning the mission itself. Who cared if it was unusual.

She would be paid. That was all that mattered.

She and Robin fell a ways behind the other three so that they entered in two distinct groups. Four guards stood at the entrance to the city, but they barely acknowledged them, each busy in their tasks. Bryn kept her head down, her pace slow, trying to act like she belonged here. Robin's face was calm, but a sheen of sweat had broken out on his brow. She could tell he was nervous.

"All right, so you've been here," she said to him, needing a distraction. "What should we watch out for?"

Robin wove through a crowd of cheerful shoppers, keeping his voice low as he answered. "Well, the Rylanders aren't the only danger here. There are smaller Crime Rings too, with fewer members. But they have nothing to lose, which makes them bolder, so keep an eye out. And then there's the garrisons of Capital soldiers. Their barracks are near the center of the city."

"Why so many soldiers? I thought this was a small town," Bryn asked.

"It is, but the Capital has cracked down on crime here in the last few months or so, after the Jenna movements."

Bryn moved closer to him as they passed through the noisy marketplace, frowning slightly. "Jenna movements through this area? When?"

"Seems they went by this way to Kamon when the Coonsian capital was out of action," Robin said. "Why, I'm not sure, but either way, they sailed past Port Rylan to get there. It made the Capital nervous, so they sent more soldiers to Port Rylan to keep an eye out."

"Interesting. No Randuins though?" Bryn asked. Capital soldiers could be avoided easily enough. Highly trained Randuin warriors could complicate things. While they usually only handled the Jenna movements, she had no doubt the Randuins would arrest the Ring-members if they were seen.

"No Randuins that I've heard of," Robin said. "I don't think there's any Jenna here for them to track. Still, it pays to be careful."

Bryn nodded.

They passed through the colorful marketplace. Bryn glimpsed Mads and the other two occasionally through the crowds. "Do the Rylanders have a base?" she asked Robin quietly.

"Yes, to the north of town. Most of their business only happens at night, though, so hopefully we'll slip past them."

"Unless they hear we're after the compass," Bryn pointed out.

"True," Robin agreed.

Bryn was about to ask more questions when her eyes landed on a cluster of posters tacked to a wall to her left, and she stopped in her tracks. Wanted posters, similar to the ones in Esile City. She recognized a few names—Dricaster and Rylanders alike. The papers were layered on top of each other, some with only names or information visible under the other posters.

One poster, peeking out above the others, bore her face.

It was a rough sketch. The person who'd drawn it couldn't have had a very detailed description. But the drawing itself had captured everything about her appearance—black hair, dark eyes, the small scar she had next to her left ear—with an accuracy that could not have come from speculation. The writing below was in the Gevarian tongue, but Bryn didn't need to read it to recognize herself.

Robin paused, confused, and Bryn quickly started forward again, her mind racing. Who had done it? Who had finally seen her in action and put a face to the feared name? She was so careful—working at night, always hiding her face during her missions, never leaving a single witness alive. Outside of the Brethren, she was only a citizen, overlooked by most and forgotten by all. No one knew who she truly was.

Her mind spiraled in confusion for an instant before focusing on one stunning conclusion. The only people who knew both her face and her reputation were Dricaster Ringmembers.

She had been betrayed.

By whom? Mads? Mads wouldn't—he was too nervous he'd be arrested himself most of the time. Dakrind? But why would Dakrind want to give up the identity of one of the best bounty hunters in the Brethren?

Those posters wouldn't remain in Port Rylan long. They'd soon circulate up and down the coastline, into the heart of the Mainland, and eventually reach Esile City. And then everything would be lost.

She had never, not once, feared arrest. There was no possibility of being caught if the soldiers didn't have a face to look for. Now that security had been torn to ribbons by the sight of her face on those posters.

"There's the orchard," Robin said, pointing.

Bryn looked up, trying to shake off this new concern. The road led right, toward the coast. A grove of apple trees stood behind a simple wooden fence. The trees were stunted and gnarled, branches bared from winter, and the overgrown weeds told Bryn the place hadn't been tended to in years.

She tried to ground her thoughts on the mission. Her revealed identity was a problem she would have to deal with later. Right now, they needed to complete their task.

She and Robin slipped through the fence and made their way to the edge of the grove. A few yards past the fence, the land dropped off in a steep cliff some fifty feet above the water. Below, the waves pounded and thundered against the rocks.

The other three Ringmembers stood waiting, the packs set in a heap by one of the trees. Cliadell's face was dark with displeasure. "We have searched the roots of every tree along the edge, Trelawney," he stated. "There is nothing here. If the compass was indeed hidden, it is long gone."

Robin pulled out the map, frowning. "Can't be. If the Rylanders already had the compass, I'm sure we would have been informed."

"Maybe we'll have to fight the Rylanders for it," Drike growled. The light in his small eyes showed that he found the idea quite appealing.

"Can't you read?" Mads said dryly, tapping a few scrawled words on the edge of the map. "This writing, Trelawney—did our informant put that there?"

Robin squinted at the page. "I'd assume so. *'Under tree, over sea.'*"

"We do not have time for riddles," Cliadell snapped. "If the Rylanders have the compass, we must get it back. Get word to your crew and we will prepare to attack."

"Oh, yes, one ship against the entire Rylander Brethren, that'll go well," Mads shot back.

Bryn moved to the edge of the cliff, her mind still reeling from the shocking sight of her face on the poster. The cold sea wind helped bring her thoughts back to reality. *Under tree, over sea.* She peered over the edge of the cliffs. The gray rock was jagged and sheer, impossible to scale. But near her foot was a distinct scuff, where something had rubbed away the grass. A rope perhaps.

"Hold on a moment," she said, moving to the pack Drike had set down. She dug inside for a moment before producing a length of rope.

"What're you planning, Valetown?" Drike asked doubtfully.

Bryn nodded at the gnarled branches of the tree above them. "Under tree—that's where we're standing right now, I'd bet. It's the tree indicated on the map, and the closest to the coast. But the clue says we have to be over sea too."

"We are over the sea now," Cliadell said.

"Not quite—we're over the beach. If we're going to get over the sea, I think we have to go—down there." Bryn gestured vaguely down the cliffside behind them. The others visibly paled at the idea. "Come on, we need to get the compass," Bryn pressed. "We can lower someone down the cliff to check if it's hidden down there at the very least."

"Who do you propose to do that, then?" Mads asked warily.

Bryn looked at him and hesitated. The Dwarve was the smallest, but he had none of her experience. She realized in a sickening moment that she did not trust any of them to lower her down the rock face. And she was quite sure they all felt the same.

"I'll do it," Bryn said after a long pause. She lashed the rope to the trunk of the tree, then set to work looping the rest of the rope around herself. She had scaled buildings this way before, pursuing bounties high up. Still, her heart sank a little at the sound of the thundering water below.

"We'll hold you," Robin said, taking the extra slack of rope. The other three moved to join him.

Bryn made a simple harness, looping the rope around each thigh and up over her shoulders, then knotted it in front of her waist. She gripped it tightly, then leaned back and let herself drop backward. The initial drop was only a few feet, but her stomach lurched. Then the others caught her, and she swung back toward the cliff side, bouncing back against the rock on her toes.

"All right, Valetown?" Drike called down.

"I'm fine," Bryn called back up. She took a deep breath and looked around. The outcrop of rock above curved inward, showing a cavern that was invisible to anyone standing above. The roots of the apple trees brushed her hair as she lowered herself down. Tiny caves pockmarked the underside of the cliff. Birds had made their nests in several of the holes; they fluttered past her face, chirping angrily at the intrusion. Bryn brushed them away, using the pockmarks as handholds as she made her way around the cavern. Aside from bits of twig or moss or the occasional nest, the upper holes were empty.

She felt a brief flare of disappointment before noticing a second row of tiny caves directly below her dangling feet. "Lower me a little more," she called up.

There was a slight jolt, then she was lowered down. The hole directly in front of her was completely empty, swept clear of sand and stone. It was better formed than the others, too, perfectly round. Certainly man-made.

Bryn took another deep breath and reached inside. The pocket kept going back. She had her entire arm inside when her fingers found something wrapped in cloth.

Almost trembling with anticipation, Bryn closed her hand around it and withdrew her arm. The object had been wrapped in filthy rags, which she removed slowly. In another moment, she was looking down at the shiny black face of a compass.

She had seen it before, in the drawing. Up until this point, she had wondered if it was all a myth. But here it was, cold in her trembling hand. She flicked open the cover to be sure, and the star-shaped emblem confirmed that it was the bounty they were searching for.

"Got it!" she yelled.

There was a distant murmur of excitement from her companions above, then the rope tightened and she was pulled up. She guided herself back up the cliff face to keep from hitting her head on the top of the cavern, then gripped the grassy ground of the orchard. Cliadell took her free hand and pulled her up.

The others grouped around her. Bryn held the compass out to Robin, who took it, staring at it in awe. "That it?" Bryn asked.

Robin nodded slowly. "Yes. This is the compass."

The instant the words passed his lips, Drike drew his sword and slashed at Bryn.

13

⌘ ⌘ ⌘ ⌘ ⌘ ⌘ ⌘ ⌘ ⌘

Brethren Broken

Drike's huge sword whistled as it sliced through the air, directly at Bryn's face. Bryn took a step back out of reflex more than anything else—her foot found empty air, and she toppled over the cliff side. She clung to the rope, struggling to slow her fall. The momentum tore the skin from her hands, but she swung to a stop—wincing in pain, she used two of the small pockmarks as handholds and clung to the cliff side.

Muffled sounds came from above her. She heard a grunt, Mads curse loudly, then the clatter of a sword hitting the rocks.

Gritting her teeth, she climbed hand over hand until she reached the cliff edge again.

Drike lay in a pool of blood, his throat slashed open. Mads knelt a few feet away, pressing his hands to a gash on his thigh. There was no sign of either Robin or Cliadell. Nor did she see the compass.

Traitors. Every one of her fears had been true.

Bryn hauled herself up the bank and snatched up her bow and an arrow, then swung to face Mads. The Dwarve watched her with a slight grin. "What, you think I'm in on this? I knew they were up to something, and figured they weren't going to tell you about it. Why

160

else would I want you and Trelawney to come behind us?"

Bryn kept the arrow on the string, but did not draw it back. "What else do you know?"

"They want the compass. All three of them, Trelawney included, but he didn't plan to kill us for it. The other two, well, they'd been planning it for a while. They let me in on their little secret on our way into town." Mads ripped a strip of fabric from his tunic and wrapped it around his injury, then got to his feet stiffly.

"Where'd they go?" Bryn demanded.

"Trelawney killed Drike, but Cliadell got the compass from him. He threw a knife at me on his way out, hit my leg. Trelawney went after him. They've both gone back into town."

Bryn looked toward the city. Somewhere in the maze of streets, Robin and Cliadell were fighting over the compass. Their bounty.

She picked up Cliadell's discarded knife—the bow would do little good in the close confines of the city—and turned back to Mads. "Then let's go find them."

They left the orchard behind and entered the crowded streets. Bryn walked ahead of Mads, careful not to get too far ahead of him. Cliadell, it seemed, had not thought to hit Mads' one good leg, which would have rendered him immobile. Instead, the Hymian's knife had hit the Dwarve's already twisted leg. Mads kept up pretty well, his dark eyes scanning the area.

There was no way to tell which way Robin and Cliadell had gone. Bryn studied the bustling town for anything suspicious, but saw nothing. They passed a group of guards, and she lowered her face as she remembered the posters. For the first time since joining the Dricasters, being recognized and arrested was a genuine fear. They would have to avoid the major roads.

"This way," she called to Mads, and turned down an alleyway away from the busy street. The houses here were shabby and run down, windows broken, cobwebs hanging in the doorframes. Mads slowed his pace and looked around with a frown. "Hurry up," Bryn said, turning back to face him.

Mads stopped. His gaze had focused on something behind her, and he took a step back. "Hold on, Valetown. Get to the side of the street and don't move."

Bryn turned sharply, ready to defend herself, but stopped when she saw what Mads was looking at.

The voices should have given them away. Cracked, weary voices, dry and lifeless like parchment, mumbling words in cadence. They muttered and wheezed as though spoken through sleep.

Then she saw them. Ten or twelve men appeared, some entering the street from the decrepit houses, others rising from behind piles of rubble. They stumbled uncertainly, peering in the bright sunlight, eyes bloodshot with wide, unfocused pupils. As one, they turned and moved toward Bryn and Mads. Their clothes were filthy and ragged, their skin caked in grime. Their mumbled words became intelligible as they drew close.

"It has been moved…find it… it is near… where is it?"

"Mads," Bryn began tensely, raising her bow.

"Don't shoot," Mads said. "Don't shoot, it makes them worse. Get to the edge of the road."

Bryn obeyed, unable to deny the growing sense of dread in the pit of her stomach. The ragged crowd moved forward, passing them by. The reek of unwashed bodies followed them like a cloud of smoke. Yet the emptiness in their eyes chilled Bryn more than anything else. Their eyes were dull and black, lifeless as coal. They streamed down the road toward the orchard without a glance at her or Mads. One of them tripped and fell—the others stepped over the body, their unfocused eyes turned ahead.

"What's wrong with them?" Bryn whispered, as the crowd shuffled past. "Are they… drugged?"

The stumbling gait and red-rimmed eyes reminded her of the inebriated greenstalk users she'd seen back in Esile. But there was something different about these men. Their gaunt faces were filled with longing, as though they followed a sweet scent just out of reach. The total lack of life in their eyes and their mechanical motions was far worse than anything she'd ever seen in a Mudger.

"No drug does that to someone," Mads said grimly, as the last of the ragged crowd disappeared. "That's dark magic, the worst of it all. It comes from the compass."

Bryn stared at him, not sure if he was serious. "The compass?"

"Meet the Wavers, Miss Valetown," Mads said, nodding at the retreating vagabonds. "The results of the compass' power."

Bryn turned away, starting back down the road. The ragged appearance and dead eyes of the Wavers had chilled her to the bone. But for them to be the product of dark magic—no, that was impossible. "A compass can point north. That's the only power it has, Mads," she stated, as much to reassure herself.

The alley led to another quiet side street, and they jogged up it. Bryn's mind was reeling from both the unexpected treachery of Drike and Cliadell and the fear of the Wavers, so that she nearly ran headlong into the group of men that sprang in front of them.

"Halt!" the leader ordered.

Bryn skidded to a stop, just avoiding collision with the men. They all wore the green and violet of the Capital. Their crossbows were lowered at her and Mads. Their leader was tall, wearing a fine uniform and a short sword at his belt. His badge marked him as the sheriff.

"Identify yourselves," the sheriff commanded.

"We're… tourists, sir," Bryn stammered. "Here to see the sights."

"We have reason to believe you are here on illegal business," the sheriff stated flatly. "Your faces are suspected to be Dricaster Ring-members of Esile City."

Bryn felt her heart drop, unable to come up with a reply. The Capital knew her face now. They knew exactly who she was, what she'd done, and what she was worth if captured.

"Ringmembers, sir?" Mads said in a bewildered tone, then punched the nearest soldier in the jaw. At the same time, a gunshot sounded somewhere nearby in the city. A flare of hope shot into Bryn's chest. Trelawney—it had to be.

"Arrest them!" the sheriff ordered. Bryn slammed the pommel of the knife into the jaw of the soldier that lunged for her, then sprinted down the street. Mads followed. Behind them, Bryn could hear the sheriff struggling to organize his troops—clearly, they were torn between pursuing her and Mads, or going to track down the gunslinger. But they wouldn't be disoriented long—they'd sort themselves out and come after her.

The street intersected with the main thoroughfare of Port Rylan. Bryn pushed past shoppers, dodged a group of small children playing in the street, and was nearly knocked down by a wagon. Too many people— she'd never find Cliadell and Robin like this.

"Hurry up, Mads!" she shouted back at him, the tension of the day sharpening her tone.

"Use your head, Valetown!" Mads yelled back. "We can't find them like this."

Bryn swung to face him, her thoughts racing. Mads was right. In the crowds, their going would be far too slow. And time was of the essence—Robin was somewhere in the city fighting Cliadell, the soldiers were after her and Mads, and the horrific group of Wavers were bent on finding the compass. There was no telling where Robin and Cliadell had gone, and the sprawling, crowded city would take a full day to search.

A burly man brushed past her. She needed to get out of these crowds, to see where she was going. Her eyes landed on the flat roof of the nearest building. The houses and shops of Port Rylan were built side-by-side, packed in along the roads. That was it.

The shouts of the pursuing soldiers came from behind. Mads would not be able to follow. She looked at him uncertainly. The Dwarve seemed to guess her trail of thought and jerked his head at the building. "Get up there and go find Trelawney. I'll head to the harbor and find us a way out of here."

Without any further hesitation, Bryn scaled the uneven brick wall until she reached the rooftop. A few people called out in surprise, but she ignored them. The sun glared off the shingles and into her face. The skyline of Port Rylan stretched out before her, a trackless jungle of roof and chimneys. With the gradual hillside slope of the town, the crowded roads and winding side streets were all visible, a perfect aerial view of the city.

Bryn ran, leaping from rooftop to rooftop. The sea wind whipped her hair and caught her cloak as it flew behind her. She heard the shouts of the soldiers below her, the startled exclamations of a few townsfolk who looked up in time to see her pass. Her boots pounded the shingles in rhythm as she made her way toward the place the gunshot had sounded from.

At last she paused, straining her ears and squinting in the sunlight. A crossbow bolt whizzed through the air past her face, and she ducked behind a chimney. A squadron of soldiers appeared on the rooftop behind her. The sheriff had alerted more of his men, and now the elusive hunter the Capital had waited so long to capture had fallen into their grasp. The bounty on Bryn's head made her a coveted prize.

"Surrender, Ringmember," one of the soldiers shouted, raising his crossbow for a second shot.

"Not today," Bryn muttered, and stepped out behind the chimney, sending her arrow into the soldier's jerkin. The man fell back as his companions surged forward.

A second gunshot split the air to her right. Bryn loosed another arrow in the direction of the soldiers and took off in that direction. Behind her, she heard the guards give chase. A crossbow bolt glanced off the shingle beside her, missing her by inches.

In front of her, the roof fell away before a wide street. She heard the triumphant shouts of the soldiers close behind.

She would not be a prisoner. This mission would be finished, and she would not give the Capital such satisfaction of bringing her in alive.

Gritting her teeth, she sprinted for the edge of the roof.

14

The Spy Unmasked

Bryn slowed her speed only slightly before jumping across the street, barely reaching the opposite roof. Her fingers caught the gutter; the rest of her body slammed painfully against the brick wall, but she pulled herself up.

Yells of disappointment came from the soldiers across the street. Another crossbow bolt tore through her cloak just above her shoulder. She dropped to her knees on the rooftop, turned, and released an arrow. It slammed into the torso of the nearest soldier; he toppled sideways to the street below with a cry.

Bryn turned and ran again, leaving the soldiers behind. But though the rooftops offered a prime vantage point, they had next to no cover. The road below her was nearly deserted, so she stopped and slid carefully down the brick wall to the ground.

The sound of pounding boots came from her left, and she ducked behind a pile of barrels. Another group of soldiers entered the road. The sheriff led them, speaking urgently. "Evacuate the harbor area— we can't let them get in the city."

"We must send an alert to Reedmount, sir," one of the soldiers told him.

"They won't get here in time. We'll have to hold our own…"

The soldiers moved past her, heading for the harbor. Bryn frowned. The town of Reedmount was the Randuin Order's headquarters. Would the sheriff call in the Randuins to deal with her? That didn't make sense—surely the Randuins had better things to deal with than a few criminals in Port Rylan. They guarded the eastern border, protecting the Mainland from the savage Jenna tribes.

This thought had just entered her mind when the sound of screams came from the harbor. Bryn climbed to the top of the barrels, peering down the hill. A single ship coasted off shore, drifting almost lazily along the half-moon harbor. The design of the sails and hull were unfamiliar to Bryn—four triangle sails that gave it the appearance of a spiked flower. But she recognized the flag, with a jolt, as belonging to the Vinskael Jenna tribe.

"What are they doing here?" she said out loud.

Another gunshot came behind her. Bryn stood at a loss for a moment, torn between pursuing Robin and Cliadell or investigating the Jenna's sudden appearance. Her duty to the mission won—she turned and ran up the street, deeper into the city.

The sound of the gunshot faded, and the excited and frightened voices of the townspeople made it hard to hear. There was no sound of conflict from the harbor. Perhaps the Jenna were only sailing through—but why?

She could see nothing from the roads. With the soldiers focused on the Jenna ship, she assumed the rooftops would be safe again.

Bryn turned, sizing up the building beside her. Before she could climb, a figure dropped from the rooftop next to her, lowering a knife at her chest.

"Stay there, Valetown," Cliadell panted hoarsely.

Bryn stepped back, raising her knife in answer. Cliadell's face was bruised, and blood streaked his blue-skinned face, but his eyes startled her the most. They were wild and bulging, as though he was straining to see through a sudden darkness.

"Stay out of this," he rasped again, "and you might live."

"Where's Trelawney?" Bryn demanded.

"Left him behind," Cliadell snorted. "He'll have the soldiers to tangle with now."

"The compass?" Bryn asked.

"Don't worry about the compass," the Hymian snapped. "Now, I'll promise to let you live if you stand down and hear me out."

"I'll do what's best for the Brethren," Bryn informed him, keeping her voice calm, though his sudden change startled her. Gone was the calculating, level-headed Ringmember she'd voyaged here with. In his place was a man driven by longing for the compass.

"Then you'll go after Trelawney, not me," Cliadell said. "Did you wonder how we got into the city so easily? Why the Rylanders let us through? Why the sheriff's men were waiting to pounce? Why your face is on every Wanted poster in the city?"

Bryn kept the knife pointed at him, but paused. Seeing her hesitation, Cliadell continued, his voice low and urgent. "It was

Trelawney," he spat. "All of it was Trelawney. He's a Rylander. He's the spy they sent to Esile. And he's going to deliver the compass to them, if he gets it."

"You're wrong," Bryn said, unable to come up with a better reply.

"How could I be?" Cliadell snapped. "The signs were everywhere. He knew everything about the mission, far before Dakrind told us. He had a detailed map of not only the Rylanders' territory, but their base town here." He gestured around him, his voice rising. "The colors they fly here under regular circumstances are those of the Rylander Brethren. The crest of the Rylanders is marked on the wall of the crew's sleeping quarters—but of course, Trelawney made sure you wouldn't see that."

Bryn tightened her grip on the knife, sickening doubt filling her mind at Cliadell's words. She fought to find some argument, anything that would prove him wrong, but she could not. "If he was a Rylander, why wouldn't he have killed us?" she asked, trying to hide her growing desperation.

"Why would he? As Mads pointed out, the Rylanders would sooner sell us to the Jenna than kill us." The Hymian's cold voice grew louder as he stepped closer. "Trelawney's a traitor through and through. You were hired to protect him, we all knew that. Well, hear me now, Valetown—you have the chance to kill him, you take it." The sunlight glinted off the point of his knife. "Or I'll kill you now."

Bryn stood her ground. Her mind reeled at his words, but she forced herself to focus on the approaching threat. Cliadell could kill her with that knife, she knew. He had trained for years to fight with these blades, in the same way she had trained with her bow. If she could buy enough time to get an arrow on her bowstring…

"Cliadell, the compass is affecting you," she said, trying to reason with him. "You aren't thinking clearly. Put the compass down now and we'll both walk out of here alive."

"I assumed you'd say that," Cliadell hissed. He lunged—Bryn parried his blow, then flung the knife, missed, and stepped aside. There was a clatter as the blade hit the cobblestones, but the brief distraction had been enough—her hands worked mechanically as she slid the bow from her shoulder and snatched an arrow from the quiver, bringing it to full draw.

Cliadell snatched up his second knife and charged. Bryn loosed the arrow, and it sank into his abdomen. The Hymian warrior gave a scream of pain and faltered, then, impossibly, ripped the arrow free and sprang at her. He gripped Bryn's collar and slashed his knife into her upper arm. Bryn kicked him in the groin and pulled free. Gasping at the pain, she whipped out another arrow and spun to face her attacker again.

In the instant she drew the bowstring back, several things happened at once. Cliadell's wild eyes focused on something to Bryn's right, and he flung his knife with a snarl. A fourth gunshot split the air as he moved, and the Hymian's body collapsed in a heap.

Robin Trelawney swore in pain as he stumbled from the shadows to the right. Bryn trained her arrow on him, and he stopped, then gave a slight grin. "You made it. Not that I'm surprised, of course—but I'm honestly glad to see you."

Bryn said nothing. Warm blood ran down her arm, and the throbbing pain in her shoulder made it hard to hold her bow steady. Trelawney was hurt too—Cliadell's final knife throw had glanced just above his hip. Blood already streaked his side, and his face was pale.

Robin's grin faded, and he glanced at the Hymian's body. "I expect he told you his side of things?"

"Prove him wrong," Bryn challenged. "You haven't exactly convinced me that you're a loyal Dricaster."

"For the cynic you are, you believed his words pretty quick," Robin said.

"For a Rylander you lie badly," Bryn shot back.

Robin braced himself against the building—he was having a hard time standing. He spread his hands. "Fine. Cliadell figured out the truth and took it poorly. That's not my fault."

"People tend to take it poorly when they're lied to," Bryn snapped, her arrow leveled at Robin's chest. "You killed Drike and Cliadell. You might be planning to kill Mads and I too."

"If I was going to kill you, I would have already done it, wouldn't I?" Robin pointed out with a slow shrug. He was growing paler by the minute. "I need you both, just like I need the compass. You have to trust me."

"You expect me to trust you?" Bryn said with a short laugh. Her heart was pounding in anger.

Robin exhaled heavily. "Fine, don't trust me. But you better make a choice fast. The Wavers will be here for the compass in a few minutes, and then we'll both be dead—but if we run for it, we can probably make it out. We can get to Drynrall, get the bounty, and go our separate ways. Is that what you want? Or are you going to kill me?"

He moved forward, swayed, then his knees gave out and he sagged back against the building. He slid his pistol back in the holster and sat there, arms spread, chin thrust forward defiantly. "Kill me then, and get it over with. Whatever you're going to do, do it fast."

Bryn aimed the arrow at him, trying to steady her trembling hands. One shot would end this act. Shut him up for good. She'd have the reward to claim and life would go back to normal.

Let it fly, her mind ordered. Let the arrow end his confusing speech. It would be so easy, all of it. And yet… and yet… she found she couldn't. Her logical mind was overwhelmed by the part of her that refused to loose the arrow.

She relaxed the bowstring. Slid the arrow back in her quiver. Knelt by Cliadell's body and searched his pockets until she found the compass. The shiny black face reflected her troubled expression a moment before she stuffed it into her trouser pocket.

Robin watched her with a confused frown. "What are you doing?"

"Making a choice," Bryn said shortly. "Now get up and let's get out of here."

A slight smile crossed the pirate's face. "Plan on turning me in to Dakrind? That's a smart plan. My bounty isn't worth as much as yours, but it's not bad."

He could decipher her thoughts so easily. Was she that easy to read? Bryn gripped his arm with her good hand and hauled him to his feet.

Mumbled voices came from the street behind them. Bryn made for the waterfront with Robin limping behind, forcing herself to not look back. All she could do was hope that Mads had found a boat that could get them back to the *Marie*.

The mumbling grew louder: "The compass… she has it… the compass… after them…"

They passed a run-down building. Dirty hands clawed at them from the darkness, and a voice called after them hoarsely. "The compass… give it to me."

Bryn ignored it, trying to calm her racing thoughts, to attribute some logic to the strange men. It could not be the compass. That was impossible. Mads must be mistaken. Perhaps the men were drunkards, or Mudgers. Madmen maybe.

"Give it to me," another voice hissed, much closer, edged with hate. "I can smell it on you."

"Hurry," Robin murmured fervently, "hurry…"

Teeth clacked behind them. A hand seized Robin's ankle and he fell. Bryn turned and fired an arrow into the face of the ragged figure in the shadows. Logical explanations. That was laughable. She had never seen anything like this. The crazed dead eyes stared up at them blankly, and her stomach twisted in fear.

She hauled Robin to his feet and kept moving. The pier stretched out before them into the harbor. As they left the town behind, Bryn noticed the Jenna ship slowly sailing west. The Jenna had not come to attack—so why were they here?

Mads was waiting in a rowboat at the end of the pier. "Got the compass?" he asked immediately.

Bryn nodded shortly, scanning the shadowed buildings at the edge of town. Ragged figures stumbled and lurched in the darkness, avoiding the bright patches of sunlight. They hid their eyes from the light, flinching back.

Robin sank into the rowboat, and Bryn climbed in after him. The pirate captain reached for an oar, but Bryn stopped him. "No. We'll row. You talk. Tell us everything."

Robin sighed and fell back against the bench as his two companions began rowing them away from the city. "Cliadell and Drike wanted the compass," he said finally. "Most people want the compass, actually. I don't know why, and I don't know anything more about our employer than what I told you already. The Dricaster employer, that is," he added.

Mads raised his eyebrows. "Dricaster?" he repeated.

"He's a Rylander spy," Bryn stated. The words hung in the air for several shocked seconds. Saying them aloud was somehow even worse than hearing them from someone else. It forced her to believe it. Forced her to come to the painful realization that Robin had lied to her. He had lied to everyone. And he had given her identity to the

Capital. She wouldn't last long with that secret shared.

Mads looked between the two of them, then gave a wheezy laugh. "Oh, that's delightful. I never would have guessed. Double crossed both Crime Rings, then, did ya?"

"Their spy," Robin said. "For both sides."

Mads shook his head. "I won't tell Dakrind. The plan still works for me, and frankly I'm just impressed."

Bryn wondered about the plan he mentioned, but she was too angry to ask. "We need to tell Dakrind, Mads. You know that."

The Dwarve looked at her, surprised. "Oh? What, you want the bounty off him on top of the stuff we'll get for the compass?"

"No," Bryn said, trying to explain her thoughts as she paddled. "He's… he's a traitor. We're required to turn him in. For the good of the Brethren."

"The good of the Brethren?" Robin repeated, raising his eyebrows. "So what if it is? What do you have to owe them? You work for them, but they don't own your integrity. And it's not like you trust them, or else, why would you use a false name?"

Bryn glared at him. Mads looked at her, startled. "That true? Valetown's not your real name?"

"Valetown is a small village outside of Elimar," Robin informed him. "It's where she's from, at least from what I've gathered. That's not a problem, but what I'd like to know is why she's been passing it off as her surname."

Part of Bryn wanted to tell him. The same part of her that restrained her from shooting him against Cliadell's warning. The sudden betrayal and deaths of her Ringmembers, the horrific crowd of hollow-eyed men that had pursued them out of the city, the throbbing pain in her shoulder—it suddenly brought to light how very tired she was, and how very much she wanted to simply rest and accept these two as allies, comrades. Friends even. These two were not like the rest of the Ringmembers, not so blinded by loyalty to the Brethren that it kept them from doing the right thing.

But she shook her head, forcing such sentiment away. This had to stop. Those ideas were dangerous. She would do what she had to do, take the bounties, and live her life. Forget about all of this.

"You," she informed Robin, "are a traitor. I don't have to tell you anything. And you," she turned sharply to Mads, "are a coward. I won't turn you in unless you try to stop me."

Mads shrugged, unperturbed, and continued rowing. Robin said nothing, only studied her for a long moment. The look in his eyes— an earnest, almost pleading expression—all but begged her to trust him and whatever plan he and Mads had in mind.

"The good of the Dricaster Brethren," he echoed finally, shaking his head disdainfully. "Bryn—do you hear yourself? You're playing their pawn. You've long turned into a mercenary for them, no thoughts for yourself. I know you're better than that."

Bryn met his eyes. "I know what I'm doing, Captain Trelawney," she said. The ice in her tone hid her sorrow and unease.

Robin continued to stare at her. "Do what you will," he said simply, after a long pause. "There's nothing I can do to stop you. But you might just regret it."

Bryn pretended to ignore him. It was easier to say nothing than to defend herself. Such defense would only show how much his words had affected her. He had seen and called out every dangerous thought she'd ever had against the Dricasters. Nothing she could say would erase his words. They called out the doubt in her own heart, doubt she shoved down for fear of being branded a traitor and being left alone again.

She trusted the Dricasters. She trusted Dakrind. Didn't she? If she could not call it trust, then she would call it a mutual need. She worked for them—killed for them—and they protected her.

A mercenary. Was that what she'd become? Killing only for the job? Never stopping to question if it was the right thing to do?

That was a foolish line of thought. Who cared if it was right—it was necessary. But she couldn't help wondering when, if there was a definable moment, she had lost her humanity.

15

An Old Adversary

"Something's wrong," Mel said as he entered the room.

Aryion, sitting on his bed across from the door and pouring over a map, looked up. "What?"

"Something's wrong," Mel repeated, sitting on his own bed. His young face was troubled. "I went downstairs to get some water, and the innkeeper asked for my help moving some crates outside. He seemed on edge."

"Did you ask him anything?" Aryion asked.

"No. I can't really figure out what's going on. Something seems different about the town today," Mel said. He sounded both confused and worried.

Aryion stood and stretched, then folded the map and slid it back inside his pack. After speaking with the town guard yesterday, he and Mel had gone to a local inn for lunch. They had exchanged small talk with the inn keeper, who offered them a room if they helped with a few jobs. After patching a leak in the roof and stacking firewood, the warm beds and clean, dry room made it worth the work.

Aryion had woken up early and begun planning what he would

ask and say to the Esile Council. Mel's concern drove his mind to a more urgent matter. He followed his apprentice down the stairs.

Last night, the tavern had been full of people eating, drinking, and visiting. The sounds of conversation and voices raised in song had filled the inn late into the night. He had expected the morning to be full of voices from the customers come for a cup of coffee or a fresh baked pastry before they began the day's work. This morning, though, the tavern was completely empty. The unusual silence sent a prickle of unease up Aryion's spine.

The inn keeper stood behind the counter, up to his elbows in suds. "Good morning," Aryion said to him. "I hear there's something up in town."

The inn keeper grunted, focused on his work. "Maybe. Whatever it is, it's already bad for business, I can tell you. Doubt it'll get better." He gestured at his empty tavern with a scowl.

"Come look," Mel said.

Aryion followed him out the door, wondering what was going on. The moment he stepped outside, he sensed something was wrong. Esile City was strangely silent. Out of the ten or twelve factories visible from the inn's stoop, only three were active and noisy. There were few conversations. The crowds that filled the streets were noticeably sparser. The sounds and activity that typically filled the city was absent, replaced by a sort of nervous energy.

He glanced around. The inn's front door looked out on the road that sloped down into the market square. It offered a fine view of the harbor beyond the buildings. He surveyed the scene. Noisy conversation was not the only thing missing this morning. There was something else, something he couldn't place.

His eyes returned to the harbor, and he realized with a jolt what it was. "The ships," he said quietly. "The Dricaster pirates—they're all gone. The only ships here are of the Capital fleet."

Yesterday, the harbor had been packed full of ships from all over the world. A number of them bore the red and gold banner of the Dricaster Brethren, marking them as Ringmembers. But this morning, the harbor was startlingly empty. In addition to the smaller sailboats and skiffs owned by the locals, the seven or eight vessels anchored at the pier were Capital warships. The green and violet banner fluttered from their masts as the breeze swept over the lonely harbor.

Aryion finally realized why the crowds were so sparse. Normally, the Dricasters would be in the town today, going about their daily lives in the guise of regular citizens. Now, most of the pirates were gone, and the whole city had noticed.

Mel studied the harbor, then looked back at his mentor questioningly. "Did the Capital come and arrest all the Dricasters?"

"Maybe some of them… but there are too many Ringmembers here for the Capital to take them all," Aryion said, truly baffled. "Besides, the Dricasters are smart. I doubt the Capital managed to track them down after all these years. And the Esile Council wouldn't want the Capital to arrest their business partners."

He fingered the hilt of his sword, his thoughts racing. Capital ships. A harbor completely vacant of pirate vessels. A city left quiet and confused by the sudden disappearance of at least a quarter of its occupants.

Maybe the Capital had indeed conducted an infiltration last night, cracked down on the criminals once and for all. But surely he would have heard that? The Dricasters wouldn't have gone quietly, that much he was certain of. There would have been signs and sounds of a recent fight.

They walked down the road. Aryion caught the shoulder of a passing merchant. "Excuse me, sir. Can you tell us anything of what's happened? The city seems rather quiet today."

The merchant chuckled. "Quiet is right, ranger. No one can make head or tail of it—not even the Council, and that's got them in a fix for sure."

"Has it," Aryion said slowly, hoping to prompt more information from him.

Thankfully the merchant seemed eager to chat. "Aye. Haven't you noticed what's up?"

"We noticed the harbor is emptier than usual," Aryion said.

The merchant nodded. "Quite is, and that's the strangeness of it. Never seen anything like it in all my years. Yesterday, every vessel in its place, every crew in a tavern—an hour past midnight, from what the dockhands say, they're gone. All of 'em, pirate and Ringmember alike."

"So it wasn't the Capital?" Mel asked, unable to keep quiet.

"Doubt it," the merchant said. "Those Randuins rode out on the east side of the city—never even came to the harbor yesterday. As for the Capital, those ships have been here for a few days, and their crews spent the evening in the local barracks up Era Road. I imagine there'll be more soldiers here soon. Sounds like the Council's panicked and sent word to the Capital. I suppose they think something's amiss." The merchant shrugged and walked away.

Something was amiss, Aryion could tell, but he doubted it was what the Council feared. Most likely, the Councilors were panicking, thinking that the pirates and Rings had banded together to overthrow them. He didn't find this very plausible. Whatever was going on, he doubted it involved an uprising against the Daffonic Crown.

He looked at Mel. "Well, on the plus side, we don't have to worry about the Dricasters tracking us down now. Come on." He led the way down the road toward the Council building.

Mel followed. "What do you think's going on?"

Aryion paused. "For the pirates and Ringmembers to disappear in the same night seems odd. But I doubt they're planning to attack the Capital, despite what the Council may assume."

"Why not?" Mel asked.

"Fauna is too far inland for the Dricasters to launch an effective attack," Aryion said. "Even if the pirates are planning some sort of revolt, they have no advantages in attacking the Capital."

"Oh," Mel said, looking thoughtful. "What if they want to attack Esile City?"

"I doubt that even more. Why would they leave Esile City first?" Aryion pointed out. "Besides, the Dricaster Ring already controls most of the city, in alliance with the Council. They would gain very little, unless they want factories and sweat shops in addition to full control of the town."

They followed the street signs pointing to the Council Hall. Aryion looked at his apprentice. The whole scenario was baffling to him, and he could tell Mel was thinking hard. "What do you make of it?"

Mel thought for a moment. "Well… I'm not sure if this is how it works. But you said before that there are rival Crime Rings. What if the pirates just left to fight somewhere else?"

"That's not a bad idea," Aryion said. He hadn't even considered that possibility. If the Crime Rings were at war, as he had guessed, it was not unlikely that the Dricasters had simply gone to launch an attack. But where?

They reached the Council Hall. At least thirty guards were posted outside, and they stiffened as the two rangers approached.

"We're here to speak to the Council," Aryion said.

The nearest soldier shook his head. "We are under strict orders to let no one in. The Council is working to understand what has happened. Leave your name and request and they will send for you at their convenience."

"Wait a moment, private." Captain Jackson appeared, waving his soldiers aside. "A good morning to you, rangers. I apologize for the confusion."

"That's all right, Captain," Aryion said. "Can we meet with the Council?"

The captain-of-guard sighed. "As luck would have it, they've locked themselves in. No one is allowed to speak with them, not even the Randuins, not until their men have confirmed there is no danger."

Aryion raised an eyebrow. "With the Dricasters?"

"Or lack of them, as I imagine you've noticed." Captain Jackson shook his head. "The Council won't allow any visitors until it's sorted out. I'm sorry about that, but orders are orders."

Mel looked up at Aryion, visibly disappointed. Aryion felt a surge of frustration, but realized there was nothing he could do about it. Still, they had come all the way to Esile City for information, and he refused to give up on that now. "Is there anyone else we could speak to? Someone who represents them?"

Jackson glanced at the Council Hall. "You might try to talk to the secretary. He keeps track of all records and who goes in and out of town. He might have news on the man you're looking for."

"Well, we'll try him," Aryion murmured, and led the way up the steps. Mel followed. Aryion stopped before the door and stole one last glance at the eerily empty harbor before walking inside.

The heavy stone door fell shut behind them. The hall was barely any warmer than outside, and quite stuffy. Aryion drew his cloak tighter around him and walked down the dimly lit hall. The clicks of their boots on the tile was the only sound.

The secretary sat at a desk at the end of the hall, and stood as they approached. "Good morning. Can I help you?"

"I hope so. We've come to speak with the Council," Aryion said.

The secretary rubbed his brow tiredly. "Of course you have. Well, I'm afraid I can only tell you what I've been instructed to—that the Council is working to understand what has happened this morning and prepare for any threats that may present themselves in the future."

"We aren't here about the missing Ringmembers," Mel said. "We were sent from Caer Sia."

The secretary raised his eyebrows. "Caer Sia, is it? Glad to see they're finally getting back to business, after the occupation and all."

Aryion took a deep breath—his patience was running thinner with every minute. "Sir… we are tasked with finding and apprehending a man we believe to be within this very city. An enemy of both Caer Sia and the Daffonic Crown."

For the first time, a glimmer of light came into the secretary's eyes. "Ah, well, there's something I can help you with." He sat down at his desk and opened a large drawer full of leather-bound folders. "These contain the records of the latest criminal cases. If an outlaw is seen here, he'd be in my records. Who are you looking for?"

"Terrax of Elvengate," Aryion said.

The secretary looked up at him, interested. "Of Elvengate, you say? Now that's strange… quite strange. Let me see…"

"Sorry," Mel said, looking between Aryion and the secretary, "but why's that strange?"

The secretary was busy shuffling through pages, so Aryion answered his apprentice. "It's a dead city. Dandio told you about Elvengate—it was ruined in the Dividing War?"

Understanding dawned on Mel's face. "Oh, right."

The history of Elvengate itself aided their mission very little, Aryion knew. But the fact that Terrax still claimed the lost city as his birthplace was unusual, and unusual meant traceable.

The secretary held up a page triumphantly. "Here it is—issued by our previous captain of guard, three years ago now. A report on Terrax' activities then. He was here causing trouble, it seems."

"He's been causing trouble for a while," Mel told him.

Aryion took the paper, reading it over briefly. The secretary was right, the case detailed here was three years old. That wouldn't help them. This file would have been before Terrax had ever gone north to join Drona. Long before the sword was stolen, or the fight with the Darkness, or the appearance of the Aces. "Is this the only information you have on him?" he asked, determined to find something more.

The secretary produced two other folders and flipped through them, skimming the pages, before nodding reluctantly. "It seems so. You think this Terrax is in Esile City currently?"

"We… thought so," Aryion said, feeling an unwelcome sensation of doubt.

The secretary shrugged. "Well, someone of his profile would certainly catch the attention of the town guard. Either Terrax is very good at staying hidden, or he is not here."

Aryion frowned, thinking. No records on Terrax in recent months. No news of him being here at all. He could be here, hiding—but Aryion doubted that. For one, Terrax knew it would be unwise to stay in one place for long. For another thing, the outlaw always had some plan, some new scheme that led to him popping up in new places. In this part of the world, news traveled fast, so if Terrax was in Esile City, the secretary would have at least heard rumors about it.

Unless Terrax had never returned to Esile City… unless he had gone to look for the Crime Rings elsewhere…

He looked up at the secretary again. "What can you tell us about the Crime Rings?"

The secretary shuddered. "Oh… well, not much. The Dricaster Brethren operated within the city up until recently—as you saw, they've cleared out today. But there are other Crime Rings, you know—the Rylanders to the south, for example."

South.

Bregg's words flooded Aryion's mind again: *"Terrax talked about going south."* Terrax had gone to find a Crime Ring, but Bregg hadn't known which one—and he'd been captured before finding out. Aryion had assumed Terrax had gone to the Dricasters, but Terrax had clearly not come to Esile City. That meant he had gone to a different town—a town like Esile City, lawless and crime-ridden.

"The Rylander Crime Ring… that is based in Port Rylan, I imagine?" he asked slowly, needing to be sure.

"They own the town, I've heard. But I've never gone that way," the secretary said. "Sounds like a rather interesting place. A pirate haven, of course, but there's enough Capital troops there to keep the peace."

A town infested with pirates and outlaws, so the town guard would have their hands full. A second Crime Ring, like the Dricasters, but far enough south to avoid the watch of Caer Sia—and just far enough east that Terrax could contact the Jenna, if Jenna he intended to hire. It was the perfect location. Terrax would be able to do whatever he pleased in Port Rylan with little fear of being tracked down.

Not when he had laid an obvious trail in the opposite direction. Leading Aryion and Mel on a wild goose chase.

"It seems rather convenient that all paths lead to Esile City," came Joesp's words from a few nights ago. The Wildkid had seen the false trail almost immediately. And Aryion, too caught up in the mission itself, had willingly ignored the warning. He had been too focused on Esile City, too certain that Terrax was here, and had never considered other alternatives. Now they had wasted days of precious time.

Terrax was not in Esile City. He had not been here for years.

Aryion clenched his jaw, furious he had not realized this earlier. Port Rylan was miles and miles from here. By the time Aryion and Mel reached it, Terrax would either be able to go into hiding or prepare his allies for counterattack.

"Thank you for your help," he said to the secretary, then turned on his heel and headed back down the hall.

Mel ran after him. "Aryion—I'm confused. I thought Terrax was working with the Dricasters. What's he doing in Port Rylan?"

"He's waiting," Aryion said bitterly. "Esile City is a lawless place, but it is so close to Fauna that the Capital will often send soldiers here—like the Randuins. That's not a risk Terrax would want to take."

"So… who did Terrax actually hire?" Mel wondered. "The Dricasters, the Rylanders, or the Jenna?"

"I'm not sure yet. It could be any of them. It might be all of them." Aryion rubbed his brow. "Whoever Terrax did hire, we can assume he has a decent number of trained mercenaries at his beck and call now."

They descended the steps. A few townsfolk had come to talk with the soldiers—Aryion could hear their confused and worried questions and the soldiers trying their best to reassure them. The whole situation sent a flare of anger into his chest. The Councilors were worried only about their own safety, with hardly any regard for the people they had been elected to look after.

But that was a fight for another day. Now he had to come up with a plan—a new plan, since the old one had been capsized by this revelation.

"So, are we going to Port Rylan now?" Mel asked.

Aryion hesitated. Part of him thought that would be a smart move. If Terrax was still in Port Rylan, maybe they could catch him.

But even as he had these thoughts, he knew that would be a reckless decision. If his guess was correct, Terrax had hired warriors to join him. He might lure the two rangers into a trap and kill them—and take the Blue Stone.

"We can't," Aryion said. He brushed snow from a bench and sat down, feeling immensely defeated. "We can't take him down alone, Mel."

"We have the Stone," Mel said confidently, patting his pocket.

"Terrax wants the Stone," Aryion reminded him. "Think. Is arresting Terrax worth the risk of losing the Stone?"

Mel hesitated. Several emotions played over his face—frustration, confusion, anxiety. "So we're just giving up?" he burst out finally.

"I don't know," Aryion said, irritated. They sat in agitated silence for several minutes.

"Maybe we can get word to someone," Mel suggested at length. "Remember what the Wildkids said—if there are Jenna in Port Rylan, we might get the Capital to send soldiers to investigate and arrest Terrax. The Randuins are here already—I bet we can get them on our side. Or if the Capital won't do it, we can send word to Caer Sia."

"The Jenna's involvement is mostly speculation at this point," Aryion said wearily. "The Capital will not send Randuins in without proof. And the Liznees can do nothing. This is an internal Daffonic issue, and the Red Dawn can't interfere in another country's matters unless requested by the Daffonic king."

They sat for several long moments, thinking. Across the street, a few soldiers were putting up fresh Wanted posters and throwing the old, damp ones away.

Aryion rested his chin in his hands. They were no longer simply arresting Terrax—now, they were potentially facing off with two Crime Rings, not to mention the possibility of Jenna. Whoever Terrax had hired, it was safe to assume he was well protected. Arresting him was not something two people could accomplish alone. Aryion refused to put Mel in that kind of situation. This mission was becoming more and more complicated with every passing minute, and for the first time since leaving Lemsonburg, he had no idea what to do.

"Aryion," Mel said, in the slow, careful tone he used when he had a potentially bad idea.

At the moment, Aryion needed any ideas—good or bad. He looked up. "Yes?"

Mel pointed across the street at the new Wanted posters on the side of the building. The sketches had been colored in to offer a somewhat more accurate depiction of the person. The descriptions below the picture were written in Erinian, the dominant language of the southern kingdoms. At least half the posters bore the red bear crest on the bottom corner, indicating that the criminal was a part of the Dricaster Brethren.

"Aryion," Mel began again, "how much do you suppose it costs to hire a few Dricasters?" He hesitated. "I know that's probably a bad idea, and probably too expensive—but you know, we could always borrow money from Caer Sia, since we're here on official business. And we could track down the Dricasters, wherever they've gone, and hire them to help us fight Terrax. Or maybe just pay them for information, or…"

But Aryion barely heard him. His eyes had locked instantly on a face on one of the posters. For several seconds, he stared at it, knowing he had misidentified the person there, knowing it was impossible.

"Hold on," he muttered, standing and moving closer, staring at the sketch of the face. There was no way in Orlell it could be…

But it was.

He would know her face anywhere.

His eyes traveled to the bottom corner of the page. The red bear snarled back at him. A Dricaster Ringmember. Oh, his father would be rolling in his grave if he knew.

For a long moment, he could hardly form words. But his mind was working rapidly, coming up with a plan. Possibly a bad plan—a crazy plan—but a plan that he found he liked.

He tore the poster from the wall, folded it gently, and slipped it in his pocket. Then, finally finding his voice again, he turned to his apprentice.

"Mel… how much have I told you about my sister?"

PART 2

Dricaster Traitor

16

Drynrall Island

"Plan on telling me anything?" Mads asked.

Bryn sat with her back against the port rail, staring at a blotch of tar on the wood in front of her, and said nothing. Though their injuries had been tended by the ship's doctor, the gut-wrenching fear of yesterday afternoon still felt fresh, dulling her mind and making it hard to form words at all. The town guard swarming the streets, the deaths of Cliadell and Drike, the throngs of staggering, dead-eyed beggars that had seemed to spawn from the shadows—every memory of their actions in Port Rylan felt raw with horror.

She'd been in dangerous situations before, of course, but always secretly, striking from the shadows, never in an open chase. She could still hear the shouts, the gunshots, the whiz of crossbow bolts flying past her, the hoarse voices of the Wavers.

Wavers. They were the ones who had inspired so much fear among her fellow Ringmembers—for good reason. Former sea-farers whose desperate fixation on the compass had caused their minds to rot away and their very Essence to be embraced by its powers. Now they lived and died for the darkness the compass was said to possess. They were hardly human anymore, the Wavers. Bryn might have felt a small amount of pity for them, if they had not tried to kill her.

Even greater than the fear of the memories was the fact that she could no longer deny the reality of the compass' dark power. Nothing else could explain what had happened to Cliadell and Drike, who had both gone into a blood rage at the first sight of it. Cliadell had continued to attack with unexplainable strength, despite the arrow protruding from his stomach. Both were Ring-members that, while Bryn hadn't fully trusted, she had always attributed a certain… stability. Yet they'd both gone wild the instant the compass was near.

But Robin hadn't. Neither had Mads. Bryn had assumed she was exempt from the compass' dark powers due to her unbelief. Yet Robin and Mads both believed in the story, and they hadn't been controlled by the compass. There must be something else, some other force that was protecting them, though she was unsure what that could be.

None of it made sense, none of it was explainable by logic, and none of it made Bryn's upcoming decision any easier.

She glanced at Mads, who sat on a barrel a few feet away, his back against the mizzen mast. "Tell you what?" she asked in response to his question.

Mads shrugged. "Oh, I don't know. Your real name, what you know about the mission that you haven't told us, what you're planning to do when we reach Drynrall…" He trailed off, arching an eyebrow.

Bryn remained silent. Not because she was angry at Mads—she realized now that out of everyone on board, Mads was the only one who hadn't lied directly to her face. She had no idea what to tell him. Every answer to his questions were complicated.

"I've told you everything I know about the mission," she said after a pause.

"Humph," the Dwarve grunted, clearly unimpressed. He got up and limped over to the tiller to talk with Richard.

"Drynrall to starboard, Cap'n," Matthew McCreery called from the crow's nest.

Bryn turned to look. The sunlight glaring off the water made it hard to see much farther ahead, but she could make out the island a few miles away. At this distance, the gradual arch of the rocky hills looked like the spine of a massive sea creature. As they drew closer, she could make out clearer details. Trees clung stubbornly to the stone cliffs. Numerous ships were anchored within the harbor. The village of Drynrall was built upon the rocky island. At first glance, one would think the village would have been washed off its island by a decent gust of wind. But the scrappy little town was made of tougher stuff than it appeared, as were the people who lived there.

At least they would not have to worry about any town guardsmen. Drynrall Island, though technically within the borders of Daffodalion, had long since been considered as its own tiny lawless country. Pirates came and went as they pleased. Ringmembers from all Crime Rings met here to do business. Aside from drunken brawls, which were quite common, there was an unspoken rule that organized fighting was strictly prohibited.

This made it somewhat safer than Port Rylan, though there was no guarantee you wouldn't be caught by someone who was after your bounty. Bryn had caught several bounties there herself. She had come to Drynrall a few months ago with Dakrind, too. He'd wanted protection, so she had waited onboard the ship while he went and met with someone.

What *had* Dakrind been doing last time he was here?

She pushed the concern away and tried to think clearly. Almost over. It was almost over. The *Burman Marie* drew up next to the pier and docked. The *Black Raven* waited at the pier across from them. Dakrind was already here, waiting for them. Waiting for the compass.

The tingle of fear in her stomach, which she had tried to push away all morning, intensified with that thought.

Robin Trelawney appeared from below, moving stiffly, one hand pressed to the bandage over the stitches in his side. He carried a sack in his other hand, which Bryn guessed contained the compass. She had noticed yesterday how the entire crew of the *Marie* had avoided the compass, openly wary of it. Pirate superstition, she'd assumed a few days ago. After seeing the Wavers, she understood. Whatever power the compass possessed, she wanted nothing to do with it. At least they'd be rid of it soon.

"We'll be back by nightfall," Robin said to John. "Stock up on supplies while we're here. We're running low on food and drink."

The first mate nodded silently. He seemed as nervous as everyone else. Bryn wondered how much Robin had told them about yesterday's strange events. From a glance, it looked suspicious. She, Mads, and Robin had returned without the other two Ringmembers, all injured, in a different boat than they'd originally planned. With the compass. If the crew believed in the legend, that the compass made you go into a killing rage, then the manner of their reappearance fit the fear.

No one spoke as they walked down the gangplank and arrived at Drynrall. Mads nodded farewell to the sailors and shook both Richard and John's hands. It was strange that despite his usually irritable manner, he had quickly made friends of the sailors on the *Burman Marie*. While Drike and Cliadell had avoided the crew and seen them as enemies, Mads had always been friendly to them. Maybe it was just to find out information. Or maybe he thought working together would be better than fighting.

As opposed to Port Rylan, which was filled with an organized, busy sort of noise, Drynrall was a cacophony of sounds. People talked and sang and shouted. A group of musicians played a few out of key instruments, their voices rising in a shanty.

"Where are we headed?" Mads asked as they paused on the road.

Robin let out a breath. "An inn on the other side of town. Hawk said he'd meet us there by noon."

Bryn glanced up at the sun—it was nearly noon already. She studied Robin as they walked. His face was pale and set, genuinely fearful.

It was the first time she'd ever seen him like this, and it both confused and concerned her. Then again, Robin knew she had to turn him in to Dakrind for treason. Bryn knew she had to. And yet… it felt so wrong to betray him. Maybe it was because she'd been protecting him this whole trip.

Besides, she reminded herself mentally, she wasn't betraying him. She was doing what was best for the Dricaster Brethren. Robin had betrayed her first. But… no, that wasn't right either. The only one he'd betrayed had been Dakrind, acting as a Rylander spy. Then again, if Trelawney was actually a Rylander, why had he been so fearful of Madam Ida when they'd passed the checkpoint?

She couldn't figure him out. Part of her wanted to ask about it, but that would mean associating with a Brethren traitor, which could brand her a traitor too.

She forced the confusing thoughts out of her head and followed Robin and Mads up the road. They passed through the main thoroughfare of Drynrall. The market was loud and busy. People sold spices, food, and novelties from all around Orlell. The smell of alcohol, tobacco, and unwashed bodies filled the air. A group of filthy children played marbles in the awning of a building.

Bryn found herself paying closer attention to her surroundings than she ever had before. That man was selling greenstalk. The vendor behind them was talking to a few pirates about the weather. To her right stood a line of wicker cages.

Bryn had passed those cages multiple times, on other visits to Drynrall. Yet now she saw them in a new light. Each cage held seven or eight figures varying in height and age, their fur damp and ragged, a wildness in their eyes as they clung to the bars.

Wildkids, waiting to be sold to either the Jenna or the furriers.

Bryn looked away and kept walking. The inn stood before them. While it was about the same size as the rest of the inns and taverns here, it was much cleaner, made of gray slate stone instead of brick. A few sailors waited outside, Ringmembers who crewed the *Black Raven*.

"Speak of the devil," Mads murmured. "What are Jenna doing here?"

Bryn looked up. Mads was right. Five Jenna warriors stood outside the door to the inn, their hands resting on their curved sabers. Their brutish faces twisted into cruel smiles as Robin approached.

"We've come to see Dakrind," Robin said, clearly caught off guard by the Jenna's presence. "I assume he's inside?"

The Jenna stepped back and ushered them inside without a word. The inn was eerily quiet. Bryn gripped her bow tighter, trying to focus on their task and not the confusion and fear she felt. Why were the Jenna here? Did they have anything to do with the strange ship they had seen in Port Rylan yesterday?

Four more of Dakrind's crew stood at the base of the stairs and led them up to the second floor. The hulking Ringmembers flanked them, closing in around Bryn, Robin, and Mads. The meaning was clear. They were completely at the mercy of Hawk Dakrind.

They reached the top of the stairs, turned left, and entered a clean, well-lit room. The tile floor had recently been swept. The window on the opposite wall looked out over the sea.

"So you made it here at last," came Dakrind's voice. He sat on the low sofa along the right wall, his boots propped up on the table in front of him.

The three of them stopped in the doorway. Without a word, Dakrind's four guards left the room.

"I admit, I wondered if it would be too difficult for so few to accomplish," Dakrind continued, standing and stretching. He seemed in good spirits. "I'm impressed to see all three of you back. The compass took care of the needed casualties, I see."

Needed casualties, Bryn's mind echoed. Was that what Cliadell and Drike had been? Even as she had the thought, she remembered her statement after her last job—calling the two guards on the clock tower "a potential security risk." That had been her reason for killing them. She'd never even given them a chance to defend themselves.

She shook herself, trying to focus. This was not the time to have regrets, to pretend she had some sense of morality.

"Drike and Cliadell turned on us, Dakrind," Mads stated. "Almost killed us, in fact, as you can probably see. Which is stupid, since there would have been enough reward for each of us."

Dakrind gave a small, unconcerned shrug. "A regretful loss, but again, a needed one. Now, where is the compass?"

Bryn looked at Robin. The pirate captain shook his head, a disappointed look on his face. "That's why we've come, Chief. We failed for now, but I promise we won't give up."

Dakrind's eyes narrowed. "What?"

"We lost the compass," Mads said.

Bryn remained quiet, eying Robin sidelong, totally confused by what was happening. What were they doing? Why were they lying so confidently to Hawk Dakrind, a person who inspired so much fear under normal circumstances?

Dakrind's face was unchanged. "You lost it?" he repeated, studying Robin.

Robin nodded, his voice level. "We recovered the compass according to the map. Drike was possessed by it immediately and almost killed Valetown. We killed him, but Cliadell stole the compass and fled. He ran into a group of Wavers, who killed him almost instantly. They took the compass and would have killed us too. We figured it would be wiser to come here and gather your forces behind us before attempting to infiltrate Port Rylan."

Dakrind's amber eyes turned to Bryn. "Is that true, Valetown?"

Bryn's mouth was dry. She had no idea what was going on, what they could possibly gain from this ruse. She wanted to nod or say something, but she seemed frozen in place.

"She's a little shocked from the whole thing, Chief," Mads said quickly. "Probably needs a good rest."

"Poor Valetown," Dakrind said softly, a hint of sarcasm in his voice. He turned back to Robin. "What's in the bag, Trelawney?"

"Badges, sir. Crests of the Rylanders," Robin said, passing the sack to him. "Madam Ida and the *Blood Swan* are currently at sea, and the Rylanders won't recognize us. These badges will allow us into the city, possibly even to their base if needed. We can get in and get a better idea of where the compass is."

Dakrind studied the silver pin in his hand. Bryn knew those were Rylander badges. They were similar to the red pins she and her fellow Dricasters wore within their coats, mostly to help someone identify them if they turned up dead.

But she knew Robin hadn't killed for those badges. He'd stolen them, stolen them from his own comrades among the Rylanders. He was practically handing Dakrind the key to take down his own Brethren.

It made her stomach twist. He could lie so easily, betray his fellow Ringmembers without a thought.

So why did she still hesitate to turn him in?

"You killed Rylanders, you say?" Dakrind asked, his voice very quiet.

Mads shrugged. "What were we going to do with 'em, throw 'em a tea party? They were a… a needed casualty, as you put it." He smirked, but Bryn could see the nervousness in his eyes.

Dakrind looked between the three of them for a long moment. Bryn waited for him to begin shouting, to berate them for 'losing' the compass, to kick them out of the Dricaster Brethren then and there.

But instead, Hawk Dakrind laughed.

"I'll give you credit, my lord," he said, looking over Bryn's shoulder to the doorway, "you are indeed a good guesser."

Bryn turned slowly.

A tall figure stood in the shadows by the door. His black hair fell past his shoulders. His silver armor was tarnished, battered after years of use. At his side he wore a long sword. His chiseled features, pointed ears, and sharp eyes marked him as an Elf.

"I have made a career off of good guesses, Captain Dakrind," the Elf said smoothly. His voice was rich, with the elegant Northern accent.

"Fellow Ringmembers, meet your employer," Dakrind said, bowing slightly to the other man. "Terrax of Elvengate."

The Elf stepped forward into the light, smiling slightly. The expression never reached his eyes—they remained as cold and black as pieces of coal.

"I apologize for leaving you in the dark," Terrax said, not sounding apologetic at all. "It was necessary, for the security of my operation. Rylanders are not the only ones who had spies. I have dwelt in Port Rylan for the past few months, in fact, and my men kept watch on both Dricasters and Rylanders." He looked at Mads with disgust. "So tell me, Dwarve… how did you lose the compass, after you so effortlessly evaded the Wavers and escaped at sea with it in your grasp?"

For once in his life, Mads seemed speechless. Terrax drew a short knife from his belt, running his fingers down the edge. "Will you not explain yourself? Or try to lie your way out now?"

"We didn't lose it," Bryn stammered, finally finding her voice. She could hardly believe her own words, but she stepped forward, moving closer to Mads. "He… he was unconscious. He didn't see what happened—he was bleeding pretty badly, and I think that's why he confused the story."

"You didn't lose it?" Terrax repeated, drawing the words out. His black eyes turned on her. "So, where is the compass then? Miss *Paya*?"

The name dropped like a stone into the silence. For an instant Bryn thought she had imagined he had said it. But Dakrind frowned in mild interest and looked at Terrax. "Her true name is Paya?"

The Elven outlaw studied Bryn skeptically. "Indeed it is, though she has long tried to be rid of the name. Fifteen years now, has it been? Sixteen? From what I hear, your family name has been somewhat redeemed. Still, the Blood Oath will forever mar your brother's name, and yours."

Robin glanced at Bryn, but Bryn could not speak. The shock of what she was hearing drove all sense from her. She could come up with nothing to prove Terrax wrong. He *knew*. How did he know? He must have traced her past to another time—sixteen years ago, living in Valetown. Traced her name and her face to that of another Paya, one marked by sixteen years of hate and killing and a history as bloody as her own.

The name itself might be hard to track, but to swear a Blood Oath came with enemies. To swear it at such a young age would have sparked tales all along the border. A fact she forever resented. The choice had driven away the only person who had ever cared for her, had forced them apart, had left her alone to contend with the world.

How Terrax knew this, she had no idea. Yet his knowledge of the truth burned a hole in her carefully drawn ruse.

"How do you know me?" she asked finally, her voice hoarse.

"Valetown is a small village, your appearance is much like his, and your history aligns quite well with certain events," Terrax said absently. "But you have not answered my question. Where is the compass?"

No one spoke. In a blur of movement, Terrax seized Mads by the shoulders and drove the knife into his chest.

Robin gave a shout and stepped forward far too late. Terrax shoved the Dwarve back—Mads stumbled back two paces before his bad leg gave out, and he fell to the ground, blood soaking his shirt front. He looked down at the injury as if bewildered, then up at Bryn. His eyes met hers, confused and shaken. "Paya?" he repeated hoarsely, and then slumped to the floor.

Bryn closed her eyes, her hands shaking.

"As you have probably gathered," Terrax said in a conversational tone, wiping his blade clean on his cloak, "I dislike being lied to. So, I will ask you once more. Where is the compass?"

"I don't know," Bryn finally managed to reply, fighting to keep her voice calm. "I don't know. They didn't tell me this was the plan."

Both Terrax and Dakrind studied her for a moment. Perhaps it was the shock and confusion on her face that convinced them she was telling the truth. Terrax rounded on Robin. "Trelawney, then. I hear you are a man of many words. Don't ask me to believe the Dwarve concocted this plan all on his own. My sources have called you quite a master of deception. Those pins," he nodded to the sack Dakrind still held, "they are those of your fellow Ringmembers, are they not? Perhaps not your fellows, but I know you spent time working for them. Even spied for them, isn't that right?"

Bryn could tell from Dakrind's reaction that this was the first he had heard of this. "You did what?" he snarled, striding up to Robin. He stood a good head taller than the pirate captain, eyes blazing in fury.

Robin did not flinch. His face was white, but he met Dakrind's gaze calmly. "This compass is not what you think it is," he said. "I've seen what it does to people. I don't know what you want to use it for, but don't do it. Whatever powers it has, whatever magic makes it work—you don't want to mess with that."

Dakrind punched him so hard he reeled back into the wall. Robin raised his hands to fend off the wild blows, but Dakrind was stronger, striking him again and again until he slumped to the ground like a ragdoll.

"You'll learn how we treat traitors, Trelawney," Dakrind hissed. He nodded to the guards—they bound the half-conscious pirate's arms behind his back and dragged him from the room.

"The compass, Miss Paya?" Terrax asked calmly.

Bryn tore her eyes away from Robin and looked at the Elf again.

He was her employer. This was her job. She must remain calm and unaffected. It had to happen this way. Mads and Robin had betrayed the Dricasters, and they both must die.

For the good of the Brethren.

She forced the emotion in her chest away. "The compass. I—I would expect it to be on board the *Burman Marie*."

"Excellent," Dakrind growled. "I'll have that ship stripped and put under guard."

Terrax nodded. "Good. Good." He was still studying Bryn. "In the meantime, Miss Paya, I have a proposition for you."

Another mission. Perfect. Just what she needed to forget about all this. "I would be honored to work for you, sir," she said levelly.

"Your Ringleader speaks well of you," Terrax said. "He calls you one of the best hunters in the Brethren. Thus, I expect you to be well-prepared for this task." He glanced at Dakrind. "Perhaps you could give us a moment?"

Dakrind nodded shortly and left the room.

Bryn was left alone with the Elven outlaw and a growing feeling of dread.

17

Darker Magic

"Would you like a drink, Miss Paya?" Terrax asked.

"No thank you."

Terrax poured himself a glass of wine and drank slowly. It left a line of red on his lips, bright as blood on his pale face. "Well. You are from Valetown, I believe? A pleasant village, though I can't say I have spent much time there."

"Yes." Bryn's gaze followed his every movement. The Elven outlaw could move calmly, speak smoothly, yet there was something in his eyes that told her he was volatile, dangerous, like a lit fuse. She'd gathered that already, after what he'd done to Mads—

A burning sensation rose from her chest into her throat, and she swallowed hard. No. No emotion, no reaction. She was untouchable, hardened. She must not let him see that he had affected her.

"How do you know me?" she asked instead, because that was one area she was still unclear on.

Terrax leaned against the small counter top, swirling the wine in the glass. "I knew you as a Ringmember before I learned of your past. I did, in fact, spend time in Esile City three years ago. I required assistance from the Dricaster Brethren. You, I believe, fulfilled a few of those tasks."

Had she really? Too much had happened in three years. Anything she would have done then had blurred with everything else, every horrible thing she'd done up till now.

"But," Terrax continued, "I had heard of your family name before. Your brother's choice to swear the Blood Oath, for example, garnered much interest among the outlaws and scoundrels of the area. The orc Hagshrub passed word of it through the neighboring towns—he seemed to find it amusing. Your brother, despite his youth, built quite a name for himself—he became almost as ruthless as you, in fact. Imagine what the Crime Rings could have made of him." He chuckled.

Bryn didn't want to imagine that.

"As for yourself," Terrax went on, "hardly anyone else paid attention to you or connected you to your current identity. Thankfully, the small population of Valetown and the rarity of the Blood Oath helped connect the dots. Your likeness to your brother and your history with the Brethren aligned with our assumptions."

"Our?" Bryn repeated, a terrible sinking feeling in her stomach. Who else knew about her true identity?

"No matter," Terrax said, brushing it past. "Now, the compass. Six hundred lupin is owed, I believe?"

"Yes, sir."

"If you complete the second part of the task, I will double the payment."

Bryn raised her eyebrows. Twelve hundred lupin. She couldn't even list all the things she could do with that. She could pay off her own bounty, she could buy a ship and start somewhere new, somewhere far away… "What do you require of me?" she asked.

Terrax smiled, pleased. "First, I suppose you must know the truth of what the compass does. You have no doubt heard of it in pirate legend?"

"A bit of it," Bryn said, remembering the story Richard had told her. "But I'm… skeptical."

"As you should be. The legend is just that—mythology, a tall tale born of pirate superstition. But of course, all such legends have their roots in truth."

It was very similar to what Robin had said before. Bryn shook her head slightly. No, she could not afford to think about Robin right now.

"The compass was made by a sorcerer," Terrax said. "One whose name you may know, being Coonsian by blood. His name was Safacon."

Bryn shrugged noncommittally. She had heard the name, but didn't know much more besides that.

Terrax continued. "At one time, Safacon had in his possession a thing of great power, a force he could not begin to understand. But by his foolishness, this Object was lost. Gone from his hands for several long years. Safacon was desperate to recover it. His men searched far and wide. Eventually, Safacon was forced to seek help elsewhere, from the same dark place that the Object had come from."

Bryn kept her face impassive, hiding her usual doubt. Part of her earlier guess was right, then. Terrax fully believed in a legend, though it was a different story than the one she'd heard before. "What place was that?" she asked, humoring him for now.

"A place I care not to speak of much," Terrax said vaguely. "It is called the Dark Realm, and the ruler of it has recently made himself known again. At his hands my forefather Liridox met his end in the Dividing War, and the kingdom of Elvengate fell." For the first time, a flicker of fear and hatred crossed the Elf's face as he spoke. Then he was calm again. "Safacon reached this dark ruler a second time, begging for assistance to find his lost Object. And so the ruler granted his wish by giving him a compass."

Terrax paused. Bryn ventured a question. "If Safacon didn't get this Object back, which the stories say he didn't… then how do you know the compass works at all?"

"A valid question, and a flaw in the story you have likely been told," Terrax said. "Contrary to pirate lore, the compass does *not* know your future enemies. No, what it seeks is something far more valuable. Star-Stones. The great Object Safacon lost was such a stone—the Jewel of Power. Thought to be crafted by man, but far older than the ancestors of mortals. When the Jewel was lost, the compass was made to find it, tracking the magic of the Star-Stones."

"But the Jewel was destroyed," Bryn said, not sure what she believed at this point. "The compass didn't find it in time."

"No, because Safacon was a fool," Terrax said disdainfully. "By his own rules of magic the compass betrayed him. Safacon gave the compass to his deputy Kado, and it led him to Caer Sia. They believed the Jewel was there. But they were wrong. The compass, you see, cannot track specific Star-Stones—it only follows the largest source of magic. There were two Star-Stones in Caer Sia at that time in history—the Stone Isilas in the High King's sword, and one of the Shards of the Blue Stone, which have only recently been rejoined into one. So the compass led Kado away from Gayrile, where the Jewel was all along."

Bryn's head was beginning to spin. Usually, when she heard a story like this, she could find a hole in it almost immediately. But this story fit so perfectly with what she knew of history that for the first time in her life she began to wonder if it was true. "So… this Kado… he lost the compass in Caer Sia when he was killed?" she asked slowly.

"Yes, he lost it there," Terrax said. "The compass entered the Crime Rings then, after thieves plundered the battle field. The legend of it had been born years before, thanks to Safacon. Not knowing the compass' true purpose, the myth of its powers spread, and its history has been a bloodbath up until now."

Just as Richard had said. The pirates didn't know what the compass did, but the darkness still affected them. "I've heard that the compass does things to people," Bryn said carefully, intrigued despite herself. "That it… does something to their minds."

"Indeed it does," Terrax said, not sounding too concerned. "There is always a price to pay for using the magic of the Dark Realm. Safacon himself fell into madness before his destruction. And I expect you have seen the same thing in the Wavers."

Bryn nodded slightly. "I didn't know why the compass affected them, though."

"The compass' powers cause hyper-fixation that leads to obsession over it. I personally believe that Safacon designed it this way, so that he would never fear Kado betraying him or abandoning his mission."

Bryn let out a long breath. This story, one of magic and darkness and death, was one she would never consider believing under normal circumstances. But what she had seen in Port Rylan, what she knew of history, and the mindless actions of the Wavers verified Terrax' story.

"What do you need me to do, then?" she asked, moving away from the topic.

Terrax smiled, and a chill of foreboding went down her spine. "There is another reason I have learned so much about your family history of late, Miss Paya. Another reason why I have told you the true powers of the compass. The Jewel of Power is destroyed, as was my attempt to gain Isilas. But there is another Star-Stone, possessed by someone I— well, let us say I have a history with this particular person."

"Oh?" Bryn asked.

"A boy," Terrax stated. "A boy who has meddled with powers he cannot control. An apprentice ranger now, though when we last met

I would not have called him much of a warrior."

"His name?" Bryn asked.

"Mel Smallbutton of Appledale," Terrax said. "You will have to track him and his mentor. They will be together, and the Stone will be with them."

A ranger. Somehow, she guessed where this was going, and, for what felt like the hundredth time, she deeply regretted taking this mission, regretted her actions in Port Rylan, regretted everything she had ever done while serving the Dricaster Brethren. Perhaps this was recompense for it all. Perhaps fate had some sick sense of humor.

"Your target," Terrax said, "is Aryion Paya, the Hummingbird, as he is known. Kill him and the boy, and bring the Stone to me."

Bryn managed to nod—it was the only action she could manage.

"They are headed to Esile City now, as my sources have stated," Terrax said. "You may use the compass to track them—it will lead you to the Stone. Bring me both the compass and the Stone in a fortnight."

She wasn't sure if she nodded that time. Her legs felt like they were made of rubber, and it took an effort to turn and move toward the door. To avoid the broken furniture where Robin had fallen. To step over Mads' body.

Dakrind appeared in the doorway. "No sign of the compass on the *Marie*," he said to Terrax, his voice dark with displeasure. "They've hidden it somewhere."

"They should be more open to trusting Miss Paya," Terrax said smoothly, looking at Bryn.

"I'll find it before we leave," Bryn said hoarsely. She could hopefully do that without killing any of the sailors who, in the last few days, had counted her as a friend. She doubted they did now.

"Have you a new assignment?" Dakrind asked her briskly.

"Yes," Bryn said.

"Excellent. We shall set sail tomorrow morning," Dakrind said.

Bryn didn't reply. The room suddenly felt like it was closing in on her, and she felt a desperate desire for air. She brushed past him and moved down the stairs, then jogged out the door, leaving the inn behind while she ran through the muddy streets of Drynrall. At last, in a quiet corner of the island, she sat down. Her thoughts reeled as she huddled on a large rock next to the water.

"Snap out of it," her mind ordered. "It's just another job. It's just another target. For the good of the Brethren."

The good of the Brethren.

Robin's voice drifted into her thoughts: *"You've long turned into a mercenary for them, no thoughts for yourself. Don't do something you'll regret."*

How she regretted it now. As unbelievable as it was to admit, she regretted it with every part of her being.

Richard had said that the compass stole your morality, made you do terrible things to gain it. While Bryn hadn't even learned of the legend until recently, she realized that this was what the Dricasters had done to her. They had forced her to abandon her own morals, to kill without thought, to do anything she had to survive. Whether it was right or wrong was irrelevant.

They had stolen something else from her too—her own choices. They had told her how to think, how to act, what to do for years.

The water lapped the rocks, splashing her face in salty spray. The cold sent a reviving shock through her body and forced reason back into her mind.

She would not kill some defenseless child. And she would not kill her brother. No matter what wrongs had been done in the past, she knew she couldn't do it. She also knew, with the same premonition, that giving Terrax either the compass or the Star-Stone would be catastrophic.

A plan. She needed a plan.

Go back to Port Rylan? Not an option. If her face was known by now, it would be wiser to avoid any major cities.

Stay hidden in Drynrall? No good. Besides, Terrax would just hire a different bounty hunter to go get the Star-Stone.

Either way her options were bad. Either way she would probably be dismissed from the Dricaster Brethren—if not killed—which would leave her with very few allies and even fewer places to go. Not when she was stranded on an island, miles and miles from the Mainland…

That was it. Out of all the things she needed, a way out was the most important one.

A ship. She needed a ship.

And for the first time all day, Bryn felt herself smile. Not in confidence, not at the wild recklessness of what she was about to do, but for the simple satisfaction that she had a plan.

18

The Captives

Despite the urge to return to the *Burman Marie*, Bryn forced herself to go back to the inn and wait. Going to the ship and subsequently returning without the compass would be suspicious. She had no real reason to go to the *Marie* outside of that purpose, and no excuse that would satisfy Hawk Dakrind. No, she must appear as resolved and unchanged as ever. Just passing the time as she would before leaving for her next assignment.

There was a small tavern on the ground floor of the inn, nearly empty. She guessed that Terrax had ordered the inn to clear out when he'd arrived. Jenna warriors patrolled the lower floor.

She ordered herself a drink, mostly for show—she was wary of even the smallest amount of alcohol right now. It might cloud her head, when she needed her thoughts clear.

So she sat in the corner by the fire, her cloak wrapped around her, taking small sips of the wine and thought through her coming strategy.

Voices broke the long silence, coming from upstairs—Dakrind's angry voice, and hints of Terrax' calm, lowered tone. They were arguing.

"If you had told me you were sending Jenna into the harbor, I wouldn't have sent my men there at all. Do you realize what you could have done?" That was Dakrind.

"My men were only there to observe. From what I hear, they caused a needed distraction for your precious Ringmembers to escape," Terrax responded coolly.

"The presence of Jenna will not go unnoticed by the Capital," Dakrind snapped. "Do you want to bring a mounted squad of Randuins down on our heads?"

"We will be gone by the time the Randuins get here," Terrax returned. "Besides that, I have been assured by my sources that the Randuins are currently in Esile City, led astray by your men's reports. If you were not so disagreeable, I would congratulate you."

"If *you* were not paying us so well, I'd bring you to the Randuins myself," Dakrind said dryly. "Don't interfere with my operations again."

"Rest assured, Captain Dakrind, I have no interest in your little plan with the Wavers," Terrax replied as they reached the base of the stairs. The Elven outlaw turned down the hall. Dakrind stood for a moment on the steps, visibly seething, then barked an order to one of his sailors.

Bryn pretended to focus on her drink. She was interested in what she had overheard. The Jenna ship she'd seen in Port Rylan had never actually attacked, which meant it was only there as a distraction. She figured she should be grateful for Terrax, or else she, Mads, and Robin would have probably been captured by the town guard. Terrax was protecting the compass, of course, not them.

But what plan did Dakrind have involving the Wavers?

Dakrind strode into the room and eyed her suspiciously. "What are you doing here?"

Bryn gave a small shrug. "Relaxing. The task is completed, and I assumed I'll need my strength for the next job." It was hard keeping her composure relaxed, forcing her usual nonchalance to reflect on her face despite her tense nerves.

Dakrind seemed convinced. "Fair enough. Did you get the compass?"

"No, not yet," Bryn said slowly. "But if the ship's under guard, they aren't going anywhere. Besides, if I take the compass now, the crew might try to come after it before we leave."

She highly doubted that. With Robin held hostage, the crew of the *Burman Marie* would likely hesitate to act. Attacking the *Black Raven*, and the Dricaster Brethren as a whole, would be an unlikely move.

Hopefully the crew would just wait it out. Hopefully the Dricaster Ringmembers were just guarding them, and hadn't done any physical harm to the sailors or ship. It would be harder to escape if half the crew was injured or dead. Hopefully everyone would just lie low until night fell, and she could free Robin.

There were a lot of *hopefully*'s in her mind this evening.

Dakrind bought himself a glass of wine and sat down across from her.

"What'd you do with Trelawney?" Bryn asked, as casually as she could.

The Ringleader raised an eyebrow. "Why do you ask?"

Bryn shrugged again. "I was only curious. I hate traitors as much as you do, and he lied to me as well."

"Indeed he did," Dakrind growled. "Well, I'll take your opinion about his fate, then, because you hate him as much as I do. Shall I turn him in to the Capital for his bounty or sell him to the Jenna?"

"You'd probably get more from the Jenna," Bryn said, keeping her voice neutral. "I don't think he had much on his bounty from the Capital."

Dakrind chuckled. "Listen to you. Well, Miss Valetown, I can always count on you to see the practical side of things. Trelawney goes to the Jenna, then." He downed the rest of the wine and leaned back with a contented sigh.

"What of his ship?" Bryn asked carefully.

"I set a few of my men to guard the ship, to be sure the crew tries nothing foolish. The *Marie* will go back to Esile. As for her crew, the usual. The two highest-ranking officers will be either executed or sold along with their captain, and the rest of the men will be released and exiled from the Brethren."

That was standard. They'd take down the three leaders of the ship, and scatter the rest of the crew. Bryn thought of John and Richard joining their captain on a Jenna slave ship, of Oliver lost and alone in the slums and alleys of Port Rylan. For an instant, her calm vanished and she felt a flash of fury. It must have shown on her face, because Dakrind frowned. "Everything all right?"

"Oh, yes. I'm just—angry at him. He is a good liar, you have to admit. He fooled us all," Bryn said, covering her slip.

"Indeed. So was Mads, which actually surprises me more." Dakrind shook his head, showing genuine regret. "I knew that Dwarve for years. Never thought he'd turn traitor. But then, he knew Terrax had hired you all, and Elves and Dwarves are long time enemies."

Bryn looked at him, surprised. "Mads knew about Terrax?" Mads had never, not once, indicated he'd known who the employer was. But—maybe he had, and she just hadn't noticed. His distrust of Cliadell and Drike, his friendliness with Robin's crew, the way he seemed to know more about the compass and the Wavers than Bryn had given him credit for...

Had it been Mads' plan all along, not Robin's? Had he only been waiting for the right chance to turn against Terrax? Would he have succeeded and survived, if she'd been on his side?

She thought of the last argument they'd had. She had called him a coward. Her face felt hot with shame. Mads had been the bravest one among them. And now he was dead.

"So, you'll send the crew to the Jenna?" she said shortly, needing a mental change in topic.

"I believe I will." Dakrind stood, stretching. "Saves me a trip to Fauna. The Jenna slavers are already here."

"How many Jenna did Terrax hire?" Bryn asked.

"I don't happen to know who Terrax keeps company with," Dakrind said distastefully. "There are around fifty here with him.

Karaka and Vinskael tribes, it seems."

That was not good. Bryn could probably avoid the Ringmember guards by the *Marie*, but she couldn't possibly avoid the notice of the Jenna warriors. They would make her plan of freeing Robin and the *Marie* that much harder.

Dakrind left the room, heading to another part of the inn. The tavern was empty aside from a few Dricaster and Jenna guards, who kept to opposite sides of the room. The tension between the two groups told Bryn something else. Dakrind and Terrax might be working together for now, but they certainly weren't allies.

Night fell slowly. Bryn feigned sleep on her chair by the fire, wrapped in her cloak, but kept one eye open enough to observe. Dakrind reappeared and went upstairs to his quarters just past midnight. The guards at the door changed watch twice.

Finally, she saw what she had been waiting for. A new guard went down a flight of stairs to the basement cellar. Several minutes later a different guard appeared, yawning.

"Your shift up already?" one of the Dricasters at the door asked him.

"Twenty minutes overdue," the other guard shot back. "And it's bloody boring work. Clement got to watch the interesting stuff, while Chief was questioning him. Trelawney's totally out now."

"Tough luck," the first guard chuckled.

Bryn pretended to wake up, stretching slowly and ignoring the lingering throbbing in her arm from Cliadell's knife. Her thoughts were racing. Dakrind had interrogated Robin. How badly was he injured? Would he be able to walk? To stand even? If not, it would be up to Bryn, by herself, to somehow get him out unnoticed and all the way down to the ship in the harbor.

She stood and headed out the door into the lantern lit town, knowing it would be suspicious for her to linger within. The guards watched her go without much interest. Robin was being kept in the cellar basement, she guessed. The guards rotated on two hour shifts. Two hours started now. If she was going to act, it was now or never.

There had to be something she could do to get the guards away from the door. Maybe she could tell them they were needed in the harbor. But even if she managed to fool the guards, she highly doubted the Jenna warriors would fall for it.

She walked down the street, her tension growing. She could practically hear the clock ticking away the minutes. What she needed was a diversion.

Her eyes landed on the wicker cages in the market.

Oh, that's a horrible idea, her mind argued. But was there a better alternative?

The Wildkids inside straightened as she drew closer, bearing sharp teeth at her. Their faces appeared far wilder in the firelight. Two Jenna guards stood posted by the cages and came to attention as Bryn moved close.

"How much?" Bryn asked, gesturing at the Wildkids.

The Jenna guard barked something in his own tongue. Bryn didn't understand it, but the meaning was clear—she was not permitted here.

"How much?" she repeated, pointing at the wicker cage.

Out of instinct, the Jenna glanced back to see which direction she was pointing. Bryn punched him under the jaw, and the Jenna reeled back against the cages. His companion swung his spear at her with a snarl. Bryn deflected it with her bow—the motion jarred her injured arm, and she winced. She drew her long dagger from her belt and slammed the pommel into his temple. The second Jenna warrior crumpled to the ground.

Bryn swung back to face the first, but the Jenna had fallen against the cage and into the grasping hands of the captive Wildkids, who had dispatched their captor almost instantly. They snarled as Bryn drew close, faces far more animal than human, eyes gleaming in the dark.

"Stay back," Bryn warned, her heart racing. Every part of her screamed that this was a terrible idea. These Wildkids would not be reasoned with. They were starved and furious after their time in the cages, and she was quite certain, once freed, they intended to kill anyone they could. "Do you speak Common?"

None of the Wildkids responded. Bryn racked her brain for a moment. She knew nothing of the Wildkid language. What language did they speak that far east, anyway?

She gestured at the dead Jenna warriors. "More Jenna—fight them here," she said slowly, trying to mime the actions with her hands.

The Wildkids said nothing, only watched her. There was no way to be sure they wouldn't kill her. But she couldn't afford to delay much longer.

Hands shaking, Bryn undid the lock on the first cage and opened the door. The Wildkid warriors sprang out, then spun to face her. These warriors were older, their hair and beards wild and scraggly, a haunted look in their eyes. Bryn forced herself to keep moving, to show no sign of fear. She unlocked the next cage. One of them, a young female with silvery fur, watched Bryn's hands with interest. When Bryn let her out, the little silver Wildkid moved to the third cage and unlocked it effortlessly.

"Good," Bryn breathed. She repeated her order, pointing at the Jenna, then back toward town. The Wildkids gave no indication of hearing her, but sprinted down a cross street in the direction of the inn.

Bryn ran back to the inn. The two guards stiffened as she approached. "The slaves got out," Bryn said urgently, interrupting their questions. "There's Rylanders here—they unlocked the cages. The Wildkids are free!"

A shadow of fear crossed the guards' faces before their reason returned. "And how is that our problem?" one of them asked bluntly. "The Wildkid slaves are Jenna profits, not ours."

"Do you think the Wildkids will care?" Bryn asked with a significant look. The guards paled as they caught her meaning. Rylanders they could fight. They would hardly have a chance against a group of revenge-hungry Wildkids.

"I'll alert Captain Dakrind," Bryn said, pressing her advantage. "You better hurry. Go alert the rest of the Jenna warriors."

The guards snapped into action and sprinted down the road. Bryn could hear them yelling, sounding the alarm. Jenna appeared from the other rooms in the inn, shoving past Bryn as they sprinted to stop the escaping slaves. Bryn let them go, hoping desperately that Dakrind and Terrax would fall for the ruse. If they didn't…

She jogged through the tavern and down the stairs. A guard stood in the cellar, lit by a single lantern on the floor. Sitting tied to a post in the center of the room, his head resting on his chest, was Robin. Asleep or unconscious, Bryn couldn't tell.

The guard looked up as she approached, frowning. "What's going on?"

"The Rylanders are leading an attack for the compass," Bryn told him swiftly. "Dakrind wants everyone to go help. I'll guard the prisoner."

The Dricaster guard eyed her carefully. Clearly, he doubted this story. Bryn felt a flash of worry and kept talking. "Look, if you don't hurry, those Wildkids will overrun the town."

The mention of Wildkids sent the guard up the stairs without another objection.

Bryn let out a tense breath, then turned to Robin, who had begun to stir at her voice. She pressed a hand swiftly to his mouth. "Don't move. Don't make a sound," she hissed in his ear.

Robin nodded slightly and remained still. Bryn dropped down behind him, slicing through the ropes, then waited, listening. The shouts of the guards outside came dimly to her ears. She could hear the sound of many feet rushing about on the upper floor. They still had to get to the harbor, get the ship ready, and get out before Dakrind sent Ringmembers after them.

"Can you walk?" she asked.

Robin nodded again and got to his feet stiffly. One hand pressed against his side. His earlier wound from Port Rylan had reopened during Dakrind's interrogation, and fresh blood stained his shirt. There was nothing she could do about it now, though.

Bryn led the way to the base of the stairs and crept upward as quietly as she could. The room was empty. The distant sounds of fighting came to her ears—clashing swords, gunfire, the shrieking cry of the fighting Wildkids, and the wilder, bloodcurdling howl of Jenna war cries.

"Hurry," Bryn hissed. They ran out the door and ducked behind the adjacent building. A group of Dricaster Ringmembers and Jenna stood in the street, shouting at each other in their respective tongues. The language barrier was causing more trouble than the Wildkids were.

They managed to slip past the arguing group, but Bryn stopped at the next house. The road was too well-lit. They'd have to go down the rocks on their right to the beach and get to the harbor that way. Bryn glanced behind her. This side of the island drooped in a gradual rocky descent before reaching the water edge. It would be treacherous, but not impassible. She hoped Robin could keep up.

They began the tedious descent down the rocks. Robin moved with a visible limp, much slower than Bryn had hoped. Bryn's heart was racing. Any moment now, she was sure, Dakrind would realize he had been tricked and would send men to pursue them. "Which way to the harbor?" she whispered.

Robin braced himself against a boulder and pointed left. "That way, maybe a mile away."

Bryn set her jaw. "We have to go faster. I don't know how long the distraction will work."

Robin nodded and followed, but his injury was slowing him down. Bryn had to stop several times to allow him to catch up. Robin noticed and waved a hand tiredly. "On second thought," he said, out of breath, "run ahead of me. Get to the ship and get them ready. You can come back this way and pick me up."

Bryn hesitated, but knew this was a better use of their precious time. She sprang lightly down the rocks to the thin strip of beach and set off at a run. By the pale light of the moon, she could see fairly well, but this didn't prevent the occasional rock or branch tripping her up. Still, she kept moving, racing toward the harbor. The sounds of battle faded behind her as she ran on.

The *Burman Marie* came into view at the pier in front of her. Three lanterns were lit, but she could not tell if it was the sailors or the Dricaster guards. Bryn jumped quietly up the pier and crept to the gangplank, peering on deck.

Two Dricaster guards stood on deck, one by the tiller, the other on the starboard rail. John Tailor was sitting on a barrel, his hands tied before him. Richard was leaning against the fore mast—the bosun didn't appear to be bound, but the guard had his crossbow pointed at him. Richard had a black eye, but neither he nor John seemed to be badly injured.

Bryn's attention turned to the two Dricasters. Both of them had crossbows, and she had no doubt that they were good shots. For an instant she debated sneaking onto the ship and taking them both down separately, but that would be too risky. She would have to trust the cover of darkness to hide her between shots.

She selected two arrows, set one on her lap, and drew back the other. The motion sent an ache through her injured arm, but she focused on her target. The arrow slammed into the back of the guard on the starboard rail—he careened forward and landed in the water with a splash.

The second guard spun around at the sound, raising his crossbow—the lantern light glinted on the cruel tip of the bolt. Bryn's hands shook as she set the second arrow to the string, but she never had to let it fly. John leapt up the moment the first guard fell and brought his bound hands down around the guard's neck. Richard sprang to aid him, but by the time he reached him the guard had already collapsed, strangled.

Bryn climbed on deck, somewhat impressed. "Are there any other guards?"

The two sailors jumped at her voice, looking at her apprehensively. "No," Richard said finally. "These two just took over their shift. Where's Cap'n?"

"He's on his way. He had me run ahead and tell you to get the ship ready," Bryn said quickly.

"What is happening out there?" John demanded.

"I'll tell you once we're out of here—please, you have to trust me," Bryn pleaded. They did *not* have time for this. "Set a course north and we'll pick up Robin on the way."

"The other Dricasters turned on us," John said flatly. He had lifted one of the crossbows, studying Bryn with evident distrust. "Are we to simply trust that you won't? You might be stealing the ship right now."

Bryn turned to the first mate, exasperated. "Your captain double crossed Hawk Dakrind, and he won't last long if we don't help him escape right now. If I were stealing the ship, I would have left my two Ringmembers alive to help me do it." She nodded towards the body of the second guard.

John and Richard exchanged a look. Finally Richard sighed. "Don't have much of a choice, I warrant," he said. "I'll rouse the crew." He looked at Bryn. "We could use your help getting the ship ready. Your Hawk Dakrind sent a troop of guards here yesterday evening, killed three of our boys to send a message."

"We will manage," John said shortly. "Go quickly." Richard nodded and retreated below.

Bryn felt a twinge of guilt in her stomach. Three sailors dead thanks to her blind loyalty to the Dricasters. "I'm sorry. But right now we need to get as far from Drynrall Island as we can."

A Jenna war cry came from the distance, reaffirming her words. Bryn turned to face John. "They didn't take the compass, did they?"

"They were looking for it," John said. "Oliver hid it from them quite well. They practically beat him senseless, though."

Poor Oliver. But she was glad he'd had the sense to keep the compass hidden. "He did well," Bryn said.

John nodded but said nothing more. He still distrusted her, Bryn could see. There wasn't much she could do about it though.

The crew, once they were told what was happening, had the ship ready in minutes. By then, Robin had limped to the pier and made his way onboard.

"We still have the compass?" was the first thing he asked.

"Aye, Cap'n. Good to have you back," Richard added with a grin.

"We're not out of this yet," Robin said. By the light of the lantern, Bryn could see the patchwork of bruises that covered his face. His clothes were ragged, and a large red stain had spread down the length of his leg. He seemed determined to assume command, though. "Set a course for the mouth of the Westerlyn. Be quick."

He stepped up to the tiller as the ship swung away from the pier. Bryn waited by the port rail, watching the town for any signs that they'd been seen. But there was no outcry, no alarm.

The *Burman Marie* slipped away from Drynrall Island with the sound of lapping waves and Jenna war cries in her wake.

19

Outcast

The exhaustion was practically a palpable thing for everyone onboard the *Marie*, but Robin refused to rest until Drynrall Island was far behind them. They sailed steadily northwest, back toward the Mainland. By the time the coastline came into view ahead, dawn had spread a pink and orange flush across the sky, reflecting on the water.

Still they sailed on. Robin kept them close to shore, where the shadows thrown by the trees kept them somewhat hidden from any watching eyes.

Bryn helped any way she could. In addition to the three sailors who had been killed by the Dricasters, many others had been wounded, including the ship's doctor, Harry. Bryn settled below decks, patching up those who needed medical assistance. She had hardly ever used this skill for anyone but herself, and she was surprised to find it rewarding.

Oliver, though battered and bruised himself, insisted on helping her. He had hidden the compass under the sleeping Whiskers, the same way he had hidden the firearms from the Rylanders. Despite the boy's tendency to chatter, Bryn had to admire his quick thinking.

At last they reached the mouth of the Westerlyn River and sailed a little ways up the bend before anchoring in a secluded cove. The river's gradual curves and the dense wall of trees hid them from any passing ships. Robin seemed fairly confident they would be safe.

"The *Black Raven* won't catch up to us for a day at least," he said to Bryn. She had finally convinced him to take a break and have his injuries treated in his cabin. "Hawk will have to ask around, figure out which direction we went. His crew wasn't planning to leave for another day, so they'll have to work to get ready."

"Good. The Wildkids should slow them down too," Bryn said.

"I hope. That was a good plan," Robin told her.

Bryn nodded slightly and focused on threading the needle. Robin's stitches in his side had broken during his interrogation with Dakrind and needed to be redone. The quiet task helped her gather her thoughts. She had many questions, but wasn't sure where to start.

"So... Miss *Paya*," Robin prompted after a long silence.

She glanced up at him. "Yes." Her tone implied she didn't want to talk about it, but Robin only raised an eyebrow.

"If you expect me to trust you after everything that happened, the least you can do is tell me who you are. Reassure me you aren't some high-profile bounty who's hiding behind a false name," he said.

Bryn threw him a look. "First of all, I didn't know what Dakrind had planned. Secondly, you know just as well as I that there are situations where it's better to hide one's identity. Hold still," she added, beginning to stitch the wound.

She had applied a numbing balm to the skin, but he still winced. "Confound it, Bryn, that hurts!" he snapped.

"Cliadell's knife missed everything vital, but your stitches reopened after all the running around last night," Bryn said, unbothered. The sailors she'd helped earlier had responded in similar fashion. "Next time, maybe shoot him before he throws his knife at you."

Robin sighed and leaned back against the wall. "Fine... fine. At least answer my questions—helps distract me from it. I'll answer yours."

"That seems fair," Bryn said, focused on her task. "How long have you been a Rylander?"

Robin thought for a moment. "Longer than I've been a Dricaster. Seven years, eight years maybe. Figured I could work for both Crime Rings and get double the pay if I was careful enough. It worked for a while, until the Rylanders figured me out. Why did you lie about your surname?"

Now it was Bryn's turn to hesitate. "I didn't want... to be associated with certain people. For their own safety, and for mine. Why do the Rylanders want the compass?"

"I'm not sure," Robin said slowly. "The employer communicated to us through letters only, just as secretive as Terrax. We —the Rylanders and I—never met him. I know the letters came from central Coonsia, near the Flatlands, but not much else. I'd assume this person wants the compass for the same purpose Terrax does. Did you learn anything from Terrax?"

Quite a bit, Bryn thought, and tried to narrow it down. She continued stitching carefully while she told him what Terrax had explained in Drynrall, about the compass' true powers and origin. She was a little shaky on the parts about the dark magic—she still wasn't sure what to make of it. But she explained it as best she could, as well as Terrax' drive to get a Star-Stone.

Robin looked surprised when she finished. "It's strange, sure, but it fits," he said. "Safacon lost the Jewel, and he would have done anything to get it back. It also explains why the compass behaves the way it does."

Bryn frowned slightly. "What do you mean?"

"Richard told you the legend, about the compass pointing to your future enemies, instead of north," Robin said. "Since the compass bears Safacon's crest, the legend was encouraged, and people just killed whoever it pointed to. But the compass would have pointed to Caer Sia for years, since there were two Star-Stones there at the time."

"One and a half, technically," Bryn said. "Sit up," she added, and wrapped a snug bandage around his side. "There's something I still don't understand about the compass and the Wavers. You said the compass can control people. I didn't believe that at first, but after seeing what it did to Cliadell and Drike, I can believe it. I guess I don't see how…" she trailed off, not sure how to phrase the question.

"How you and I are still here?" Robin asked.

"Well, you and your crew," Bryn said. "I can explain my own survival—I never really believed in the compass until now, much less obsessed over it. But what about you all? You knew the legend, and you believed it was true."

Robin nodded thoughtfully. "I've been thinking about that. There's a difference between knowing something's real and knowing something's dangerous, though." He frowned. "I used to think like you. I didn't believe in anything I couldn't see and touch. Then I learned about the compass, saw what it did to the Wavers—well, that answered the question on whether or not the supernatural is real."

Bryn listened intently, surprised to hear how much of his thoughts echoed her own. Robin went on. "I might not have understood what made the compass work, but I knew it was wrong—it was dangerous, far more dangerous than anything mortal. Even if I didn't understand it, I knew the only way to guard my mind—and my heart—was to cling to the little bits of Light I could see."

Bryn frowned, not quite understanding. "What light?"

Robin gestured around them uncertainly. "Well… you're Coonsian, you grew up learning about the High Light too. I'm still figuring it all out, but you can feel what things are good and bad. You can sense it. Like you can sense about the compass."

Bryn didn't argue there. Even if she hadn't physically felt something with the compass, she had seen what it had done—and that was a power she didn't want anything to do with. But it wasn't enough to just avoid it. She needed to focus on other things—a stronger power, one of light and life. A faith she had long abandoned.

"I suppose I'm still figuring it out, too," she murmured. "Your crew are the same way?"

"Most of 'em know the truth now," Robin said. "Whatever darkness controls the compass, we'll cling to the Light to avoid it." He stood stiffly and pulled on his shirt. "Another question. How did Terrax know your name?"

Bryn took a breath. "There's someone he's looking for. A boy, who apparently has a Star-Stone. Terrax has been tracking him for a while now."

"That doesn't explain how he knew your name," Robin said.

"Terrax was in Esile City a few years back. He connected me with someone from Valetown," Bryn said, knowing her vague answers wouldn't satisfy him.

"So you know this boy he's after," Robin guessed.

"No, I don't. The boy—he's an apprentice ranger, it seems." She forced herself to finish. "My brother is training him."

Robin raised his eyebrows. "Brother?"

"The ranger known as the Hummingbird. Aryion Paya." Even his name was an effort to say. "He swore the Blood Oath when we were fifteen, then left Valetown."

The simple statements brought an onslaught of painful memories with them. That recurring dream. The tiny hand pulled from hers. The smoke in the room. The contempt and dislike of her father, killed by the orc chieftain. The weakness in her mother, weakness Bryn had promised herself she would never settle for.

Robin looked impressed. "Light above, that's your brother? He helped the Liznees reclaim Caer Sia, did you hear about that? He's practically a hero in the north."

"That's nice. No, I didn't know that. We haven't spoken in years—I thought he was dead," Bryn said. There was a brief pause. "What were you and Mads planning?" she asked after a beat.

"Well, the plan's fallen apart now, but I'll still tell you. Mads talked about leaving the Brethren."

"No he didn't," Bryn said incredulously.

"Trust me, he wanted to." Robin sat at his desk and folded his arms on the table. "He hid it so well no one would have suspected him, but that's the only way we could have escaped Dakrind's notice. Mads found out Terrax was the one who was after the compass, and planned to double cross him. The plan was that we'd get the compass in Port Rylan and leave clues that we'd been killed by Rylanders. Then we would leave—go northeast up the Durbin Strait and leave the Crime Rings behind."

Bryn stared at him. "Why didn't you?"

"Because of you," Robin said with a shrug. "Couldn't exactly double cross Dakrind without you in on it. We needed you to commit."

"Then why didn't you kill me, like you killed Drike and Cliadell?" Bryn asked.

"Drike and Cliadell were only there to spy for Dakrind. They never would have joined the plan—the compass' powers had them by the time they reached Port Rylan. You on the other hand, you were focused on the mission, and you weren't about to kill us for it." Robin smiled slightly. "Besides, I didn't want to kill you."

"I appreciate that." Bryn smiled back before catching herself. "So… what's your plan now?"

Robin bent over the map on his desk. "That's what I'm working on now. We can hardly go back to Port Rylan. The Rylanders figured out I'm a spy way before Dakrind did—that's partly why I needed you to come on this whole hellish trip."

"I assume Terrax will be looking for us soon, too," Bryn pointed out. That could be a problem. Terrax' force of outlaws and Jenna mercenaries would be watching the southern seas to regain the compass.

"Right," Robin said with a weary sigh. "And the Dricasters will come after us as well. That rules out Esile City."

Bryn studied the map. "Why not go up the Durbin Strait, like you planned before?"

"We might, but now that I know the Jenna are on Terrax' side, it'd be safer to avoid that area," Robin said heavily. "Once Terrax finds out we've gone, the Strait will be crawling with Jenna ships."

"Where are we currently?" Bryn asked.

Robin tapped the map, indicating the mouth of the Westerlyn. "Here. There's not much in this area, so at least we can hide out for a while. This is no-man's land—between Dricaster and Rylander territory. Any further west, though, we get a little too close to Esile City for my liking."

"And mine. But I think we have to go back to Esile eventually."

Robin looked at her inquiringly. "We do?"

"We want to get out of the Brethren and not have to worry about Dricasters coming after us," Bryn said slowly. "Dakrind wants the compass. I'm thinking we can arrange to trade our freedoms for the compass."

"Not a bad idea," Robin said. "But that does leave the problem of giving Hawk Dakrind, and thus, Terrax, the compass."

"I don't know how we can avoid that," Bryn said with a shrug. "Worst case scenario, the compass overcomes them and they become Wavers."

Robin stared at her for a long moment, shaking his head slowly. "There has to be a better option than that." He thought for a moment, face showing his uncertainty. Bryn realized in the same moment that they had yet to learn anything about Dakrind's plans. She suspected he wanted the compass for himself, though there was no real proof of that. The conversation she'd overheard before escaping Drynrall implied that Dakrind wanted something with the Wavers, though she had no idea what that could be.

"We'll think of something," she said out loud. "For now, ransoming the compass is the best plan I have."

"Well, in the meantime," Robin said, turning back to the map, "the crew needs a rest." He traced the winding line that marked the Westerlyn River. "We'll sail upriver to Waypath. It's a pirate town, like Drynrall, with no town guard. But it's smaller and quieter. We can hide out there for a day or so, then get going again once we have a better plan."

"Good," Bryn said.

Robin rolled up the map, looking satisfied. "I'll tell the boys. They'll enjoy having a day off." He hesitated slightly, as though the next words were an effort. "Thank you."

Bryn frowned. "For what?"

"Getting us out of Drynrall. I was sure you'd head out on your own and leave. We'd probably all be dead if not for you," he said.

Being thanked for saving someone's life was an entirely new thing for Bryn, and she was surprised to find she liked it. The smile she had pushed away earlier threatened her face again. "Oh… well, you're welcome. Take it as payback for not killing me after Port Rylan."

"Which could technically be considered payback after I saved you from Cliadell," Robin said.

Bryn raised an eyebrow. "Saved me? You're the one with the knife wound in your side."

He shrugged. The manic glint was back in his blue eyes, and the sunlight lit his smile. "Suppose I should be thankful for the knife wound. Else I might never have got to talk with you."

Richard called from above, and Robin was up the steps before Bryn could think of anything to say—if indeed she could think of anything that would explain the odd fluttery feeling deep in her chest. "Pirates," she muttered irritably, then followed him on deck.

The scene outside drove all other thoughts away. The sailors had gathered on the stern, peering back toward the sea. The slight bend of the river offered limited view of the ocean beyond, but Bryn could see what had worried Richard. A fleet of ships, nearly thirty in all, were heading east.

"Dricaster ships," John muttered, peering through his spyglass. "I would guess they are heading for Drynrall."

Robin watched the ships, his jaw set. "You're probably right," he told John after a long pause. "The question is, why?"

Bryn studied the passing fleet. Sails billowing in the morning wind, red banners streaming from their masts as they sailed resolutely ahead. She recognized some of those ships—they were usually anchored in the Esile harbor.

She assumed Dakrind would call for backup to hunt the compass down, but there was no way he could have got word to them this fast. Thus, the fleet must have arranged to sail east several days prior. But why? What could prompt them to travel deep into enemy territory to meet with their Ringleader?

What the reason could be, she wasn't sure. At least the ships hadn't seen the *Marie* hiding in the river bend.

"We don't have much time," Robin said. "Set a course upriver. We're going to Waypath."

The journey upriver was a tedious one. In addition to fighting the gradual current, the shallower parts of the river forced them to go slower. But by mid afternoon, the river widened, and they reached Waypath.

The river bulged in a natural reservoir, offering the ideal port for any ship sailing inland. Most of the ships anchored at the pier were small boats—skiffs and rowboats, single-mast and designed for the narrow river. There were two other pirate frigates, slightly smaller than the *Marie*. A few people looked at them with interest and surprise as they arrived.

"You're sure we'll be safe here?" Bryn asked uneasily, following the eyes of the watching townsfolk.

"Safer than we'd be in Port Rylan," Robin said. He leaned against the port rail, studying the town.

The forest grew so thick around the village that Bryn could only make out the occasional house or shop. When they disembarked a few minutes later, she could better view the town of Waypath. A small circle of wooden buildings and ruined stone walls made up the township. More houses and shops filled the forest around it. A few people milled along the dirt roads. Through the trees, Bryn could see the lights from several campfires that illuminated circles of tents and covered wagons. Gypsies from Gevari, she guessed, or other roving bands of outlaws come to shelter for the winter.

The soft yellow light of the afternoon sun, the pleasant damp smell of the forest, and the overall peace and quiet eased her nerves. They would be safe to rest here, at least until they headed west again.

20

The Road to Westerlyn

Months ago on the quest for the Shards, when Aryion had told Mel the story about the Blood Oath and his history with Hagshrub, he had left out a few details. Most of them related to his twin sister, Brynlee Paya.

The twins were born in the early hours of a winter day, to a mother so weak she nearly died during the birth and a father who could barely provide for them. Aryion and his sister had been raised with nothing besides expectations. Their father knew well the cruelty of the world, and took it upon himself to teach his children how to be strong and how to fight. At least, he taught his son. The daughter, who he had neither expected nor wanted, had been passed by, ignored. Still, she was determined to keep up with her brother as much as she could. She could learn and run and fight just as well as Aryion. And so the two were a team. Despite their father's partiality, the twins were always together, relying on each other, facing the world together.

Until the winter of their fifteenth birthday. When the orcs had come and destroyed the last fragments of family and hope they clung to.

This was a story Aryion had long tried to forget. To push aside.

According to his father's teachings, the only way to deal with the wrongs of yesterday was to strive to forget them. It didn't matter what harms had been caused—forgetting was easier than reconciling.

But he was tired of trying to forget.

Wherever she was, whatever had happened to her, Aryion had been uncertain for years. He had tried to forget her. To forget his own actions. To focus on pursuing the orc chieftain who had wronged them and fulfill the Blood Oath that bound him.

And then he'd met Mel, and been caught up in the quest for the Shard, and everything had changed.

Aryion no longer wanted to forget the hurt. The Blood Oath no longer bound his honor. He wanted to find Bryn, if she was still alive, and strive to heal the breach between them.

Now was his chance to do it.

Now he knew she was alive, knew what she had done with her life.

A Dricaster Ringmember. It surprised him, but only because he knew his sister. She'd had such a strong conviction of right and wrong growing up, and he was startled that she would abandon that to become a bounty hunter. Then again, he'd thrown away such convictions himself to impulsively swear the Blood Oath and leave her alone all those years ago.

And so he told Mel everything. His apprentice listened with wide eyes but didn't interrupt.

"I didn't want to tell you this before, and I'm sorry for that," Aryion said as he finished. "I suppose… I wasn't sure what you would think of me."

To bear a Blood Oath was bad already. To admit that he had abandoned his twin sister was worse in Aryion's mind. Worse than the things he had done in the years between his pursuit of Hagshrub and joining the quest. Everything he had done, everyone he had killed, he had excused at the time as necessity. Now that the Blood Oath was past, he realized how low he had sunk.

"That's all right," Mel said immediately, as Aryion knew he would. "I never asked about it. And… well, it's past now. My dad always says you can't do anything about the past, so you should do everything you can to make things right for the future."

How different things were for Mel. His family, happy and whole. His sister whom he adored. His parents always watchful of him, worried while he was gone, overjoyed on his rare visits.

Aryion smiled at him, grateful despite himself. "Well, thank you. And your father is right."

He stood and took a breath. They had returned to the room in the inn, and the window looked out at the harbor, just visible in the fading light. The strange silence made him wonder about the Dricasters' plan again. He wondered, also, if his sister was involved in it. That thought would have to wait for now. Personal matters aside, they had to focus on the mission to find Terrax.

Mel's idea was a good one, if a bit risky. Hiring a Dricaster—multiple Dricasters, even—would give them a better chance against Terrax and his forces. It would also answer the question if the Dricasters were working with Terrax, which Aryion still wasn't sure about. The problem now was that there were no Dricasters in Esile City, which meant they needed a different plan.

"Is that what we're doing now?" Mel asked. "Going to track down the Dricasters?"

"No, that's hard enough under normal circumstances," Aryion said. "They are planning something, and clearly did not want to be seen leaving Esile City."

Mel thought for a moment, his brow furrowed. "You don't think we could… I don't know, interrogate someone again? Try to get information?"

Aryion smiled slightly. "We could try. But the Dricasters are notoriously tight-lipped. Even their contacts outside of the Brethren are sworn to secrecy on pain of death. We could interrogate, bargain with, even threaten a captured Ringmember, and he would still tell us nothing."

Mel looked up as another thought occurred to him. "How do you know all this about the Ringmembers, Aryion?"

Aryion focused on unlacing his boot. He had expected this question to come eventually, and now struggled over his answer. He could lie. Ignore the question. Answer vaguely.

Answer vaguely won out. "Bearing a Blood Oath comes with enemies, Mel."

Mel frowned, clearly not satisfied. "You mean the orcs? Did Hagshrub tell the other orcs about you?"

"I assume he did. Either way, the news spread." He took a breath, bracing himself for yet another painful recounting. "I swore the Blood Oath when I was only fifteen. In my mind, I thought it was a logical choice. I never assessed the other consequences it would have. As the years began to pass, with no sign of Hagshrub and no closer to being rid of the Oath, I began to regret it. But I knew I had to fulfill it, so I began to resort to… other means."

He paused. Mel didn't say anything, only listened with intense curiosity. "The Rings are full of assassins, brigands, thieves, and bounty hunters—but they're also the best source of information in Daffodalion. The country is too large to count on rumors alone, and there are so many orc tribes to keep track of. So I began completing… favors… for the Rings in exchange for information on Hagshrub."

Mel's eyes were wide. "You were a Ringmember?"

"No, I never joined any of the Brethrens. Some of the tasks were harmless enough—delivering news, repairing equipment. Others were—well, about as bad as the Blood Oath itself."

Aryion trailed off. The secrets he had shared in the last few hours were draining. He felt worn down, ashamed of his past, and very, very tired. "I was willing to do anything to succeed," he said, unable to meet his apprentice's eyes. "Those years, those tasks—they were a means to an end, a goal I thought to be good. I finally realized what I'd become and headed north to track Hagshrub alone. A few months later I got wrapped up in the whole business with the Shards and the Aces, and here we are."

Silence fell for several minutes. Aryion glanced at Mel—the boy's face was shocked, confused, and bore a trace of anger. "Did you work for Terrax then?" he asked finally. "The secretary said Terrax was in Esile City three years ago. Did you complete favors for him too?"

"I might have. I was never told exactly who I was working for."

Mel pushed his hair back from his forehead and took a deep breath. Aryion could not tell if it was the fact that he hadn't told any of this before or the fact that he might have helped Terrax that upset Mel more—though he could guess it was the latter.

"It's fine," Mel said after a long moment, his voice strained. "It's fine. What's our plan?"

"It does not have to just be fine," Aryion said quietly. "I'm sorry I never told you. Are you angry?"

"I don't know. Not at you. I asked about it." Mel sat down on his bed, looking down. "It doesn't matter what I feel—we need to focus on catching Terrax. He's our mission now."

Aryion hesitated. "Is that what you've learned from me? To ignore your own thoughts?"

"No…" Mel admitted slowly. A little of the fire went out of him.

"My father used to say things like that," Aryion said. His voice was low as memories swirled through his mind. "To suppress every emotion and doubt, and just do your job. No matter if the task was wrong or not. I used to follow that belief so closely—I used it to justify what I was doing." He paused. "Mel… it's good to have doubts sometimes. To question what you are doing. It shows integrity, something I've had to relearn in these last few months."

Mel was silent. There was more behind his eyes that he wasn't telling, but Aryion guessed what he was thinking. He continued gently. "When you're young, you think well of everyone. The world can do no wrong. Then something happens, something ugly and dark, and you tell yourself that's the way things are. You never allow yourself a chance to process it. Pushing it away only makes it return worse."

He knelt on the floor before Mel, putting a hand on his shoulder and looking up into his eyes. "I don't want you to feel as though you have to push the hard emotions away. There's a time to be stoic, and there's a time to show feelings. I don't want you to become hardened to the emotion or the doubts." He looked away. "I don't want you to turn into me."

Mel shook his head. His words came fast, a torrent of emotions all at once. "I'm sorry. Didn't want to talk about it. It's just—I hadn't really thought about that for so long. I finished the quest for Drisilas, and then I was home—and then I was on the quest for the Shards. And then Bregg brought it up."

Aryion studied him, understanding. "Your friend?"

"Llyrion," Mel said in a choked sort of voice. "And I—I know it's weird for it to affect me now, and I barely even knew him. I just— on the last quest—first Norrin—and then you almost…" His voice broke, and he looked away.

Aryion had never talked to him about that part of the battle. He knew Mel had fought the Ace-Lord while he had been dueling Hagshrub. From Aryion's perspective, the end of the battle came in scattered fragments, like a nightmare he could never fully remember. Knife in ribs. Black fog, white ice. Mel's scream. Blue light, the Ace-Lord snarling. Blood on the floor. Mel's frightened face, faint voice, fading away…

"You don't have to tell me about that," he said quietly. "Just know… I'm here."

Mel took a shaking breath. "It's not that. I mean—I've always heard it's wrong to… to want revenge like that. Like the Blood Oath. But Terrax is—Terrax killed—why does Terrax deserve to be brought in alive?" he finished finally.

Aryion met his eyes again. The long-suppressed pain and grief was blazing there behind the tears. "I don't have an answer for that," he admitted finally. "I don't think Terrax deserves life any more than your friend Llyrion deserved death." Mel closed his eyes and lowered his head. A few tears slipped down his cheeks. "But… if I've learned anything," Aryion continued slowly, "I don't think it's our place to decide who lives and who dies. Vengeance isn't something we're meant to control. Trust me, it is quite a burden to bear."

There was a long silence as they sat in the shadowed room. There were no words, nothing to say. The silence spoke for itself. It mourned what was lost, yet waited in hope for the good to come. Aryion found that hope was easier to embrace once he let the pain fade away. He could tell Mel felt the same.

Mel straightened and seemed to compose himself. Determination and hope had replaced the anger in his eyes. "Okay, so—what's our plan now? Where do you think the Dricasters went?"

Aryion nodded, glad to see the resolve in his apprentice's eyes. The pain was still there, but he could tell Mel's thoughts were clear. "Let's set aside the Dricasters for now, and focus on the first part of your question. You tell me—what do we do when the original plan has fallen apart?"

"We adapt," Mel answered promptly. "We take the parts of the plan that still work and adjust it to fit the new information." This part of training was something Aryion had drilled into him. Too often the plan needed to be adjusted, and flexibility was a valuable skill.

"Good," Aryion said, pleased. "In this case, we should look at our whole plan." He spread the map on his bed, tracing the road from Appledale to every town they had visited. "We were told to go to Lemsonburg and interrogate Mr. Bregg."

"And we did that," Mel said.

"Then we planned to go south, picking up information on our way to Esile City," Aryion continued, tracing the winding line of the river.

"Did that," Mel nodded, catching on.

"Our next phase of the plan was to arrest Terrax," Aryion said. "As Terrax is not in Esile City, and seeing as he seems to have a significant number of warriors behind him now, we'll have to move to the next step."

He looked up at his apprentice. "If my guess is right, we can assume that the Randuins fell for the same trick as we did. Terrax laid them a false trail that brought them here, looking for Jenna, when the Jenna are actually elsewhere."

"And now the Randuins are investigating the Esile Council," Mel said.

"Yes. I doubt Terrax counted on that, but it still works to his advantage. It means the Randuins will be too busy here to pursue him or any Jenna he hired." Aryion studied the map again. "Our plan to stop Terrax has now interwoven with the Wildkids' plan to catch the Jenna."

"So now we get to join the Wildkids?" Mel asked hopefully, a small grin appearing on his face.

Aryion returned the smile. "I believe it is our best move. Without aid, we cannot hope to bring Terrax in. With a squadron of Wildkids, we might have a chance," Aryion said. He traced a circle around a forested area. "This is the Westerlyn Woods. The town of Westerlyn is right here." He tapped the outline of a town to the west of the forest. "A few miles south of Westerlyn, on the other side of the river, is a pirate town called Waypath."

"Waypath—that's where we were planning to meet the Wildkids already, right?" Mel said. "Why isn't it on the map?"

"It's a secret town. A few outlaws set it up to be able to hide from the Capital soldiers. It's acted as a sort of safe house for decades now—a place for pirates to get supplies, or for outlaws to lie low. I actually went there, years ago. I think if we can take a carriage to Westerlyn, I can get us the rest of the way to Waypath."

"And the Wildkids will meet us there?" Mel asked.

"Yes, just like we planned. Once we rendezvous with them, we can decide our next move."

"What about the Dricasters?" Mel asked. "Do you still think we should hire them?"

"Only if necessary," Aryion said. "Updating our plan to fit the circumstances is one thing. Hiring a mercenary to complete our assignment for us isn't something I could easily explain to your parents—or the High King, for that matter." He smiled wryly. "Anyway, though Waypath is secretive, that does not mean it is safe. I hope the Wildkids can lie low there, but we will have to watch for Ringmembers."

"Can't be worse than Aces," Mel pointed out with an unconcerned shrug. Aryion threw him a wry glance, but he was glad to see Mel's usual unwavering determination. His earlier anger and sorrow had faded, eased by explaining his thoughts aloud. Vengeance no longer weighed so heavily on him. He was ready to continue the mission.

"No worse than Aces," Aryion agreed, "but still potentially dangerous."

· · · · · ·

The following morning they headed to the station to wait for the carriage to Westerlyn. The civilians seemed to have grown used to the strange silence of Esile City now, and people were almost relaxed. With the Dricasters and pirates gone, the city was a safer place than usual. The only people still concerned over it was the Council, who still seemed to fear an uprising.

"I've been thinking," Mel said as they ate breakfast at the station. "If the Randuins can prove the Esile Council is involved with the Crime Rings, maybe the Capital can finally do something to stop all the crime here."

"Maybe," Aryion agreed. "I am not sure what would happen then, though. We didn't come here to overthrow the Esile Council or get involved in Daffonic politics."

"We didn't come here to investigate a Jenna invasion, and that's what we're considering," Mel pointed out with a grin.

To this thought, Aryion had no argument. He was heartened by the Randuins' presence in Esile City, despite the fact that it had happened entirely by coincidence. Even if the Esile Council would not protect their own, the Randuins could keep the city safe.

The carriage marked for Westerlyn arrived, and Aryion arranged their ride east. The town of Waypath was unmarked on the station master's map of destinations, but if they found the river, they could follow it south until they found the town.

As the carriage started east, Aryion studied Bryn's poster again. The language was written in Erinian runes, which he couldn't decipher, but it was clear what the poster advertised. He recognized that the numbers placed his sister's bounty at just over four hundred lupin, and felt a mixture of admiration and worry. *What in Orlell have you been up to, to get a bounty that high?*

He wondered, if the need arose, if he and Mel would need to make contact with the Dricasters. He also wondered if it would lead them to speak with Bryn. It was strange when he thought about it, knowing she had been working for the Dricasters all this time. While he was completing tasks for them, she would have been working for them in the shadows. Their paths would have come very close to crossing many times. Perhaps it was best that they hadn't.

Thinking of Bryn reminded him of the conversation from last night. It had been unpleasant, but now that it was out of the way, he felt strangely liberated. The secrets he had borne for so many years were shared now, and he felt that some of the weight had gone.

The carriage followed the road east, skirting the sprawling borders of the Capital and then dropping into rolling wilderness again. They stopped at a tiny village on the outskirts of the Capital and then took a second carriage, which would take them to Westerlyn. Aryion planned to stay there for the night, then continue in the morning.

On they went. The carriage bumped steadily east. Rain fell throughout the day. By the time they reached Westerlyn, the light was fading.

Aryion had just enough money to pay for a room in an inn, which was something to be grateful for. It was growing colder by the minute, and the rain had begun to mix with snow. They walked through the lamp-lit streets. The inhabitants of Westerlyn were a mix of Dwarves and humans. No one seemed to pay attention to the two rangers. Then again, Westerlyn was used to strangers passing through.

The inn was smaller than that of Esile City's, a single story building with a few rooms. The beds were low to the ground with flat, bumpy mattresses. But it was warm and dry and better than camping in the frigid rain.

Aryion lowered his pack to the ground and stretched, stiff from the long carriage ride. Mel flopped onto his bed, not even bothering to take off his wet cloak. "Do you suppose there are any Dricasters here?" he asked with a yawn.

"Maybe," Aryion said, coaxing a fire to life in the little hearth. "We are safe for the time being. Try and get some sleep."

Mel obeyed and was snoring softly within minutes of lying down. Aryion sat on the bed across from him, thinking. Waypath was hard to find under regular circumstances. Now, with the Dricasters up to some sort of mischief, rumors of Jenna, and Terrax on the loose, there was no telling what sort of guard or patrols would be prepared as they approached the city. He wondered if he could convince the Wildkids to risk their own mission to help them catch Terrax. What if they refused? He and Mel would have come all this way for nothing.

He would deal with that possibility tomorrow. For now, he lay flat on his back and stared at the ceiling while the snow fell without and the shadows deepened within.

21

Red and Scarlet

Bryn waited in her cabin for several hours after they docked in Waypath. She needed rest, and wanted a moment to process all that had happened. The adrenaline of the night and the work aboard the *Marie* had distracted her from the looming truth of what they'd done. She had rebelled. She had joined forces with a Brethren traitor, defying Hawk Dakrind—Hawk Dakrind, a man whose wrath was so feared among the Rings.

What the consequences would be for this, she had not yet guessed. It was likely that Dakrind would pursue them, as Robin assumed. As for when, she wasn't sure. As she'd overheard in Drynrall, Dakrind seemed to have a plan of his own, and she was fairly certain he needed the compass for that.

Well, she thought, the time for rest was over. She would need to be on her guard, now that they were all Brethren traitors. She checked the injury on her arm. The wound still ached, but the bleeding had stopped and the cool air helped ease the pain. She put her coat over her shoulders, the small Dricaster pin remaining stubbornly attached inside. That, she promised herself, would be removed only when they were away from the Dricasters for good.

Dusk was falling over Waypath. Most of the sailors were enjoying a much-needed rest before supper. John and Matthew were on watch. They glanced her way as she walked on deck, but said nothing. The tension seemed to have faded now that they were away from Drynrall, but she could tell they still didn't know what to think of her. Three of their shipmates had been killed by Dricasters. There was nothing she could say to help that hurt.

She looked toward the village. Smoke from hundreds of campfires hung in the air over Waypath, blending with the fog and tainting the sunbeams orange. The smell of cooking meat drifted over the water.

Richard appeared from below, smoking his pipe. He greeted Bryn cordially enough and turned to John. "Cap'n wants you and I to go ashore for a bit. See if we can pick up any news."

John nodded. He looked absolutely exhausted. There were dark circles under his eyes, and he had a nasty cough.

"I'll go," Bryn said, with a glance at John. The first mate frowned, surprised, and she continued, "Robin will need you here to help plan. I'm not much use in that."

This was true, but she could also tell that John needed a break.

Richard shrugged, and John, after a pause, agreed. "Keep your head down," he said shortly to Bryn. "Your face may be known here as well."

Bryn hadn't thought of that. Waypath had no town guard, but there was nothing to stop an ambitious bounty hunter from coming after her if they recognized her.

At least she could hope that no one knew her real name. She doubted Terrax would spread that around—it could reveal too much about his own operation.

She followed Richard down the pier and into the streets of Waypath. "What sort of news are we listening for?" she asked, turning her attention back to their task.

"Cap'n wants to know why all those Dricaster ships are out and about," Richard said. "It can't just be for the compass. There must've been some type of gathering in Drynrall."

Bryn frowned. Dakrind had never mentioned coordinating a Ringmember gathering—but then again, there was a lot Dakrind hadn't mentioned. "What kind of gathering?" she asked.

"That's what we're trying to figure out," Richard said, keeping his voice low. Gypsies and travelers milled the streets of Waypath.

Bryn slipped past a cluster of raggedly dressed women and jogged to catch up to Richard. "So, Robin thinks the Dricasters gathered in Drynrall?" she asked, trying to better assess the situation. The fleet of ships sailing east that morning had been a strange sight, but she hadn't thought about it much further. She could understand why Robin wanted to learn more about them, though.

"I'd bet so," Richard said. "Where else would they meet? That far east is Rylander territory, you know. Drynrall Island is the only place they'd be able to gather unnoticed, if they were set on going east. Dakrind must have arranged something."

Bryn thought for a moment, trying to work out the timing in

her head. Esile City was a four day trip to Drynrall Island—maybe three, if the sea allowed. A mail carrier could bring a message across land in a day or so, if his horse was fast. So that all added up to four or five days just to get a message back to Esile City—double that for everyone to come to Drynrall, as Dakrind requested.

Nine days, give or take.

Nine days ago, she'd been… where had she been? She had just accepted the bounty to kill the Gevarian Mudger on the eve of the new year. Dakrind had assigned her that job like normal, but he'd been distracted, his desk messy, scattered with papers. She had thought little of it then, but the memory jarred a whole new line of thinking in her mind.

"I'm getting a drink," Richard said, turning toward a wooden building on the left. "Want one?"

"Umm… sure," Bryn said distractedly, following the bosun into the building. She noticed that all the structures in Waypath were small and simple, with interlocking wood walls and plank ceilings. The two small tables were the only furniture pieces; people sat on barrels, packs, or saddle bags.

She and Richard got their drinks—whiskey for Richard, coffee for Bryn—then sat against the wall. "Why's the town built like this?" Bryn asked.

Richard gestured at the interlocking planks of the ceiling. "Way-path's not really a town, see. More like one big camp. Everything here is designed to be taken down and moved fast if need be. It's kept the Capital from pinning it down and establishing a town guard here."

Bryn studied the room, impressed, then returned to her thoughts. "Dakrind would have had to send word for the Dricasters to join him in Drynrall nine days ago at least, but I think he organized it before," she said.

Richard looked at her, interested. "You think so? What do you make of it?"

"I think Dakrind's planning something," Bryn said slowly, trying to get all her thoughts in order. "And the more I think about it, the more sure I am that his plan bodes ill for Terrax."

Richard raised his bushy eyebrows, catching her implication. "You think he plans to turn on him?"

Bryn lowered her voice—the little tavern was noisy with conversation, but she wasn't taking any chances. "I heard Terrax and Dakrind arguing when we were still in Drynrall. They might be working together, but I can tell you they aren't friends. Dakrind knew about Terrax and the compass, even though he didn't tell us much." She paused. "I think he's still trying to find out *why* Terrax wants the compass."

She remembered the way Terrax had dismissed Hawk from the room before he'd told her about the Star-Stone. Dakrind had seemed displeased, but Bryn hadn't thought much about it then.

"I think Dakrind's figured out that the compass is more valuable than he thought—and now he's trying to find out what it actually does," she continued quietly. "If everything had gone to his plan in Port Rylan, Mads, Robin, and I would all be dead, and Cliadell and Drike would have brought him the compass. Then Terrax could send them after the Stone, which would mean they'd bring both the Stone and the compass to Terrax in Drynrall…"

"And Dakrind's men would be there, ready to take them back," Richard finished as Bryn trailed off. He gave a low whistle. "That's not a bad theory."

A trio of gypsies had set up in the back of the tavern and begun to play a shanty. Their voices were joined by the customers, filling the evening with song.

You'll hear her shanties in the cold,
You'll taste the fear of a sailor's soul
And you'll see her prow on a stormy morn
Watch for the Red Canary

"What's the Red Canary?" Bryn asked, glancing at Richard. The bosun was tapping his toe to the beat of the song.

"A ghost ship," Richard replied with a wink. "They say she was the flagship of the Nøkken, the queens of the Sea-Spirits. Tales say she went to battle with the Viriki."

"Who's…"

"Jenna gods," Richard said, shaking his head. "What *did* you learn in school, if you don't mind my asking?"

"My father didn't believe in teaching mythologies or history," Bryn said. "He said the past didn't matter. I was taught practical studies—reading and writing, mathematics, strategy, fighting."

Technically, she had taught herself to fight. Her father had refused to teach her—he said it was impractical for a woman to leave the home. But Bryn would watch him spar with Aryion hour after hour, until her brother's young hands had been scored with cuts and bruises and he'd doubled over for breath. Bryn would patch him up and they would practice together, late at night so their parents would not find out. Swordplay, archery, hand-to-hand combat, night after night.

She shook her head, moving past the memory. "So, the *Red Canary* fought with the Jenna gods, and lost, I assume? And now it's a ghost ship?"

"So the legend goes," Richard said. "The ship was once a guardian of goodness and life. When the dark rulers rose to power around the time of the Dividing War, they sent the ship to the depths. But they say you'll still see the *Red Canary* in your last seconds before death, come to carry you to the afterlife."

"That's not true, though," Bryn said doubtfully.

Richard shrugged. "Oh, the stuff about the Viriki and sailing to the afterlife is fishy, sure. But people what see the *Red Canary* and live to tell of it say sometimes she's not always come for the bad. Sometimes she's come to guide your ship through a rough patch, or bring you through a hurricane what rocks your ship within an inch of life. Whatever she is, she ain't mortal, I can tell you."

Bryn was about to tell him the story was ridiculous, but considering how pirate mythology had misinterpreted the tale of the compass, she decided against it. What Robin had said was true—there was always some grain of truth in those old tales. And Terrax' words had assured her that the supernatural world was as real as the mortal.

"What about you?" she asked instead. "How'd you come to learn all these legends?"

Richard chuckled and shook his head. "Years of listening, Miss Valetown. Been on the seas for my whole life, I have. I was first mate on the *Scarlet Consort* in my younger days."

Bryn looked blank, and Richard sighed. "Don't even know her, no doubt. The *Consort* was the Capital's flagship for nearly a decade, Miss Valetown. They kept her in the navy even after her time was past, and I stayed on the crew, until the Dricasters decided they wanted her. The *Black Raven* caught her in open seas."

"Dakrind stole the *Scarlet Consort*?" Bryn repeated, interested.

"That he did," Richard said. His normally cheerful face was grim, and his voice was heavy. "Crippled her just enough so she could still sail, and sold the surviving crew to the Rylanders."

That was standard practice for a captured ship, Bryn knew. "Then how'd you end up on the *Marie*?"

The bosun, she had noticed, greatly enjoyed storytelling. Richard leaned forward, in his element. "Well, Cap'n Trelawney had just done a deal with the Rylanders. He was taking a cargo east—a cargo of people."

He shook his head. "Slaves, bound for the Jenna. Trelawney dropped us off with the Vinskael Jenna tribe off the southern coast of Sikhazi, got the pay for us, then stole us back when it was dark."

Bryn shook her head incredulously. "And kept you on crew?"

"He gave us the choice to stay onboard and work for him or go free. I didn't have much place to go, naturally. This was several years ago, the height of the War of the Strait. If I went back to the Capital they'd ship me out to battle again, and I was through fighting for a Crown that didn't give two pence about its soldiers." Richard spread his hands. "So I took Trelawney's offer, and I've been bosun for the *Marie* ever since. Glad to be serving a captain like Trelawney—he's a good one."

"He is," Bryn said, startled to realize she agreed. The thought brought that strange fluttery feeling back to her chest, which she tried to ignore. "So, the *Scarlet Consort*—she's still with the Dricasters?"

"Aye, she is," Richard said. "Captained by one of Dakrind's idiot men, and she hardly sees any action now. I've a mind to get her back one day if she's ever captained by someone more capable."

"No fancy to be captain yourself, then?" Bryn asked, surprised.

"None," Richard said with a shrug. "And certainly not under the Dricasters."

"Well, hopefully we'll all be away from the Dricasters soon," Bryn said.

The musicians were playing a new song now, a driving, marching rhythm. The melody was vaguely familiar—Bryn was certain she had heard it before in Esile City. They sang of a harper come to sing and play for the queen of the Nøkken—a maiden called Mariana. The song ended on a strange, uncertain note, the story interrupting itself. There was no telling if the harper had succeeded in his task.

Whether or not the stories about the Nøkken or the *Red Canary* were true, Bryn found a strange satisfaction in their whimsicality. She had always blamed her logical, unyielding mindset on her own character, but she began to wonder if it came from her father. Yes, he had taught her and Aryion to be strong and level-headed, raising them to know the harshness of the world. But at the same time, he had robbed them of the simple, imaginative childhood they should have had. Learning these stories—myth and truth alike—was freeing.

"Well, we'd better get going," Richard said. He drained the last of his drink and stood. "Need to get some supplies."

Bryn followed him. The sun was sinking low in the west, and the chill smarted as they walked down the muddy roads. It was so cold the mud had frozen, with tiny icicles raising the turf a half inch from the ground. The ice crunched under their feet as they walked.

A wiry man dressed in furs sat by a fire, his back to his wagon. His olive-toned skin was flushed slightly in the chill, but his dark eyes were alert. "I a'help you?" he asked promptly, in the lilting accent of a Gevarian.

"Come for vittles, and for information," Richard said, tossing him a small sack of coins.

The Gevarian looked pleased. "I've got oats, rice, dried beef for now," he said, nodding to the barrels at his right. "Got a few men a'comin' in tomorrow with a'few types of brandywine and cider."

"Just the food for now, if you please," Richard said. "And any word you might have picked up about the Dricaster Brethren."

A mischievous light shone in the Gevarian's dark eyes. "Aye now, whatcha interested in Dricasters for? Not 'ere for de bounty on me, eh?" He hefted a sack of rice and passed it to Richard. "The Dricasters have left Esile City, though I assume you've a'heard of that by now. Got the Council's feathers all rustled, they 'ave."

"Why'd they leave?" Bryn asked, taking the rice from Richard.

The Gevarian winked. "Uprising is what the Esile Council fears. After what a'happened up north in Sia, they've reason to a'worry, I thinks." He handed over another sack, which Richard hefted onto his shoulder.

"Have you seen any Dricasters here today?" Bryn asked.

"Eh, not so far," the gypsy said. "But they're shifty ones, them Dricasters. Might not 'ave known 'em if they were a'here."

"Thanks," Richard said, tucking a barrel under his burly arm and starting back down the road.

Bryn followed, thinking. "No Dricasters yet," she said slowly.

"Nope," Richard said, sounding satisfied. "Gypsies hear every-thing, so I'd bet he's right. It also seems no one's heard about us fleeing Drynrall yet, which means Dakrind is mobilizing slower than we thought."

Or he's just good at keeping secrets, Bryn thought, but she didn't say it aloud. Richard could be right. It was unlikely the news could have spread that quickly.

The last red light of evening lit the stone ruins on the hill above town as Bryn and Richard returned to the *Burman Marie*. Harry had built a fire on shore a few yards within the trees and was roasting a fresh catch of fish. Whiskers the ship cat sat on the pier next to the gangplank, watching a school of tiny fish with great interest.

John was speaking to Robin as Bryn approached—the first mate threw her a glance and paused. Bryn frowned slightly. "Everything all right?"

"Everything's fine," Robin said, and turned to Richard. "Hear anything of interest?"

"A few shanties in the tavern, and the Gevarian we bought the goods from said he hasn't seen any Dricasters pass through yet," Richard said. "Sounds like the Dricasters leaving Esile has set the Council on edge. No one's quite sure why they've gone east, though."

"What if it's an uprising?" Oliver asked excitedly, popping his head up from the stairwell.

"It's three lashes for eavesdropping, Oliver," Robin said without looking—Oliver snickered and vanished.

"Could be an uprising," Richard said thoughtfully.

"That seems illogical," John said, his brow furrowed. He folded his arms across his chest. "If the Dricasters were going to revolt, they would go toward the Capital, not away from it. Drynrall Island is miles from anywhere the Capital would care to protect."

"I don't think it's a revolt," Bryn said. "If it was, there would be more planning, and Dakrind would have told the Ringmembers about it so we would be ready."

"You believe he would have told you?" John asked dryly.

Bryn met his eyes. "I was the best bounty hunter in the Brethren. Even if Dakrind didn't have a complete plan at the time, he would have at least mentioned it."

"And yet he told you nothing about what he was planning in Drynrall," John stated. The distrust was evident in his tone. "You claim you were equally betrayed by Dakrind, despite the fact that they let you go unscathed?"

Richard turned away awkwardly and carried the supplies down the stairs. "Let it lie, John," Robin said, shaking his head. "I told you, she didn't know. And Hawk let her go because he needed her for another task, right?" he added, looking at Bryn.

"Well… no, not exactly," Bryn admitted. "Dakrind didn't know about the job Terrax wanted me to do."

John studied her with a mixture of distrust and dislike, and Bryn wished she could explain herself better. It did look suspicious. She was the only one out of the four loyal Dricasters to escape alive and uninjured—if you didn't count the gash from Cliadell's knife in her arm. But that had only come because Cliadell was rebelling against his fellow Ringmembers, and Bryn had still been loyal at that point. Yes, she had freed the *Marie*, but she'd needed to get off the island some-how. Dakrind had evidently intended to let her off without punishment.

"If I was still on Dakrind's side, why would I have freed Robin?" Bryn asked finally, trying to come up with something to make him trust her. "Or why would I have killed my own Ringmembers to get the *Marie* out?"

John stared at her a few more moments, then shook his head slowly. "Your disloyalty to the Dricasters is no guarantee that you are loyal to us," he stated.

Bryn felt an uncomfortable prickle. Robin looked between John and Bryn and shook his head. "Whatever her intentions were, we can't afford to be at each other's throats. Not until we're away for good."

John turned away without another word. Bryn bit her lip, frustrated. The first mate's words cut to the core. She could prove she was against the Dricasters, sure. But proving that she was on the same side as the *Marie*? That was a difficult feat. Especially because she still wasn't sure what would happen after they'd escaped Dakrind's watch. She couldn't stay on the *Marie* forever, even if she was welcome, which she doubted.

Harry called out that dinner was ready. Bryn bundled up in her cloak and joined the others on shore around the blazing fire. After days of living on cold, bland rations, the roasted fish and wild rice was as good as a king's feast.

Matthew McCreery pulled out his lute and, joined by a few other crewmembers, struck up a rousing jig. Some of the gypsies from the neighboring camps came to listen and sit by the fire, whooping and clapping to the beat of the songs. A hot meal, cold drink, and a comforting sense of safety produced a wondrous change in the weary sailors. Even John seemed in better spirits.

Bryn sat at the edge of the blaze, the warm light on her face, watching her companions. The crewmembers passed the instruments around the circle to any others who could play, and the songs varied. Everyone here was from a different region of Orlell, where the music was as diverse as the people. They sang several shanties, a Gevarian harvest hymn (no one could pronounce the words correctly, but the gypsies only laughed and sang louder), and two Elven battle epics.

The lute reached Robin, who shook his head and began to pass it by, but his crew protested. "Oh, come on, Cap'n!" the sailors insisted. "The Song of the Stars!"

"You're the only one who knows it all," John added with a chuckle.

Robin protested a few moments, but Bryn could tell he was enjoying himself. "Oh, all right," he said finally, and plucked the beginning notes. With the quiet thrum of the lute, the mood changed. The mirth and liveliness faded into the shadows. The fire crackled, accompanying the melody. The crew sang along softly, their low voices accompanying Robin's:

'Ere the Ace-Lord in his line,
'Ere the world be born of light,
'Ere the world be told of time,
Then the Stars walked land and sky
They in the Land Immortal dwell

Bryn had heard this song time and time again. It was always the last song to be sung in the taverns along the border, the chorus that quieted the crowds of Esile in even the most boisterous of pubs. Yet here, something was different. For the first time, she found herself really listening as the verses that told of the Stars, the ancient goodness and Light, and the coming of darkness into the world. Robin's low voice echoed in her mind, accompanied by her mother's from many, many years before.

> *'Ere the Dark ones leave His trust,*
> *'Ere their hatred forged for us,*
> *When War toiled, our minds forgot,*
> *Kingdoms split as mortals fought*
> *All they the Land Immortal dwell*

Sorrow. That was what she found anew in the song tonight. A deep, ancient sorrow for all that had been lost. Yet hope too. A hope she had long since abandoned, a reckless hope that dared to believe that maybe, just maybe, it would all end well. If they could avoid and overcome the dark powers of the compass. If they could cling to the Light.

She pulled up her hood, both to shelter her ears from the cold, and to hide the tears that threatened her eyes. They were not tears of sadness, though the song called up every memory of every horrible event in her life. The hope stirred her heart, and the sorrow transformed into happiness. Peace even.

Here, in a circle of pirates and outlaws, all singing the same song, she felt peace.

She could not think of the future now. She could not think about leaving this behind, returning to the harsh cold world on her own. She could deal with that decision later.

For now, she stared into the fire as the last notes of the song dropped into silence.

22

The Black Raven

"I think I found something," Mel said.

Aryion looked up from packing his bedroll, his cold fingers struggling to fasten the straps. It was freezing this morning. They had left the inn at Westerlyn behind yesterday and spent the majority of the day walking east. There had been no sign of Dricasters on the road, which confirmed Aryion's guess that they had kept to sea and not landed on the Mainland to go after the Capital. While the thought reassured him a little, it left the nagging confusion of what the Dricasters could be doing.

With no sign of Waypath, he and Mel had camped off the trail last night, cold, tired, and discouraged. The chilly sunlight of a new day rejuvenated him slightly. Today was the day they would meet with the Wildkids—of course, if they could find Waypath. In the light of morning, that task seemed less daunting.

"What is it?" he asked in response to his apprentice.

Mel nodded to the left. "I walked down the road this morning after I filled up the water flasks. It leads to a clearing. There were lots of tracks and marks on the ground. At first I thought it was an old campsite, but it's way too big." He paused, frowning. "There's nothing there, just tracks and muddy grass."

Aryion straightened, feeling a slight surge of hope. If Mel had found what Aryion hoped he had, they were not as far off as he had feared. He fastened the straps of the bedroll and shouldered his pack. "Show me."

The sun was shining this morning, but dark storm clouds lurked on the horizon. The road was iced over, making it slippery, but it was better than slogging through mud. In a few minutes, Mel stopped, gesturing to a wide open clearing. As he had described, the area was large—a circular gap in the woods at least a quarter mile wide. The trees and brush had been felled and cleared away. In some places, the ground was scored by the indentations where small buildings had stood, their tracks slightly concealed by dead leaves and bramble.

"Look," Mel said, and Aryion turned to him. His apprentice crouched beside a small mound of soil that nearly covered the remnants of a camp fire.

"Good eye," Aryion murmured. He studied the terrain. More dents gouged in the ground, mapping out the foundations of the structures that had been built there. More mounds of soil that disguised where fires had been.

He turned to Mel. "What do you make of it?"

Mel looked up. "Someone had a camp here, I think. A big one— almost as big as the Appledale township. Maybe a gypsy caravan?" he suggested, then stopped and frowned again. "I've never heard of caravans setting up buildings."

"It's a good idea," Aryion said. He studied the trail, which slanted south slightly. "I think this is where Waypath used to be."

"It's gone?" Mel sounded alarmed.

"Relocated," Aryion said. "Waypath was constructed so that it can be packed up and moved quickly—that's the reason why it's so hard to find, and why it's on so few maps. The maps that do include it can only show a radius of the area where it's likely to be."

"Oh," Mel said. "Why did they move the town, then?"

"Maybe the Capital tried to send guards here. Or maybe it's connected to the business with the Dricasters, which would be my guess," Aryion said, studying the tracks on the trail. Leaves had been swept over it, but the icy mud had preserved the furrows left by the wagons. "Seems like they moved closer to the river. Come on," he said, leading the way down the road.

Mel followed, glancing back at the strange empty place where the town had once been. "Aryion? If they moved closer to the river, doesn't that mean the Dricaster pirates could sail to it?"

Aryion paused. In his excitement of finding the footprints of Waypath, he hadn't considered this. He had assumed they would find out what the Dricasters were planning after they stopped Terrax and the Jenna. But if the Dricasters had indeed sailed east, there was nothing stopping them from going to Waypath. From Waypath, it was a day's sail to Port Rylan, which was where they assumed Terrax had gone. What if Terrax had come to meet the Dricasters elsewhere?

For the first time, the possibility crossed his mind that the schemes of the Crime Rings and the issue with Terrax were intertwined.

"We'll see," was all he said to Mel, trying to hide the growing worry in his mind.

......

"Please, Miss Valetown?" Oliver pleaded.

Bryn, stoking last night's fire to life, took one last sip of lukewarm coffee and turned to him. "I'm not sure I'd make a good teacher, Oliver."

"But you're the only archer we've ever had on board," the cabin boy persisted. "I might not get to meet another bounty hunter what uses a bow, you know."

The night had passed uneventfully. Bryn had awoken early yet well-rested for the first time in days. Robin and John had gone to buy more wares from the gypsy vendor, since a new load of supplies had arrived this morning. Most of the other sailors were either stretching their legs in town, or relaxing in camp beside the harbor. This left Bryn a moment of rest, warming up while she talked to Oliver.

Oliver had been asking ever since they'd left Drynrall for her to teach him to shoot a bow. He had taken an interest in Bryn's bow from the moment she'd come on board. But the armory of the *Marie*, though well-stocked in all manner of spears, swords, and stolen firearms, was lacking both bows and arrows.

Bryn stood and splashed the dregs of her coffee onto the beach. "I can show you, Oliver, but my bow is too heavy of a draw for you to learn with."

"I can do it," Oliver said confidently.

He probably could, Bryn thought, but he was unaccustomed to the sixty-pound draw weight, which would cause his release to be off and all shots to go awry. And she was trying to conserve arrows. "They probably sell bows here in Waypath," she said as she bent her bow back to string it. "You'll need to learn on something lighter, just until your form is correct and your muscles are stronger."

Oliver looked disappointed, but nodded. "All right, but couldn't you still show me? I'll teach you how to shoot a rifle," he offered.

"I know how to shoot a rifle," Bryn said with a slight smile. She had learned a few years ago, after Hawk Dakrind had acquired his first batch of firearms. "If you can find yourself a bow to use, then yes, I will teach you," she promised.

The cabin boy brightened and ran back to the ship to find Richard.

Bryn tested her bowstring experimentally. The wound in her arm was still tight and sore, but she could draw her bow. Satisfied, she had just begun to follow Oliver back on board when movement on the river to her right drew her eyes.

A ship, black as night, oars out and pounding the river water to a froth, propelling them to Waypath. The morning light glinted off the silver inlays on her prow, caught the gleam of swords in the hands of the sailors on deck. The golden bear of the Dricasters snarled from her red banner fluttering in the wind.

The *Black Raven* had come.

For an instant, Bryn stared at the approaching ship in shock. She had expected Dakrind would track them down eventually, but she hadn't expected it to be so soon. Now he was here, come for the compass and likely eager to kill them all.

With that thought, she turned and sprinted up the beach toward the road into town. A crowd of people stood in her way, gawking at the ship—she wove through them, running back towards the vendor she and Richard had visited yesterday.

Robin and John were walking back down the road, carrying baskets of supplies. Concern crossed their faces as they saw her.

"Dakrind's here," Bryn said immediately, keeping her voice low but urgent.

Robin's face went white, but he recovered quickly. "Get to the ship. We need to get out now, before they—"

A deafening boom cut him off, followed by the sound of splintering wood. Shouts of alarm came from the harbor. Bryn's heart lurched—Dakrind was firing on the unprotected *Marie*.

"…attack," Robin finished, dropping the supplies, and sprinting back toward the harbor.

"Wait!" Bryn cried, chasing after him and John. Idiot, she thought furiously, he's going to get himself killed. At the moment, she could tell Robin didn't care, overcome with fear for both his ship and his crew. He shoved through the crowds toward the docks.

Bryn caught up to John first, gripping his arm. "Mr. Tailor, wait.

We need to think this through."

The first mate pulled free, irritated. "Wait? While Dakrind destroys our ship?"

"Dakrind's not after the *Marie* at all," Bryn said, jogging alongside him through town. "He's here for the compass. He knows we have it, so he'll come for us, not waste his time on the ship."

John hesitated. "He seems occupied with the ship at the moment," he pointed out.

"It's to draw us out. I've seen him do this before. Dakrind wants to cause as much chaos around us as he can, force us to expose ourselves." She took a breath, forcing her racing mind to calm. "We can't go rushing into this fight without thinking first."

"Well, I agree with you there," John said shortly. "I am not standing by while Dakrind kills the crew. Not again."

There was a second bellow of cannon fire, another crunch of wood. Bryn winced involuntarily, then turned to John again. "We won't stand by. Find the men in town. I'll get the others off the ship while you mobilize the crew. You have firearms. We might be the only ones who stand a chance against Dakrind."

John paused, glancing toward the harbor, then finally nodded. "Very well. You protect the captain."

Bryn nodded, and they ran the rest of the way to the docks.

The *Burman Marie* sat at an odd angle, tilted slightly in the water, wallowing like an injured swan. It was difficult to tell how bad the damage was from shore. Fire blazed at her stern, and Bryn could see the sailors hastening to put it out. Robin had already reached the pier and leapt on board his ship. Bryn followed him; behind her, she heard John calling for the sailors to join him in preparation of battle.

Richard was on deck—blood streaked his face from a gash on his brow, but he didn't seem badly hurt. "First round tore through the back of the berth," he was saying to Robin as Bryn boarded the ship. "Four men hurt, one dead."

"The compass?" Bryn asked.

"I have it," Robin said, holding it up. He watched as the *Black Raven* turned and began to sail towards them almost lazily. Bryn could see a tall figure dressed in black at the helm, a red-plumed hat on his head. His gold beads glinted in the sun. Dakrind. She caught the white flash of his teeth as he smiled in satisfaction, his gaze fixed on the *Marie*.

"Shall we return fire, Cap'n?" Richard asked uncertainly.

"We won't stand a chance, not with the *Marie* in this condition," Robin said, frustrated. "Off load the guns and join John and the others on shore. I won't have the ship caught in the cross fire if we can avoid it."

Richard nodded and moved to obey, calling for the crew to aid him. Bryn watched as the *Raven* drew closer, the details gradually coming into focus. There was something different about the other ship's decks, but she couldn't tell what it was.

Dakrind's voice reached them, echoing over the water, cold with hate. "Robin Trelawney, you have one chance to surrender before I sink your ship and leave you here to contend with the Wavers. Hand over the compass, and your crew will be spared."

The mention of the Wavers sent a thrill of fear through Bryn. She exchanged a startled look with Robin before he turned back to Dakrind, cupping his hands around his mouth. "Looks like your mind is starting to crumble with old age, Dakrind," he called. "There's no Wavers in Waypath. Makes it one of the few enjoyable towns on the southern coast."

"That will change very quickly if you do not comply," Dakrind replied smoothly. "Give me the compass now, while you have the chance."

"What's he on about?" Robin muttered to Bryn, then shouted, "I'm bringing the compass to Terrax directly. That's the usual arrangement, before you decided to interfere. I'm to receive my pay from him."

"There will be no pay to receive if you're dead," Dakrind spat. "Hand over the compass, Trelawney, or the Wavers will tear your ship to pieces."

Bryn snatched a spy glass from a passing sailor and peered through it, a terrible suspicion rising in her mind. She focused the glass on the decks of the *Black Raven*. There were cages on board the ship, wicker cages like the ones in Drynrall Island. But the prisoners inside were not Wildkids. The distance blurred their appearance slightly, but Bryn could see the wild eyes, the haggard forms, the clacking teeth.

Wavers. Dakrind had loaded the *Raven* with Wavers.

Her stomach lurched in horror as she realized the truth. The ships they'd seen sailing east, the entire fleet of Dricaster vessels… they hadn't come to fight Terrax' Jenna. They had come to retrieve the Wavers, to ship them to wherever Dakrind needed, then release them like a herd of infected animals. An army of mindless warriors—and if Dakrind had the compass, he could direct them wherever he wanted.

"Head to Port Rylan if you're so interested in Wavers," Robin yelled. "I'm sure they'll give you a welcome."

"He's not joking," Bryn whispered, handing him the spyglass. Robin peered through it, and Bryn saw his face pale.

They stood on a crippled ship with no way to escape and no chance to avoid the Wavers. Bryn could see them seething and clawing the bars of their cages, whipped into a frenzy by the proximity of the compass. Fear such as she had never known filled her. If they stayed, they would certainly be killed, and they would likely be gunned down the minute they tried to flee downriver.

Then, at the same moment she had the thought, a volley of fire arrows launched from the tree line, slamming into the *Black Raven's* decks. Sailors screamed in pain and fell forward into the water, crossbow bolts protruding from their bodies. Dakrind disappeared behind the gunwale. His crew was thrown into confusion.

"Was that John?" Bryn demanded incredulously, reaching for the spyglass.

"Can't have been John," Robin muttered. He was studying the shore through the spyglass.

Bryn squinted into the shadows of the trees until she saw them. An army of shadowy figures, bearing crossbows and dressed in leather armor, streamed onto the beach in a coordinated attack, shooting at the *Raven*. She thought they were Jenna for a moment, but realized that was wrong—the warriors were human. Most of them. Their leader strode out of the trees, tall and foreboding, silver fur bristling. Madam Ida, leading a small army of Rylanders and raining fire upon the *Raven*.

"Blast it all," Robin said. "What are *they* doing here?"

Dakrind appeared again, bellowing orders to his crew. The *Raven* swung broadside to the Waypath township and fired another round. The crowd of Rylanders pulled back as cannonballs tore through the trees and huts alongside the waterfront. Civilians cried out in fear.

"On shore, now!" Robin barked. "Let's go."

Bryn followed as the sailors left the *Marie* behind and hurried to join the group on shore. The thunder of the *Raven*'s guns made her teeth rattle, and the very ground of Waypath shuddered under the force of the cannons. Despite this, the Rylanders continued their attack. Bryn had no idea why they were here, but now was not the time to speculate. A battle between Crime Rings had erupted on the shores of the Westerlyn River.

. . . . . .

The two rangers had walked in the peaceful silence of the woods for so long, Aryion had begun to relax. The smell of the damp trees, the chirping of birds, and the winter sunlight made it easy to forget that they might be walking into potential danger.

The unexpected rumble of cannon fire brought every fear rushing back.

Both of them froze. Aryion listened for a moment as the distant booming died down. For a moment, he thought he may have heard wrong. But the sound was unmistakable.

Mel looked at his mentor, wide-eyed. "Who has cannons this far south? I thought only the Liznees had them."

Aryion stood still, a cold foreboding in the pit of his stomach. "Pirates, most likely," he said finally. "There were firearms stolen during the Aces' occupation of Caer Sia. I imagine some of them made it south."

They began to run. Another smell filled the air as they went west—an acrid, stinging stench that made his eyes water. Burned tar. Not a ship's tar, though—this was stronger. Likely used to patch a roof or window sill. A house was burning.

"Stay close," he ordered. Mel shadowed him as they ran. Months of training had strengthened him so that he could maintain this pace for hours, and he was almost as fast as Aryion now.

But they did not have to run for long. Abruptly, they crested a small hill and got their first glimpse of the battle below.

The hill sloped down to a gradual flatland, where the town of Waypath was fully visible through the trees. Fire lit the north side of the township, and debris littered the river harbor. Aryion had half expected to see that the Wildkids had beaten them here, and were engaged in battle with the Jenna. But there was no sign of Wildkids nor Jenna in Waypath. Instead, a tall black galleon cruised through the water, cannons blazing as it fired at the town. Six rowboats had left her behind, moving toward shore.

Aryion stared at the scene below, overwhelmed with déjà vu for a moment. It was so like the fight in Kamon, with the rowboats speeding to the beach and the stench of oil smoke and the cries of fear. But the Kamon battle had at least been fought by two prepared sides. This attack was upon a defenseless town full of defenseless people and, as far as Aryion could tell, totally unprovoked.

"Aryion, look," Mel said urgently, pointing at the black ship. A red banner streamed from the central mast. "That's a Dricaster ship."

Aryion stared at the flag in confusion. Mel was right. But why would the Dricaster Brethren launch an attack on a town full of gypsies and outlaws?

That question would have to wait. "Come on," he said, and he and Mel sped downhill.

23

Fire and Steel

By the time the *Marie*'s crew had assembled on the hill slope looking down at the river, Dakrind's men were approaching the shore.

John Tailor had acted quickly and organized an efficient counter attack. Most of the crew had been in the camp on the beach when the *Black Raven* had first arrived, so they hadn't been in the line of fire. On the slight rise above the camp was a crumbled heap of brick buildings, the remnants of some port that had stood here before being abandoned. The sailors had taken cover behind the brick wall, which was tall enough to offer shelter and offered a prime shot down at the approaching pirates.

"Steady, boys," John ordered. He crouched next to Bryn, a rifle held steady on the top of the wall, watching as the rowboats drew closer.

Bryn nocked an arrow to her string but did not draw it yet. The *Black Raven* had turned back upriver, firing at the Rylanders hidden in the trees. The Rylanders, though outgunned, had already caused significant damage—black smoke rose from the *Raven*'s starboard side, and two of her sails were in ribbons. But the ship could still maneuver and fight, and that was exactly what Dakrind must intend.

She doubted he had expected to fight the Rylanders, though. Bryn was still struggling to understand why the rival Ringmembers were here at all.

"Here they come," Robin murmured, bringing Bryn's attention back to the battle.

The rowboats ground against the shore, and the pirates ran through the shallow water up to the beach, snarling and brandishing weapons. The sharp crackle of gunshots ran down the line of sailors behind the wall. Bryn drew back her arrow and stood, sighted, then released. She ducked behind the wall again before seeing if she had hit her target. The wall badly inhibited her view. By the time she drew back her next arrow and peered over the wall again, the pirates had hidden behind trees and rubble, out of sight except for when they had to step out to shoot.

Robin fired his pistol a second time, then crouched down to load another charge. A sailor on the other side of John gave a choked cry and fell, a crossbow bolt in his chest. Rounds of gunshots came from Dakrind's men—they matched the weaponry of the *Marie's* crew, but they had more men to fight. Robin's men were badly outnumbered.

"Does Dakrind really have Wavers on board?" Matthew asked uneasily.

"Seems he does," Robin said with a heavy sigh. "We can't let the *Raven* dock here. If those things get out, they'll tear the town apart to get the compass."

"That is likely what Dakrind has planned," John pointed out. He swung back to face over the wall and fired again. Somewhere near the beach, Bryn heard the dull thump of a body hitting the ground. The first mate, in addition to being prompt and thorough onboard, was also an expert shot.

"Dakrind knows if the Wavers get the compass, he'll never get it back," Bryn said. She was still struggling to make sense of Dakrind's logic. Perhaps he believed he could control the Wavers… but that was impossible. From what she had gathered, the Wavers were so far gone they could no longer form coherent thoughts aside from the drive to get the compass. They wouldn't follow orders and fight for Dakrind.

Then again, maybe Dakrind didn't have to control them. He probably hoped the Wavers would kill everyone here before killing each other to gain the compass. They'd do all the dirty work for him, she thought with disgust, then realized that had been her exact job before she'd left the Brethren.

Boom! Boom! Boom!

The blasts shook the ground as the *Raven* fired at the defenders uphill, closer than before. Bryn risked a glance over the wall. The black ship was turning slowly downriver, clearly intending to provide cover for the pirates on the beach. She didn't see the Rylanders, and wondered for a moment if they had all been killed.

This thought was rejected as she saw the flickers of movement through the trees, a mere arrowshot from their position.

"Watch your left!" she shouted, pulling Robin down just in time. A hail of crossbow bolts whizzed through the air from their unprotected left. The Rylanders had a better position, able to fire down at the backs of the *Marie's* crew. They wanted the compass too, and they clearly intended to kill them for it.

"Back!" Robin shouted hoarsely. "Back, boys, hurry!"

Bryn released two arrows in rapid succession. One missed, but the other slammed into a Rylander aiming at John. The *Marie's* crew fled back, away from the beach, finding better cover nearer to town. Bryn noticed that the gypsies and outlaws of Waypath had assembled to fight too—the destruction of the northern half of their village had whipped them into a fury. They sprinted to meet the Rylanders in the trees, armed with a wide variety of weapons.

"That'll slow Madam Ida down," Robin commented, out of breath. The crew huddled behind the brick wall. At least half of them had been injured in the Rylanders' sudden attack. Four sailors lay still and unmoving at their previous position, crossbow bolts protruding from their bodies.

Bryn set her jaw, frustrated. Men were dying, and she could do nothing to help from here. There was hardly any visibility for her to shoot.

That thought reminded her of Port Rylan, when she had run blindly through the crowded streets looking for Robin, until she had thought to climb…

Her eyes landed on a sturdy-looking wood hut to her right, on the other side of the street. The tall trees around it would cover her, and she could still see through the boughs to shoot down anyone who attempted a rush on the brick wall.

The open street between her and the cabin was four paces wide. Four paces of open space where she would most certainly be shot at. She turned to John. "Cover me—I'm going up on the roof."

John nodded, understanding her plan.

Bryn edged to the end of the wall, then took a breath and sprang clear. Her boots pounded the gravel street as she ran. Gunshots exploded in the air around her. She heard the crack of John's rifle behind her, and Dakrind's crew turned their attention on the wall. Then came a nearer gunshot, a short cry of pain—

She reached a tree and turned back in time to see John fall, his rifle clattering to the ground.

Robin cursed loudly and ran to his fallen first mate. Bryn started back, but Robin waved her on. "Go! Get up there and shoot!" he barked.

Bryn obeyed, startled to feel the throb of pain in her chest. John had not trusted her. He had blamed her for the deaths of the crewmembers. And yet Bryn had felt a sense of responsibility for the whole crew from the moment they had left Drynrall. She had promised herself she would keep them safe, defend them, keep them alive, as she did for Robin.

And she had failed.

The pain was replaced by fury. She reached the rooftop, drew back an arrow, and let it fly at the Ringmembers on the beach.

. . . . . .

The thunder of cannons, billowing black smoke, and the stench of burned goods assaulted Aryion's senses as he and Mel reached the edge of the battle field. As Aryion had observed earlier, this fight resembled the Kamon battle in some ways. But in others, it was wildly different. For one, the Kamon battle had been well-planned and organized by both sides—a bloody fight, yes, but a cleverly concocted one.

The battle in Waypath could only be described as chaos.

The pirates who had arrived in the black ship were one group of many. After firing on a second, smaller ship in the harbor, they had in turn been attacked by a group of crossbow-wielding warriors in the trees. The black ship had sustained damage, but nothing so severe she could not return fire, which was exactly what had happened. At the same time, Aryion noticed a third group of pirates firing from behind a long brick wall. Though outnumbered, they were holding their own, armed with rifles and pistols, and fired quick, direct shots at any attackers.

And then there were the gypsies and outlaws of Waypath. Though taken by surprise, the destruction of part of their village had enraged them. They were scattered throughout the town, hiding behind trees, charging into the fray, loosing arrows and hurling daggers.

Four armies, blending and mixing in a whirlwind that was nearly impossible to follow.

"Stay low," Aryion said, and he and Mel moved to hide behind a large stump. They were on the south side of the town, the river harbor to their right. From here, they could watch the fight on the beach.

"Whose side are we on?" Mel asked. His eyes were wide as he watched the fray.

Aryion studied the battle for a few moments, trying to come up with an answer, but he had none. It was impossible to tell who was on whose side—they all seemed to be fighting for themselves. He saw two gypsies hacking away at each other with swords, a pirate shoot one of his own crewmates, a crossbow bolt take down a man on the same side.

"Just… wait and watch," he said, though he had no idea what to do. They had come to Waypath to find and meet with the Wildkids, not to engage in a battle between pirates and Crime Rings. If the Wildkids were not here, he and Mel would have to find them quickly and escape before this battle got any further out of hand.

Something crashed in the woods to their left—a group of fiery-eyed outlaws sprinted toward them.

Aryion sprang up and pushed Mel behind him. "Run! Toward the river!"

Normally, he would have squared up and calmly fought the outlaws. Probably would have won. But confusion, tension of the last few days, and fear for his apprentice drove away any confidence he usually felt.

Instead, he turned and ran with Mel toward the harbor.

. . . . . .

Bryn had five arrows left.

Dakrind's crew had spread up the shore, hiding behind heaps of rubble and firing occasional shots. The Rylanders, as far as Bryn could tell, remained on the north side of town. They had taken cover in a crumbling brick building in the trees and were shooting down at Dakrind's crew. Thankfully, they could no longer hit the *Marie*'s crew from that position. The bloodbath of sword play to the left had ceased—bodies of Rylanders, Dricasters, and inhabitants of Waypath littered the beach and road.

The appearance of the Rylanders had clearly caught Dakrind off guard and likely ruined his plan to release the Wavers. Since the Rylanders wanted the compass too, Bryn doubted he would risk such an attack. But the Rylanders were at a disadvantage without their ship. She wondered what had become of the *Blood Swan*, not that the graceful pirate ship would have had much advantage against the *Raven*'s cannons.

Either way, the best thing the *Marie*'s crew could do now was wait. Let the Ringmembers fight this battle out and then escape when they could.

But they couldn't wait for long. The Rylanders could fight Dakrind's crew all they wanted, but they knew by now that Robin had the compass. Eventually they would leave their cover behind and charge the crumbling wall where Robin's crew sheltered.

Maybe the crew could reach the *Marie* and slip away downriver…

That thought vanished with a quick glance at the ship. The *Burman Marie* wouldn't be able to flee anywhere. She could sail—hopefully—but it would be a slow limp to the coast, where they'd have to stop and make repairs.

They needed more manpower, but Bryn didn't know where they would find that. As deserters, the *Marie's* crew were hated by both Crime Rings. And the Waypath inhabitants would hardly be able to offer aid.

She looked at the *Black Raven*. Dakrind seemed content to continue firing at the Rylanders in the trees. The ship drifted closer to shore, her prow pointed directly at Bryn. Bryn looked toward the river. A cluster of small huts and trees—that was all that stood between her and the water.

And the *Raven's* guns.

"Curse it, Dakrind," she muttered. She leapt to her feet, grabbed her bow, and dropped down from the rooftop.

Boom! Boom! Boom!

Another round of cannon fire began in the same moment she moved. The area behind her exploded. Fragments of wood whistled through the air, stinging across her back. A wave of hot air flung her forward, and she crashed down in the mud between two buildings.

Boom! Boom! Boom!

Bryn lay face down in the mud, covering her head. Cannonballs tore through the wall in front of her, showering her with wood splinters. She gritted her teeth and waited for the building next to her to collapse and bury her. But, miraculously, it stood. Through a hole in the wall, she watched the *Black Raven* continue to float downstream, firing occasionally at the town.

As soon as she was sure the guns were no longer trained in her direction, Bryn sprang to her feet and turned to the left to run.

Instead, she crashed into a tall man in a mottled gray cloak.

24

Old Allies Not Forgotten

Bryn stumbled two paces backward, winded by the collision. Muddy water dripped into her eyes—half blinded, she brought her bow back to full draw, squinting to make out who she had run into.

"Look out!" came a new voice—unfamiliar, young, and scared. It reminded her of Oliver's voice, but the accent was different.

There was a hissing whisper of a sword being drawn, and Bryn saw a flicker of blue light. She wiped her eyes with the shoulder of her cloak, clearing her vision.

Two people stood in front of her, both in the garb of rangers. A boy crouched to her right. His tawny hair was tousled, and he had his hand in to his pants pocket. Something glowed blue through the fabric.

Bryn's eyes snapped away from his to face the other stranger. He was tall, with dark hair and dark eyes, holding his sword at the ready, his other hand raised in a placating gesture.

"Don't shoot—don't shoot." This voice was familiar—low and calm, with a northern accent. Somewhat like Robin's—no, that wasn't why the voice was familiar.

This voice came from another time, another place, accompanied by memories of training late at night and laughter and growing up with her best friend at her side—

She stared at him for several seconds, stunned. *Impossible,* her mind screamed, *you can't be here. You shouldn't be here. Why are you here?* He was still talking—at least, she could see his mouth moving, but any words seemed to have been swept away.

Bryn let the bowstring relax, lowering the arrow. "Why are you here?" she demanded, because it was the first thing she could come up with.

He frowned, confused, before the confusion was replaced by shock, then recognition. "Brynlee?"

Bryn had no idea how long they might have stood there, staring at each other. The young boy stepped forward, looking at Bryn with wide, interested eyes. "That's her?" he asked.

He was so much younger than Bryn had expected—maybe eleven or twelve years old. Terrax must have been mistaken. Was this really the bounty she would have been sent to kill? Her eyes were drawn to the pinprick of blue light in his pocket, which brought her back to reality. Dakrind was here for the compass, and the compass would lead him to—

"You need to leave," she ordered. "You both need to leave, now, before they come for that Stone—"

"We—I didn't—you're—" Aryion was speechless. Her brother was never speechless. The boy looked surprised too—what had Terrax said his name was? She couldn't remember.

"You know about the Stone?" the boy asked at the same time, concern crossing his face.

"A lot of people know about the Stone, and they're going to kill you if you don't run," Bryn informed him, looking at Aryion.

Aryion finally managed to find words. "What is going on here? Do your Ringmembers intend to besiege the beggars of Waypath?" There was a note of contempt in his voice.

A round of gunfire came from nearby, and all three of them flattened against the wall of the building. "I'm serious," Bryn hissed, ignoring her brother's jibe. "You need to run right now, before Dakrind gets here."

"Who's…" the boy began.

"The Dricaster leader," Bryn informed him. "Hired by someone very dangerous to find *that*." She pointed her bow at the Stone in his pocket.

A look she had not seen in many years crossed Aryion's face. He put a protective hand on the boy's shoulder, looking intensely at Bryn. "They are after him?"

"They're after both of you," Bryn said, staring at her brother in surprise. Protecting—that was what he did now. So he must have fulfilled the Blood Oath. Killed Hagshrub and moved on with life.

"Who is?" Aryion demanded.

"Someone named Terrax. Look, we don't have time for a discussion. You need to get out of here before they come," Bryn said.

But they both reacted at the name. "Terrax hired them?" the boy said in shock. "We're trying to find him—is he here? Does he have

Jenna? Are those his soldiers?" He pointed at the *Black Raven.*

More gunfire. Bryn stood at a loss, not sure what to do. Here was the one Terrax had been so eager to track down and kill. Here was her brother, whom she had not spoken to in years. He was grown up now, taller than she was, with a beard and tired lines on his face and their father's sword in his hand.

But beyond was Robin and his crew, fighting for their lives against Hawk Dakrind—

She could sense her brother wasn't going to leave, but she couldn't let him get involved in this fight. They would place the Stone right in Dakrind's hands.

"I'll tell you everything later," she said. "But not right now. Right now we need to get out of Waypath. That ship in the harbor," she pointed to the *Marie,* "that's our best way out."

Aryion took a breath, seeming to put aside his questions for now. "Fine… fine, Lee." He had always called her that growing up, even though Bryn had protested against the nickname. "Who's on your side?"

"There's a crew of sailors pinned down behind a wall uphill— maybe fifty, maybe less," Bryn said. "If you want to help, we need to get them back to the ship and get ready to run."

"Is the ship damaged?"

"Yes, but I think she can still sail," Bryn said.

"You think?" Aryion repeated warily.

"We don't have a better option," Bryn said. "There's a small trail that leads away from town, through the trees and to the harbor. You might be able to get the wounded out that way."

Aryion met her eyes. Something passed between them that Bryn could never fully explain, some agreement or acknowledgment that lay unspoken. Their missions had intertwined, and any personal business must be set aside.

He nodded to her, and Bryn vanished into the trees, running back toward the wall.

. . . . . .

"I don't see any Jenna here, at least," Mel observed.

Aryion shook himself slightly. His mind was still reeling from the unexpected appearance of his sister. It made it that much harder to focus as he and Mel slipped through the woods toward the ship Bryn had pointed out.

"What makes you think there would have been Jenna here?" he asked.

"The Wildkids said there were Jenna in the area," Mel reminded him. "If there were Jenna here, we could assume Terrax was here too. But I don't think he is. I don't think he'd want to risk fighting…" he paused, gesturing uncertainly at the chaos of battle, "… them."

"It's a good point," Aryion told him, glad that his apprentice had kept his focus. It was a small thing to be grateful for. The battle was confusing enough without having to worry about catching Terrax now.

He glimpsed the path through the thick brush ahead of them. The trail wound parallel to the river, overshadowed by dense walls of trees. The trees completely hid the path from any watchers, allowing for a relatively safe escape route. But that also meant that they would be unable to see any approaching attackers.

He and Mel pushed through the boughs and stepped onto the trail. A group of ragged sailors were making their way slowly down the path, and stopped abruptly as they saw the rangers. Their leader, a burly pirate with side burns and a cut on his brow, moved forward. "Who're you?" he demanded gruffly, reaching for his pistol.

Aryion raised his hands in a peacemaking gesture. "We're on your side. Bryn sent us."

The sailor frowned slightly. "Did she? And aren't you her spitting image," he commented, half to himself. "Minus the beard, of course."

"Very funny, Richard," one of the other sailors sighed.

"We need to get the ship ready to leave," Aryion told him, ignoring the comment. "I think Bryn plans to protect your retreat, and we've come to help you."

Richard nodded slightly. "Right, then." He nodded back down the road. "If you rangers can give us some cover, we're trying to get the wounded out this way."

"We can do that," Aryion said, and he and Mel jogged back down the trail toward the sounds of battle. The overgrown path and deep shadows thrown by the trees made it difficult to move quickly. Aryion hoped the retreating pirates would be hidden by the forest. He assumed the Ringmembers would focus on fighting each other, but he wouldn't put it past them to come after the wounded.

The sailors were not the only ones using this trail to escape. The inhabitants of Waypath were fleeing the conflict too. Outlaws, gypsies, and peasants hurried past, some carrying rucksacks of goods, others supporting their wounded friends.

"This way," Aryion called to a group of gypsies, who were hiding behind a broken hut. They looked at him blankly.

"I don't think they understand Common," Mel said.

"You think?" Aryion asked dryly. He repeated the words, gesturing down the road. The ragged group hesitated, still unsure. But they seemed to understand what he meant, and started down the path into the shadowed trees.

The river was the only option for the people of Waypath, Aryion realized. On foot, the journey to a civilized town would take days. Their best chance was to get to the harbor, board their little boats and skiffs, and sail further up, deeper into the vast wilds.

The thought reminded him of what Bryn had said earlier, and brought to light a flaw in the plan. If she and the sailors could get their ship out of the harbor, then what? Judging by the coiling smoke rising from the stern, he doubted they could outrun the black ship. They'd be gunned down and sunk before they ever reached the coast.

It didn't make sense to him. That black ship flew the Dricaster colors. His sister was a Dricaster, wasn't she? What had happened that led to this battle in the first place?

"What have you gotten yourself into, Brynlee," he muttered to himself.

A commotion behind them pulled him back out of his thoughts. Cries of fear came from down the road in the direction of the retreating wounded. As the rangers paused, the sharp crack of a gunshot came next.

"Help the other wounded," Aryion told Mel quickly. "I'll go see what that's about."

Mel hesitated, but obeyed. Aryion sprinted down the trail in the other direction. He drew his sword as he ran, prepared to see more Ringmembers, or Jenna maybe. What he saw instead brought him to a skidding halt.

The path drooped down slightly, heavily overshadowed by trees like a wooded tunnel. The injured sailors he and Mel had met with earlier huddled down on the left side of the road. A few of them had drawn weapons. The burly pirate, Richard, had a pistol lowered at the trees on the other side of the road.

"Not another move," he ordered the figures in the shadows, but his hand shook slightly.

Aryion's eyes caught the slight movement in the shadows of the trees, and he saw what Richard was pointing at. The figures seemed invisible at first, so perfectly blending with the deep colors of the forest.

Wildkid warriors. They numbered at least fifty, Aryion guessed, though the shifting light made it hard to be certain.

"Hold your fire!" he called.

Richard glanced at him, his face pale with fear. "You mad, ranger? You ever seen what they can do? They'll rip us apart without a second thought."

Aryion moved between Richard's gun and the Wildkid he was aiming it at, who remained in the trees. His initial thought had been relief, that perhaps it was Joesp's group that had arrived. But Richard's words brought a harsh truth back to his mind. He did not know these warriors. They were a far larger force than a reconnaissance group. No… this was a war party.

"They'll rip you apart faster if you start shooting at them," he told the sailor, keeping his voice calm and measured. He stood, sword raised slightly, trying to make out the forms in the trees. The Wildkid warriors spread down the side of the road, keeping to the shadows. Sunlight caught the occasional glint of spears and daggers, or of bared teeth.

"This battle does not concern you," Aryion said, fighting to maintain the calm in his voice. There were far too many warriors for him to take alone. He didn't see any of the three Wildkids they had met in Yellow Bank, which made it safe to assume this was a different force entirely. "We are not your enemy. Go back to the coast."

He wasn't sure they understood him. Joesp and his brothers had spoken Common, but they had come to spy. This group had come to fight.

The Wildkids had emerged from the trees, forming a semi-circle and blocking the road from both directions and cutting off any retreat. Richard swore behind Aryion, his voice tight with fear. Aryion remained still, watching the warriors, racking his brain for a plan.

At last, a voice broke the tense silence.

"Who are you, ranger?"

It was a female voice, young and wary, spoken with the slightest accent. A Wildkid warrior with black fur stepped into the light. She carried a bow and had a quiver of arrows at her hip. Her vivid green eyes studied the group carefully.

Aryion kept his sword up. "I am called the Hummingbird," he said simply. "Who are you?"

"I am leading this mission. We are here to scout."

"This is a lot of warriors for a scouting party," Aryion commented as the Wildkid continued moving forward.

"I thought rangers had better things to do than battle Crime Rings," the young Wildkid replied crisply. "If you are the ranger I thought, at least."

Aryion kept his sword up, but curiosity entered his mind now. This Wildkid spoke as if she had heard of him before. How? He didn't think that any news of his actions on the quest for the Shards would have traveled that far southeast. So she must have heard of him somewhere else.

"I never said I was here to battle Crime Rings," he told her. She was close enough to reach out and touch his sword now. "I am, however, sworn to protect the Mainland kingdoms, which means it is my duty to know what you're doing here at all. Entering Daffodalion with a war party in these times does not seem wise."

The Wildkid stopped, the tip of Aryion's sword resting against her chest, and smirked slightly. "Well, I never said I was wise. Smart, sure, but that's mostly compared to Rygal."

"You know Rygal?" Aryion asked slowly.

"Dusty!" Mel's excited voice came from Aryion's right, and he turned abruptly. The young apprentice ran down the road, completely oblivious to what was happening, grinning from ear to ear. "Dusty—I was hoping you'd be here—we met your brothers, did Aryion tell you that?" He stopped, noticing the tense situation and the wariness on both faces.

"You *know* them?" Richard said in disbelief.

"Aryion, it's fine, honestly," Mel said, sounding exasperated. "You can put your sword down."

Aryion hesitated, rattled. The tension of everything happening made it hard to think clearly, but he was beginning to understand that this group of Wildkids were on their side.

The Wildkid smiled as she saw Mel, then met Aryion's eyes again, took the flat of the blade in two fingers, and moved it aside gently. "Trust me, ranger?" she asked.

"Not yet," Aryion said, "but I trust Mel." He sheathed his sword. Despite his words, he felt reassured. Dusty's green eyes were calm and civil, shining in the shadowed forest light. Her warriors had not come here to fight—not yet, at least. Though the question still remained of why she was here at all.

The Wildkid warrior looked between Mel and Aryion. "My brothers mentioned they met with you in Yellow Bank. They said you wanted to meet with us here."

Aryion nodded slightly. "Yes, though I'm not sure now is the time to discuss it." He turned to Richard. "Get your men to the ship," he told the sailor, who nodded and continued their way down the road. Aryion looked to Dusty again. "Are your brothers here?"

"Yes, but they're engaged in battle on the other side of the town," Dusty told him. "We had camp a mile or so from Waypath. When the Dricasters got here and began firing, we went to see what was happening. We split up when the Rylanders appeared."

"The sailors are almost out, Aryion," Mel reported. "Bryn and the others are still pinned down behind that brick wall. I was going to help them, but I wanted to make sure everything was all right here."

"At least one ranger can keep his head," Dusty said wryly.

"How many warriors are with you?" Aryion asked, ignoring the comment.

"Sixty-four in the town," Dusty told him without hesitation. "And you were right, this isn't our battle to fight. We came to investigate the Jenna in Port Rylan, since the Randuins were busy in Esile City."

"Then what brought you this way? You're miles west of Port Rylan," Aryion said with a frown.

"Well, we didn't find any Jenna in Port Rylan. No Jenna, no Ringmembers, and no Wavers, which concerned me. We rowed upriver to get supplies here, to avoid the Capital's notice." Dusty studied him carefully. "My brothers mentioned you are looking for Terrax."

"Have you seen him?" Aryion asked.

"No. We have confirmed, at least, that he's hired Vinskael and Karaka Jenna to aid his cause, whatever that could be. We can discuss that later." She glanced back toward the harbor. "You mentioned retreating to the ship?"

The mention of the ship reminded Aryion of their current situation. "The ship—of course." He thought for a moment. "You said you sailed upriver?"

"Yes. Our canoes are hidden in the forest," the Wildkid replied.

A surge of hope filled Aryion's chest. There was the answer. "Good. That's good. The smaller pirate ship in the harbor is our way out, but she's damaged. The black ship will probably give chase once she tries to flee."

"Not if we cover your retreat," Dusty said with a wink.

Aryion smiled. "Exactly. I doubt the Ringmembers will want to stick around and fight Wildkids. But hurry."

Dusty turned and called a series of orders to her warriors in the Wildkid's language. The group vanished into the trees again. Dusty turned back to the rangers. "Be careful. It's good to see you, Mel—we'll catch up once this is over." She looked at Aryion, giving a crooked grin. "Good to meet you, Hummingbird." With that, she followed her warriors.

Aryion let out a breath and started back toward town. "Let's get the rest of the wounded out, and hope this is over soon," he said to his apprentice. "I don't know if I can manage any more surprises today."

"Me neither. I was right, though," Mel said with a grin. "About Dusty. I told you you'd like her."

25

Parley With Dakrind

As soon as the two rangers had headed down the forest path, Bryn slipped through the trees and the ruined buildings until she reached the edge of the street. Here she paused, listening carefully for a few moments. The open space between her and the brick wall would leave her exposed to potential fire. But the silence told her the battle had reached a stand-still. Bodies of Ringmembers, pirates, and townspeople littered the road.

Dark clouds had covered the sun—rain was coming. The *Black Raven* crouched on the far end of the harbor, smoke rising from her starboard rail. The Dricasters who had come ashore had retreated back toward the river's edge. Bryn could catch glimpses of them hiding behind the ruined cabins and burned trees. She didn't see the Rylanders at first, but finally noticed a large group of them sheltering in a larger structure a hundred yards or so uphill. As for the gypsies and outlaws, most of them had already fled the area. Aryion and his apprentice had hopefully directed the survivors to the river.

The rangers' arrival offered them a small advantage, Bryn thought, and right now they needed as much help as possible. They still had no way of escaping the *Black Raven*—at least, they couldn't outrun her. She had begun to come up with an alternative strategy.

She waited another moment, then sprinted across the road and slid behind the brick wall.

John sat propped against the wall, his face deathly white, his teeth gritted in pain. Blood showed through the filthy rag pressed against his collarbone.

Robin knelt next to him, and looked up as she arrived. His face was tired and streaked in mud, but he appeared uninjured. Beyond him, a line of weary pirates crouched, some holding weapons, others nursing injuries or tending to the wounded. Bryn did a quick head-count of the remaining men behind the wall. Forty five. Twenty had gone with Richard back to the ship. They'd lost twelve men already today, and she knew there were more injured.

"How are we holding out?" she asked quietly, already knowing the answer.

Robin let out a breath. "Not well. There's no chance of us getting to the *Marie* from here. We'll be gunned down the minute we show ourselves."

"The *Marie* is in no condition to sail anywhere," Bryn pointed out.

Robin scowled in the direction of the harbor. "She can hold."

"She can," Bryn said, "but your crew can't."

"You think I don't know that?" Robin snapped. He stopped, composing himself.

Bryn spoke, keeping her tone low but urgent. "We can't fight them. But there might be a way to get out of this. Like how we avoided the Rylanders."

Robin glanced up at her, his face unsure but interested. Bryn went on. "Dakrind's here for the compass. I don't think he'll let us out of here alive unless he has it. We might trade the compass for our freedom."

Robin was shaking his head before she finished. "That's all very well, but how do you explain that to the Rylanders? They're here for the compass too. And Dakrind will need more to convince him not to kill us—knowing him, he'll dump the Wavers here and flee with the compass, bargain or no."

Bryn started to argue, then stopped, realizing he was right. "Do you have a better plan?" she asked instead.

Robin glanced over the wall toward the line of Dricasters on the beach, then back at Bryn, and gave a slight smile. "Not really. But I can buy you time. Get the crew out of here and get the *Marie* as far from Waypath as possible."

"What about you?" Bryn demanded.

"I'm going to parley with Dakrind and stall for time. I'll catch up with you." He gave a slow shrug. "Who knows, maybe if I turn myself in, he'll let the rest of you escape."

Bryn grabbed his arm. "That's suicide! And you know Dakrind won't let us off that easy."

John coughed and tried to push himself upright, but the motion made him groan in pain. Robin looked down at his injured friend, desperation on his face. "I know Dakrind won't let us go. That's why you need to run while you can." He pulled the compass out of his pocket and set it in her hands. "Try to help John. Don't let them get the compass, and don't you dare give up."

"You're saying you plan on turning yourself in to Dakrind without the compass?" Bryn said incredulously.

"It's better than nothing. Now go, that's an order." He stood abruptly, looking toward the riverfront.

Bryn shook her head. "That's very noble of you, Captain Trelawney, but you know it won't work." She pulled him down behind the wall again, trying to think.

Footsteps on the road behind her made her turn. She was startled to see the young apprentice approaching, out of breath and looking quite cheerful. "What are you doing here?" she demanded, both surprised and irritated. "I told you to go to the ship."

The boy looked at her and shrugged. "We did go to the ship. Aryion's there now. He told me to see if you needed help."

Robin looked up at Bryn, absolutely lost. "Who's this?"

"He's the one Terrax is after, which means he needs to leave," Bryn said, giving the young ranger a meaningful look. The boy—she couldn't remember his name—didn't seem to notice.

"I will leave, but not without all of you. Your ship is ready to run as soon as you're all on it."

"I'm well aware of that," Robin said dryly. "The problem is the fact that Dakrind will start blowing holes in her the minute she tries to leave the harbor."

"He'll probably try," the young ranger said with a grin. "But we have a troop of Wildkids ready to cover our retreat."

Bryn looked at him blankly, unable to register what he'd just said. Robin looked just as stunned. "You did what now?" he stammered.

"Wildkid warriors," the boy said, drawing the words out for emphasis. "They're here to help us—sort of. Aryion worked it out. Anyway, we need to get on the ship and go."

Bryn finally found her voice. "That's great, but the Wildkids won't be able to protect us from both Crime Rings. We'll need something more." She paused, thinking hard. The Wildkids could stall the pursuit, and likely inflict plenty of damage on both Rylander and Dricasters alike. But the fact remained that they were outnumbered and outgunned. The Wildkids' wooden canoes wouldn't stand a chance against the *Raven's* guns.

Fighting would not be the answer. They needed a different plan.

Robin's patience ran out. "If you think of something, great. Right now, I'll go speak with Dakrind while you retreat."

"Don't—" Bryn began, but he had already stood and stepped forward, down the slope toward Dakrind's men. Bryn looked at the boy—Mel, that was his name—and gestured to the wounded crew behind the wall. "Help them get to the *Marie*. Hurry." Mel nodded and moved down the line.

Robin stepped away from the wall, hands up, studying the waiting pirates in the ruined beach-side huts below. "Gentlemen! I've come to parley with Dakrind. Where is he?"

There was a long pause, then Hawk Dakrind appeared from the shadows of a smoking cabin. His black cloak caught the breeze, as though made of smoke too. He folded his arms over his chest, voice low and cold. "The right to parley does not apply to traitors, Trelawney."

"Well, the right to bargain then," Robin said. "You'll be interested, I assure you."

Dakrind glared at him so fiercely his eyes seemed to blaze red. But he nodded. "Very well. Make it quick."

Bryn tore her eyes away from the scene to check on the others. Mel had worked quickly and was effectively directing the weary sailors from cover to cover until they reached the safety of the forest. Despite his youth, he evidently had some experience, Bryn noticed with surprise.

Matthew McCreery, the second mate, was still behind the wall, nervously watching his captain around the corner. Bryn called him over and knelt before John, who was barely conscious. "Get him to the ship. He's still alive, and we won't leave him behind."

Matthew nodded and gripped John under the arms, pulling him upright. John grunted in pain and protested feebly. "No…leave me here… the captain will need help…"

"I'll do my best to help him," Bryn told him.

John's fevered gaze met Bryn's eyes, desperation and determination blazing there. "You need a plan, Miss Valetown," he said hoarsely. "Try to remember… why all parties… are present. Try to find incentive…"

Matthew half-carried him away from the wall, moving carefully along the path Mel had pointed out. Bryn turned back to Robin and Dakrind, her mind working over John's words. The first mate was right—they needed a plan. Find incentive for them to let us go, she thought, figure out what they wanted. Well, they were all here for the compass, weren't they? But there was only one compass, and she knew both Crime Rings wanted it desperately.

Robin was still talking. "Dakrind, you have to know by now that I don't want the compass. If I did, why wouldn't I have just run with it after getting it in Port Rylan?"

A rustle of movement to the left drew Bryn's eyes. The Rylanders had left their cover and were watching from the tree line uphill, their crossbows held loosely. They seemed interested in what Robin was saying, but that did nothing to reassure Bryn. There were easily fifty Rylanders, all armed. She couldn't possibly defend Robin from so many, much less defend herself.

"The answer is, I don't want the compass at all," Robin continued after a drawn-out pause. "However, I do want my pay. I admit I didn't trust our employer to deliver on his payment, which is why I didn't bring you the compass directly on Drynrall Island. Now that it's clear that the employer is real and prepared to pay, I propose a bargain."

"Go on," Dakrind said. He sounded bored, which wasn't a good sign.

"I'll bring you the compass," Robin said. "We will meet in Esile

City in a week's time, where I'll give you the compass and you'll give me my pay. And you'll let myself and my crew go without trouble."

A growl of complaint came from Dakrind's waiting crew. Bryn could tell they despised the idea of letting Robin off the hook free of consequence after his betrayal.

"If you don't want the compass, as you say," Dakrind said, his voice dripping with sarcasm, "why not hand it over now, and I'll give you your pay myself? The employer left the reward in Drynrall for Miss Valetown, wherever she is now. Six hundred lupin, here and now, for the compass."

Robin hesitated a second too long. "I—I'd rather hand the compass to the employer directly. Ringmember security and all that. Besides, what's to stop you from killing us after I give it to you now?"

"What indeed," Dakrind said darkly.

Robin still wanted to flee east, Bryn assumed. That was why he wanted to send Dakrind in the wrong direction—back west to Esile City. But there was no chance at all that Hawk would fall for that trick.

Neither would the Rylanders. Madam Ida stepped forward, her one good eye blazing in fury. "And what of your second employer, Trelawney?" she snapped. "Seven hundred lupin for the delivery of the compass, as discussed by the Rylander Brethren? What's to keep us from taking the compass now and receiving our pay, and leaving you and your ship here to sink?"

This was the first Bryn had heard of the Rylanders receiving pay for the compass. She had assumed that someone would have hired the Rylanders, but she was impressed to hear that their employer was paying a hundred more lupin. It made it all the stranger that Robin would have taken a job from the Dricasters at all.

She glanced behind her—the last group of crewmembers had retreated, headed for the ship. Mel appeared behind a building and gave her a thumbs-up. Bryn motioned for him to follow the wounded, and he nodded and vanished.

Bryn looked back toward Robin, knowing he wanted them to flee. But she knew it wouldn't work. It was not only the matter of leaving Robin behind that was a problem, it was the fact that there was nothing Robin could offer Dakrind to keep him from pursuing and sinking the *Marie*, then killing them all. Besides, even if they evaded Dakrind and the Dricasters, they'd have to contend with the Rylanders. They wanted the pay their employer had promised, whatever the reason the Rylander employer wanted the compass. She guessed it was along the same lines of why Terrax wanted it. And Terrax, of course, wanted the compass for…

A thrill seemed to run through her body as a plan hit her.

Robin hesitated, glancing between the two Ringleaders, his confidence wilting under their vicious glares. "Now… hold on a moment, Madam Ida," he stammered nervously, clearly sensing that he was about to be shot by about fifty different people. They had run out of time, Bryn could see. The time to act on her sudden revelation must be now.

She swung over the blockade and moved to stand beside Robin. "Wait—wait—"

Dakrind stared at her, startled, then laughed. "Oh, Miss Valetown, and here I assumed they had killed you. What in Orlell do you think you're doing? Protecting a traitor to the Brethren for no pay at all? Don't tell me it's out of some sense of duty." He straightened. "Now, hand over the compass, and I'll let you rejoin the Dricasters without consequences."

Rain began to fall, filling the air between her and the Ringmembers. Bryn ignored it, ignored them all, and focused on her words. "We have the compass, but there's evidently a slew of people who want it. You want the compass," she nodded to Dakrind, "Terrax wants it, and your employer," she looked at Madam Ida, "wants the compass, too. We can fight this battle all day long, but in the end, only one of us will walk away with it."

"Sounds about right," Madam Ida growled, silver fur bristling.

"You'd take the compass over any bargain we can offer, then?" Bryn pressed on. "Over anything… but what if instead of the compass, I gave you what it… *actually* leads to?"

Robin threw Bryn a swift, nervous glance. Bryn continued. "The compass doesn't point to your potential enemies. You're all smart enough to know that's just pirate legend. What it leads to is something far more valuable." She let the silence drag out for a moment before finishing. "Star-Stones."

Dakrind's face remained impassive, but Bryn could see a wrinkle of interest forming on his brow. Madam Ida looked startled. "Star-Stones?" she repeated.

"Star-Stones," Bryn confirmed. "A force more powerful than the compass itself. If you had a Star-Stone, you'd be unstoppable." She hesitated. "And that's exactly what Terrax intends to become."

Dakrind didn't bother to hide his interest now. "What are you implying, Miss Valetown?"

Bryn kept her voice level and confident, but loud enough that they could all hear her. "Terrax plans to use a Star-Stone to take over the Crime Rings. Once he has the compass, he will follow its lead to the Stones and the southern coast would be his."

She studied Dakrind. "You've assumed this for some time, haven't you? You've been planning to turn on Terrax. He'll expect that, mark my words. The compass and the Wavers stand no chance against a Star-Stone. Terrax will overthrow you and destroy every Ring without a thought."

A tense silence followed her words. Bryn could see the faces of the listening Ringmembers wrinkle in thought as they pictured what she was describing. The devastation and death that such a thing implied showed in their worried expressions.

Bryn took a calming breath before continuing. "Here is my bargain. Go back to Terrax and arrange for him to meet us in Esile City. We will come with the Stone then. Once we've arrived," she looked at Dakrind, "you will kill Terrax and take the Star-Stone for yourself."

"And we are expected to stand and watch?" Madam Ida asked

with a sneer.

"Only for the moment, while we deal with Terrax," Bryn said. "After that, you can have the compass for yourself. You can either give it to your employer and receive the payment for it, or keep it yourself to find other Star-Stones."

She paused, trying to ignore the anxious throbbing of her heart, and watched the faces of the two Ringleaders. Both looked skeptical. But she felt a surge of hope because they both seemed to be considering her proposal.

"Quite a bargain, Miss Valetown," Dakrind drawled finally. "But the word of a traitor is no assurance to me. What proof do I have that you'll follow through on your deal and not betray the Brethren again?"

"Take the compass," Bryn said, holding it up. Dakrind and Madam Ida stared in shock. Gasps and excited whispers ran through the Ringmembers behind them.

Bryn stood still, the compass cold in her hand. Robin threw her a quick, alarmed look, but she pressed on, keeping her voice calm. "You can hardly expect me to fail both Crime Rings, can you? As of this moment, I owe the Rylander Brethren the compass and the Dricasters a Star-Stone. If I don't deliver, you know I have nowhere to go."

"Indeed," Dakrind mused. The last comment wasn't a false statement, and Bryn knew it. The only thing that had prevented the Rylanders from tracking her down years ago had been the protection she'd had as a Dricaster Ringmember. That protection no longer existed. If she failed them now, the entire Mainland—and likely most of the island colonies—would become enemy territory.

Dakrind turned to the Rylander leader. "What say you, Madam Ida?"

"It is satisfactory," Madam Ida said briskly. "We will give her a fortnight to deliver either the compass or its reward. But what of the Wavers, which you stole from our territory?"

"Don't become sentimental now, Ida," Dakrind said dryly. "They are of no concern to you."

"Perhaps not, but the damage you inflicted upon my ship while taking them is my concern," Madam Ida replied, her eyes blazing as she stared at Dakrind. "Do you intend to turn them against us and release them upon our territory again?"

"If you have the compass, you don't have to worry about that," Bryn pointed out. "You can control the Wavers yourself." She glanced at Dakrind. "You know you can't control the Wavers without the compass, right?"

"Indeed," Dakrind said again, this time with a deadly calm in his tone. He and Madam Ida stared one another down for several moments before Dakrind turned to Bryn. "Well, Miss Valetown, it seems we have an accord. You shall have the compass returned to you for a Star-Stone, delivered to Esile City in five days' time."

Bryn hesitated. "I asked for a week's time."

"And I say five days, besides a token of promise that I won't unleash the Wavers here," Dakrind said icily. "Now, the compass."

He stepped forward. Bryn met his eyes as she placed the compass in his outstretched hand. There was no satisfaction there, only an intense desire that chilled her. For a moment she wondered if she had done the right thing.

Then Dakrind's hand closed over the compass, and it was too late to turn back.

"See you in Esile City," she said with a quick nod, then turned and walked away. Behind her, Dakrind shouted an order to his men to return to the *Black Raven*, while the Rylanders retreated in clean, ordered ranks. Bryn let out a tight breath, unable to believe that they had left the confrontation unscathed and alive.

The rain fell harder as she and Robin headed toward the pier. The *Marie* was visible through the dull gray light.

"I thought we had a plan," Robin muttered.

"I do have a plan," Bryn told him. She could sense the nervous tension in his voice. It was a valid concern. She could hardly believe what she had just done.

"Some plan," Robin said dryly. "Give away the compass, hang everyone's life on an impossible task—how exactly do you expect us to find a Star-Stone without the compass, Bryn?"

Bryn reached the pier, trying to push away her anger. Anger at the Crime Rings in general, anger at the doubt in Robin's voice, and anger also at the uncertainty inside herself. The bargain was risky— perhaps too risky. "I'm not the one who's made enemies of both

Crime Rings," she said briskly. "Now I'm trying to fix that—and the least you can do is trust me."

"You think I don't regret that?" Robin stopped—Bryn kept walking, but slowed her pace so she could hear his words. "That decision has already cost too much. Fifteen of my crew—my men—have paid for my poor choice with their lives."

Bryn turned, startled. Robin stood, arms folded over his chest, and didn't meet her eyes. The pain and guilt in his stance made her regret her harsh words. "Your men trust you," she said quietly. "They don't hold it against you. If this works, none of them will have died in vain."

There was a brief silence. Robin finally let out a tense breath. "Very well. Doesn't seem like I have a choice. I just hope you know what you're doing."

Bryn nodded and turned away, before she let her own uncertainty show.

On the far side of the river, visible in glimpses through the fog, a small fleet of canoes waited. The rain made it hard to see the figures inside, but Bryn knew they were full of Wildkid warriors.

Mel had said Aryion had made a plan with the Wildkids—when or how, she had no idea.

They jogged up the gangplank. Three Wildkids stood silently next to the mizzen mast, clearly expecting them. Richard and Matthew were waiting on board too, and looked relieved to see them. "Glad you made it back, Cap'n," Richard said. "Do we have a plan?"

"Do we," Robin muttered. He gestured to the Wildkids. "Where on Orlell did they come from?"

The two sailors looked in the direction he was pointing, then looked back at Robin. "Thought they were part of the plan," Matthew said. "The ranger reassured us that they're on our side."

"Ranger?" Robin repeated, absolutely confused now. He looked at Bryn. "You've teamed us up with a ranger?"

"Sort of," Bryn said uncertainly. "It's part of my plan—the part about the Star-Stone."

"So there actually is a Star-Stone, like you told Dakrind?" Robin asked.

"There might be," came Aryion's voice behind Bryn. "But first, I believe explanations are in order."

26

Questions Answered

The strange little gathering in Robin's cabin reminded Bryn of the meeting they'd had back in Esile City. It shed light on all that had changed since that first day, too. Of the five Dricasters that had begun the venture, she and Robin were the only two left alive, and now they were both branded traitors. Richard and Matthew were the only two sailors that attended the meeting.

In addition to them, there was a young Wildkid woman with black fur who introduced herself as Dusty of the Mara-N'Tell. There were two other young warriors with her—a male with rust-red fur named Nellioh, and a small, silver-coated girl called Graysil who seemed vaguely familiar to Bryn, though she couldn't guess why. They stood in the corner, quietly observing. Mel stood near them, seeming happy to be in their company.

Robin sat at his desk, studying the group for a long moment. "Well," he said finally, breaking the silence. He eyed Aryion carefully. "Where'd you spring from, then? You're not a Dricaster."

"I am a ranger," Aryion said evenly. "My apprentice and I were sent from Caer Sia to locate and apprehend Terrax of Elvengate. The trail has led us here."

Robin frowned slightly, then seemed to understand. "Oh, *you're* the Hummingbird?" He looked between Aryion and Bryn for a moment. "Yes, I can see it now."

Aryion and Bryn glanced at each other. As they were not currently speaking to each other, it made no sense to acknowledge the relationship. Aryion seemed to have sensed that Bryn was in no mood to talk to him. On Bryn's part, she could not put into words the emotions she felt. She could think of nothing to say, and let the silence stretch. But the air between them almost shivered with tension.

"We were sent to find Terrax," Aryion repeated after a pause. "I thought he was in Esile City, but our allies," here he glanced at the Wildkids, "had heard rumors of him being in the south. So we left Esile and traveled here."

"Well, you can bet he'll be back in Esile in a few days," Robin said. "If your sister's deal turns out any good at all."

"What deal is that?" Dusty asked, her face showing interest.

Robin placed his elbows on his desk and looked at Bryn expectantly.

Bryn sighed. "I made a deal that involves both the Dricaster and Rylander Brethrens—hopefully, to keep them off our tails for now. We're going to Esile City, where I've told Dakrind that we'll deliver the Star-Stone to the Dricasters. He wants to use it against Terrax. Then, he'll give the compass to the Rylanders so they can receive their reward."

"No," Mel said flatly. Bryn looked at him, surprised by the finality in his tone. "First of all," Mel said, "the Stone doesn't work like that, and secondly, you can't give Dakrind the Stone."

"We're in a tight place here, kid," Robin said impatiently. "Unless you plan to help us track down another Star-Stone within five days, you have the one we need."

"No," Mel repeated.

"*You're* in a tight place?" Dusty asked Robin incredulously. "Have you seen the state of the rest of Orlell right now?"

Bryn frowned, confused. "What do you mean?"

Aryion answered. "This Stone does more than you think. To you, it might just be another bounty. In truth, it's one of the only hopes for survival we have."

"Against… what, exactly?" Richard asked, sounding intrigued.

"The Ace-Lord. Kahlifis. The Master of Death, or whatever you want to call him," Mel said shortly. "Point is, you can't have the Stone."

Aryion put a hand on his shoulder to calm him and looked at Bryn. "How would that plan help your current situation at all? If you have made enemies of both Brethrens, I doubt they will let you free even after you've fulfilled this bargain."

"I doubt they will," Bryn said. "But I just told you what I told Dakrind. I haven't told you what my actual plan is."

That got everyone's attention. Bryn went on, setting up the scene. "The fact that Dakrind and Terrax are two of the most mistrusting people in Orlell makes it difficult to count on surprise. It's safe to assume they're already expecting us to turn on them. And that's exactly what I intend to do."

"Even though they expect it?" Matthew asked with a frown.

"Yes, because it will distract them from the other part of the plan we'll be up to," Bryn said.

Now everyone looked confused. Bryn continued, trying to place her thoughts in order. "We have five days. We can make it back to Esile City in three. Once back, the Dricaster Brethren will be mobilized in the city and aware of what is happening, so we'll have enough Ringmembers to discourage any counter attack from Terrax' Jenna."

"Not bad," Aryion said wryly, "just one problem. The Dricasters aren't in Esile City."

"Not yet," Bryn said. "They went east to prepare with Dakrind. My theory is that he planned to turn on Terrax in Drynrall. Our taking the compass ruined that scheme. Now, Dakrind will update his men on what has happened at Waypath, and they'll return to Esile City to wait for Terrax and the Stone."

"Do we know where Terrax is?" Mel asked with a frown.

Robin answered. "He's gone back to Port Rylan. He's trying to hire the Rylanders to work for him."

Bryn looked at him, surprised by this statement. "How do you know that?"

Robin nodded back in the direction of Waypath. "John and I met with an… informant while we were buying supplies this morning. Terrax seems to have got wind of the Rylander employer. Whoever this employer is, they want the compass too, and they're paying the Rylanders seven hundred lupin to get it. Now Terrax is trying to bribe the Rylanders to work for him instead, so that he has more people tracking the compass."

"The Rylanders are whipped into wrath against the Dricaster Brethren," Dusty added. "We overheard news on our way west. Hawk Dakrind, it seems, entered Port Rylan and rendered the Rylanders' flagship immobile. I assume that is why the Rylanders were here today."

Bryn raised her eyebrows, interested to hear this. Likely, Terrax had heard that the Rylander employer paid better than he did. He would have to either match or raise the reward to convince the Rylander hunters to give him the compass. "How did your informant know about this?" she asked Robin.

"I'll tell you later," Robin said. "We get to Esile, rally the Dricasters, and then…?"

His words trailed off, prompting her to continue. Bryn hesitated. The fragments of her heart that still screamed for loyalty and servitude to the Dricaster Brethren rejected her plan. For an instant she struggled against herself, but she put the fear aside and managed to finish. "And then… with all the Dricasters together… we inform the Capital."

Everyone stared at her in shock. Even the Wildkids looked surprised. Robin looked stunned. "The Capital?" he repeated finally, as if he had misheard her.

"The Capital has tried to stop the Brethren for decades," Bryn said. "All they need is the location to besiege. We'll blow the Crime Ring's cover and the Council will drive the Dricasters out of Esile."

"Now that's a plan," Aryion breathed. "The Council is already on edge. They believe the Crime Rings intend to overthrow them. They'll probably come and fight the battle for us without a second thought."

Robin looked at Bryn, shaking his head very slowly. "That's the highest form of treason I've ever heard of," he said finally.

"No different than you giving Dakrind those Rylander pins in Drynrall," Bryn pointed out. "The Dricaster Brethren will survive—the Capital won't be able to take them all down. But they'll have to regroup and start afresh somewhere new." She could hardly believe the words she was saying. Robin was right. This was the highest level of betrayal a Ringmember could commit.

"All right," Robin said after a long pause. "All right. So, we set the bears on the bee hive. What about Dakrind's Wavers?"

"I'm still working on that," Bryn admitted.

The long pause was broken by the Wildkid's voice. "We could help," Dusty said, glancing at her warriors. "I heard about your actions in Drynrall, Miss Paya. Whatever your intentions were, you freed eight of our captive Clanmates, one of them my younger sister." She nodded to the young Wildkid with silver fur. Bryn remembered her as the one who had figured out how to unlock the cages. "My people owe you. I have nearly seventy warriors with me on this mission, and we would be glad to take vengeance on the Dricasters."

Bryn felt a flare of hope. A force of Wildkids could mean the difference between survival and death against the Wavers. Yet even as she had that thought, she thought of what such a thing would cause. The Wildkids were not here to become involved in a battle between Crime Rings. Their purpose was far more important—and a fight in Esile City could jeopardize their budding alliance with the humans of Daffodalion.

"I appreciate the offer," she said. "But you know you can't join us in this battle. Fighting Mainlander citizens—even Dricasters—could ruin any chance of joining with your old allies."

Dusty frowned slightly, clearly disappointed to be excluded. Bryn went on. "If what you said earlier is true, and the world is in a tight place, then there's a greater good your warriors are involved in. I don't think this is your battle to fight."

"She's right," Aryion said, putting a gentle hand on Dusty's shoulder. "Any involvement your people have in this could reflect badly on your alliance efforts. We'll take your warriors' help to protect the ship to the coast, but then you have your own orders to follow."

"Look on the bright side," Robin added, as Dusty still frowned. "With the Dricasters involved in a battle in Esile City, your journey north will be much safer than usual. If you're hoping to get to Caer Sia, now is the time."

Dusty still looked disappointed, but she clearly understood they were right. "Very well." She looked at Bryn. "In that case, I think your best option to stop Dakrind's Wavers will lie in the help of the Esile Council. Their forces will be able to stall them while you deal with the compass."

Bryn nodded, knowing getting the Council to help was easier said than done.

"What about Dakrind and the Star-Stone?" Robin asked.

"I don't think that's too hard to figure out," Mel said with a shrug. "Dakrind will need the Stone to be convinced of the plan. I'll take it to him."

"Absolutely not," Aryion said immediately.

"I won't give it away," Mel said, looking hurt that anyone would suspect he would.

"I know you won't. I also fully intend to return north with you in one piece," Aryion said firmly.

"But this plan won't work if they can't stop the Ringleader," Mel said.

"He's got a point there," Robin said, looking thoughtful. "Not only that, we still need the compass to satisfy the Rylanders."

"I can take him the Star-Stone," Mel said. "When the battle starts, I can grab the compass and get away. We can arrest Terrax and give the compass to the Rylanders."

Robin sighed. "As… skilled… as you probably are, kid, that's not going to work. Dakrind will know something's up the minute you arrive."

"What if I went with him?" Bryn asked slowly. "I'll turn in both the Star-Stone and its keeper. He's worth something to the Capital, aren't you?" she asked, the last words directed to the young ranger.

"Probably not the Capital," Mel said, "but Caer Sia, I bet. I did spend most of last year helping them." He was remarkably calm.

Aryion was *not* remarkably calm. "Under no circumstances will you place a ransom on his head, not even as bait for a trap," he snapped at Robin. "You don't understand who he is. You don't understand what the Stone is."

"If you have a better suggestion, ranger, I'm all ears," Robin said. "As it is, this doesn't sound like a bad plan. We won't actually place a ransom on him, we'll just make Hawk *think* we have." He studied Mel in a new light. "How much would you say you'd be worth to Caer Sia, kid?"

"Don't answer that," Aryion said flatly.

Mel shrugged.

"Probably enough to barter with Dakrind for our freedom, at least," Bryn said, catching Robin's trail of thought.

"That doesn't matter, because the ransom won't exist," Aryion insisted.

"Well, it *will*," Robin said patiently. "But only as long as the Esile Dricaster base exists too. When a Crime Ring is upended, it takes months for them to get back on top of details—like keeping track of bounties, for one. There'd be a bounty on your kid for, oh, let's say ten minutes—long enough for Dakrind to erase the debts on the rest of us. When the Dricaster Ring goes down, so does the bounty."

Aryion was beginning to look like a hunted animal backed into a corner. "I don't… we can't… it doesn't matter, then," he persisted. "If you say Mel's bounty will die with the Esile base, so would your debt."

"Well, not quite," Robin said. "Mel's bounty will be gone for good, at least. As for our debt, I'm sure Dakrind will still want us dead either way. But with his base revealed, his Crime Ring in chaos and, likely, most of his fleet incapacitated, he won't be able to do much about it."

"I'll be fine," Mel said cheerfully. "I'll be in and out."

"I think you've been spending too much time with Rygal," Dusty said with a wry smile.

"You have no idea," Aryion told her wearily. He still looked worried.

"I'll keep him safe," Bryn promised him quietly. Aryion met her eyes, fear and uncertainty written in every line of his face. But he finally relented.

"Very well," he said wearily. "You and Mel go, meet with Dakrind and Terrax, and ideally escape with the compass, the Stone, and your lives. Then what?"

"Then Terrax is yours to take," Bryn said. "We'll probably have to fight our way out."

"Probably," Robin echoed with a sigh. "And Dakrind will *probably* have the *Marie* shot with more holes than a block of bad cheese."

They needed more firepower, especially if they were going to successfully escape the Dricaster fleet. That could be an issue.

"If I may, Cap'n," Richard ventured, stepping forward, "as we've already suspended personal morals for now, what with betraying the Dricasters and all…"

"Go on," Robin said.

"Let's commandeer a ship," Richard suggested. "A fast one, one of Dakrind's fleet, so she'll be equipped with cannons. Have the *Marie* anchor right next to her the day before, and take her when her crew goes ashore to assist Dakrind when the fight starts."

Robin folded his arms. "You're thinking the *Scarlet Consort*?"

"Aye, Cap'n," Richard said with a grin. "No better ship in the sea for the job, I can tell you."

Robin finally smiled. "All right, Rich, I like it. You take a third or so of the boys and commandeer the *Consort*, and stay clear of the fight. If things go sour, you might be our only way out of Esile."

"What's to stop Dakrind from shooting the *Scarlet Consort* too?" Aryion pointed out with a frown. "It's not a bad plan, but we'll need more than two ships if we are intending to take down the Dricaster fleet."

"I think there will be more in Esile City," Dusty said. She looked at Aryion. "You mentioned that the Randuins are there now, investigating the Council's actions. Perhaps you can convince them to join the fight."

"It'd be worth a try," Aryion agreed. "If they have a mounted squad of dragon riders, we might stand a chance."

"They might," Bryn said, though she doubted it. The Randuins in Esile City were only investigating possible Jenna. It was unlikely they would have brought dragons along.

"Let's hope this works," Robin told him, "because if not, we'll all be in serious trouble."

Bryn studied the group. They still looked wary and nervous, but excitement lit their faces too. "Well then," she said. "Any other details we're forgetting?"

"Just the matter of the compass," Robin said, looking her in the eye. "If we get it back, we hold onto it. I can arrange for the second employer to pay the Rylanders their reward. That should satisfy them in place of the compass itself."

Bryn frowned slightly, but decided she would ask him about it later.

"In the meantime," Matthew said, "do we have a heading?"

"The *Marie* won't get far like this," Robin said. "We'll have to spend an additional day here to repair her." He looked at Dusty. "I don't suppose you and your warriors would be able to help?"

"Oh, I'm sure we can lend a hand," Dusty said. "You are, after all, escorting the New Blood and the Star-Stone west. I'd say that falls into our best interest as well as yours."

Bryn didn't recognize the term 'New Blood,' but saw Mel look at Dusty with a gratified smile. Aryion looked pleased too.

The others left Robin's cabin. Bryn lingered behind, needing a few questions answered. As soon as everyone had gone, she turned to the captain. "You didn't tell me about the informant."

"No," Robin agreed, "because I'm still trying to figure it out."

"Who was it?"

"Someone working for the Rylander employer. I don't know much." Robin stood, leaning against his desk. "What I do know is that whoever hired the Rylanders is dangerous. Much more so than Terrax. Knowing too much about it could put you in danger." His tone was genuine and sincere. A little of Bryn's anger faded. He had not lied to her—not deliberately, at least. Still, retaining information for her safety only worked so well.

"If this employer is as dangerous as you say, it might be worth informing the person who's protecting you," she said slowly.

A faint smile crossed Robin's face. "All right. I'll tell you, I promise. But let's get this business over with the Dricasters first before we worry about the Rylander employer. Fair enough?"

Bryn thought about insisting he tell her now, but realized he was right. There were more pressing matters to attend to. She nodded.

"Bryn," Robin said, as she turned to go, "I shouldn't have snapped at you. You've done very well. You've kept us alive all this time and I'm grateful for that."

His apology caused the last of her anger to fade. She returned his smile. "You have your crew to watch out for," she said. "You shouldn't blame yourself for those you've lost. I know it's hard." She shrugged sadly. "Part of the reason I've never liked working in teams, actually."

"Well, I suppose this mission has been unusual for both of us," Robin remarked. He stood and strode up the steps.

Bryn followed. They would speak on the details of the plan more later. She needed to think and mull over all the pieces, make sure it was fool proof and every variable had been accounted for.

She would think of that later. For now, she allowed her mind to wander and wonder over who had hired the Rylanders.

PART 3

The Second Employer

27

Protectors

A vague sense of anticipation woke Bryn the next morning. She couldn't place where the sense came from at first, until she remembered. Five days began today. Five days to return to Esile where, if all went well, this entire mess would become an unpleasant memory.

The *Burman Marie* remained docked at the pier in Waypath. The little harbor was almost empty aside from a few small fishing vessels. Nearly all the inhabitants had fled the township. Those who remained were busy in the town, deconstructing the surviving buildings and packing up goods. The town would have to move again, that was inevitable. By nightfall, Bryn guessed, everyone would have cleared out, leaving only the brick ruins and lonely piers.

The *Marie's* stern had sustained four large holes just above the water line. Water sloshed within her lower levels, but there had been no permanent damage to her hull. There were tools and supplies kept aboard for these kinds of situations, which meant the repairs would likely take no longer than a day. Robin seemed optimistic.

Those who were uninjured set to work repairing the ship, directed by Robin. Some of the older Wildkids, who Dusty told them had repaired a wrecked Jenna vessel years ago, joined the work. The beach near the pier swarmed with activity, with men moving to and from the ship carrying armloads of wood planks.

The flooding in the hold of the ship meant that most of their supplies had been ruined. Aryion and Mel went ashore with Matthew and some of the others to hunt and forage.

Bryn was starting to feel useless for the first time the whole journey. She found Robin on shore, cutting more planks with Richard. "How can I help?"

Robin paused, leaning on the saw, then glanced at the ship. "Could you… would you mind taking a look at John? Harry's down with him, but…" He trailed off, concern evident on his face.

"I'll do what I can," Bryn said, and headed back to the ship.

The back corner of the berth deck had been turned into a sort of hospital wing. The wounded lay in their hammocks, which had been lowered to the ground to allow an easier time treating the sailors' injuries. Harry, the ship's doctor, was inside, moving between injured men. He looked up as Bryn approached.

"How are they doing?" Bryn asked.

Harry wiped sweat from his bald head. "Lost three in the night. Most of the injured weren't badly hurt, thank the Light—I patched 'em up yesterday. These eight are recovering, but slowly." He knelt beside John, who lay on his side. The first mate was very still, pale as a ghost. His skin was clammy and hot to the touch, and his eyes flickered weakly.

"Will he…" Bryn started, taken aback by John's condition.

Harry let out a breath. "He's holding out, Miss Valetown. He was coming down with an ailment as we left Drynrall—I think it was the stress of it all that did it. The injury's just pushed him to the edge, and his body's too weak to fight the sickness."

Bryn put a hand on John's forehead, which burned with fever. Harry was right. The injury itself, she could see, was not a mortal wound. He'd been shot by one of Dakrind's pirates. The bullet had hit just under his right collarbone, between his shoulder and neck. Painful, but not fatal.

"You removed the bullet?" she asked, studying the injury. The wound had stopped bleeding, but it was badly swollen, and bruises had spread across his chest.

"No, it passed through," Harry said. "I made sure to remove any cloth or debris while treating it."

Bryn examined the injury, thinking. She'd never treated a bullet wound before, but it seemed like Harry had already done everything that needed to be done. The wound had been cleaned. That was good—she'd seen people die of infection long after being shot.

"Did you disinfect it?" she asked.

"All out," Harry said heavily. "We used the last of the disinfectant after Drynrall, and we weren't able to buy any in Waypath."

"Then we can use whiskey."

Harry raised an eyebrow, but left to fetch it.

"And get some cool damp cloths," Bryn called after him. That would not be difficult. The frigid morning temperatures already threatened to freeze their water supplies.

Harry returned, and they carefully maneuvered the first mate onto his back. His eyes flickered weakly, unfocused and clouded. "This is going to sting," Bryn warned him, not sure if he understood. She doused the wound as gently as she could. John tensed and gave a faint groan, too weak to form any words.

"Hold on," Bryn murmured, her hands trembling. Harry rinsed the wound with water while she laid the cool cloths on John's chest.

The first mate had roused slightly from either the pain or the cold. "The others… all right?" he asked hoarsely.

"Yeah, the others are fine," Harry told him. "They're mighty worried for you, though."

"The captain…" John started to ask.

"He's alive," Bryn reassured him. "The fighting is over. We're repairing the ship now."

John relaxed slightly. Bryn laid a cloth on his forehead and looked at Harry. "I think sleep would be the best thing for him now. Do you have any greenstalk extract?"

Harry frowned. "Might have a little. I'll look."

Greenstalk was dangerous in large amounts, which turned it from a painkiller to a highly addictive hallucinogen. A small amount would cause deep sleep, which was what John needed most now.

Harry returned with the vial and gave John two drops. "Anything else?"

Bryn gave him a small smile—Harry looked almost as worn out

as John. Between cooking, cleaning, and patching up his crewmates, he must be exhausted. "I think that's all for now," she said. "I'll re-bandage the wound. You can go ashore and take a rest."

Harry nodded gratefully and left.

Bryn spread the numbing balm over the injury and fetched a few clean cloths. She could tell the drug was working. John's eyelids were heavy, and his whole body had relaxed. "Harry said… you are going to… turn the Dricasters over," he said groggily.

"Yes. That's the plan," Bryn said.

John laughed softly. "Dricaster traitor. I thought you were… still on their side. I'm sorry."

Bryn was not sure if he was thinking clearly, but his apology was comforting. "That's all right," she said. "I can't exactly blame you. Your job is to protect the crew."

John smiled and nodded, drifting off. "Yes… yes. And you," he said, forcing his eyes open, "your job is to protect the captain… he might not say it… but he thinks highly of you… he truly…"

Bryn applied the bandages, hoping John hadn't noticed how she had blushed. John didn't finish. His eyes were closed, and he breathed deeply.

She bandaged the wound while her mind swirled, wondering over the thousand possibilities that John could have alluded to. Wondering over the strange sensation that seemed to have awakened in her. Wondering over the secrets in Robin's eyes. Wondering, too, over her own response, what she could possibly ever say or do.

"I'll protect him," she told John quietly. She put a hand on his brow—the fever had lessened. Satisfied, she returned above decks.

. . . . . .

Repairs were finished by evening. A brisk northerly breeze tugged at the bundled sails, as though urging the *Marie* to return to sea. Bryn was eager to get going again, but the sailors had spent the entire day repairing the ship and were worn out. She helped Harry prepare supper, and the sailors and Wildkids gathered around the fire on shore for the meal.

John Tailor slept through the entire afternoon. He woke just before supper, and Harry gave him some broth. The fever still lingered, but the color had returned to his face and he seemed a little stronger. He wanted to know their strategy, so Bryn summarized their mission to Esile. He looked impressed and only cautioned against becoming too friendly with the Capital.

"You are still a wanted criminal," he reminded her as he drifted off again. "Be sure you have a safe location to hide when this is all over."

It was good to know John wasn't angry at her anymore. But his words only brought Bryn's attention back to the thought that had filled her mind that first evening in Waypath. Where would she go after this business with the compass was over? She certainly had no home among the Crime Rings, Dricaster or no. She'd seen what years of service to the Brethren had done to her, and she wanted no more to do with it.

But she realized, in that case, her options were severely limited.

She ate her dinner silently, thinking through the plan and watching the interactions on the beach around her. Mel fit right in with the sailors, joking and laughing with the others and listening to Richard's tales. He and Oliver had quickly become friends, and seemed to be having some sort of contest on who could tell the wildest story. Oliver had years of listening and learning from Richard, but it seemed Mel had experienced quite a few of his own adventures.

Aryion sat a little ways from the group near Bryn, his back to a tree, watching his apprentice with a half-smile. Mel had launched into a story about riding a kragon into Caer Sia to drive out invaders, and the crew listened open-mouthed. The young ranger became more and more animated as the story went on, flapping his arms to mimic wings and describing the height so well that even the staunchest sailors turned pale.

"Where'd you pick him up?" Bryn asked quietly, glancing sideways at her brother.

Aryion smiled and looked down. "You might say he picked me up. We were both involved in a mission last year."

"Ah, the quest to join the Shards?" Bryn asked wryly, adding a little dramatic emphasis to the words. "He's already recounted most of the story."

"Yes, that quest," Aryion said with a nod.

There was a moment of silence. There were so many things to say, so many questions to ask, that Bryn was suddenly overwhelmed.

How could any words heal the wrongs of sixteen years? But it was Aryion who spoke first.

"I want to tell you about the Blood Oath," he said quietly.

Bryn looked at him, waiting. She knew about the Blood Oath. It was a promise, taken only under the most solemn of circumstances, for once sworn it could never be taken back. Sworn wisely, it was not always a negative thing. But Aryion had sworn it for vengeance. He had explained everything to Bryn then—about the Oath being an unbreakable vow, about it overruling everything else about one's life, about it becoming a warrior's purpose.

She steeled herself for those excuses now. But what he said was vastly different.

"It was wrong of me to leave you. I was so… angry, after the orc attack. I wanted to make Hagshrub suffer. I swore the Oath on an impulse. I wasn't thinking clearly, and… I am sorry, Lee."

Bryn looked at her hands. "Why didn't you take me with you?"

"Because I thought you would be safer away from me. Taking the Oath brought enemies. I didn't want to put you in danger, or force you to live in fear."

"But you did," Bryn said quietly. "You left. I couldn't protect you. I thought you were dead." Her voice caught, and she looked away to hide the sudden, burning tears.

"I left because I thought it would protect you," Aryion said softly. "I can see now that I was wrong." He placed a hand on her shoulder. "If I could go back and do it over again, believe me, I never would have taken the Oath. I never should have left you. I'm so sorry."

Those simple words cut through the shell of ice that had encased her heart for years, a shell that had forbidden her to feel any anger, any sorrow, any loneliness that she should have felt in response to the wrongs of the past. Feeling these emotions afresh hurt, but it was the right kind of hurt. A freeing sort of pain.

She took a shaking breath and cleared her throat. "You know I would have come with you," she said. "You know I would have come and tracked Hagshrub with you. We could have caught him together. You didn't have to bear the Oath alone."

Aryion looked away, his eyes bright. "I know."

There was a long pause. "You fulfilled the Oath, I assume," Bryn said finally.

"Yes. With help." Aryion glanced at Mel.

"Who is he?" Bryn asked, nodding toward the boy.

"My apprentice," Aryion said. "The one called the New Blood, if the title means anything to you. And currently, the greatest enemy of the Aces."

"The Aces?"

"You remember the stories Mother would tell us? The legends?"

"Some of them," Bryn said. Their mother would tell them tales before bed, allowing their minds to slip into dreams to the sound of her voice.

"Well, many of them weren't just legends. The Ace-Lord, the Stars, the Stones, the prophecies—they're *real*, Lee. As real as you and I."

He smiled slightly. "I know you never believed them. But from what Captain Trelawney has told me of the compass, you can't exactly deny the unbelievable anymore."

"I know," Bryn said. She let out a breath. "Robin told me that the compass can affect you even if you don't believe in it. He said the only way you can avoid those powers is to have something better in you—to hope in the Light." She frowned slightly. "I'm still figuring that out."

"You believe it's true?" Aryion asked.

"Yes," Bryn said, startled to realize she did. If such dark powers were real, she wanted to trust in the Light. She looked at Aryion again. "You mentioned prophecies?"

"Yes. There's one in particular that waits for us back in Caer Sia. We don't know what it holds yet, but we sense that time's running short."

"Before what?"

Aryion looked at her grimly. "Before the war."

Bryn looked at Mel. He had finished telling his story, and was now listening with wide eyes as Oliver spoke of the legend of the Nøkken. The scene of the sailors, their faces lit by firelight, eating and drinking and soaking in the story, was such a peaceful one that she felt a twinge of doubt. What Coonsian war could ever involve them this far south in Daffodalion? How could it affect them all? Even the attack in Caer Sia had been dealt with—the Shards joined, and the Ace-Lord driven back. But Aryion's words made her wonder what sort of power could envelope them all in such a way.

She noticed the Wildkid warriors had risen and were moving away from the camp. Dusty caught her and Aryion's gaze and motioned them toward the beach. They followed, leaving the camp full of enraptured sailors behind.

The Wildkids had gathered on the dock, some of them already seated in their canoes. Robin and Richard were waiting for them.

"We wanted to wish you all farewell and good luck," Dusty was saying as Aryion and Bryn approached.

"You're heading out, then?" Aryion asked.

Nellioh nodded. "Our mission leads us north. There are allies in Coonsia—the Alfona people of the Magno forest, and some of the Elven villages. We'll make our way to Caer Sia eventually, but there are others we need to speak to first."

"Be careful," Bryn warned. "The Dricasters will be busy enough in the next few days, but there are other Crime Rings and dangers in the north."

"We will." Dusty glanced between Bryn and Robin. "Where do the waters take you next, Captain?"

"Oh, you never know," Robin said with an unconcerned shrug. "Right now I'm hoping we can get in and out of Esile City in one piece."

"That would be fortunate," Dusty agreed with a short laugh. She looked at Aryion. "Have you told them of the events in the north?"

"A little," Aryion said.

"Sounds like you Coonsians are prepared to fight this war through," Robin said, looking at Aryion. "Even you and the kid?"

"We must. We all must, for the good of Orlell," Aryion said.

The good of Orlell, Bryn's mind echoed. Such a different mindset than her narrow, selfish view of the Brethren's wishes. Doing something for the good of Orlell called for selflessness, for greater good to prevail, for sacrifice.

It was something that Bryn wasn't sure she could ever bring herself to do.

"It might be safer in the south," she said to Dusty, though she guessed nothing would change the Wildkid's plan. "Your people's lands would be far from the war."

"Maybe for a little while," Dusty said. "But I know the Ace-Lord won't stop with Coonsia. He plans to conquer all of Orlell."

Aryion nodded in agreement. "I'm afraid the future fight will involve everyone, no matter your homeland. There's no neutral side anymore."

His tone had a subtle question there, one that Bryn couldn't answer yet. This was a bigger choice than the decision of where to go after they left Esile. This was a choice of life or death.

"Your crew fought bravely here in Waypath, Captain Trelawney," Joesp said. "We could use men like them. Brave, loyal soldiers."

Robin thought for a moment, his arms folded over his chest. "I need to do what's best for my crew," he said after a long pause. "I'm not sure getting involved in a war with the Aces is the best thing for them now."

"I understand that," Dusty said with a slight nod. She glanced up, studying the moon's position in the clear winter sky. "Well, we must be off. Good luck to you all."

"Good luck, Dusty. And thank you," Aryion said.

Dusty and her brothers shook each of their hands in turn, then climbed into a canoe. The watchers on the pier watched as the line of canoes began to row upriver. For one moment, the moonlight lit them enough for Bryn to see Dusty, looking back at them with a slight smile and a waving hand.

Then the shadows fell over them again, and the Wildkids sailed upriver under the cloak of night.

28

Days At Sea

As the *Burman Marie* reached the coast the next morning, they saw the Dricaster fleet again.

The ships passed by a mile or so from the river mouth, heading northwest for Esile City. The *Marie* hung back in the shadows of the Westerlyn River while the crew watched the fleet move past. Bryn stood by Robin with an arrow on her string. "Those the same ships?" she asked, though she already knew the answer. Even at a distance, she recognized most of them.

Robin was peering through his spyglass. "They are," he answered her after a few seconds. "Heading back to Esile, looks like."

"That's good though, right?" Mel said. The young ranger clung to the ropes with Oliver, both of them watching the distant ships sail past. "We want the Dricasters all together in Esile City."

"It's not bad," Robin said, but he didn't elaborate. Bryn could guess what he was thinking. Dakrind had taken Wavers out of Port Rylan, but there was no way he could have fit them all on the *Black Raven*. That was why he'd ordered the other Ringmembers to assist him.

If each of those ships carried a hundred Wavers on board…

Bryn didn't want to finish the thought. She hoped instead that

Dakrind had abandoned the plan with the Wavers now that their bargain had been made.

It was a weak hope, but the best one she had.

They left the river mouth behind and started out for Esile in the wake of the Dricaster fleet. Bryn spent the afternoon pouring over maps of Esile City with John, who had recovered greatly overnight. Richard offered input too, and the map of Esile City was soon covered in notes marking strategic positions and dangerous streets. Bryn usually made plans like this before beginning an assassination mission. Any variables had to be eliminated. But this time the stakes were higher. She was responsible not only for her own life, but for Aryion's, and Mel's, and Robin's, and the entire crew of the *Marie*.

Aryion joined them below decks, and she showed him the schematics of the city. "These are the guard barracks," she told him, circling a building on the eastern side of town. "I'm assuming all the soldiers the Council sent for will be here. After you alert the Council, I'd say this is the best place to plan your attack."

Aryion stroked his beard thoughtfully. "We met with the captain-of-guard when Mel and I were there. How many soldiers should we expect to be there?"

"Three hundred, maybe more," Bryn said. Three hundred soldiers against the entire Dricaster Brethren and however many Wavers Dakrind had brought into the fight. That could be a problem.

Aryion didn't bring that up. "We'll have to evacuate the waterfront area," was his only concern. "Most likely the Dricasters will flee into the city once the Capital seizes their ships. I don't want them to slip away amid the townsfolk."

"Good. Make sure you do it before the fight starts. The town guard can help with that," Bryn said.

She tried to reassure herself. They had a plan, a good one. Even Aryion had warmed up to it, and he seemed confident that it would work.

That didn't ease Bryn's nerves, though. She tried to appear calm and collected, more for the sake of her brother than anyone else. He was entrusting the protection of his apprentice to her for a time, and she wanted him to trust her.

Mel seemed calm enough. Bryn had been skeptical of him when he had first arrived, but the boy had impressed her. He was sure of his actions, kind to everyone, so cheerful that even the most irritable sailors would smile in his presence. And he was eager to help. He joined Oliver in his duties, helped Harry make meals, and would have taken turns rowing if he'd been able.

Before supper, he tracked Bryn down in the berth deck to go over the plan again. "We shouldn't expect Terrax to act predictably," he informed her gravely, his young face serious. "He's been after the Star-Stones for years now. I don't know what he'll do when he finds out we've brought one into Esile—he'll probably turn on Dakrind as soon as he learns about the Stone."

"I can understand that," Bryn agreed. She remembered Terrax' calculating eyes, his unpredictable manner in Drynrall, and shivered.

"You faced Terrax before?" she asked.

Mel nodded. "Yep, about a year ago. He was trying to get a different Star-Stone then."

Bryn raised an eyebrow. "But you beat him?"

"Sort of," Mel said. "He retreated after the Darkness turned up."

Mel had regaled the sailors with the story of Drisilas and the Darkness earlier that day. While the story seemed far-fetched, Mel was quite serious, and Bryn could no longer doubt him. "You've fought Terrax recently, then," she said. "What do you expect he'll do?"

"That's what I'm trying to figure out," Mel said. He leaned against the bench, his brow furrowed, fidgeting with the hilt of his dagger the same way Aryion did when he was thinking hard.

Bryn hid a smile. "I'll bet you're right," she said after a pause. "About Terrax turning against Dakrind. They might be working together, but they aren't allies. There's a very good chance they'll turn on each other the moment the Stone is in Esile."

"Maybe they'll both finish the other off, then," Mel said optimistically.

"Maybe," Bryn mused. Dakrind against Terrax—that would be an interesting fight. She had no idea who would win.

Harry appeared from the kitchen and announced that dinner was ready, and the galley quickly grew noisy as the sailors came below decks.

"The main thing to remember," Mel said as they got their plates of food, "is that Terrax is smart. He'll have a plan to deal with us, and with Dakrind, probably. The sooner we can figure that plan out, the better. Aryion always says that information is more valuable than fighting skills—if you know what your enemy is thinking, you'll have a better chance of beating him."

"Sounds smart," Bryn said. That was something their father used to say, she thought with a smile.

She ate her supper in silence. It grew stuffy below decks after a while, and she headed up to get some air. Standing on deck, the soft northerly breeze refreshed her weary mind. A thousand stars twinkled above the water.

"Fine night out," Robin commented behind her. He stood leaning against the tiller, finishing his meal. From somewhere deep in the darkness, a haunting melody began, so faint Bryn wondered if she had imagined it. She threw a glance at Robin, who smiled. "The Nøkken," he said. "They're singing to the Stars."

Bryn stared across the water, listening to the eerie voices. Wilder than a human's song, like the Jenna warcries, but this was a gentler, quieter sound. The song tugged at her heart and whispered words in an ancient language. At last it faded away, leaving only the faint echoes. Her thoughts returned to the present.

"What can you tell me about the Rylander employer?" she asked finally. She had put off this question thus far, trying to focus on each day's plan instead. This moment of quiet felt like the opportunity to discuss it.

Robin thought for a moment. "I can't tell you everything yet.

Not because I don't trust you," he added, as Bryn started to protest, "but because this is a dangerous business. So dangerous that even knowing it might get me killed later."

"By whom?" Bryn asked.

"By the one who hired the Rylanders." Robin stepped nearer to her and lowering his voice. "Here's what I can tell you. The Rylanders were contacted by an anonymous source who placed a bounty of seven hundred lupin on the asset, either to deliver the compass, or bring proof of its destruction."

Bryn frowned, startled. "Destruction?" she repeated. "Why would they want it destroyed?"

"That's what I'm still trying to figure out," Robin said truthfully. "For whatever reason, the employer wants the compass destroyed. Which, in truth, might be a better course of action than letting anyone keep it."

"I thought you wanted to keep it," Bryn said slowly.

"I did at first. I didn't believe the stories about the Wavers," Robin admitted. "After seeing what we did in Port Rylan, I knew the compass was bad news. Whatever magic gives it its powers, that's not something we want to mess with. I'd rather destroy it than hand it over to Dakrind."

Bryn looked away, embarrassed. "You know that was the only way he would have agreed to the deal."

"Yes, I know that now. I just wish you would have told me before. It would have reassured me that you're still on my side."

Bryn sighed. "After everything that's happened, you have to know that I'm on your side."

"I know that now," Robin said again. "I didn't really believe it until you brought up using the Capital against the Dricasters. That showed me that you meant it."

There was a pause. "I was wanting… to ask you something," Robin said at length.

His voice held a different note than Bryn had heard before. She looked at him curiously, waiting for him to continue.

"After we get out of Esile," Robin said slowly, "after we beat Dakrind and hopefully escape free… what do you plan to do?"

Bryn gave a slow, uncertain shrug. "I'm still working on that. I suppose I don't exactly have a place anymore."

"Did your brother talk to you?"

"Yes, he and Dusty want to recruit us into Coonsia's war."

Robin laughed shortly. "He brought it up to me again today. He asked me what you thought of it, and I told him to ask you."

Bryn frowned, puzzled. "Why'd he ask you what I think?"

One could have heard a pin drop in the silence that followed. Robin stared at the toes of his boots. "I think… he thought that we are… that is, that you and I are on… friendlier terms than reality."

"Oh."

"Silly thought, I told him." Robin reddened.

"Yes," Bryn said, forcing a smile. "Don't, ah, think anything of it. He's always been like that."

"Ah."

"A… silly thought, you told him?"

"Yes. Not that you are—silly, I mean—just the suggestion that we—that we are—" Robin gestured vaguely with his hands and shrugged.

"Of course," Bryn said. She had never seen him act so shy and embarrassed—it was quite different from his usual swagger. She was glad it was dark out. Had it been lighter, Robin would have seen that her face was as red as his own.

"I, ah, talked to John," she said instead, then regretted bringing that up because it reminded her of what John had started to say in his fevered state the day before: *He might not say it, but he truly…*" but John had gone to sleep before finishing, leaving Bryn wondering what on Orlell he had been about to reveal. Here was the opening— the best chance she would have to ask Robin if he knew what John had been about to say. More importantly, to know if her guess was true. But maybe it was better to not, because she didn't know how she'd respond to his answer.

"I talked to him today, too. He told me he approves your strategy," Robin said. "And he said he apologized to you, and I told him good for him."

Another awkward pause. "Was that… all you were going to ask me?" Bryn asked finally.

Robin let out a short breath. "No. I was going to offer you a job here on the *Marie*, in case you're undecided after our business in

Esile is over. You could be our… our battle leader or something."

Bryn smiled slightly. "I'll think about it. I don't know if I really fit in here—this whole team thing is still new to me."

"Of course." Robin stared at the ground.

"Besides, you'd… you'd probably all get tired of me," Bryn added, forcing a laugh.

Robin said nothing to that, which gave Bryn all the answer she needed. She could not explain why her chest felt so tight, why her breath suddenly came short, why she felt so tense.

They were only about a pace apart. He was looking out at the moonlit waves. The silver light reflected off the dark water, lit his face, filled his eyes.

Common sense fought with curiosity, and for the first time in Bryn's life, curiosity won. "Why are you asking me this?" she asked softly. "Did you think I'd…"

She let the sentence trail off. Robin looked up and met her eyes. For a fraction of a second, the light showed his every emotion. Worry, sorrow, pain… and something else, something she told herself she must be imagining.

Then his face was impassive again. He took a deep breath. "I just… wanted to know what you'd planned is all. If you need a safe place to go to ground after we take down the Dricasters, know that the *Marie* will always welcome you."

"Well… thank you," Bryn said. She turned away before she said anything more, asked any more questions that came with such complicated answers.

To make friends was already difficult for her. To care for someone again—truly care for someone—came painfully. Years of loss, of hurt, of betrayal had hardened her heart to any such emotion. It was the same reason she had avoided working with others until now. They might be a team, but only some of them would survive. That was the brutal nature of her job.

And those were Ringmembers, people she barely knew yet felt such guilt for their deaths. What about people she loved? She had lost her parents. She had lost friends when she had left Valetown years before. She had lost Aryion—now that she had him back, she felt afraid to allow herself to love and care again.

And Robin…

No, she thought as she lay in her hammock late that night, no, she could no longer dismiss those feelings as concern for his well-being. It had long since turned into something else. Yet to acknowledge it, to act on it—that came with a vulnerability and a terrible fear that once she did, she would lose him too.

The horrors she had experienced at the hands of the orcs that killed her parents had hardened her to the point that she was afraid to grow close to anyone. Afraid to form any sort of attachment or relationship with anyone. That fear of potential loss lent itself to the doubts about her newfound feelings for Robin Trelawney.

• • • • • •

Morning brought little relief to her conflicted feelings, but the activities of the day made it easier to hide them. The wind remained steady, blowing north. The *Marie* had to tack into the breeze, moving west in a zig-zag pattern. The going felt painfully slow.

Bryn tried to distract herself from her growing worry about whatever waited in Esile City. She had collected some wood while they were in Waypath, and set to work making new arrows. She found a stash of Coonsian broadheads in the hold of the *Marie* (John said they had come from the same place they had acquired the firearms.) Bryn sharpened and polished the rust until the steel was sharp and battle-ready.

Once the arrows were done, Bryn fulfilled her promise to teach Oliver to shoot. The cabin boy had acquired a bow after the battle in Waypath, and he and Bryn set up a few targets on the wall of the berth deck. Mel joined them—he was a solid swordsman, but his archery skills were sadly lacking.

"Never was your strong suit, was it," Bryn couldn't help remarking to Aryion. He laughed—a sound she realized she had missed, and it made her laugh too.

She instructed both boys in archery for a few hours. There was only one bow for them to share, since Bryn's was too heavy for them to learn on. Oliver and Mel took turns. By the end of the practice, the wall of the berth had multiple dents and gashes left by stray arrows. But the targets were pierced and bore the signs of successful shots, too.

Mostly, though, Bryn spent that day with Robin.

He remained at the wheel, guiding the ship west. The weather was cold and clear, a bright sun setting before them and painting the western sky red and orange.

"Good sign," Robin said, nodding to the sunset. "Now, if the sky's red in the morning, that means there's bad weather coming. But red at evening is a good sign."

He did most of the talking. He talked about the *Burman Marie*, how he had won her in a race with a Liznee captain—"Believe it or not," he said with a crooked grin. He talked about growing up in Cattrick Fief, a coastal town on the northwestern tip of Daffodalion. He talked about crewing the *Marie* with only John and Matthew, who had worked the docks in Cattrick Fief with him when they were boys. He talked about spending weeks fighting through a storm, and the relief when the sky turned clear again. But it was a short lived relief, he added wryly, because the next few days were spent repairing the *Marie*.

"She's a strong one, you know," he said, patting the tiller affectionately. "She's always willing to keep going. Even with holes in her deck and her sails in ribbons, you patch her up and she'll keep at it."

And Bryn sat and listened in a comfortable silence. Neither of them talked about the future, about difficult choices to come or the adversaries they must defeat. In fact, Bryn realized, it was the first normal conversation they'd had at all—nothing relating to compasses or dark magic or bounties.

Night fell. The driving wind made it unwise to anchor at sea, so Robin brought them to the shore a few hours after sunset to rest.

They built a large fire near the tree line, out of the wind, and had a hearty meal. Matthew brought out his lute, and struck up song after song.

Bryn sat next to Robin, staring into the fire. Aryion sat across from her, listening to the songs. Mel dozed off, the cat on his lap, his head on his mentor's shoulder. Matthew strummed the quiet chords to the tune about the *Red Canary*.

The coming struggles felt far away. Even if this day would be her last, Bryn was grateful for it.

Far across the sea, the haunting voices of the Nøkken filled the air, their song accompanying the lute as darkness settled.

29

Esile Waiting

Bryn took the dawn watch with Richard the following morning, so they both saw the fiery red sunrise. The beauty of it, and the comforting way it warmed their backs held a deceiving calm. But she remembered what Robin had said the day before about red skies at sunrise, and felt a stir of unease.

Richard stood with his arms folded, his pipe gripped between his teeth. "Don't like the looks of that," he murmured, glancing back the way they'd come.

Bryn studied the red-orange sky. To their right, angled north slightly, she could see an ominous wall of clouds scudding toward the tip of the Horn, as though they were amassing for confrontation too. The *Burman Marie* would probably round the Horn before the storm reached it, but if they hoped to retreat back the same way, the weather could be a problem. By the size of the storm clouds, she guessed it would sweep inland too.

The sun cleared the eastern horizon, hovered for a few minutes above the sea, and was then shrouded behind clouds. The sudden chill and hazy darkness turned Bryn's unease to worry. As the *Marie* rounded Esile's Horn and the smoky outline of the city came into view far, far across the water, she had the uncomfortable sensation that they were sailing into the open jaws of a great beast.

The crew worked quickly as they rounded the Horn. Robin moved to the tiller, his fingers tapping the wheel as he studied the distant city. He let out a slow breath. "Right, then." He turned to Aryion, who stood silent and hooded behind him. "I'll have Matthew row you to shore. Go to the Esile Council and do whatever you have to to convince them to help—we need the Council behind us for the soldiers to join us."

Aryion nodded and looked at Bryn. "You are certain the Dricaster's base is still in the same place?"

"The hat shop on Third Street," Bryn said. "They shouldn't have any reason to move it. The secret door is behind the second bookshelf on the right."

"Good." Aryion moved to join Matthew as the crew lowered the rowboat. He gripped Mel's hand and looked his apprentice in the eye. "Be safe and be smart. I'll find you once the Capital soldiers attack the Dricasters."

"I will. You be careful too," Mel added.

The tall ranger nodded shortly and swung over the rail to join the second mate in the boat.

Bryn had spent most of last night running through every aspect of their plan in her mind, hoping to catch any errors or details they had overlooked. She realized one now, and turned to Robin. "I think Dakrind will try to create a diversion, so we have to be smart. Try to involve the townspeople as little as possible—keep the fight in the harbor. If we bring the battle to Esile City, any civilian deaths will be at our hands."

"Good point," Robin said with a half smile. "I'll add it to my list of things to remember today."

"Stay in the harbor, get the *Scarlet Consort*, and stay alive," Bryn listed off. "That's not too long of a list."

He smiled, but his eyes showed his nervousness. "Easy enough, isn't it, Bryn."

Bryn had noticed he only ever called her by her first name if he was either irritated or worried. She guessed the latter. But what did Robin have to worry about? He wasn't the one going to face Hawk Dakrind.

"Everything all right?" she asked, keeping her voice low.

Robin looked at the approaching harbor. "Your plan to involve the Capital is a good one. But let's not forget… this is Hawk Dakrind we're dealing with. I don't think he'll turn us in to the Council, but I'm willing to bet he's got some other scheme to work against us."

Bryn nodded slowly. "He'll have the Dricasters."

"He'll have the Dricasters and Light knows what else," Robin said. "All I'm saying… be ready for anything."

Something about the way he said this caught Bryn's attention. It sounded like he spoke less about Hawk Dakrind. Between the words she read a message: *Trust me, Bryn.*

She would have to. It was the only way the plan might work.

"I'll be careful," she said. "Are you with me?"

"Always," he said, and guided the *Marie* into the harbor.

Bryn scanned the other ships in the harbor. Seven or eight Capital warships, the green and violet banner snapping in the wind from their masts. But they weren't the only ones. The entire Dricaster fleet had returned.

She told herself it was a good thing the Dricasters were here. Hopefully they'd all be settled in their den, resting from the long voyage, and Dakrind would brief them on new tasks.

But the way the ships seemed to stand at attention, the way their crews nodded shortly to the *Marie's* sailors, the ominous silence blanketing the harbor like snow… it seemed dreadfully like a waiting army.

. . . . . .

The secretary looked up in clear shock as Aryion entered the Council Hall and watched as the ranger approached.

Aryion barely acknowledged him, only strode down the long hallway, his cloak billowing from his shoulders, a half-smile playing on his face in satisfaction of the plan to come.

"Good morning to you," the secretary called to him, before he could throw open the doors to the meeting room. "I, ah, assume you'd like to meet with the Council?"

"A good assumption," Aryion said, "but not quite right. I would not *like* to meet with the Council. I am *going* to meet with the Council."

And with that, he flung open the heavy doors.

The secretary leapt to his feet and rushed after him as he entered the meeting room, protesting frantically. "Sir—sir—I beg your pardon—you can't just—"

Aryion ignored him entirely, turning his attention to the people in the room.

All eleven Council Members stared at him with startled eyes. All were men, all easily over seventy years old, most of them with long gray or white beards and sluggish faces. Two of them were sipping wine. Tobacco smoke hung heavy in the air. Another man, tall and burly and wearing a uniform, stood before them, giving some sort of report.

From what Aryion had heard, the Councilors had been nervous and on edge before, when the Ringmembers had vanished from Esile. But that fear had evidently faded now that the Dricaster ships were back in their proper places. Aryion wished he had considered that. The Esile Council never worried over the crime in the city—it was the Crime Rings' business and that was the way things were. As long as no threat was posed to the Council, no thought was given to stopping the Dricasters. This would make convincing them to help that much harder.

One of the Councilors squinted at him. "What do you think you're doing, mister?"

The panicking secretary took Aryion's elbow, trying to lead him back out. Aryion pulled away, knowing he had to speak fast. "Gentlemen.

I come with urgent news regarding the Dricaster Brethren and an uprising against the Daffonic Crown. I have reason to believe that the Crime Rings are even now assembled in preparation for battle. It is my firm recommendation that you evacuate the harbor area and prepare counter attack as soon as possible."

He watched their faces as he spoke. He hoped his words would rouse them, startle them—something. What he didn't expect to see was the disinterest and obvious doubt.

"And who, pray, are you?" the Councilor nearest him asked dryly.

Aryion bowed shortly, rankled. "Aryion Paya, the Hummingbird, sir. Ranger of Coonsia."

"Of Coonsia," one of the other Councilors echoed doubtfully.

"Seems they've finally got their business back in order, have they?" the first Councilor asked. "Have you come to negotiate the profit we lost while they were… how did they put it… 'occupied'? Tell your king that we require full compensation for our losses during that time. We request—"

"I've not come about money," Aryion said, fighting to curb his rising anger. The jibe about the occupation and their disdain over what had happened in Caer Sia filled him with fury.

"Excuse the intrusion, good Councilors," the secretary stammered awkwardly. "I couldn't stop him—the guards let him in—"

"I've already sent your guards to set a perimeter around the Council building," Aryion interrupted. "I was told that Captain Jackson is not on duty today."

"He's been dismissed," another Councilor informed him. "Discharged from duty for disrespect to the Council."

"He's what?" Aryion echoed in disbelief. But he could guess what had happened. The Council had found out about Captain Jackson giving Aryion and Mel information. They'd dismissed him before he shared any more secrets or opinions.

"A perimeter will not be necessary," said a third Councilor. He wore a finely embroidered jacket and seemed to be in charge. "We have received news only an hour ago that the Dricaster Brethren have returned and have no intents of hostility against the Council."

Not against the Council, Aryion thought. And then he understood. The trouble with the Dricaster Crime Ring, every ounce of illegal activity here, was enough to get the Councilors replaced and cause the Capital to launch a formal inquiry. As long as the business remained secret, though, the Council could get away with sharing profits. And if someone had reassured the Council that they were safe, they had no reason to report the Dricasters to the Capital.

Someone had got here before him. Someone had worked out some kind of deal with the Council.

"I expect this news came from a reliable source?" he asked coldly.

"Oh, a gentleman of great importance," the lead Councilor said vaguely. "The Dricasters were away on some business in Waypath, that was all."

Waypath. That was a secret town, an outlaw lair. The Council wouldn't know about Waypath... unless someone had told them.

Dakrind.

Aryion stood for a moment, absolutely at a loss. They needed the Council's support. The *Burman Marie* was counting on it, Bryn and Mel were counting on it. He studied the faces again, his desperation mounting. All he saw was the same doubt, the same distrust, the same indifference.

In every face but one.

The burly man who had been standing when he'd first arrived met Aryion's gaze. The man was taller than he was, his face weathered and bearded. His uniform, Aryion saw now, was more than simple formality, made of plated leather. Subtle armor. This was a warrior. A crest adorned the left breast of his jerkin—a holly leaf, with a vertical sword.

"I would recommend you listen to this ranger, good Councilors," the man said mildly, studying Aryion carefully. "It's unwise to dismiss such a report so quickly without investigation."

Aryion was studying the crest on the man's uniform, trying to place it. Flags and crests ran through his mind—not the Capital's colors, but not Coonsia's either—farther east—

He stared at the crest for a few more moments before he finally connected it to what it stood for. The green holly leaf, the silver sword—that was the crest of the Randuin Order.

Warriors from the east, the Randuins were highly trained, protecting Daffodalion's borders from the Jenna. They had come to Esile to investigate a report regarding Jenna—a false report, Aryion was certain of now—but they had stayed to investigate the activity of the Council. Jenna or no, he knew they'd be interested to know about the Dricasters and their business partners. The main purpose of the Randuin Order was to protect the people of Daffodalion. Most importantly, the Randuins answered not to a baron or a Council, but directly to the Daffonic Crown.

"We were well assured of our safety, Commandant Daeva," one of the Councilors said briskly.

"Assured, but not confirmed," the Commandant pointed out. "Dricasters are loyal to themselves, not to the Esile Council… unless you have more to tell me."

The Councilors hesitated, looking nervously at each other.

"This is not your sector, Randuin," the lead Councilor snapped, finally finding his voice. "We appreciate your aid. But as you can see, there are no Jenna in Esile City, so you had best be on your way. You are excused. As for you, Hummingbird," the Councilor turned steely eyes to Aryion, "your report has been invalidated. Good day to you."

The Randuin Commandant slipped out of the room with a short nod. Aryion hesitated, not sure what to do for a moment. The Council would not help. Dakrind's promise had satisfied them, and they couldn't care less what happened to the civilians of Esile City.

The solution was clear. If the Esile Council would not help, he must look elsewhere.

He turned and strode out of the door, leaving the Councilors and the stammering secretary in the room, and entered the main hall. "Commandant?"

The tall warrior was halfway down the hall, and turned with a slight frown. "Yes?"

Aryion reached him and took a breath. "I understand you are here seeking Jenna?"

The Randuin Commandant straightened, his face serious. "Indeed we are, though we've had very little success. As far as I can tell, there are no Jenna in Esile City."

"Not yet," Aryion said.

The Randuin's bearded face went from serious to suspicious. "How do you know this?"

Aryion met his gaze. "I have news from several first-hand witnesses that an enemy to both Caer Sia and the Daffonic Crown has hired Jenna warriors. Terrax of Elvengate. He's formed an alliance with the Dricaster Brethren."

Commandant Daeva raised an eyebrow. "First-hand witnesses, you say?"

"Yes, sir. Now, I must beg your aid. It is my duty to see that the populace and country is protected, and if the Esile Council will not do it, then I must ask for your assistance."

. . . . . .

Bryn paused right outside the door that led down into the hidden lair of the Dricasters and looked at Mel. "All set?"

The boy nodded. Bryn had bound his hands behind his back with a special kind of knot that came free if Mel tugged a strand. She figured she would be doing most of the fighting, if it came to that, but it would be important to have Mel ready to fight too.

Bryn took a deep breath, squared her shoulders, and descended down the stairs.

She kept her eyes straight ahead, on the door to Hawk Dakrind's office. She gripped Mel's shoulder in one hand, while the other brushed the bow slung at her shoulder. It took every ounce of her willpower not to scan the room for trouble or stare at any Ringmembers. She must appear calm. She must appear confident.

Most importantly, she must appear absolutely in control of the situation.

"There's no one here, Bryn," Mel whispered.

Bryn drew herself out of her focus and swept her eyes around the room. The hall was completely deserted. Tables had been swept clean of dishes and belongings. The banner had been taken down.

The Dricasters were not here.

"A pleasure as always, Miss Valetown," came a cold voice.

Bryn turned slowly. What she saw made her stomach lurch.

Hawk Dakrind sat at a table in the shadows, the compass dangling from his hand like a pendulum. His amber eyes were strangely dim, like a pane of dirty glass. They met Bryn's gaze dully, empty of all life, bottomless pools with dark circles. It was like looking at a wax replica of a person, it was like looking at…

"Wavering isn't so bad," Dakrind said almost lazily. "You get used to sleepless nights and tasteless drink. The power of the compass makes you so much stronger. It would be interesting to see what such a thing could do to an already powerful warrior." He smirked.

Bryn fought to keep her voice casual. "Where are the others?"

"They are engaged at present," Dakrind said shortly. "I assume you came to fulfill our bargain."

Mel threw a quick glance up at Bryn—he clearly realized something was off. Bryn gathered herself in an instant and nodded, pressing forward with the plan. "Yes. I've brought the Stone, as promised. And I've brought something else, if you care to extend our deal."

Dakrind's fevered eyes glittered with interest. Bryn could hardly believe this was the same man she had faced only five days ago in Waypath. That Dakrind had been frightening, but with a natural sort of power. This man was a horrific shadow of what had been, a shell filled with the same darkness that powered the compass.

The same darkness that had powered the Jewel.

She pulled out the Blue Stone. The soft blue light filled the room, so pure and gentle that it soothed her nerves slightly. "Here is the Stone. I have also brought its keeper—Mel Smallbutton, known as the New Blood. You will find he is worth much to Caer Sia, more than enough to pay off the debt owed by Captain Trelawney and myself."

She pushed Mel forward—not hard enough hurt, but hard enough to sell the story. Mel scowled back at her and squirmed slightly, playing the part of a defeated and angry prisoner.

Dakrind stared at the Stone for a long moment. In the pause, Bryn saw the light reflect off his eyes, cutting through the deadness that filled him. Then the moment passed. Dakrind squinted at the blue light, an ugly expression coming over his face. "Put that away," he snapped. "I accept the Stone in exchange for the compass. But I do *not* agree that a Coonsian whelp is worth as much as my hatred for you and Trelawney."

"Well… let me offer something else," Bryn ventured, stalling for time. This was bad. There was no way she and Mel would both get out of here—even less likely that they would escape with the Stone and the compass.

Dakrind stood so quickly the bench lurched back from the table. "No, Miss Valetown. The Stone is mine. The compass is yours. I allow you to walk away with your life, however long it lasts after the Brethren comes after you."

"I don't accept," Bryn said, taking a half step back. "Our deal is valid only on the condition of our canceled debts."

"Then you should have included that in the original bargain," Dakrind sneered. "It seemed you overlooked that part of it. Much as you overlooked the fact that I have great influence with the Esile Council."

A cold fear gripped Bryn's heart. Mel looked back at her, alarm on his face. Dakrind noticed and chuckled. "And I assume you planned for the boy to snatch the Stone from me after you had given it over? Fool. Betraying your Brethren is bad enough, but I thought you had more sense. *I* went to the Council only this morning. *I* assured them of their safety—fat, pompous fools, they were easy to flatter and deceive. *I* shall kill Terrax myself and rid the Mainland of those Jenna filth. And when the Stone is mine, *I* shall raise an empire of Esile."

Bryn looked into Dakrind's maddened eyes. "Even with Terrax' outlaws and the Dricasters," she said slowly, "you know that won't work. The Capital will come and kill you all. The Ringmembers will be outnumbered."

"Not anymore," Dakrind said smoothly. "Not with the Wavers on my side."

He raised the compass and smiled, and Bryn's blood ran cold.

"They were easy to gather, with the compass' powers drawing them close," Dakrind continued. "Their minds may be rotted, but they are still mortal, and thus gullible. They will do as I command, and once they have served their purpose, I will be rid of them for good."

Bryn looked into the Ringleader's emotionless eyes. Aryion had told her about the Hazes, who had come to Coonsia many years ago. He had said the dark spell Safacon had placed on them heightened their strength and skills. But the spell had also enhanced everything dark about a person, amplified it.

As she looked at Hawk Dakrind, she realized that was what the compass had done to him. The Waver had always been within him. His evil glared in her face, exposed, obvious. He glanced back at a side door and called out. "Varic?"

A Ringmember appeared, stumbling slightly, his eyes holding the same dull light as Dakrind's. "Aye, sir?"

"Summon the Wavers," Dakrind said. "And send for Terrax."

"That will not be necessary," a cold voice said from the doorway. Terrax entered the room, staring at Dakrind with hate. Behind him came a large group of Jenna warriors, their dark eyes gleaming in anticipation of the fight.

The Ringmember Varic left the room without a second thought. Thunder rumbled outside, and the wind picked up as the storm swept inland. Bryn looked at the two men staring one another down, at Mel whose face was a mix of fear and fury, at the compass gripped in Dakrind's fist.

Then, from the window to her left, she heard the first of the screams, and saw the first wisps of smoke.

30

Esile Burning

At the first signs of fire, the clock tower struck one, signaling the Jenna and Ringmembers into battle.

It was the Jenna who had started the fire, likely at Terrax' command, Aryion guessed. Jenna warriors streamed from their hiding places in the shadowy buildings, armed to the teeth. Several shops and an oil refinery directly downhill from the soldiers' barracks were ablaze. As Aryion watched, the whale oil ignited with a *whoosh* and the harbor-facing windows exploded in a shower of glass.

This brought the Jenna forward, eager to attack, and the surprise of the townsfolk turned into panic when they saw them. Esile City was far enough west that it had been decades since any Jenna had posed a threat here, but they were not so far south as to have not heard of the devastation of the Kamon battle months before. People screamed and fled and fell before the Jenna warriors, trying to escape as the invaders ran through the streets in a storm of slashing swords and blood-curdling war cries.

But the Jenna did not have the city to themselves for long. Despite the gray midday light, the appearance of Terrax' Jenna mercenaries brought the true rulers of Esile City out of their lairs.

Ringmembers poured from their ships in the harbor, appeared from taverns, leapt out of secret hiding places and drain covers like rats, all moving swiftly to engage the Jenna. Another crew of pirates disembarked from the *Black Raven*, moving purposefully into the city.

With them came the Wavers.

As opposed to the lurking shadows they had been in Port Rylan, the Wavers were organized now, electrified by the proximity of the compass. They surged among the Ringmembers, who drove them into the city like a herd of wild animals. They outnumbered the Ringmembers at least five to one, but any thought of turning on their captors had been driven away by the desperate desire to gain the compass.

Aryion stood on the balcony of the tower next to the barracks, looking down the hill and watching as the throng of Wavers approached. Dakrind had been busy, he thought. The hordes of Wavers streamed into Esile City like ants. Bryn's guess had been right. Dakrind had used his entire fleet to carry the Wavers. They must have gone south, along the coast, capturing Wavers on the way to use in battle.

He was not sure if Dakrind could control them. Kado had done something similar with the Hazes, after all, as Rygal had recounted to him from his first adventure. But as he watched the Wavers, he realized they weren't here to fight for Dakrind. They were causing panic and chaos, sure, but one look at their deadened eyes and stumbling movements told him that they had come for one thing and one thing only.

The compass.

For an instant, an unwelcome fear entered his mind, urging him to go get Mel and get out of Esile while they had the chance. But that thought was quickly banished. Their mission to capture Terrax had been put aside—right now, the people of Esile City needed help.

He turned to face the soldiers in the guard tower. Their location was about a half mile or so from the town square, where the main fray of battle was. At his orders, Esile's town guard had gathered here. There were also twenty Randuin warriors who had joined him at the orders of the Commandant. He could tell they were uneasy about the change in plans—after all, the Randuins had only come here to investigate, not to fight a full-scale battle.

In total, the defenders numbered just over two hundred, armed with crossbows and swords. Their fear and unease was almost palpable.

"Fighting might not be our best option, sir," Captain Jackson said as Aryion turned away from the balcony. The former captain-of-guard had been packing his things to leave when Aryion had arrived. He'd been dismissed and demoted by the Council, but one word about who they were going up against and he was determined to lead his men in battle. "There's too many of them. It might be better to round up the townsfolk, barricade here, and wait it out."

Aryion let out a breath. Jackson had a good point. The guard tower was well-fortified, and he doubted the Wavers would find any interest in it since the compass was elsewhere. "The Jenna are still a problem," he said. "I doubt the Wavers will cause us trouble—they're here for something else entirely."

One of the Randuins frowned, interested. "Something else?"

Aryion opened his mouth, about to explain more, then stopped. They were running out of time. "Yes. Anyway, we must deal with the Ringmembers and Jenna before they burn the city." He gestured at the barracks. "I like the idea of using this place to guard the civilians. If we can evacuate the waterfront homes, we can bring the townsfolk here."

He pointed towards the harbor. "Commandant Daeva has alerted the rest of the Randuins—they're in the barracks on the other side of town, and they're under his orders. I suppose we have the Council to thank for that," he added wryly. After all, if the Council hadn't panicked and sent for reinforcements when the Dricasters had first disappeared, they would have been even more outnumbered.

"Then what?" Captain Jackson asked, interested. The other soldiers in the room had come closer, listening intently to the plan. The fear in their faces had been replaced by determined resolve.

"Once the waterfront is cleared of civilians, the Randuins and the Capital ships can destroy the Dricaster fleet," Aryion said. "We'll cut off their retreat and face them by the harbor."

That felt like a painfully high risk. Though they were probably better manned, the eight Capital ships would hardly stand a chance against the entire Dricaster fleet—not to mention their cannons. Commandant Daeva had gone back to the Randuin barracks, though, Aryion remembered. Perhaps the Randuin had another trick up his sleeve.

Captain Jackson folded his arms, thinking. "What will we do about the Wavers?"

Aryion hesitated. Bryn's plan included taking the compass back south, which potentially meant she'd have to flee an angry crowd of Wavers. Unless Captain Trelawney had anything to do with it, he thought—the pirate also seemed interested in having the compass for himself.

"I think the Wavers will leave Esile," he said aloud. "We'll have to deal with them later. For now, we have to hurry before those Jenna do any more damage. The Commandant is counting on us to clear out the waterfront buildings as quickly as we can."

. . . . . .

At the same moment the factory windows exploded next to the hat shop, Dakrind bellowed an order, and several things happened at once.

Numerous side doors flung open and Dricasters charged into the room, guns blazing. Terrax shouted, and a hail of crossbow bolts and arrows struck the Ringmembers as the Jenna surged forward. Dakrind pointed his pistol at Terrax just as Terrax flung a knife at Dakrind—both missed and they each dropped for cover.

Bryn saw all this in the instant that she grabbed Mel and pulled him down behind an overturned table. They huddled behind it as the room erupted in gunfire, war cries, and screams of pain and rage.

"Stay down," she warned Mel. She nocked an arrow to her

bowstring and listened, trying to pick out specific voices amid the cacophony so she'd know where to shoot. It was impossible. They were surrounded by two hostile sides—she would run out of arrows trying to protect them, and she and Mel would both die.

"The compass," Mel whispered. He sat with his back against the table, clutching the Stone with both hands against his chest. "We have to get the compass."

"I know!" Bryn hissed back. She slid around the table to loose the arrow, then ducked behind it again before seeing who she hit.

"Nice shot, Miss Paya," came Terrax' voice—he sounded cool and calm above the chaos.

Bryn nocked another arrow to her string, planning to fire in the direction of the Elven outlaw's voice. He kept talking, his drawling tone grating on her tense nerves. "I see you have found another task to occupy you. Tell me, was it Caer Sia who hired you to protect the New Blood, or does your Ringleader hate you so much? It's a dangerous job, you should know. Do you understand what protecting him could cost you?"

Bryn tried to ignore him, but his dry words reached her ears even over the din of battle. She shot around the side of the table again. The sounds of the fight muffled the arrow's flight, but she thought she heard it thunk into the wall. She ran her shaking fingers over her quiver of arrows, counting—fourteen arrows left.

Maybe if they made a run for it…

"The New Blood brings pain everywhere he goes," Terrax continued.

"Have you heard of the many who have fallen protecting him? Captain Llyrion Tarash, Norrin of Arkran—even your own brother, I hear, nearly met his end guarding the New Blood. Surely you cannot believe the lies of the Prophecy that he will bring about good. Not when everyone around him dies."

Bryn assumed, later, that the main reason she was able to keep her head was because she had no idea what Terrax was talking about. Aside from trying to distract her, his words had no real effect on her.

But his words were not aimed at her.

Mel sprang up, launching himself over the table, his face twisted in anguished rage. His dagger glinted in one hand, and from the other shot rays of blue light.

"Mel, stop!" Bryn yelled, reaching after him.

Mel ignored her. Crossbow bolts and gunshots filled the air around him, yet he seemed to be protected by a translucent shield of blue light. He charged directly at Terrax. Four outlaws rushed to stop him but were flung back by the force of the Stone's power. Terrax stood in the shadow of a doorway—Bryn saw satisfaction cross his face as Mel appeared.

She swung herself over the table to stop him—a round of gunfire crackled the air as she did so, and she ducked behind a pillar at the side of the room. Mel lunged forward, his dagger glancing off the silver armor concealed by Terrax' cloak. Terrax seized his wrist, dragging him forward. Mel swung his other hand in a wild punch, the Stone's light leaking between his fingers. Terrax blocked the blow, wrenched the boy's sword arm behind him, and grabbed Mel's other hand.

They struggled in the doorway, fighting for the Stone. Terrax was stronger—he shoved Mel's face into the door frame and tore the little blue Star-Stone from his grasp. Mel gave a cry of anger that was cut short as Terrax raised his sword, pressing it against the back of his neck.

Bryn held her bow at full draw, arrow ready. Terrax hauled Mel in front of him, using him as a shield, and smirked at Bryn. "Not a movement from you, Miss Paya," he snarled. "I have what I want. You concern me no more." He edged toward the door, forcing Mel forward. The boy's face was streaked with blood, and fear had replaced the wild fury in his eyes.

Bryn let the arrow fly—it glanced off Terrax' armored back with a clang as he fled the room. She sprinted after him without thinking. Several guns fired at once, and she ducked behind another pillar just in time. Her heart was racing. The compass was a minor issue compared to what was happening now. Terrax had taken the Stone—he had taken Mel.

She gritted her teeth and looked around the room. Terrax' Jenna mercenaries were still fighting the Dricasters, but she was sure the moment she moved, all weapons would be trained on her. If she was fast enough...

She looked to the right—the door was ten paces away. Doubt filled her. There was no way she would reach it unscathed. It would be wiser to wait the fight out and leave once everyone was exhausted. But Mel wouldn't last that long. Terrax didn't want him for ransom, he wanted revenge for his foiled plot a year ago—he would make his death long and slow.

"High Light help me," she whispered, not sure if her prayer would be heard. But she felt a strange peace settle over her as she said the words.

She took a deep breath, slid the arrow back into her quiver, gripped her bow, and bolted for the door.

A crackle of gunfire followed her out the door. Three crossbow bolts whizzed around her head. She grabbed the doorframe and had nearly made it out when a gunshot sounded right behind her, and a blinding pain exploded in her left shoulder blade, hurling her forward.

She crashed into a bookshelf as she stumbled through the door, heart throbbing. Agonizing pain shot from her shoulder down her back. The world twisted in knots before her eyes, and her vision blurred. She could feel warm blood running down her back. Terrax' voice came faintly from above… the upper story… Mel…

"High Light help me," she gasped again. The pain did not lessen, but again, she felt that unexplainable sense of clarity.

Choking down a cry of pain, she got to her feet and stumbled toward the stairs that led to the upper story. The suite of rooms above the hat shop, previously inhabited by the owners, were now the residence of the Ringleader and were used as a secure place to deal business.

Bryn forced herself up the stairs. Her bow dipped close to the floor, and she tried to raise it. The movement sent a flare of agony down her back, and she bit back a scream. There was no way she could shoot with her injury, which meant she would be very little help. But Mel was in danger. She had promised Aryion to keep him safe—she had to fulfill that promise, no matter the cost.

She opened the door to the upper room. It was finely furnished, with a couch against the wall on her left and several cabinets of wine against the opposite wall. Huge paneled windows across from the door opened onto a balcony that looked out over the harbor. Her entire flat could probably fit here with room to spare.

Terrax stood in the middle of the room facing her, the blade of his sword pressed against Mel's throat. The Elven outlaw shook his head slowly, almost in regret, as he saw her. "I tried to warn you, Miss Paya," he said with a slight shrug. "If you had let us go I may have returned the favor. Now I'll have to kill you too."

Bryn tried to raise her bow again. Her left arm trembled so much that she could hardly hold the bow steady, but she leveled the arrow at the outlaw. Terrax watched her with a sardonic smile. "Determined, aren't we? Look at you, trying to make a noble choice. Trying to pretend you are anything but what you are."

His voice grew low. "I remember you, bounty hunter. I hired you three years ago. The tasks you carried out in my employment, the things you did, the people you killed—do you remember them? Do you remember their faces? Do you really think all will be forgiven and forgotten after what you've done?"

Bryn drew back the arrow. Her injured back screamed in protest, but her aim steadied at Terrax' neck. "Let him go," she ordered, her voice hoarse but firm with a strength she didn't know she possessed.

Mel shoved the blade of Terrax' sword with his bare hand and forced it down. Terrax slashed for his neck, but Mel ducked clear, rolling out of the way.

At the same time, Bryn saw a figure climb onto the balcony. Robin silently hauled himself up and aimed his pistol into the room. The barrel lowered directly at Bryn.

For an instant Bryn's mind could not make sense of what she was seeing. Robin was going to kill her.

She let the arrow fly at Terrax in the same instant Robin's gunshot filled her ears. She thought she felt the air of the bullet's passage whipping past her face, then someone cried out behind her. She turned—Dakrind stepped back behind the doorway, bleeding from his side, his face a mask of hatred.

If Robin had not been there, Dakrind would have killed her.

"Get down, Bryn!" Robin barked.

Bryn crouched behind the sofa. Her arrow had missed, shattering the window behind Terrax. Mel was across the room from her, hiding behind a chest of drawers. To her right, through the door-way, she caught glimpses of Dakrind. His face came in and out of shadow as he glared into the room.

Robin knelt behind a small bookshelf near to the sofa. Bryn had no idea why he was here—he was supposed to stay with his ship—

but she had never been happier to see anyone in her life. Robin looked at her and mouthed the words, "All right?"

Bryn nodded, trying not to show how much pain she was in. Shooting her bow had almost made her faint, which wouldn't have helped the situation.

"You're at another dead end, Terrax!" Dakrind called into the room. He made no move to enter. Bryn wondered if he feared Robin would shoot again, but that didn't seem right. There was plenty of cover between him and Robin if he wanted to attack. What was he waiting for?

"I am right where I want to be," Terrax replied smoothly. "I have the Stone. Your presence here tells me that my Jenna have likely overwhelmed your pitiful Ringmembers. Unless you have come to die, I recommend you leave."

Dakrind gave a rasping laugh, his half-Waver features distorting in pain and frenzied excitement. "Wouldn't you like that."

Sounds of movement on the stairs caught Bryn's attention. The noises of battle in the lower levels were faint from here, but the occasional gunshot told her the fight was still happening. Who was climbing the stairs, then?

Dakrind raised his voice. "If you've come for the compass, Trelawney, I recommend you get in line."

"Gladly," Robin called back. "Put the gun down and let's form a queue, shall we?"

Someone was climbing the stairs. Multiple people, Bryn realized. The repetitive thuds of their boots on the steps sounding like the beating of drums. That wouldn't be the Jenna or the Dricasters—they knew to move quietly. Perhaps Capital soldiers had come to help. But then… why would the soldiers come up here, ignoring the obvious sounds of battle below?

"Hand over the Stone, Terrax," Mel said, his voice tense. "You don't know what it can do."

Terrax laughed. "On the contrary, New Blood, I know *exactly* what it can do. Or at least, what it is capable of. You don't think the Jewel was the only Star-Stone that could channel the Dark Realm's powers, do you?"

Bryn made eye contact with Mel—he looked worried. Up until now, she had assumed Terrax wanted to use the Stone as a weapon. But now it sounded like he meant to use it for something else.

But she didn't have the chance to finish the thought. There was something far worse to worry about now.

The footsteps grew louder, and now she heard other sounds mixed in. Muttering. Shuddering breaths. Whispered words. Clacking teeth.

Her blood ran cold.

31

The Cursed

Aryion stood on the road leading to the harbor and watched the fray of battle before him.

Rain pounded down upon the city. The wind rocked the waiting ships in the harbor and churned the quiet waters of Esile Bay into a boil. Black clouds roiled overhead, and the occasional crackle of lightning lit the horrific scene.

Though outnumbered, Aryion was pleased to notice that the town guard had hardly needed to fight anyone so far. At the first appearance of the Wavers, the Jenna warriors had attacked the Ringmembers. As for the Ringmembers, it was quickly clear to Aryion that they wanted nothing more than to rid their city of Jenna and once again have Esile to rule.

The two groups were too focused fighting each other to pay any attention to the small squadron of soldiers evacuating the civilians from the harbor area. The fire in the oil refinery had spread to the neighboring shops, but the soaking torrent of rain prevented the flames from igniting the houses on the other side of the street. The Capital soldiers formed a protective barrier between the frightened townsfolk and the wild fighting beyond.

Waypath all over again, Aryion thought grimly, watching the bloody battle.

He stood slightly in front of the barrier of soldiers that protected the retreating townsfolk, sword lowered, keeping a careful eye on the battling warriors at the water's edge. The main body of Wavers had gone further into town, following the compass' draw. He had to resist the urge to run and make sure Mel was all right. Bryn had promised to protect him, and he would have to trust her.

Captain Jackson stood next to him, studying the fight uncertainly. "The Ringmembers don't seem too worried about us or the civilians," he commented.

Aryion shook his head. "We aren't a threat to them. They out-number us at least ten to one. If they wanted to kill us, they would have done it already."

Jackson looked at him, concerned. "Then why haven't they?"

"The Jenna," Aryion said. "The Ringmembers know the Jenna are a greater threat. I assume the town guard is their back up plan. They'd rather you own the town than the Jenna."

"Rather noble of them," Jackson said wryly.

Aryion looked to the right, where the bay opened north to the sea. He could see the *Burman Marie* waiting there, thankfully unharmed. Next to her was the other ship Robin had recommended they seize— the *Scarlet Consort*. That part of the plan, at least, had happened as in-tended, though they hadn't needed the extra firepower at all so far. The unexpected arrival of the Wavers had thrown a wrench in Robin's plan to flee with the compass. He hoped that was why Robin had left the *Marie*, as Aryion had noticed a few minutes ago. Robin would let Bryn know what was happening. Of course, if the Wavers were following the compass, she'd find out soon enough.

He noticed the Dricasters were slowly falling back, toward the piers and the waiting ships. That was strange. They might be outmatched by the Jenna, but he hadn't expected them to flee the town without more of a fight.

He understood what they were doing the moment the first ship angled slightly and turned broadside along the waterfront next to the harbor.

"Get down!" he shouted, and the soldiers dropped down just in time. A round of cannon fire came from the Dricaster ship as the Ringmembers fired upon the Jenna. Howls of pain and rage filled the air. Brick and cobblestone were flung everywhere, striking many who tried to flee.

"Pull back!" Aryion barked. They were exposed here. The Ringmembers, he realized, did not intend to let the town guard stand by. They'd kill both them and the Jenna in a barrage of cannonfire and have the town for themselves.

Where were the Randuins?

Far across the water, he saw the Capital warships riding the roiling waters, hastening to their aid. They wouldn't get here in time, Aryion realized numbly. What could they do either way? The Capital soldiers were both outnumbered and outgunned.

And the Dricasters evidentially knew it. Their ships, tied at the docks, barely needed to move to be in firing position. Cannonballs tore through the buildings behind him. The north edge of the line of retreating civilians were hit hard—many bodies fell back into the smoke.

The townsfolk, disoriented and terrified, began to scatter. Captain Jackson ran toward them, raising his hands. "Listen! Listen!" At his voice, the frightened civilians looked to him for direction. "We'll take Era Road and head to the barracks," Jackson said. "Go there in a quick and orderly fashion. We'll cover you."

The civilians hurried to obey. A few town guardsmen headed to the front of the group, ushering them uphill to safety.

"I'm not sure how much cover we can give," Aryion said. He was impressed with the way Captain Jackson had regained control of the situation, but they were still in trouble. "We don't stand a chance against those ships."

Jackson let out a breath. "It's the only hope these people have of escaping, sir. If we can buy them ten minutes, they'll make it out."

He moved to stand between the retreating townsfolk and the warriors, watching the infuriated Jenna and the jeering Dricasters. Aryion joined him without another word. The Dricaster fleet had moved back from their moorings, turning broadside to the town. Two ships had left the harbor and sped to engage the oncoming Capital vessels, their red banners snapping in the wind like streaks of blood against the gray sky.

Aryion remembered the devastation a single Dricaster ship had caused in Waypath. The full strength of the fleet would likely wipe out half the city.

But the people would live. That was more important.

He watched the ships anchor in position, watched the cannons angle toward them, and hoped that somehow Mel would make it out all right.

But instead of thundering cannons, a flare of fire erupted on the opposite deck of the nearest ship.

Aryion took a reflexive step back. He could see the Dricaster pirates swarming over the deck to put out the flames, could hear the rise of confused and startled voices of the other crews.

Across the water, the Capital warships surged closer, moving into position. But the fire had not come from them. None of the Capital ships carried cannons, Aryion knew. He stole a glance at Jackson, and saw a look of sudden hope on the captain's face.

Then a second bolt of flame slammed into the tar-soaked ship, igniting the decks, and he realized the assault had come from above.

Through the clouds, Aryion saw them. Dragons. Descending with the rain in a tight, ordered formation as they attacked the Dricaster vessels. Not the lumbering, stupid beasts he'd seen on occasional trips through the Lago desert, nor the snarling lizards that inhabited Gayrile—no, these dragons came from Reedmount, intelligent, precise, and deadly in battle. An airborne cavalry of fire and steel.

He watched, speechless in shock and awe, as they swept low over the enemy ships. Randuins rode on their backs, flashing swords in hand.

Some of the Dricasters ships tried to angle their cannons up at them, firing a few rounds. The Jenna attempted no counter attack at all—too well did they know the skill and fury of the dragon riders. They turned and fled. A ragged shout of victory rose from the watching soldiers and townsfolk. Aryion looked up to watch the mounted Randuins circle overhead and felt himself smile as the rain fell on his face.

"Thank the Light," Jackson breathed.

The dragons' initial blasts had caused chaos among the Dricaster fleet, which was all the encouragement the approaching Capital ships needed. The confused Ringmembers were easily overcome. The ships wallowed in the harbor, their surviving crews swimming, defeated, to the shore.

The squadron of dragons landed on the road to the harbor, their riders dismounting and hurrying to arrest the beaten Ringmembers. Commandant Daeva swung out of the saddle of a muscular gold dragon, issuing quick orders to his men. Then he turned and strode up the road to the weary soldiers before him.

Jackson saluted. "Harbor area evacuated, sir," he reported.

"At ease, Captain. Good work," Commandant Daeva said with a smile, shaking his hand. He turned to Aryion. "An excellent plan, master Hummingbird."

"You're here not a moment too soon, I can tell you," Aryion said tiredly, shaking his hand.

"Well, let my men take it from here," Commandant Daeva said.

"I'll help you, sir," Jackson offered, though he looked exhausted.

"Take a rest, soldier," Commandant Daeva said gently. "Tend to your men. We can handle the Jenna. After all," he added as he swung into the dragon's saddle, a wry smile on his face, " it *is* what we came here for in the first place."

. . . . . .

Thunder of storm and gunfire came from the harbor, but Bryn hardly noticed it. She crouched behind the sofa, watching in horror as the Wavers appeared.

A great crowd of Wavers streamed into the upper story of the hat shop, clogging the doorway in their desire to reach the compass. Dakrind entered the room surrounded by them, protected on all sides, a cruel smile on his face. No one moved. Terrax' face was dark with displeasure. Robin looked angry but not particularly surprised. Mel had not moved at all, only sat with his back against the wall, his eyes wide.

Dakrind held up the compass, and the Wavers stopped. "Steady," he ordered them softly. "This is what you want. You must have it. It will be yours."

The Wavers watched him, slack-jawed, like a pack of starving dogs. Bryn felt a chill of fear. She wasn't sure if the Wavers still possessed some thought, or if their minds became clearer with the compass. Either way, they waited around Dakrind, crowding the room, listening intently.

"First," Dakrind said in a voice just above a whisper, "retrieve for me the Star-Stone. Then you will have the compass."

The Wavers tore their eyes from the compass and faced Terrax, whose displeasure had turned to real fear. They took a step toward him, slowly, almost hesitantly.

Then, as one, they turned and flung themselves upon Hawk Dakrind.

Their muttering voices rose into wordless screams and howls. Their fingers tore and clawed, ripping cloth and skin. Their teeth clacked shut upon the backs of their companions as they fought wildly for the compass.

Dakrind screamed—Bryn saw him writhing under the pile. He clutched the compass, trying to fend off the attackers with his free hand, but there were far too many. The compass slipped from his grasp.

The Wavers dove upon it. More of them poured through the door. Bryn watched in horror as their drive to gain the compass turned into rage, and they began pummeling and clawing each another instead.

"Close the door!" Robin yelled hoarsely.

Bryn tried to move, but her knees had gone weak with terror, and she slumped back. Mel jumped up and threw his shoulder into the door, forcing it closed in the faces of the oncoming Wavers. The door shuddered as the Wavers on the other side fought to push it open.

"I can't hold it!" Mel cried.

The compass was kicked in the madness, and went sliding under the sofa where Bryn hid. The Wavers lunged, groping under the couch, pinning Bryn against the wall. Shaking, she reached under the sofa and gripped the compass—it was slick with blood.

A gunshot split the air, and Mel ducked with a cry as the bullet hit the door above his head. Dakrind staggered to his feet, a trail of smoke rising from his pistol. Blood and claw marks streaked his face, and his eyes were wild and unfocused. The Waver inside him had taken control at last. He turned and shot at Terrax, who had retreated for the balcony. The bullet hit Terrax' armor with a ringing clang, and the force of it knocked him to the ground.

Dakrind drew out a second pistol and fired again, hitting the outlaw's arm. Terrax rolled back into cover with a hiss of pain, the Stone slipping from his grasp. Robin seized it and jumped up— "Kid, catch!" he shouted, and tossed the Stone to Mel.

In the same instant that Mel caught it, Dakrind turned and shot Robin squarely in the chest.

Robin fell, disappearing behind the cabinet.

Something inside Bryn seemed to shatter into a thousand pieces, as though her heart was made of glass. She gripped the compass so hard the metal bit into her hand, her vision blurred with tears of pain—not pain anymore, she realized, it was a grief she had long refused to feel choked her throat.

She placed her feet against the sofa and shoved it forward, into the Wavers, then stood and drew back an arrow. Her target had been Dakrind's throat—her injured shoulder betrayed her at the last second, and the arrow slammed into Hawk's upper arm. He let out a bellow of pain and stumbled, then turned his wild eyes on her. The sight of his bloodied face, the arrow protruding from his body, the maddened murder in his eyes were so similar to those of Cliadell back in Port Rylan that Bryn froze for an instant, unable to react, unable to dodge the coming gunshot that would end her desperate fight.

Then another gun fired, and Dakrind jerked sideways. One hand came up to the left side of his chest, as though startled to find the blood there, then his knees buckled and he collapsed. Bryn turned.

Robin knelt on the floor. A small plume of smoke rose from the tip of his pistol as he lowered it wearily.

The Wavers had torn the sofa to ribbons in pursuit of the compass. Bryn didn't notice them, barely noticed her own pain, only crawled the remaining distance between her and Robin, unable to believe what she was seeing. She touched his face with a shaking hand, too relieved to form words. "Are you—are you—"

Robin's shirtfront was torn from the bullet, but she saw no blood. He pulled apart the fabric, revealing a silver breastplate that bore the Liznee crest. Dakrind's bullet had left a dent in the center. "I told you," he said with a painful grin, "we picked up some stuff in Caer Sia."

Bryn laughed, even though it hurt. Tears spilled down her cheeks, but she hardly noticed.

The sound of fingernails on the door snapped her back to reality. Mel had his back against the door, holding it closed. He gripped the Stone in both hands, hunched around it, shielding it with his whole body. Bryn wondered for a moment if he could make the Stone shield all three of them, the way he had used it briefly when he'd charged Terrax. But something about his actions then told her that wasn't something to use the Stone for. No—if they were going to beat Terrax and the Wavers, they would have to do it on their own.

The surviving Wavers in the room had finished tearing apart the sofa and now realized the compass was no longer there. Slowly, they turned to Bryn, glazed eyes locking on her own.

"Bryn!" Mel screamed. Filthy hands had begun to force the door open, clawing at the wood.

The Wavers surged toward Bryn. She fell back, and Robin gripped her arm. "The compass, Bryn," he ordered over the cacophony. "Give me the compass."

Bryn sprang painfully to her feet, barely registering his words. "What?" she yelled.

"Give me the compass!" He had his hand in hers, trying to force her fingers open—Bryn pulled away, the old dark doubts filling her mind. Of course he wanted the compass. If he had it, now that her plan had gone to pieces, he could simply retreat and flee on his ship. He would leave her and Aryion and Mel here to die.

She jerked her hand away, looking at him hard, trying to read his face. Robin looked surprised, then he met her eyes and lowered his voice. She expected him to try to persuade her, to challenge her, to threaten even. All he said were three words.

"Trust me, Bryn."

The words entered her mind and challenged the doubts that had sprung up. Trust. She had demanded it of him, yet never gave it back. He had followed her plan, time and time again, because she had asked him to trust her—and now he was asking the same.

The Ringmember side of her ordered her to flee. He was a pirate. He was not trustworthy.

But she fought against it and placed the compass in Robin's hand.

He ran toward the door, pushing through the Wavers.

Terrax attacked Bryn before she could see what Robin was doing. She raised her bow like a quarterstaff, blocking blow after blow from his short sword. The force of it jarred the wound in her back. Terrax was eerily silent—there were no calm words, no sly tone. He had come to kill her and nothing else.

He slashed again. Bryn managed to dodge, but she was backed into the corner. Terrax' eyes blazed in hatred as he swung again and again. His sword cut across Bryn's upper arm, and she fell back, unable to do anything against the wild attack.

Across the room, the door finally splintered—Mel sprang away from it as the Wavers began to pour inside. The distraction was enough for Bryn to duck down, away from Terrax. The Elven outlaw moved to follow her, then stopped, staring in shock at something. Bryn's eyes followed his gaze.

Robin was kneeling in the center of the room, placing the compass on the floor before him. Wavers rushed for him, reaching out, but he paid them no attention. He raised his sword above his head—as the first Waver clawed his neck, Robin brought his blade down upon the face of the compass.

There was a sound like thunder, a rumble that shook the entire building. A bright white flash shot from the compass, accompanied with a magnified sound of breaking glass. Strange shadowy wisps shot in all directions, black darts that shattered the remaining windows and flung everyone to the ground.

The Wavers froze, rigid, shielding their eyes from the white light. Black shadows leaked from the compass like oil, spreading across the floor. It took Bryn a moment to realize that the Wavers had *become* the shadows. They fell, fading away, darkness engulfing the bodies on the floor.

For an instant, no one moved. The silence was deafening after the noise of battle. Rain pattered on the shards of broken glass. Bryn blinked, her vision refocusing after the blinding light. Robin crouched a few feet away. Where the compass had been, fine black ash streaked the floor.

The shadows remained.

Darkness filled the room like gray fog. Bryn crawled to Robin's side, gripping his shoulder. Terrax looked up at the growing blackness, his face suddenly drawn with fear.

Then, through the shadows, came a low, rippling laugh that chilled Bryn to the core. White ice crusted the ash of the compass. Cold gripped the room. Terrax shrank back against the wall, eyes wide.

A low voice spoke from the shadows, uttering words that terrified Bryn as much as confused her.

The signs are scarred,

The Messenger has come,

The Twelfth will rise.

And then, as the shadows blanketed the room in a black veil:

Are you sure you want to play this game?

Terrax gave a cry of terror and fell face down. Bryn could hardly breathe over her panic. She and Robin huddled together, unable to understand the wordless terror that filled them in the voice's presence.

Then came a flash of pure blue light, and another voice, young, yet full of authority, filled in the room. "Be gone, Kahlifis. We see your illusions for what they are. You have no power here."

The Stone shone with a flash of light, and the shadows receded. The storm outside had ended. Winter sunlight poured through the broken windows. Bryn blinked.

Mel stood by the door, the Stone raised over his head. He looked pale and frightened, but the strength and tone in his voice struck her with awe. If she had ever doubted this boy, she saw him in a new light now. The New Blood. The hope of Caer Sia.

She wondered if she ought to bow, but decided against it.

32

A Report for the Randuins

By the second morning after the fall of the Dricasters, the fighting had ceased, the fires had been extinguished, and much had changed.

The corruption within the Esile Council had finally been exposed. All eleven Councilors had been relieved of duty within hours of the end of the battle. Without the threat of Dricasters or Councilors to bind them, many Esilians had come forward with information and news that had long been prohibited. For the first time in many years, a feeling of relief and security settled over the city.

A brief gathering had been called that afternoon between the newly appointed Councilors and the Capital generals. Aryion attended the meeting at the request of Commandant Daeva. Mel, as ever, went with him.

"So, you say this was an uprising, Hummingbird?" General Mobbs asked. He had led the garrison from the Capital, come to aid in the aftermath of the battle.

"As far as we can tell, yes, sir," Aryion said. "We've assessed now that the Dricasters were aided by pirates from Port Rylan."

"Pirates?" another general repeated. "And are the rumors true that they were assisted by an undead force?"

420

"Who said they were undead?" Mel whispered to his mentor.

Aryion smiled slightly. Mel would get used to such wild rumors soon enough, he thought. "No, sir. They were quite mortal. Unstable, perhaps, but more misled than evil."

Mel had recounted the sequence of the fight with the Wavers, along with the extraordinary power displayed by the compass and the Stone. Much of the Wavers' history was still unknown—when they had first appeared, how they had come upon the compass, when they had fallen prey to its dark powers—Aryion could only speculate. But whatever the answers were, the Wavers were gone now—truly gone, taken to the dark place they had obsessed over. Despite the circumstances, he felt a stir of pity for them.

"I still don't know what this whole fiasco was about," General Mobbs said with a frown. "Even if the Esile Council and the Dricaster Brethren had an agreement, it makes little sense that the Dricasters would attack the city unprovoked."

"From what we can tell," Commandant Daeva said, stroking his beard thoughtfully, "the Dricasters had planned an uprising for several months now. They mainly used the Council for protection, and the Council used the Dricasters for funds. It was hardly an alliance. The Crime Ring would always have done what was best for the Crime Ring."

"What of the Jenna, then?" one of the new Councilors asked. "Was it the same tribe involved in the Kamon battle?"

"No, these were the Vinskael Jenna, a smaller tribe and more prone to mercenary contracts. They have fled to the sea," Commandant Daeva said. "My guess is they were hired by Terrax, with no real commitment to his cause. We sent scouts to follow their ships and be certain they return to Sikhazi, and I doubt they will come back to Esile without Terrax to pay them."

The generals nodded. The secretary sat beside Commandant Daeva, taking notes. He had retained his position once it had been found that he knew nothing about the Council's involvement with the Crime Rings.

Aryion looked at the Commandant. "Did your men explore the Dricasters' base? I am sure many of our questions could be answered there."

"They searched it thoroughly," Commandant Daeva said with a nod. "We found pages of plans for an uprising, numerous illegal substances, and maps detailing the hidden locations of other bases. I can send my men to continue the investigation," he added, with a glance at Mobbs.

The general shook his head. "No, I believe that can wait. There are more pressing matters to attend to than clearing out the Crime Rings."

"With the Dricasters out of action," the secretary ventured hesitantly, "I assume the other Crime Rings will take several months to resume business. A major—ah, partner in crime—has been removed from them." He chuckled at his own wit.

Mobbs chose to ignore this. "As for the traitor Terrax, I would like to know your thoughts," he said to Aryion. "I know you and your apprentice were sent from Caer Sia to apprehend him. If you prefer to take him back to Caer Sia for detainment, we can provide a regiment of guards. However, Terrax is a Daffonic traitor as well. Without any disrespect to Sia, I understand the city is still recovering from a recent attack?"

Aryion nodded. General Mobbs was right. Caer Sia was still vulnerable, and it was on the brink of war with the Aces. Aryion had half hoped Terrax would have been killed in the battle, to avoid the decision of what to do with him. Now the time for decision had come. Yet he realized, in the same moment, that the choice was not his to make.

"Mel?" he said, turning to his apprentice. "You are the one who defeated and captured Terrax. By Daffonic custom, you are allowed to choose his fate."

Mel was silent for a long moment. Aryion saw numerous emotions playing over his young face, and could only imagine the conflict in the boy. Terrax had done more than kill and destroy. He had robbed Mel of a simple childhood, thrust him into this world of battle and death far sooner than anyone would have wished. He had killed one of Mel's friends. He had nearly killed many more in Caer Sia by working for Pellion Drona. If Mel requested his execution, it would be more than justified.

Mel let out a long breath. "I don't think… I don't think killing him would accomplish much. It won't change what's done." He paused, seeming to gather his thoughts. "Don't kill him. He needs to be imprisoned. And you're right, sir," he added to General Mobbs. "Caer Sia is still recovering. The last thing I'd want to do is take Terrax back into Sia." He looked at Commandant Daeva. "Hand him over to the Randuins."

Aryion felt a surge of pride. He turned to the Commandant. "Will that be acceptable?"

"Indeed it will," the Randuin said with a nod. "It's a clever move, lad," he said to Mel. "I think Terrax would prefer death to prison—his pride would demand it. Perhaps in Reedmount he will come to a better frame of mind."

"A life sentence gives him plenty of time to think it over," Mel said matter-of-factly. The generals laughed.

"I have one other request," Aryion said. "Your Captain Jackson. I understand he was discharged by the previous Councilors. After his service in this attack, I expect those charges can be revoked?"

One of the new Councilors, a young Elf with dark hair, looked uncomfortable. "I'm sorry, ranger," he said. "Despite Captain Jackson's actions, we can't go back on a judgment of dishonorable conduct, even though the charge may be false."

"Well, allow me to help the matter for you," Commandant Daeva suggested. "Reedmount has recently found itself in need of a new captain-of-guard. I'd like to offer the position to Jackson. His actions well commend him for the job."

The generals looked pleased, as did the Councilors.

"Thank you for your help, Commandant," Aryion said, shaking the burly warrior's hand. "We are grateful for it."

Commandant Daeva nodded with a smile. "A pleasure to work with you, rangers."

"There's one last thing I have to ask, Hummingbird," General Mobbs said as Aryion and Mel started for the door. "You told the Randuins the location of the hat shop and the secret entrance to the Dricaster base. How did you come to know that?"

Aryion paused. "An anonymous tip," he said simply.

Mobbs frowned. "Have you any ideas who it was from?"

"Not a clue, General. It may have been a concerned citizen, or a rival Ringmember."

"Hmm," Mobbs murmured. "Well, it might be worth trying to track down that tip. Commandant, could you send a few of your men to look into it?"

"I'm afraid not, General. We're tied up in a rather important case of our own, as I told you."

Mobbs sighed. "Well, in that case, I suppose we'll never know. Though I do wish we could at least thank him—whoever it was."

"As do I," Aryion said, and left the Council hall with a smile on his face.

. . . . . .

The *Marie* and *Consort* were moored just north of Esile City, in a quiet, secluded cove. Aryion had assured Bryn that the Capital was more focused on helping the people of Esile City than tracking down a few renegade pirates, but she still felt nervous waiting for too long so close to Esile. She assumed the meeting with the generals had been productive, and tried to push down her growing worry. What if the Capital wanted to track them down? What if the new Council was just as corrupt as the last? What if Terrax escaped?

"It'll be all right," Robin reassured her as they waited on the ship. "They're rangers, after all. It's not as if they have bounties on their heads."

"I know," Bryn replied. She stood slowly, wincing at the pain in her back. Two days had turned the burning agony into more of a dull ache, but it still hurt. Harry had patched her up when she and Robin had returned to the *Marie*, both bruised and battered but cautiously optimistic.

With the Dricaster Brethren in ruins, she had decided to explain her true identity to the crew of the *Marie*. She had always been worried the truth would destroy the newfound trust they had in her, but to her surprise, a great calm seemed to have come from her honesty. The crew forgave her lie, the secret was out, and everyone seemed grateful to move forward.

She spotted Aryion and Mel walking down the path toward the cove, and she and Robin descended the gangplank to meet them. Aryion was smiling, which told her the meeting had been successful. "How did it go?" she asked.

"Quite well," Aryion said. "Terrax is to be taken to Reedmount. The Randuins have assured us they will detain him there."

Bryn felt a stir of unease. "Are you sure?" There had been corruption in the Esile Council, and there could very well be corruption in the Capital too. What if someone freed Terrax?

Robin was nodding, impressed. "That's a smart move," he said. "Reedmount is more secure than most—Caer Sia included. Those dragon riding maniacs will keep an eye on him."

"You're certain?" Bryn asked again, still not convinced.

"As certain as I can be. Try not to worry about it," Aryion said. "The Randuins are not the Esile Council. They are more honest than most and better warriors than nearly everyone."

"He's right, Bryn," Robin said. "Don't worry about Terrax. If there's any good eggs within the Capital, it'd be the Randuins."

Since Robin was usually skeptical of any form of authority, Bryn decided to trust their decision.

"So what now?" Mel asked eagerly.

"We're heading north, up the Mata Strait," Robin said. "I assume you two will need a ride back to Caer Sia?"

"Thank you, but no," Aryion said. "The journey by carriage will be a quicker one, and I'd recommend you two stay clear of major cities for now. You're safe enough in Esile City, and quite anonymous, but I can't say the same for the rest of the Mainland." He smiled slightly at the two of them.

"Well, in that case, good luck to you both," Robin said, clapping Aryion's back lightly.

"Stay out of trouble," Aryion told him.

"Same to you," Robin said with his crooked grin, then swaggered back up the gangplank to the deck of the *Marie*.

Bryn rolled her eyes in Robin's direction and turned back to see Aryion studying her with a knowing smile. "What?"

"Nothing," Aryion said with a shrug.

Bryn glared at him. "If you're thinking that we're… well…"

Mel looked alarmed. "But you are, aren't you? I think he likes you, at least. Aryion was sure of it. We had a bet on it."

Bryn switched her glare to the young ranger, who looked more confused than anything, then back at Aryion, who wore a suspicious smile. "You're both idiots," she said finally.

"Granted, but we're not blind," Aryion said.

Mel snorted with laughter. Bryn finally allowed herself to smile. "What's next for you two?"

Aryion's smile faded slightly, and he became serious. "We must return to Caer Sia. The second stage of the Prophecy is coming, and we also need to aid in the Wildkids' alliance efforts. If war is coming, then the Stone should be in a more secure place."

Bryn studied them, knowing there was nothing she could say to change his mind. She also knew that now was not the time for her to make any decisions regarding her role in the war. There were other matters to attend to, other things to resolve, she thought, with a glance back at the ships. "All right. Well… stay safe."

She embraced her brother, then Mel. They hesitated a moment longer. It seemed, even after sixteen years, they were still unaccustomed to parting. "Thank you," Aryion said after a pause. "For helping us both."

Bryn smiled slightly. "Consider us even. Thank you for helping with the Dricasters." She paused, then unpinned the Dricaster badge and placed it in his hand. "Most pirate ships in the north will know how to reach the Dricasters. If you ever need me, show them this pin, and they'll fetch us."

"Very well. Be safe," Aryion said.

They bade one another farewell, and Bryn walked onboard the *Burman Marie*. When she looked back, they had gone, fading into the forest like shadows.

33

A Captain for the Consort

The *Marie* and *Scarlet Consort* sailed up the Mata Strait side by side.

The bitter chill of Esile City was replaced with warm, tropical weather as they entered the Kamo Bay. They docked at the island city of Kamon for supplies. Bryn stood on board the *Scarlet Consort*, thinking over her plan for the next few days. A light breeze rippled the ship's sails, and the boards creaked and sang with the rhythm of the waves.

The warm sun and quiet peace of the place made it easy to forget there was a coming darkness in the world. It had been days, but Bryn could not stop thinking about what Aryicn had said about his concern regarding the second stage of the Prophecy. She didn't know much about prophecies—Mel had told her a little—but she worried that it would mean more fear, more pain, more death in a world that was already struggling.

At least the compass had been destroyed, she thought. That reminded her of their deal with the Rylanders They needed to arrange for payment to go to the Rylander Brethren somehow. She still hadn't brought this up to Robin. Most likely, they would have to sail back south to Port Rylan to arrange payment. This potentially put the entire crew of the *Marie* in danger—after all, they were still wanted criminals to the other Crime Rings.

She could not ask the crew to risk such a task. A solution had formed in her mind, but she was putting off bringing it up.

For now, she breathed deep the sweet floral smells of Kamon and tried to enjoy the sensation of freedom. She was free. Free of the heavy secrets that had weighed her down for years. Free of the false identity and the killing and hate that had bound her. Free of the Dricasters for good.

She turned to Richard. The bosun stood on deck nearby, a wide smile on his rugged face as he stood on board his long-lost ship. "Have you decided that you want to captain her after all, Rich?" she asked.

He shrugged. "Oh, maybe for a bit. Nothing permanent, I hope. Need to find her a captain that'll care for her like her previous one."

"That would be fortunate," Bryn agreed.

Richard studied her. "I think you'd be a good captain, Miss Paya." Bryn laughed, but he persisted. "Honestly now. You've the wits and the brains, and you're more than capable of telling anyone what to do."

Bryn turned away, blushing at his praise. "I don't know anything much about captaining. I'm sure you'd want someone more capable."

"Ah, you're too modest now," Richard said, grinning. "Heard you telling Oliver the tale of how you once commandeered a supply barge all on your lonesome. That takes skill, that."

"That was a long time ago." Bryn hesitated. She knew her way around a ship, yes, but that hardly qualified her for the role of captain. And yet taking command of the *Consort* could be the solution to her plan regarding the Rylanders.

"The job sort of varies by person," Richard continued. "You'd have me at the helm at the start. Maybe pick up a few men to help crew her, and all you have to do is shout loud and have a heading."

Bryn laughed again. "Is that all?"

"Oh, you'd have your fair share of work," Richard chuckled. "Think about it. I'm quite happy to be first mate on board, if you're taking names for the job."

"So you're recruiting me as your captain? I thought it was the other way around."

Richard shrugged again. "Not that you have a better option. I know the *Consort*, Miss Paya." He paused. "If you're wondering about it, talk to Cap'n."

Robin. Yes. She needed to talk to him. The thought caused her smile to fade slightly.

Robin returned to the *Marie* shortly, carrying a bundle of supplies and talking cheerfully with John and Matthew. The *Marie's* first mate had recovered quickly, though he still moved slowly. He and Matthew smiled at Bryn as they passed her as she waited on the pier and headed up the gangplank.

"Make sure to load it below," Robin called to them. "That blasted cat keeps sleeping on the gear." He turned to Bryn with a smile. "Now I could get used to this," he said, gesturing at the bright sunshine. "Can't stand the cold."

"Yes," Bryn agreed, following him onboard the *Marie*. The two ships angled away from the pier, riding the northern breeze. Bryn let the moments stretch as they turned the *Marie* up the Strait.

Finally, as they left Kamon behind, she moved to stand by Robin. "I have a plan about the Rylanders. But you're not going to like it."

Robin looked at her, catching the serious tone in her voice. "You do?"

"We need to finish the deal," Bryn said slowly. "You said the Rylander employer was willing to pay for either the compass' delivery or its destruction. I think I can arrange for him to pay the Rylanders directly, instead of us. That should satisfy them in place of the compass itself."

Robin was quiet. "We can't go back to Port Rylan. I doubt Madam Ida would let us out again, deal or no."

"No," Bryn agreed. She took a deep breath. "But I can. Let me have the *Consort* and twenty crewmembers. I can deal with the Rylanders. And you all will be free."

Robin looked at her with a frown. "That's your plan? Leave us and go south?"

"I can't ask you to put your men in danger again," Bryn said. "You have men who are wounded. The *Marie* needs repairs. And you're still wanted by the Rylanders."

"You don't have to go to Port Rylan alone," Robin said. "We could go there. Together." He studied her meaningfully. Ever since escaping Drynrall, they had been a team. Sticking together had been the best course of survival. Now, Bryn realized, with a painful tug at her heart, the safest thing would be to part ways.

"Your men need you here," she said gently.

"Yes, well, we need *you* here," Robin said bluntly. "You've been watching our backs from the start, protecting us, caring for us—not like we've done anything to deserve that, though. What would we do if you didn't come back? If the Rylanders…" He trailed off.

"We?" Bryn asked with a faint smile.

Robin shook his head, his face bright red. "Never mind that. And what's this business about you taking the *Consort*? I didn't agree to that."

"You'd already offered for me to stay, didn't you?"

Robin looked at her quickly, hiding his surprise and hope too late. "Oh, did I. Does that mean you're accepting the offer to stay on the *Marie*?"

"No," Bryn said. "Not on the *Marie*. That's your ship, and she's already got a mostly capable captain. However, the *Consort* is a different matter."

Robin smiled his usual cocky grin. "However, Miss Paya, *I* commandeered her. So, technically—"

"So, technically, I've been watching your back this whole venture and thus have every right to demand some sort of payment, as you said earlier," Bryn said smoothly.

Robin arched an eyebrow. "Well, I technically saved your life after Port Rylan. In which case my debt is slightly paid."

"Saved my life?" Bryn repeated incredulously. "When?"

"By deciding not to kill you," Robin said with a shrug. "You weren't in on the original plan, you know."

"Your generosity is duly noted," Bryn said dryly. "Your debt still stands, though."

"Let's talk payment, then," Robin said, spreading his hands. "How can I repay you, my lovely Ringmember Paya?"

"Captain Paya to you. The *Scarlet Consort* was commandeered by Richard, not you. She's his now."

"Yes, but Richard doesn't want to be captain of her, which means she's under my command as well. We'll hold onto her until I find someone capable of captaining," Robin said.

"Funny, Richard all but recruited me to stay and captain her."

Robin looked shocked. John, who was at the helm, snorted with laughter, something Bryn had never heard him do. Robin looked back at the *Scarlet Consort*, which was trailing them. "Richard did what?" he yelled in that direction.

"What, Cap'n?" came Richard's distant and confused voice.

"She does have a valid point, Captain," John said.

Robin scowled at him, but Bryn could tell he was hiding a smile. "Below with you, John, or I'll have you keel-hauled."

John went downstairs with his hands in his trouser pockets, whistling off-key.

Robin looked at Bryn, running a hand through his hair. "All right. The *Scarlet Consort* for you. You can have twenty to crew her for now, and Whiskers if you can stand her yowling. And I'll throw Richard in for good measure for being exceedingly pushy."

"You should have heard my brother," Bryn laughed. "He and Mel had a bet on it."

"A bet on what?"

Bryn shrugged, suddenly a little shy. "Well, on us, I suppose."

Robin chuckled and shook his head. They stood side by side, looking out over the water, a small space between them.

"I appreciate your offer to handle the Rylanders," Robin said after a pause. "But I can't ask you to risk that. Port Rylan is dangerous."

"I know it is. Because you gave the Rylanders my face," Bryn stated. It was the one thing she hadn't brought up yet. She had set it aside ever since they'd escaped Drynrall, knowing there were more important things to address. She couldn't exactly feel angry about it—she was a wanted criminal now either way.

Robin paused. "Yes, I did. I described you as best I could in exchange for those Rylander pins I gave Hawk."

Bryn shook her head wearily. "You didn't think that might cause problems for us now?"

"Maybe," Robin said, "but I don't think you'll need to worry."

Bryn stared at him. "What are you talking about? I saw the posters in Port Rylan. Aryion told me there were some in Esile City, too, written in Erinian."

"Can you read Erinian?"

"No," Bryn said, confused by the change in subject.

"What about Gevarian? That's what the Port Rylan posters were written in. Can you read Gevarian?" Robin asked.

"No," Bryn said again, suddenly uncertain.

"Well, John can. John!" Robin called.

The first mate reappeared at the stairs promptly. "Yes, Captain?"

"Can you tell Miss Paya what her posters say, in both the Erinian and Gevarian dialects?" Robin asked, a satisfied, knowing light in his eyes.

John looked quite pleased to be asked. "Of course I can, Miss Paya. Both posters contain the same picture, but different information. The posters in Esile City have the name and description of a certain Rachel Smith—an outlaw who died years ago, it seems. In Port Rylan, the posters contain the same false name and description but a different location to look for you."

Bryn looked between the two of them, a little hope coming back to her.

"Thank you, John," Robin said, and the first mate walked back to the prow. Robin looked at Bryn. "The Rylanders will figure out they have the wrong information sooner than later. The posters might have your name and general appearance, but it's all jumbled up, attached to the wrong people. Most of the locations lead to a Jenna tribe."

"So you told them I'm a Jenna. Thoughtful."

"Oh, don't be difficult. No one goes after Jenna. Except the Randuins, but they're busy enough as is. Like I was saying, the Rylanders will figure out their information is incorrect and they'll get rid of the posters in a few months at most. Anyone who does try to track you will be led into the heart of Jenna territory."

Bryn shook her head slowly, trying to hide her immense relief. The cheerful freedom she had felt before was slowly returning. "You can be very clever at times," she said shortly, unable to hide her smile.

"I have occasional moments," Robin said with a small smile. "If it wasn't impertinent to point out, I'd say you owe me now."

"I do indeed," Bryn said, shaking her head. "Perhaps I could repay that debt, if I agree to follow through with whatever plan you have to deal with the Rylanders?"

"That seems reasonable," Robin said. "The question is, would you trust that plan?"

"Your plan? Of course not. It's probably reckless and dangerous and I'm sure I won't like it," Bryn said. Robin frowned slightly. Bryn leaned closer to him and smiled again. "However, I do trust you, Captain Trelawney. It's taken me long enough to see it."

"Took you the whole trip!" came Oliver's cheerful voice, interrupting the moment. The cabin boy swung from the foreyard above them, looking jubilant.

"It's five lashes for eavesdropping on private conversations, Oliver!" Robin said without moving. Oliver's only reply was a snicker as he dropped down to the deck and scurried down the stairs—likely, Bryn guessed, to spread the delightful gossip with the crew.

She straightened, shaking her head. "Well, if the matter of the *Consort* is settled, then tell me about this plan of yours with the Rylanders. Do I need to play the part of a slaver again to keep you safe?"

"Oh, not this time," Robin said with a wink. "I can only be captured by a lovely slaver so many times. It'll ruin my reputation otherwise."

Bryn turned and faced him. For an instant, she was tempted to roll her eyes, or reply with a snappy comeback.

Instead, she stepped close, put her arms around Robin's neck, and kissed him. There was an interested murmur from the sailors on deck, which neither of them noticed or cared. Bryn pulled away and saw Robin's startled but pleased expression.

"That," she told him, "is only to shut you up."

With that, she turned and moved toward the port deck.

Robin stood behind, for once at a loss for words. John came back on deck, glancing sidelong at Robin. "I believe she will do you well, Captain," he said simply.

"You have far too many opinions for a first mate, John," Robin stated, and turned back to the helm.

34

Task Completed

"There's one last thing to take care of," Robin said.

They had spent the past day sailing steadily north. It was now midafternoon, and the tropic forest had been replaced by the vast emptiness of desert flats on both shores.

Bryn sat on the steps leading up to the helm and glanced back at him. He stood leaning on the wheel, a grim resolve on his face. She had expected this. Though he'd reassured her she did not have to return to Port Rylan, Bryn knew action was still needed. "Our deal?" she guessed.

Robin nodded. "I've arranged to meet my informant three miles past the edge of the Flats—the middle of nowhere, it seems."

Bryn frowned slightly, thinking. "When did you arrange that?"

Robin sat down next to her. "Waypath. You remember I mentioned the informant?"

Bryn's mind had been so occupied with planning their strategy to handle the trouble in Esile for the last few days that she had almost forgotten that. The mysterious informant Robin had met with in Waypath had told him that the employer would be satisfied with either the compass or its destruction. This was the first she had heard of meeting with the informant directly, though.

"You didn't tell me about this meeting," she said slowly.

"No," Robin said, "because I wasn't sure we should follow through with it."

"Why not?"

Robin let out a breath. "Like I told you after Waypath. The Rylander employer—there's something strange about them, whoever they are. Something dangerous. They knew about Terrax—knew he had gone to Port Rylan, which no one else knew at the time. More than that, they knew we'd be in Waypath… with the compass."

A chill ran down Bryn's spine. She tried to ignore it. "They didn't demand the compass when you met with them, though?"

"He didn't. It was just one man. Alone, no guards. He didn't ask for the compass. He just wanted to know what we were planning to do with it."

"What did you tell him?"

"I made up a tale about meeting with Madam Ida first. He didn't seem surprised. He just told me that Terrax was no longer on Drynrall Island, and that the employer would be waiting for us after we finished our business in Esile." Robin nodded north, toward the wide expanse of flat land.

Bryn frowned, thinking. None of this new information eased her growing concern. She could tell Robin felt the same. "Well, the payment from the employer should satisfy Madam Ida, at least," she said, then paused. "Do you trust the employer?"

"Not particularly. Sure, they didn't just kill us and take the compass in Waypath, but this whole business seems strange. So did the informant. You should have seen him—he seemed… off."

"Off? Like the Wavers?" Bryn asked, suddenly uneasy. What if they were dealing with another Dakrind, another employer possessed by desire for the compass? What if the Rylander employer meant to kill them the moment they stepped on shore?

"No, not like the Wavers. He seemed sane enough. Just…" Robin thought for a moment, searching for the right word, then gave up with a shrug. "I don't know. I doubt they'll kill us. But that doesn't make this safe."

Bryn agreed. The amount of details the Rylander employer had known frightened her. The Crime Rings kept their secrets close. No one could have known such things otherwise. So how exactly had this person known all this? More importantly, how much did they know about her and her companions?

But Robin was right. They had made a bargain back in Waypath, and they needed to fulfill that.

By nightfall, they reached the rendezvous point Robin and the informant had arranged. A slight hill framed the shore to the right. Beyond it, the land faded into the dead grayness of the Salem Flats, empty and dry, utterly desolate. The moonlight shone silver on the ground.

They anchored the two ships. Bryn and Robin went ashore. Robin carried a small satchel filled with fine black ash—the only thing left of the compass. Bryn hoped it would be ample proof that they had completed their assignment.

They crested the small rise between the Strait and the Flats. The land fell away before them. A fire blazed a hundred yards or so away, the yellow light framing a lone figure.

There waited the mysterious employer.

She took a breath and gripped her bow.

"It'll be all right," Robin said quietly. "Are you with me?"

"Always," Bryn replied softly. "I'm not sure about this, though."

"I'm with you there," Robin agreed. "Still, he's agreed to meet us, alone, peacefully. Let's have it over with."

They walked down the hill and drew closer to the fire. The figure came into focus as they approached. A man, Bryn saw, about Robin's height and build but a few years younger. That surprised her. He wore a fine gray jerkin, a sword at his side, and a hat with a bright blue plume. He had blond hair and a well-trimmed beard. The brim of his hat shaded the top half of his face.

"Good evening, Ringmembers," he called. His voice was calm and polite.

"Good evening," Robin called back. "I assume you are our employer?"

"Not quite," the man said, smiling. "I am but a servant to them. However, I am here to give you your pay in exchange for the bounty. I assume you have acquired the compass?"

Robin held out the satchel. "Destroyed. Best proof we have of it."

The man opened the satchel and took a pinch of ash, feeling it. He nodded slowly. "Ah, well done. My Lord will be pleased."

There was something strange about the man, Bryn thought, but she couldn't figure out what. His voice was calm and even. His movements were easy, not the shuddering of the Wavers as she had first feared. But there was something—she couldn't place it.

The fire flared, and the stranger's face was visible in the light. His eyes were pale blue, hollow and empty. Not a dead emptiness like the Wavers—a strange hollowness as if a power controlled him, enslaved him.

Enchanted him.

"Is that satisfactory?" Robin asked, giving no indication that he was as unnerved as Bryn was.

"Indeed it is," the man said.

"Then I hope we can arrange to send the payment directly to the Rylander Brethren," Robin said.

The man seemed unsurprised. "Certainly, if that is more convenient. We assumed that would be best. Neither of you are on friendly terms with the Crime Rings anymore, I understand?" he asked.

His conversational tone almost lessened the implication of his statement. Bryn exchanged a quick, uneasy look with Robin. Robin met the man's eyes. "That's not important," he said crisply. "What's important is that your employer knows not to spread rumors like that around."

The man nodded. "Of course. We are well accustomed to keeping secrets. Thank you for your services, Ringmembers."

He extended a hand. Robin shook it briskly, as if he were afraid of being burned, and turned away. Bryn followed, trying to cement an image of this strange man in her mind. Blond hair, blue plume in hat, hollow blue eyes.

And there was one other detail, she reminded herself—the crest on the breast of his jacket.

A triangular emblem, a symbol Bryn didn't recognize.

She and Robin turned and walked back toward the water.

Behind them, the enchanted man looked back into the shadows beyond the fire. "Is this satisfactory, sir?" he asked.

A shadowy shape flickered into focus, and a smooth, cold voice replied. "Indeed it is. The compass' power has been returned to its rightful master."

The enchanted man glanced back at the retreating figures. "Shall I send for the Ringmembers' assistance again?"

"Not now. We have other pressing matters." The fire flared again, and the light glinted off the second speaker's tarnished armor, half-decayed face, and purple-red eyes alight with an eager smile.

The Ace-Deputy nodded to himself. His master would be pleased indeed.

On the crest of the hill, Bryn paused, hearing some echo of the ancient voice that chilled the air behind her. She saw the fire, saw the man they'd met with, saw a strange slithering shadow that seemed to fade into the darkness like smoke.

Then, far across the Flats, a deeper darkness seeped from the twilight sky and swept over the land. Descending shadows leaked from the air, swallowing the Flats in icy dark. In the faint light she saw the silhouette of a ruined castle, miles away. She saw movements that she could not explain. Shadows sweeping about its walls, raising the ruins, re-birthing the strength until its towers scraped the sky. A crackle of silver lightning split the gathering clouds, lighting the skeletal structure that had suddenly been raised. An echo of laughter came from the distance, and she recognized it as the same laughter that she had heard upon the compass' destruction.

The chilling voice repeated the message in her mind:

The signs are scarred,

The Messenger has come,

The Twelfth will rise.

Then came a rumble of thunder, and total darkness shrouded the Flats again.

"Bryn?" She jumped. Robin stood slightly down hill, looking up at her with concern. "You all right?"

Bryn's heart was racing. She did not understand what she had just witnessed, could not explain the fear she felt, only knew that somehow, the compass' destruction had played into the hands of a deadly force. Such power could not be matched. The war was futile. There would be no victory.

"I…" she stammered, unable to speak.

Then an eerily sweet melody rose from the sea to her left. The song of the Nøkken. Her eyes rested on a shape gliding through the darkness, and she stared in wordless awe.

A ship. Glittering red and gold through the darkness, drifting through the shadows and fog. Pale sails filled with invisible wind, carrying her onward.

Watch for the Red Canary, came the words of a cheery song from days before. And then she understood.

One was not meant to watch in fear, but in hope. Waiting for its coming. Waiting for the glimmers of goodness and light that still remained in the world. Trusting the Light.

Bryn stared at the ghostly ship for a moment, watching as it vanished into the fog, and was startled to feel an unexplainable comfort settle upon her. Whatever darkness had risen beyond her, whatever fear there was to come, she no longer waited in apprehension. The darkness would not last forever. Somehow, the war would be won. Somehow, the words of the Prophecy, the hope and faith of the mortals, and the promises of the High Light would prevail.

She turned to Robin and nodded. "Yes, I'm all right. Now let's go. The sea is waiting."

Epilogue

Caer Sia. One week later.

"It's time," Iriam said.

Aryion stood near Mel, studying the ancient scroll on the table before them. He glanced up at the Neutral, whose face was more serious than usual. "You are certain the second stage is set?"

"I can be certain of little," Iriam said with a faint smile. "However, the events of the last few months lead many of us to believe that yes, the time has come. Even if we are wrong, I believe you are ready to read the Prophecy, Mel."

Mel frowned slightly. "What do you mean? Didn't you say I was ready before?"

"In some ways, you were. In others, you were not. You have grown and learned much since then. You now better understand the power of the Stones and your own role in the world. You have matured."

Mel grinned, embarrassed. "I don't know about that."

Aryion returned his smile, but inwardly he agreed with every one of Iriam's words. Mel *had* changed since their quest for the Shards. He had learned much on this mission. He was different from the boy who would have used the Stone to threaten a prisoner. He was more sure of himself. Responsible. Confident in his actions. He no longer sought revenge, not even against Terrax, but rather justice.

Aryion was proud of him.

"Do you know anything more about the compass than what

you've told us?" Mel asked, still hesitating before the scroll.

Iriam paused, a thoughtful look in his red eyes. "From what you describe, the information Terrax told the Dricaster Ringmembers was quite accurate. Its likeness and behavior is similar to Safacon's other devices. And you say it bore Safacon's crest?"

"I described it to Rygal, and he said it was," Aryion said.

Iriam nodded slowly. "Mel's description of the compass' destruction is remarkably similar to that of the Jewel's when it was broken. And you heard the voice again?" he asked Mel.

"Sort of. It was different this time." Mel let out a breath. "It was the Ace-Lord's voice, I know that for sure. But he sounded… happy that the compass was broken."

"Such a thing would please him," Iriam said gravely. "The compass' dark powers belonged to the Ace-Lord, as the Jewel's did. And like the Jewel, the destruction of the compass has returned that power to the Aces."

Aryion felt a stir of unease. "How much power?"

"I cannot say yet. I can assure you, however, that it pales in comparison to the hope of the Prophecy," Iriam said.

Mel fingered the weathered page and nodded. "In that case… here goes."

He opened the scroll.

The New Blood will return…

Glossary/Pronunciation Guide

Appledale ....small town in Daffodalion

Aryion Paya (AR-ree-on PY-ah).................... ranger. Also known as the Hummingbird

Black Raven...Hawk Dakrind's ship

Bryn Paya (brin PY-ah).................former Dricaster assassin, skilled archer

Burman Marie (BUR-man ma-REE)..................... Robin Trelawney's ship

Caer Sia (care SEE-uh).................the capital of Coonsia, home of the Liznee people

Coonsia (COON-see-uh) ....country on the Mainland of Orlell

Daffodalion (DAFF-oh-DAHL-lee-in) ....Coonsia's neighbor, the largest country on the Mainland

Dricaster Brethren (DREE-cast-ter)......Crime Ring located in Esile City

Drynrall Island (DRIN-rahl).............. pirate haven off the southern coast

Dusty... a fiery and skilled Wildkid warrior

Esile City (EE-sile).............................. large industrial Daffonic city

Fauna...............................capital of Daffodalion, also referred to as the Capital

Graysil (GRAY-sill)...................................Dusty's youngest sister, gray fur

Hawk Dakrind (hawk DAK-rynd).... leader of the Dricaster Crime Ring

Iriam (EER-ree-ahm)............................. Neutral, advisor to the High King

Jenna................................ a wild race of tribal warriors from Sikhazi

Joesp (JO-esp)........................ Wildkid warrior, Dusty's brother. Black fur

John Tailor.. first mate on the Burman Marie

Lemsonburg (LEM-sen-burg).. *Daffonic city*

Madam Ida... *leader of the Rylander Crime Ring*

Mads Moda (mads MOH-duh)................. *Dwarve, Dricaster Ringmember*

Matthew McCreery.....................................*second mate on the Burman Marie*

Mel Smallbutton... *young ranger apprentice*

Nellioh (NELL-ee-oh)................*Wildkid warrior, Dusty's brother. Red fur*

Newuel (NEW-wull)............... *Wildkid warrior, Dusty's brother. Gray fur*

Oliver Thomas.................................... *chatty cabin boy on the Burman Marie*

Port Rylan...*southern Daffonic port city*

Randuin Order (RAN-du-een)........... *courageous sect of warriors based in eastern Daffodalion*

Richard Darvi... *bosun on the Burman Marie*

Robin Trelawney...*captain of the Burman Marie*

Rowlen Daeva (ROW-len DAVE-ah).........................*Randuin Commandant*

Rylander Brethren (RY-lan-der).............*Crime Ring located in Port Rylan*

Sikhazi (si-KAHZ-zee)................................... *eastern country, home of the Jenna*

Terrax (TERR-axe) .... *an elven outlaw*

Waypath....................................... *hidden pirate haven in the Daffonic woods*

Acknowledgments

A word must be said for four writers—Ted Elliot, Terry Rossio, Stuart Beattie, and Jay Wolpert—whose story blossomed into one of the greatest swashbucklers to ever reach 2003's screens and, years later, inspired an over-eager 13 year old to write a pirate tale of her own. Yes, dear Pirate fans, I hope you find glimpses of that film interwoven through this Orlell Chronicles swashbuckler.

The Curse of the Compass would not have been possible without, again, the ever-present support of the Orlell launch team (Orlellios, as we'll call you now!) Thank you for your encouragement and enthusiasm.

Mom, thank you once again for your early edits that helped hone the story. (The blue pens make it easier to read your notes—please, retire the orange pen for good.)

To my fellow writers of the Calvary McMinnville Writer's group, thanks for reading and editing sections of the book. Special thanks to Shelli Owen for your feedback and grammatical edits (I got rid of most of the m-dashes).

And to Levi, whose encouragement, humor, and love glimmers throughout this story, thank you for everything.

www.ingramcontent.com/pod-product-compliance
Lightning Source LLC
Chambersburg PA
CBHW011122190726
48289CB00012B/2871